BARRY N. MALZBERG, EDITOR

THE BEST TIME TRAVEL
STORIES OF ALL TIME

BARRY N. MALZBERG is the author of more than thirty SF novels and more than 250 SF short stories, as well as thrillers and erotic novels under his own name and various pseudonyms. He won the John W. Campbell Memorial Award for his 1972 novel, *Beyond Apollo*. His fiction, like his critical writing, often casts a bleak and mordant eye on matters, particularly the state of the science fiction field; indeed, his 1982 collection of critical essays, *The Engines of the Night*, outlines Malzberg's progressive disenchantment with the genre, in light of the course it had taken during the 1970s. Behind that despairing surface, however, lies a deep dedication to the idea of science fiction—its possibilities, its ideals, its finest moments—that lends his criticism the weight of authority: it is born of love.

ALSO AVAILABLE

Published by ibooks, inc.:

THE BEST
TIME TRAVEL·STORIES
OF ALL TIME

BARRY N. MALZBERG
Editor

ibooks
new york
www.ibooks.net

DISTRIBUTED THROUGH SIMON AND SCHUSTER. INC.

A Publication of ibooks, inc.

CONTENTS

CONTENTS

INTRODUCTION

PARADOX, A PARADOX: Of course time travel is an impossibility. The paradoxes are devastating, they pyramid. Return to the past to meet oneself; alter the past and the very future from which the alteration sprang has itself been changed or destroyed. Kill your grandfather and you kill the man who, through line of descent, made it possible for you to kill him: could not have happened. Introduce new technology or its knowledge to the unblemished past and there is no past as understood. Not workable. Physicists can prove this with lines and computations; mathematicians and logicians can disprove time travel with equal facility. Doesn't work. Never could have worked. Science fiction's formulation insists that an extrapolation be at least logical. No such logic here. Time travel exists only at the level of fantasy. Elves and dragons and magic ring. The Princess in the tower. The witch's curse, the poisoned kiss, the thunder of unicorns in the distance.

A MOST UNSEEMLY PARADOX: Still, its possibility, its implications have functioned as one of the staples of the science fiction genre. Wells's Time Machine is a travelogue of course, sunk in social commentary and devoid of paradox but Wells falls outside a genre whose origins are well codified in the pulp magazines. Heinlein's *By His Bootstraps*, a catalogue of the bizarre; the hero of all ages bouncing through the corridors to lecture younger versions of himself was a sophisticated treatment of paradox published as early as 1941. *By His Bootstraps* was already a parody, a mockery of the theme (which put-on might have reached its apogee in Robert Silverberg's 1968 Ballantine novel, *Up the Line*). H. Beam Piper's Paratime Police, shuttling through history to avert impending disasters, the Bureaucrats of James Blish's (1954) Beep working out boy-meets-girl/mother-of-the-world scenarios to keep the timeline stable. Implausibilities founded upon a foundation impossibility but extraordinarily sophisticated, self-aware implausibilities. Perhaps this is another definition of science fiction.

THE MEMORY HOLE: Time travel, after all, is part of the human condition. Were we to ban all of these stories on Grounds Of Major Implausibility we would still have memory, every act of which is time travel; we would have wishes, hopes, expectations which operate the other way; we would have all of the refractions and compounding of threatened desire. If contemplating a pregnancy is not time travel, what is it? Insurance actuaries as members of the Paratime Police. Deeply embedded.

Here are fourteen stories on time travel. "The best of all time?" Why not? A marketing ploy? No, it is other than a marketing ploy, let us all aver every extension of desire; every recollection of darkness or light is for its moment "the best." Generations of fans and enthusiasts should give raucous endorsement to this anthology. "Bring it up the line, kid." One of the most raucous endorsers must—at this very moment—be the thirteen-year-old editor.

How would it all turn out? I wondered. If only I could travel in time and know. What will become of me?

—Barry Malzberg
March 2002
New Jersey

THE BATTLE OF LONG ISLAND

NANCY KRESS

As does Silverberg's "Hawksbill Station," this novelette incorporates important elements of the historical novel, but here history has been conjoined to the present rather than, as with Silverberg, the reverse. Like all of the most achieved fiction, this story is ultimately not really about what it initially seems to be about and the concluding scenes—which would have far less power outside of the context of imaginative literature—are devastating in consequence.

Nancy Kress's first stories and novels appeared in the late 1970s; her Nebula award in 1986 for her short story "All Them Bright Stars" increased her visibility, and a subsequent novella, "Beggars in Spain" (later novelized) won both the Hugo and Nebula. Showing equal strength—a rare occurrence in science fiction—in both short and long forms, she is one of the four or five most important science fiction writers to have emerged since 1980.

Over by the mess tent one of my younger nurses is standing close to a Special Forces lieutenant. I watch her face tip up to his, her eyes wide and shining, moonlight on her cheekbones. He reaches out one hand—his fingernails are not quite clean—and touches her brown hair where it falls over her shoulder, and the light on her skin trembles. I know that later tonight they will disappear into her tent, or his.

Later this week they will walk around the compound with their arms around each other's waists, sit across from each other at mess, and feed each other choice bits of chow oblivious to the amused glances of their friends. Later this month—or next month, or the one after that, if this bizarre duty goes on long enough—she will be pale and distraught, crumpling letters in one hand. She will cry in the supply tent. She will tell the other nurses that he fed her lies. She will not hear orders, or will carry them out red-eyed and wrong, endangering other lives and despising her own.

She will be useless to me, and I will have to transfer her out and start over with another.

Or maybe it won't happen that way. An alternate future: He will snap at his buddies, volunteer for extra duty near the Hole, become careless with some red- or homespun-coated soldier stumbling forward with a musket or bayonet. He'll kill somebody or—less likely—get killed himself. Or maybe he'll just snap at the wrong person—his captain, say. He'll be transferred out. If he kills an Arrival, General Robinson's wife and daughters are members of the D.A.R.

The two people by the mess tent, of course, don't see it this way. They like the same movies, were snubbed by the same people in high school, voted the same way in the last presidential election. Both volunteered for duty by the Hole. It follows that they're in love. It follows that they understand each other, can see to the bottoms of each other's souls. The other military couples they know—the ones who have divorced, or who haven't; the affairs on leave; the angry words on the parade ground at dawn—have nothing to do with *them*. They are different. They are unique.

When people can see the truth so plain around them, why do they persist in believing some other reality?

"Major Peters! You're needed in Recovery! Quick!"

I leave my tent and tear across the compound at a dead run. We have only three people in Recovery: one of the weird laws of the Hole seems to be that they seldom come through it if they're going to recover. Musket balls in the belly or heart, shell explosions that have torn off half a head. Eighty-three percent of the Arrivals are dead a few minutes after they fall through the Hole. Another 11 percent live longer but never regain consciousness. That leaves us with 6 percent who eventually talk, although not to us. After we repair the flesh and boost the immune system, the Army sends heavily armored trucks to move them out of our heavily armored compound to somewhere else. The Pentagon? We aren't told. Somewhere there are three soldiers from Kichline's Riflemen, a field-grade officer under Lord Percy, and a shell-shocked corporal in homespun, all talking to the best minds the country thinks it can find.

This time I want to talk first.

The soldier who has finally woken up is a grizzled veteran who came through dressed in breeches, boots, and light coat. It's summer on the other side of the Hole: The Battle of Long Island was fought on August 27, 1776. Unlike most Arrivals, this one staggered through the Hole without his rifle or bayonet, although he had a hunting knife, which was taken away from him. He'd received a head wound, most likely a glancing shell fragment, enough to cause concussion but, according to the brain scan, not permanent damage. When I burst into Recovery, he's sitting up, dazed, looking at the guards at the door holding their M-18s.

"The General and Dr. Bechtel are on their way," I say to the guards, which is approximately true. I sent a soldier walking across the compound to tell them. My phone seems to be malfunctioning. The soldier is walking very slowly.

"General Putnam?" the new Arrival asks. His voice is less dazed than his face: a rough, deep voice with the peculiar twist on almost-British English that still sends a chill through me all these months after the Hole opened.

"Were you with the Connecticut Third Regiment? Let me check your pulse, please, I'm a nurse."

"A nurse!" That seems to finish the daze; he looks at my uniform, then my face. When the Hole first opened, there was wild talk of putting the medical staff in Colonial dress—"To minimize the psychological shock." As if anything could minimize dying hooked to machines you couldn't

4

imagine in a place that didn't exist while being stuck with needles by people unborn for another two centuries. Cooler heads prevailed. I wear fatigues, my short hair limp against my head from a shower, my glasses thick over my eyes.

"Yes, a nurse. This is a hospital. Let me have your wrist, please."

He pulls his hand away. I grab his wrist and hold it firmly. Two Arrivals have attacked triage personnel and one attacked a Recovery guard; this soldier looks strong enough for both. But I served in the minor action in Kuwait and the major ones in Colombia. He lets me hold his wrist. His pulse is rapid but strong.

"What is this place?"

"I told you. A hospital."

He leans forward and clutches my arm with his free hand while I'm reaching for the medscan equipment. "The battle—*who won the battle?*"

They're often like this. They find themselves in an alien, impossible, unimaginable place, surrounded by guards with uniforms and weapons they don't recognize, and yet their first concern is not their personal fate but the battle they left behind. They ask again and again. They have to know what happened.

We aren't supposed to tell Arrivals anything not directly medical. No hint that this is more than a few days into their future. That's official policy. Not until the Military Intelligence experts are finished with whatever they do, wherever they do it. Not until the Pentagon has assured itself that the soldier, the Hole itself, is not some terrorist plot (whose, for Christ's sweet fucking sake?). We're "not qualified for this situation." (Who do they imagine is?) Those are my orders.

But he hasn't asked for very much future: The Battle of Long Island was over in less than 24 hours. And I, of all people, am not capable of denying anyone the truth of his past.

"The Colonists lost. Washington retreated."

"Ahhhhhhhhhhh. . . ." He lets it out like escaping gas. In Bogota, in the '95 offensive, lethal gas wiped out 3,000 men in an hour. I don't look directly at his face.

"You were hit in the head," I say. "Not badly."

He puts his hand to his head and fingers the bandage, but his eyes never leave mine. He has a strong, fierce face, with sunken black eyes, a hooked nose, broken teeth, and a beard coming in red, not gray. He could be anywhere from forty to sixty. It's not a modern face; today the Army would fix the teeth and shave the beard.

"And the General? Put survived the battle?"

"He did."

"Ahhhhhhhh. . . . And the war? *How goes the war?*"

I have said far too much already. The soldier sits straight on his bed, his fierce eyes blazing. Behind us I hear the door open and the guards snap into salute. In those Colonial eyes is a need to know that has nothing in it of weakness. It isn't a plea, or a beseeching. It's a demand for a right, as we today might demand a search warrant, or a lawyer, or a trial by jury—all things whose existence once depended on what this soldier wants to know. He stares at me and I feel in him an elemental power, as if the need to know is as basic as the need for water, or air.

"How goes the war, Mistress?"

Footsteps hurry toward us.

I can't look away from the soldier's eyes. He doesn't know, can't know, what he's asking, or of whom. My mouth forms the words softly, so that only he hears.

"You won. England surrendered in October of 1781."

Something moves behind those black eyes, something so strong I draw back a little. Then they're on us, General

6

Robinson first and behind him chief of medical staff, Colonel Dr. William Bechtel. My father, who has denied me truth for thirty-five years.

I have never stood by the mess tent with a young soldier. If you join the Army at 20, right out of nursing school, and you stay in it for nineteen years, and you never wear a skirt or makeup, there is only one question your fellow soldiers come to ask. I know the answer; I am not homosexual. Neither, as far as I can tell, am I heterosexual. I have never wanted to feel anyone's touch on my hair in the moonlight.

Dr. Bechtel was assigned to duty at the Hole the day it appeared. If I'd known this, I never would have requested a transfer. I was en route to the U.S. European Command in Stuttgart; I would have continued on my way there. I use my dead mother's surname, and I don't think General Robinson knows that Bechtel is my father. Or maybe he does. The Army knows everything; often it just doesn't make connections among the things it knows. But that doesn't matter. I run the best nursing unit under fire in the entire Army. I'd match my nurses with any others, anywhere. I myself have performed operations alongside the doctors, in Bogota, when there were five doctors for three hundred mangled and screaming soldiers. I never see my father outside the OR.

The new Arrival's name is Sergeant Edward Strickland, of the Connecticut Third Regiment. No modems are permitted in the Hole compound, which used to be Prospect Park in Brooklyn, but officers are issued dumb terminals. The Army has allowed us access to its unclassified history databanks. By this time we all know a lot about the Battle of Long Island, which a year ago most of us had never heard of.

Strickland rates two mentions in the d-banks. In a 1776 letter to his wife, General Israel Putnam praised Strickland's "bravery and fearlessness" in defending the Brooklyn Heights entrenchments. A year later, Strickland turns up on the "Killed in Action" list for the fighting around Peekskill. A son, Putnam Strickland, became a member of the Pennsylvania Legislature in 1794.

My father never had a son. The criminal charges against him resulted in a hung jury, and the prosecutor chose not to refile but to refer the case to the Family Court of Orange County. After he was barred by the judge from ever seeing me again, he lived alone.

In the afternoon, a Special Forces team shows up to make a fourth assault on the Hole. During the first two, medical staff had all been bundled into concrete bunkers; maybe the Pentagon was afraid of an explosion from antimatter or negative tachyons or whatever the current theory is. By the third attempt, when it seemed clear nothing was going to happen anyway, we were allowed to stay within a few yards of the Hole, which is as far as most Arrivals get.

And farther than the assault team gets. The four soldiers in their clumsy suits lumber toward the faint shimmer that is all you can see of the Hole. I pause halfway between OR and Supply, a box of registered painkillers in my hand, and watch. Sun glints off metal helmets. If the team actually gets through, will they be bulletproof on the other side? Will the battle for Brooklyn Heights and the Jamaica Road stop, in sheer astonishment at the monsters bursting in air? If the battle does stop, will the assault team turn around and lumber back, having satisfied the Pentagon that this really is some sort of time hole and not some sort of enemy illusion? (Which enemy?) Or will the team stay to give General Israel Putnam and his aide-de-camp Aaron Burr a strategy for defeating twenty thousand British veterans with five thousand half-trained recruits?

Head nurses are not considered to have a need to know these decisions.

When the assault team reaches the shimmer—I have to squint to see it in the sunlight—they stop. Each of the four suited figures bends forward, straining, but nothing gives. Boxlike items—I assume they're classified weapons—are brought out and aimed at the shimmer. Nothing. After ten minutes, three soldiers lumber back to the command bunker.

The fourth stays. I wouldn't have seen what he did except that I turn around as three British soldiers fall through the Hole from the other side. An infantryman first, blood streaming from his mouth and nose, screaming, screaming. By the time I reach him, he's dead. The other two come through twenty feet east, and as I straighten up from bending over the infantryman, his blood smearing my uniform, I see the Hole guards leap forward. A musket discharges, a sound more like an explosion than like the rat-a-tat-tat of our pieces. I hit the dirt. The guards jump the other two redcoats.

Beside me, just beyond the dead Brit, I see the assault-team lieutenant finish his task. He's undogged the front of his suit, and now he reaches inside and pulls out something that catches the sunlight. I recognize it: Edward Strickland's hunting knife. He lobs it gently toward the Hole. It cuts through the shimmer as easily as into butter and disappears.

"Major! Major!" One of my young nurses runs toward me. For the second time I crawl up from the English soldier's body.

Another musket discharges. A fourth British soldier, an officer, has stumbled through the Hole and fired. The ball hits the young nurse in the chest, and she staggers backward and falls in a spray of blood just as the *rat-a-tat-tat* of assault rifles barks in the hot air.

* * *

We're in OR all afternoon. I think that's the only reason they don't get to me until evening. My nurse, Lt. Mary Inghram, dies. The British major who killed her dies. One of the other British soldiers dies. The infantryman was already dead. The last Brit, a Captain John Percy Healy of His Majesty's Twenty-Third Foot under the command of Lord William Howe, is conscious. He has arterial bleeding, contusions, and a complex femoral fracture. We put him under. To treat him and to autopsy the other three English soldiers, we have to remove heavy winter uniforms, including watch coats and gloves. The cockade on Healy's tricorne is still wet with snow.

I am just finishing at the dumb terminal when the aide comes for me. I haven't even showered after OR, just removed my scrubs. The terminal screen says JOHN PERCY HEALY, THIRD SON OF VISCOUNT SHERINGHAM, 1747–1809. (1) ARRIVAL IN VIRGINIA WITH TWENTY-THIRD FOOT, 1781, JUST PRIOR TO CORNWALLIS SURRENDER AT YORKTOWN. *see Burke's Peerage.*

"Major Peters? The General wants to see you in his quarters, ma'am."

1781. Five years after the Battle of Long Island.

"Ma'am? He said right away, ma'am."

What battle had Captain Healy been fighting on his side of the Hole?

"*Ma'am. . . .*"

"Yes, soldier." The screen goes blank. After a moment, red letters appear: ACCESS DENIED ALL PERSONNEL UNTIL FURTHER NOTICE.

General Robinson's quarters are as bleak as the rest of the compound: a foamcast "tent" that is actually a rigid, gray-green dome, furnished with standard-issue cot, desk, locker, and terminal. He's made no effort at interior decoration, but on the desk stand pictures of his wife and three daughters. They're all pretty, smiling, dressed up for somebody's wedding.

Bechtel is there.

As I stand at attention in front of the two men, I have a sudden memory of a doll I owned when I was a child. By the time the doll came to me from some other, forgotten child, its hair was worn to a fragile halo through which you could see the cracked plastic scalp. One eye had fallen back into its head. It wore a stained red dress with a raveling hem where one sleeve should have been. My mother told me much later that whenever I saw the doll around our house, I picked it up and carried it everywhere for a few days, but when I lost it, I didn't hunt for it. When it appeared again at my father's trial, it must have seemed natural to me to once more take hold of its battered, indifferent familiarity, I think now that I didn't understand to what use it was being put; I don't remember what I thought then. I was four years old.

Nor do I remember anything about the actual trial, only what I was told much later. But I know why I remember the doll. I even know why I think of it now, in the General's bunker. After the trial, my mother took the doll away and substituted another with the same shape, the same dress, the same yellow hair. Only this doll was new and unused, its red satin dress shiny and double-sleeved. I remember staring at it, puzzled, knowing something had changed but not how, nor why, it was the same doll—my mother told me it was the same doll—and yet it was not. I looked at my mother's face, and for the first time in what must have been the whole long mess of the trial, I felt the floor ripple and shake under my feet. My mother's smiling face looked suddenly far away, and blurred, as if she might be somebody else's mother. I remember I started screaming.

The General says, "Major Peters, Sergeant Strickland says you were the first person to talk to him after he gained consciousness. He says you told him the American colonists won the Revolution and that England surrendered in 1781. Is that correct?"

"Yes, sir." My shoulders are braced hard. I look directly at the General, and no one else. The General's face is very grave.

"Were you aware of explicit orders that no medical personnel shall supply information concerning these men's future, under any circumstances?"

"Yes, sir. I was."

"Then why did you disobey the order, Major?"

"I have no good reason, sir."

"Then let's hear an ungood one, Major."

He's giving me every chance to explain. I wonder if General Israel Putnam was like this with his men, all of whom followed him with a fanatic devotion, even when his military decisions were wrong. Even when a movement started to have him court-martialed for poor military judgment after the disaster of Long Island. Robinson watches me with grave, observant eyes. I might even have tried to answer him if Bechtel hadn't been there. Bechtel is responsible for the conduct of his entire medical staff, of course, and for a sudden, horrified moment, I wonder if that's really why I disobeyed orders. To get back at my father.

But I can't say all that out loud, not even if Bechtel were still posted halfway around the world.

"No reason at all, sir," I say, and wait for my reprimand, or transfer, or court-martial. I'm not sure how seriously the Army takes this gag order with Arrivals. I've never heard of anybody else disobeying it.

The General shuffles some papers on his desk. "There is a complication, Major." He looks up at me, and now I see something else in his eyes besides fairness. He is furious. "Sergeant Strickland refuses to talk to anyone but you. He says he trusts you and no one else, and unless you're present, he won't cooperate with Military Intelligence."

I don't know what to say.

"This is obviously an undesirable situation, Major. And one for which you may eventually be held responsible. In the meantime, however, you're needed to assist in the debriefing of Sergeant Strickland, and so you will report immediately to Colonel Orr and arrange a schedule for that. If that represents a conflict with your other duties, I will arrange to relieve you of those."

Relief fills me like sunlight. No court-martial. If I cooperate, the whole thing will be overlooked—that's what the offer to keep my nursing duties means. Robinson doesn't want an issue made of this one slip any more than I do. Slavering beyond the perimeter of the high-security compound, along with the Brooklyn Zoo, are hundreds of journalists from around the world. The less we have to say to them, and they about us, the better. No duty goes on forever.

"Yes, sir. There will be no conflict of duties. Thank you, sir."

"You logged onto the library system last night."

"Yes, sir." Of course log-ons would be monitored. The Army knows what I discovered about the Brit captain. The Army knows that I know they know. I like that. I joined the service for just these reasons: Actions are measurable, and privacy is suspect.

"What did you learn about Captain Healy?"

I answer immediately. "That he must come from a different past on the other side of the Hole. A past in which events in the Revolution were somehow different from ours."

Robinson nods. The carefully controlled anger fades

from his eyes. I have passed some test. "You will say nothing of that speculation to Sergeant Strickland, Major. Anything you tell him will concern only history as it exists for us."

He's asking me to not do something I would never have done anyway. I am the last person to offer Strickland a doubtful past. "Certainly, sir."

"You will answer only such questions as Colonel Orr thinks appropriate."

"Yes, sir."

"There will be no more anomalies in any communication in which you are involved."

"No, sir."

"Fine," Robinson says. He rises. "I'm going for a walk."

Without dismissing me. The General knows, then. He has cross-filed the personnel records. Or Bechtel told him. Bechtel requested this "walk" to leave us alone for a moment. The skin over my belly crawls—Robinson *knows*. I stare straight ahead, still at attention.

A long silent moment passes.

Bechtel makes a noise, unclassifiable. His voice is soft as smoke. "Susan—I didn't do it."

I stare straight ahead.

"No matter what the judge decided. I never touched you. Your mother wanted the divorce so bad she was willing to say anything. She *did* say anything. She—"

"Will that be all, sir?"

This time there is no soft noise. "Susan—she *lied*. Doesn't that matter to you?"

"She said you lied," I say, and immediately am furious with myself for saying anything at all. I clench my jaw.

My fury must somehow communicate itself to my father. In the stiffness of my already stiff body, in the air itself. He says tiredly, "Dismissed," and I hear in the single word things I don't want to examine. I walk stiff-legged from the tent.

After the trial, I never touched the doll in the red dress again.

My first interview with Sergeant Edward Strickland, Connecticut Third Regiment, First Continental Army, takes place the next morning. He's been moved from Recovery to a secure bunker at the far end of the compound, although he still has an elevated temperature and the remains of dysentery. Even in a standard-issue hospital gown he doesn't look like a man from our time. It's more than just the broken teeth. It's something unbroken in his face. He looks as if asscovering is as foreign to him as polyester.

"Sergeant Strickland," commands the Military Intelligence expert, Colonel Orr. Unseen recording equipment whirs quietly. "Tell us all your movements for the last few days, starting with General Putnam's fortification of the Brooklyn Heights works."

Strickland has apparently decided he is not enlisted in this Army. He ignores the colonel and says directly to me, "Where am I, Mistress Nurse?"

Orr nods, almost imperceptibly. We've rehearsed this much. I say, "You're in an Army hospital on Long Island."

"What date be today?"

"July 15, 2001."

I can't tell if he believes me or not. The fierce black eyes bore steadily, without blinking. I say, "What work did you do before you joined the Army, Sergeant?"

"I was a smith."

"Where?"

"Pomfret, Connecticut. Mistress . . . if this be the future, how come I to be here?"

"We don't know. Three months ago soldiers from the

Battle of Long Island began to stumble into a city park out of thin air. Most of them died. You didn't."

He considers this. His gaze travels around the foamcast bunker, to my glasses, to the M-18 held by the guard. Abruptly, he laughs. I see the moment he refuses the idea of the future without actually rejecting it, like a man who accepts a leaflet on a street corner but puts it in his pocket, unread, sure it has nothing to do with his real life.

He says, "What losses did we suffer at Long Island?"

"A thousand dead, seven hundred taken prisoner," I answer, and he flinches.

"And the enemy?"

"Howe reported sixty-one dead, twenty-nine missing."

"How did the enemy best us?"

"Surprised you with a flanking march down the Jamaica Road, with a force you couldn't possibly match."

"How did Put retreat?"

"By water, across the river to New York."

It goes on like that, reliving military history 225 years dead. Six months ago, I knew none of it. Orr doesn't interrupt me. Probably he thinks that Strickland is learning to trust us. I know that Strickland is learning to trust his own past, checking the details until he knows they're sound, constructing around himself the solid world that must hold this mutable one.

From the direction of the Hole comes the muffled sound of musket fire.

This time it's a Hessian, one of the mercenary forces serving the British under De Heister in front of the Flatbush pass. He's the first Hessian to come through the Hole. Screaming in German, he fights valiantly as the OR personnel put him under. By the time I see him, swaddled in a hospital gown in Recovery, his face is subdued in the unnatural sleep of anesthesia, and I see that although as big as Strickland, the Hessian mercenary is no more than 16. By our standards, a child.

Strickland walks in, accompanied by the MI colonel and a very attentive MP. Are they trying to build his trust by giving him the illusion of free movement within the compound? He's the first Arrival who's ambulatory and still here. I think about how easily the Special Forces lieutenant slid Strickland's hunting knife back through the Hole, which not even our tanks had been able to penetrate, and I bet myself that Old Put's Sergeant's free movement has no more latitude than Put himself did on the Jamaica Road.

Strickland gazes at the Hessian. "A boy. To do their fighting for 'em." The rough voice is heavy with sarcasm.

"From De Heister's troops," I say, to say something.

"Put always traded 'em back."

"It must have been hard for them, to go so far from their homes," the nurse on duty says tentatively. She has a high, fluttery voice. Strickland looks at her with irony, a much more surprising expression on that rough face than sarcasm, and she flushes. He laughs.

The German boy opens his eyes. His blurry gaze falls on Strickland, who again wears his own breeches and shirt and coat, with the strip of red cloth of a field sergeant sewn onto the right shoulder. The Hessian is probably in a lot of pain, but even so, his face brightens.

"Mein Felowebel! Wir haben die schlact gewinnen, ja?"

The Military Intelligence colonel's eyes widen. Strickland's face turns to stone. Orr makes a quick gesture and the next minute both Strickland and I are being firmly escorted out of Recovery. Strickland shakes off the MP's arm and turns angrily to me.

"What did he mean, *'Mein Felowebel'*? And, *'Wir haben die schlact gewinnen'*?"

I shake my head. "I don't speak German."

Strickland looks at me a moment longer, trying to see if I'm telling the truth. Evidently he sees from my face that I am. We stare at each other in the sunlight, while I wonder what the hell is happening. Orr emerges from Recovery long enough to snap an order at the MP, who escorts Strickland back to his quarters.

In my own quarters I fish out the German-American dictionary I bought when I thought I was being sent to Stuttgart instead of Brooklyn. It takes a long time to track down spellings in a language I don't speak, especially since I'm guessing at the dialect and at words I've only heard twice. Outside, two passing soldiers improvise a songfest: "There's a Hole in the battle, dear Gen'ral, dear Gen'ral; there's a Hole in the battle, dear Gen'ral, a Ho-oo-ole." Finally I piece together a translation of the German sentence.

My sergeant! We won the battle, yes?

I try to think about everything that would have had to be different in the world for Frederick II of Hesse-Kassel to furnish mercenaries to the Colonial patriots instead of to the British. I can't do it; I don't know enough history. A moment later, I realize how dumb that is: There's a much simpler explanation. De Heister's Hessian could simply have deserted, changing sides in midwar. Loyalties were often confused during the Revolution. Desertion was probably common, even among mercenaries.

Desertion is always common.

My mother was born in 1935, but she didn't graduate from college until 1969. All her life, which ended in a car crash, she kept the conviction of her adopted generation that things are only good before they settle into formula and routine. She marched against the draft, against Dow Chemical, against capitalism, against whaling. She was never for

anything. Shoulder to shoulder with a generation that refused to trust anyone over thirty, this thirty-three year old
noisily demonstrated her hatred for rules.

All my childhood I never knew if I was supposed to be
home for dinner by 6:00, or 6:30, or at all. I never knew if
the men she dated would return again, or be showered with
contemptuous scorn, or move in. I never knew if the elec-
tricity would suddenly be cut off while I was doing my al-
gebra homework, or when we would move again in the
middle of the night, leaving the gas bill shredded and the
rent unpaid. I never knew anything. My mother told me we
were "really" rich, we were dirt poor, we were wanted by
the law, we were protected by the law. At 17, I ran away
from home and joined the Army, which put me through
nursing school.

My mother is buried in Dansville, New York, which I
once saw from a Greyhound Bus. It's a small town with
orderly nineteenth-century storefronts and bars full of
middle-aged men in John Deere caps. These men, who pay
their mortgages faithfully, stand beside their bar stools and
argue in favor of capital punishment, confiscation of drug
dealers' cars, the elimination of Welfare, and the NRA. On
summer weekends they throw rocks at the Women's Peace
Collective enclave off Route 63. The Dansville cemetery is
kept neatly mowed and clipped. I chose the burial plot myself.

Captain John Percy Healy of His Majesty's Twenty-Third
Foot is kept under close guard. Strickland couldn't get anywhere near him, even if he knew that Healy and his winter-
clad Battle of Long Island existed. Nor can he get near the
Hole, although he tries. The summer sun is slanting in long
lines over the compound when he breaks away from the MI
colonel and the bodyguard MP and me and sets off at a

dead run toward the Hole. His head is down, his powerful legs pumping. As each leg lifts, I see a hole in the sole of his left boot flash and disappear, flash and disappear.

"Halt!" shouts Colonel Orr. The guards at the Hole raise their weapons. The MP, whose fault this escape is, starts to run after Strickland, realizes he can't possibly catch him, and draws his gun. "Halt, or we'll fire!"

They do. Strickland goes down, hit in the leg. He drags himself toward the Hole on his elbows, his body thrashing from side to side on the hard ground, a thin line of blood trickling behind. I can't see his face. The MP reaches him before I do and Strickland fights him fiercely, in silence.

Three more soldiers are on him.

I've seen more direct combat nursing than any other nurse I've met personally, but in OR I can't look at Strickland's eyes. If he had reached the Hole, he could have gone through, and I'm the only person in the room who knows this. Not even Strickland knows it. He only acted as if he did.

Dr. Bechtel sends for me the next morning. He's the chief of medical staff. I go.

"Susan, I think. . . ."

" 'Major,' sir. I would prefer to be called 'Major.' Sir."

He doesn't change expression. "Major, I think it would be a good idea if you requested a transfer to another unit."

I draw a deep breath. "Are you rotating me out, sir?"

"No!" For a second some emotion breaks through—anger? fear? guilt?—and then is gone. "I'm suggesting you voluntarily apply for a transfer. You're not doing your career any good here, with Strickland, not the way things have turned out. There are too many anomalies. The Army doesn't like anomalies, Major."

"The entire Hole is an anomaly. Sir."

He permits himself a thin smile. "True enough. And the Army doesn't like it."

"I don't want to transfer."

He looks at me directly. "Why not?"

"I prefer not to, sir," I say. Is a nonanswer answer an anomaly? I can feel every tendon in my body straining toward the door. And yet there is a horrible fascination, too, in staring at him like this. Somewhere in my mind a four-year-old girl touches a one-eyed doll in a raveled red dress. *Here. He touched me here. And here. . . .* But did he?

The four-year-old doesn't answer.

"Strickland is asking to see you," he says wearily. "No—*demanding* to see you. Somewhere he saw Healy's uniform. Being carried across the parade ground from the cleaning machine, maybe—I don't know. He won't say."

I picture Healy's heavy watch coat, his red uniform with the regimental epaulets on both shoulders, his crimson sash.

"Strickland's smart," I say slowly, and immediately regret it. I'm participating in the conversation as if it were normal, I don't want to give him that.

"Yes," my father says, a shade too eagerly. "He's figured out that there are multiple realities beyond the Hole. Multiple Battles of Long Island. Maybe even entirely different American Revolutions. . . . I don't know." He passes a hand through his hair and I'm jolted by an unexpected memory, shimmery and dim: my Daddy at the dinner table, talking and passing a hand through his hair, myself in a highchair with round beads on the tray, beads that spin and slide. . . . "The Pentagon moves him out tomorrow."

"Strickland?"

"Yes, of course, that's who we've been talking about." He peers at me. I give him nothing, wooden-faced. Abruptly he says, "Susan—ask for a transfer."

"No, sir," I say. "Not unless that's an order."

We stand at opposite ends of the bunker, and the air shimmers between us.

"Dismissed," he says quietly. I salute and leave, but as I reach the door, he tries once more. "I recommend that you don't see Strickland again. No matter what he demands. For the sake of your own career."

"Recommendation noted, sir," I say, without inflection.

Outside, the night is hot and still. I have trouble breathing the stifling air, I try to think what could have prompted my father's sudden concern with my career, but no matter how I look at it, I can't see any advantage to him in keeping me away from Strickland. Only to myself. The air trembles with heat lightning. Beyond the compound, at the Brooklyn Zoo, an elephant bellows, as if in pain.

The next day the Hole closes.

I'm not there at the time—0715 hours EDT—but one of the guards retells the story in the mess tent. "There was this faint pop, like a kid's toy gun. Yoder hit the dirt and pissed his pants—"

"I did not! Fuck you!" Yoder yells, and there are some good-natured insults and pointless shoving before anybody can overhear what actually did happen.

"This little pop, and the shimmer kinda disappeared, and that was it. Special Forces showed up and they couldn't get in—"

"When could they ever?" someone says slyly, a female voice, and there are laughter and nudges.

"And that was it. The Hole went bye-bye," the guard says, reclaiming group attention.

"So when do we go home?"

"When the Army fucking says you do."

They move Strickland out the next day. I don't see him. No one reports if he asks for me. Probably not. At some point Strickland decided that his trust in me was misplaced, born of one of those chance moments of emotion that turn out to be less durable than expected. I wasn't able to help him toward the Hole. All I was able to do was tell him military information that may or may not be true for a place and time that he can't ever reach again.

Curiously enough, it is the Brit, Major John Healy, to whom we make a difference.

He is with us a week before they move him, recovering from his injuries. The broken leg sets clean. Military Intelligence, in the form of Colonel Orr, goes in and out of his heavily guarded bunker several times a day. Orr is never there while I'm changing Healy's dressings or monitoring his vitals, but Healy is especially thoughtful after Orr has left. He watches me with a bemused expression, as if he wonders what *I'm* thinking.

He's nothing like Strickland. Slight, fair, not tall, with regular features and fresh-colored skin. Healy's speech is precise and formal, courteous, yet with a mocking gaiety in it. Even here, which seems to me a kind of miracle. He's fastidious about his dress, and a military orderly actually learns to black boots.

Between debriefings, Healy reads. He requested the books himself, all published before 1776; but maybe that's all he's permitted. *Gulliver's Travels. Robinson Crusoe.* Poems by somebody called Alexander Pope. I've never been much of a reader, but I saw the MGM movie about Crusoe, and I look up the others. They're all books about men severely displaced. Once Healy, trying to make conversation, tells me that he comes from London, where his family has a house in Tavistock Place, also a "seat" in Somerset.

I refuse to be drawn into conversation with him.

On the day they're going to move him, Bechtel does a complete medical. I assist. Naked, with electrodes attached to his head and vials of blood drawn from his arm, Healy suddenly becomes unstoppably talkative.

"In London, the physicians make use of leeches to accomplish your identical aims."

Bechtel smiles briefly.

"In *my* London, that is. Not in yours. There is a London here, I presume, Doctor?"

"Yes," Bechtel says. "There is."

"Then there exist two. But there's rather more, isn't there? One for the Hessian. One for that Colonial who attempted escape back through the . . . the time corridor. Probably others, is that not so?"

"Probably," Bechtel says. He studies the EKG printout.

"And in some of these Londons, we put down the Rebellion, and in others, you Colonials succeed in declaring yourself a sovereign nation, and perhaps in still others, the savages destroy you all and the Rebellion never even occurs. Have I understood the situation correctly?"

"Yes," Bechtel says. He looks at the Brit now, and I am caught by the look as well—by its unexpected compassion.

The vial of blood in my hand seems to pound against my temples.

My mother told me, when I was eight, that my father had caused the war then raging in Vietnam.

I say nothing.

"Then," Healy continues in his beautiful, precise, foreign voice, "there must exist several versions of this present as well. Some of them must, by simple deduction, be more appealing than this one." He glances around the drab bunker. Beyond the barred window, an American flag flies over the parade ground. Couldn't we have spared him the constant sight of his enemy's flag?

Then I remember that he probably doesn't even recognize it. The stars-and-stripes wasn't adopted by the Continental Congress until 1777.

"This compound is not the whole of our present," Bechtel says, too gently. "The rest is much different."

Healy waves a hand, smiling. "Oh, quite. I'm convinced you have marvels abounding, including your edition of London. Which, since I cannot return to my own, I hope to one day visit." The smile wavers slightly, but in a moment he has it back. "Of course, it will not be even the descendent of my own. I must be prepared for that. In *this* history, you Colonials fought the Battle of Long Island in the summer."

"Yes," Bechtel says.

"My own history is apparently quite unrecoverable. Your historical tactician tells me that no connection appears to exist between this place and whichever of those histories is mine. And so I cannot, of course, know what might have happened in the course of my own war, any more than you can know." He watches Bechtel closely. All this is said in that same mocking, light-hearted voice. I can hear that voice in London drawing rooms, amid ladies in panniers and high-dressed curls, who know better than to believe a word such an amusing rake ever says.

Bechtel lays down the printout and steps toward Healy's cot. Instinctively the Brit reaches for the coat of his uniform and pulls it around his shoulders. Bechtel waits until Healy is draped in his remnants of the British Empire. Then Bechtel speaks in a voice both steady and offhand, as if it were calculated to match the careless facade of Healy's own bravery.

"You must choose the reality you prefer. Look at it this way, Captain. You don't know for sure who won the war in your time, or who survived it, or what England or the United States became after your November 16, 1776. Your past is closed to you. So you're free to choose whatever one you wish. You can live as if your choice *is* your past. And in so doing, make it real."

I move carefully at my station, feeding Healy's blood samples into the Hays-Mason analyzer.

Healy says, with that same brittle gaiety, "You are urging me to an act of faith, sir."

"Yes, if you like," Bechtel says. He looks at me. "But I would call it an act of choice."

"Choice that I am not a prisoner *de guerre*, from a losing army, of a war I may or may not have survived?"

"Yes."

"I will consider what you say, sir," Healy says, and turns away. The epaulets on his shoulders tremble, but it may have been the light. From the parade ground beyond the window comes the sound of a jeep with a faulty muffler.

"I've finished here," Bechtel tells the guard, who relays the information over his comlink.

They remove Healy in a wheelchair, although it's obvious he doesn't like this. As he's wheeled past, he catches at my arm. His blue eyes smile, but his fingers dig into my flesh. I don't allow myself to wince. "Mistress Nurse—are there ladies where I'm going? Shall I have the society of your sex?"

I look at him. Not even a hint of how Lieutenant Mary Inghram died has leaked to the outside press. Her parents were told she died in an explosives accident: I signed the report myself. When the Pentagon takes the Arrivals from our compound, they vanish as completely as if they'd never existed, and not even an electronic-data trail, the hunting spoor of the twenty-first century, remains. Ladies? The society of my sex? How would I know?

"Yes," I say to Healy. "You will."

The tent is empty except for Bechtel and me. I clean and

stow the equipment; he scrubs at the sink. His back is to me. Very low, so that I barely hear him over the running water, he says, "Susan. . . ."

"All right," I say. "I choose. You did it."

I walk out of the bunker. Some soldiers stand outside, at parade rest, listening to their sergeant read the orders for move-out. Guards still ring the place where the Hole used to be. In the sky, above the Low Radar Barrier, a seagull wheels and cries. The elephant is silent. I have never seen my father since.

You might think I should have chosen differently. You might think, given the absence of proof, that like any jury empowered by the Constitution of the United States, I should choose the more innocent reality. Should believe that my father never molested me and that my mother, who is now beyond both proof and innocence, lied. The trial evidence is inconclusive, the character evidence cloudy. If I choose that reality, I gain not only a father, but peace of mind. I free myself from the torments of a past that might not even have happened.

But I would still be *this* Susan Peters. I would still watch my nurses tremble with love in the moonlight, and I would still see clearly the deceptions and hurt ahead, the almost inevitable anger. I would still recoil if a man brushes against me accidentally away from the hospital, and still pride myself on never wincing at anything within a hospital. I would still know that I chose Army nursing precisely because here dangerous men are at their weakest, and most vulnerable, and in greatest need of what I can safely give them.

I would still know what Strickland learned: The Hole always closes.

One version of the past has shaped all my of choices. If I decide it never happened, what remains? Will I exist? I,

Susan Peters, who runs the best combat nursing unit in the entire Army? I, Susan Peters, who have earned both the Commendation Medal and the Distinguished Service Cross? I, Susan Peters, who can operate on a patient myself if the doctors are occupied with other screaming and suffering men? And *have*?

I, Susan Peters.

Who was sexually abused by her father, ran away from home, joined the Army, became a nurse, served honorably in the Special Medical Unit assigned to the Battle of Long Island, and have never lied to a patient except once.

And maybe it wasn't a lie.

Maybe there *will* be ladies where they are taking Captain John Percy Healy of His Majesty King George III's Twenty-Third Foot. Maybe Healy will stand with some young woman, somewhere, in the moonlight and touch her face with gentle fingers. It's possible. I certainly don't know differently. And if there are, then it wasn't even a lie.

THE MAN WHO CAME EARLY

POUL ANDERSON

Time out of time—time travel as a multiple or single inconvenience—is perhaps the most pervasive theme to emerge from the stories included here, the stories being representative of the finest work on the theme. It is the stark, forthright realism of this story—which, its premise granted, plays as starkly as Eugene O'Neill's *The Iceman Cometh,* and for many of the same reasons—which astonished its readers in 1956 and which continues, fifty years later, to be shocking. There are many good treatments of this theme—Ted Thomas's "The Doctor"/*Orbit Two* comes to mind—but this casually brilliant story has never been superseded.

Poul Anderson (1926–2001) over his 54-year publishing career, took every honor that science fiction and fantasy had to offer; he was productive to the very last days of his life (stories appeared in *Analog* and *The Magazine of Fantasy & Science Fiction* the month after his death). He was an SFFWA Grandmaster, multiple winner of Hugo and Nebula Awards and acclaimed almost equally as a fantasist. It is now possible, in seeing the full arc of his creative life, to put him on the same level as Asimov, Clarke and Heinlein, the so-called "Big Three" over a thirty-year period. His work will certainly live as long as that of anyone who has to date written science fiction.

Yes, when a man grows old he has heard so much that is strange there's little more can surprise him. They say the king in Miklagard has a beast of gold before his high seat which stands up and roars. I have it from Eilif Eiriksson, who served in the guard down yonder, and he is a steady fellow when not drunk. He has also seen the Greek fire used, it burns on water.

So, priest, I am not unwilling to believe what you say about the White Christ. I have been in England and France myself, and seen how the folk prosper. He must be a very powerful god, to ward so many realms . . . and did you say that everyone who is baptized will be given a white robe? I would like to have one. They mildew, of course, in this cursed wet Iceland weather, but a small sacrifice to the house-elves should—No sacrifices? Come now! I'll give up horseflesh if I must, my teeth not being what they were, but every sensible man knows how much trouble the elves make if they're not fed.

Well, let's have another cup and talk about it. How do

you like the beer? It's my own brew, you know. The cups I got in England, many years back. I was a young man then ... time goes, time goes. Afterward I came back and inherited this, my father's farm, and have not left it since. Well enough to go in viking as a youth, but grown older you see where the real wealth lies: here, in the land and the cattle.

Stoke up the fires, Hjalti. It's getting cold. Sometimes I think the winters are colder than when I was a boy. Thorbrand of the Salmondale says so, but he believes the gods are angry because so many are turning from them. You'll have trouble winning Thorbrand over, priest. A stubborn man. Myself, I am open-minded, and willing to listen at least.

Now, then. There is one point on which I must set you right. The end of the world is not coming in two years. This I know.

And if you ask me how I know, that's a very long tale, and in some ways a terrible one. Glad I am to be old, and safe in the earth before that great tomorrow comes. It will be an eldritch time before the frost giants fare loose ... oh, very well, before the angel blows his battle horn. One reason I hearken to your preaching is that I know the White Christ will conquer Thor. I know Iceland is going to be Christian erelong, and it seems best to range myself on the winning side.

No, I've had no visions. This is a happening of five years ago, which my own household and neighbors can swear to. They mostly did not believe what the stranger told; I do, more or less, if only because I don't think a liar could wreak so much harm. I loved my daughter, priest, and after the trouble was over I made a good marriage for her. She did not naysay it, but now she sits out on the ness-farm with her husband and never a word to me; and I hear he is ill pleased with her silence and moodiness, and spends his nights with an Irish leman. For this I cannot blame him, but it grieves me.

Well, I've drunk enough to tell the whole truth now, and whether you believe it or not makes no odds to me. Here . . . you, girls! . . . fill these cups again, for I'll have a dry throat before I finish the telling.

It begins, then, on a day in early summer, five years ago. At that time, my wife Ragnhild and I had only two unwed children still living with us: our youngest son Helgi, of seventeen winters, and our daughter Thorgunna, of eighteen. The girl, being fair, had already had suitors. But she refused them, and I am not one who would compel his daughter. As for Helgi, he was ever a lively one, good with his hands but a breakneck youth. He is now serving in the guard of King Olaf of Norway. Besides these, of course, we had about ten housefolk—two thralls, two girls to help with the women's work, and half a dozen hired carles. This is not a small stead.

You have seen how my land lies. About two miles to the west is the bay; the thorps at Reykjavik are some five miles south. The land rises toward the Long Jökull, so that my acres are hilly; but it's good hay land, and we often find driftwood on the beach. I've built a shed down there for it, as well as a boathouse.

We had had a storm the night before—a wild huge storm with lightning flashes across heaven, such as you seldom get in Iceland—so Helgi and I were going down to look for drift. You, coming from Norway, do not know how precious wood is to us here, who have only a few scrubby trees and must get our timber from abroad. Back there men have often been burned in their houses by their foes, but we count that the worst of deeds, though it's not unheard of.

As I was on good terms with my neighbors, we took only hand weapons. I bore my ax, Helgi a sword, and the two carles we had with us bore spears. It was a day washed clean by the night's fury, and the sun fell bright on long, wet grass. I saw my stead lying rich around its courtyard, sleek cows and sheep, smoke rising from the roofhole of the hall, and knew I'd not done so ill in my lifetime. My son Helgi's hair fluttered in the low west wind as we left the buildings behind a ridge and neared the water. Strange how well I remember all which happened that day; somehow it was a sharper day than most.

When we came down to the strand, the sea was beating heavy, white and gray out to the world's edge, smelling of salt and kelp. A few gulls mewed above us, frightened off a cod washed onto the shore. I saw a litter of no few sticks, even a baulk of timber ... from some ship carrying it that broke up during the night, I suppose. That was a useful find, though as a careful man I would later sacrifice to be sure the owner's ghost wouldn't plague me.

We had fallen to and were dragging the baulk toward the shed when Helgi cried out. I ran for my ax as I looked the way he pointed. We had no feuds then, but there are always outlaws.

This newcomer seemed harmless, though. Indeed, as he stumbled nearer across the black sand I thought him quite unarmed and wondered what had happened. He was a big man and strangely clad—he wore coat and breeches and shoes like anyone else, but they were of odd cut, and he bound his trousers with leggings rather than straps. Nor had I ever seen a helmet like his: it was almost square, and came down toward his neck, but it had no nose guard. And this you may not believe, but it was not metal, yet had been cast in one piece!

He broke into a staggering run as he drew close, flapped his arms and croaked something. The tongue was none I had heard, and I have heard many; it was like dogs barking.

I saw that he was clean-shaven and his black hair cropped short, and thought he might be French. Otherwise he was a young man, and good-looking, with blue eyes and regular features. From his skin I judged that he spent much time indoors. However, he had a fine manly build.

"Could he have been shipwrecked?" asked Helgi.

"His clothes are dry and unstained," I said; "nor has he been wandering long, for no stubble is on his chin. Yet I've heard of no strangers guesting hereabouts."

We lowered our weapons, and he came up to us and stood gasping. I saw that his coat and the shirt underneath were fastened with bonelike buttons rather than laces, and were of heavy weave. About his neck he had fastened a strip of cloth tucked into his coat. These garments were all in brownish hues. His shoes were of a sort new to me, very well stitched. Here and there on his coat were bits of brass, and he had three broken stripes on each sleeve; also a black band with white letters, the same letters on his helmet. Those were not runes, but Roman—thus: MP. He wore a broad belt, with a small clublike thing of metal in a sheath at the hip and also a real club.

"I think he must be a warlock," muttered my carle Sigurd. "Why else so many tokens?"

"They may only be ornament, or to ward against witchcraft," I soothed him. Then, to the stranger: "I hight Ospak Ulfsson of Hillstead. What is your errand?"

He stood with his chest heaving and a wildness in his eyes. He must have run a long way. At last he moaned and sat down and covered his face.

"If he's sick, best we get him to the house," said Helgi. I heard eagerness; we see few faces here.

"No . . . no . . ." The stranger looked up. "Let me rest a moment—"

He spoke the Norse tongue readily enough, though with

34

a thick accent not easy to follow and with many foreign words I did not understand.

The other carle, Grim, hefted his spear. "Have vikings landed?" he asked.

"When did vikings ever come to Iceland?" I snorted. "It's the other way around."

The newcomer shook his head as if it had been struck. He got shakily to his feet. "What happened?" he said. "What became of the town?"

"What town?" I asked reasonably.

"Reykjavik!" he cried. "Where is it?"

"Five miles south, the way you came—unless you mean the bay itself," I said.

"No! There was only a beach, and a few wretched huts, and—"

"Best not let Hialmar Broadnose hear you call his thorp that," I counseled.

"But there was a town!" he gasped. "I was crossing the street in a storm, and heard a crash, and then I stood on the beach and the town was gone!"

"He's mad," said Sigurd, backing away. "Be careful. If he starts to foam at the mouth, it means he's going berserk."

"Who are you?" babbled the stranger. "What are you doing in those clothes? Why the spears?"

"Somehow," said Helgi, "he does not sound crazed, only frightened and bewildered. Something evil has beset him."

"I'm not staying near a man under a curse!" yelped Sigurd, and started to run away.

"Come back!" I bawled. "Stand where you are or I'll cleave your louse-bitten head."

That stopped him, for he had no kin who would avenge him; but he would not come closer. Meanwhile the stranger had calmed down to the point where he could talk somewhat evenly.

"Was it the *aitsjbom*?" he asked. "Has the war started?"

He used that word often, *aitsjbom*, so I know it now, though unsure of what it means. It seems to be a kind of Greek fire. As for the war, I knew not which war he meant, and told him so.

"We had a great thunderstorm last night," I added. "And you say you were out in one too. Maybe Thor's hammer knocked you from your place to here."

"But where is here?" he answered. His voice was more dulled than otherwise, now that the first terror had lifted.

"I told you. This is Hillstead, which is on Iceland."

"But that's where I was!" he said. "Reykjavik . . . what happened? Did the *aitsjbom* destroy everything while I lay witless?"

"Nothing has been destroyed," I said.

"Does he mean the fire at Olafsvik last month?" wondered Helgi.

"No, no, no!" Again he buried his face in his hands. After a while he looked up and said: "See here. I am *Sardjant* Gerald Robbins of the United States army base on Iceland. I was in Reykjavik and got struck by lightning or something. Suddenly I was standing on the beach, and lost my head and ran. That's all. Now, can you tell me how to get back to the base?"

Those were more or less his words, priest. Of course, we did not grasp half of them, and made him repeat several times and explain. Even then we did not understand, save that he was from some country called the United States of America, which he said lies beyond Greenland to the west, and that he and some others were on Iceland to help our folk against their foes. This I did not consider a lie—more a mistake or imagining. Grim would have cut him down for thinking us stupid enough to swallow that tale, but I could see that he meant it.

Talking cooled him further. "Look here," he said, in too calm a tone for a feverish man, "maybe we can get at the truth from your side. Has there been no war you know of? Nothing which—Well, look here. My country's men first came to Iceland to guard it against the Germans. Now it is the Russians, but then it was the Germans. When was that?"

Helgi shook is head. "That never happened that I know of," he said. "Who are these Russians?" We found out later that the Gardariki folk were meant. "Unless," Helgi said, "the old warlocks—"

"He means the Irish monks," I explained. "A few dwelt here when the Norsemen came, but they were driven out. That was, hm, somewhat over a hundred years ago. Did your kingdom once help the monks?"

"I never heard of them!" he said. The breath sobbed in his throat. "You . . . didn't you Icelanders come from Norway?"

"Yes, about a hundred years ago," I answered patiently. "After King Harald Fairhair laid the Norse lands under him and—"

"*A hundred years ago!*" he whispered. I saw whiteness creep up beneath his skin. "What year is this?"

We gaped at him. "Well, it's the second year after the great salmon catch," I tried.

"What year after Christ, I mean," he prayed hoarsely.

"Oh, so you are a Christian? Hm, let me think . . . I talked with a bishop in England once, we were holding him for ransom, and he said . . . let me see . . . I think he said this Christ man lived a thousand years ago, or maybe a little less."

"A thousand—" Something went out of him. He stood with glassy eyes—yes, I have seen glass, I told you I am a traveled man—he stood thus, and when we led him toward the garth he went like a small child.

* * *

You can see for yourself, priest, that my wife Ragnhild is still good to look upon even in eld, and Thorgunna took after her. She was—is—tall and slim, with a dragon's hoard of golden hair. She being a maiden then, the locks flowed loose over her shoulders. She had great blue eyes and a heart-shaped face and very red lips. Withal she was a merry one, and kindhearted, so that she was widely loved. Sverri Snorrason went in viking when she refused him, and was slain, but no one had the wit to see that she was unlucky.

We led this Gerald Samsson—when I asked, he said his father was named Sam—we led him home, leaving Sigurd and Grim to finish gathering the driftwood. Some folks would not have a Christian in their house, for fear of witch-craft, but I am a broad-minded man, and Helgi, at his age, was wild for anything new. Our guest stumbled over the fields as if blind, but seemed to rouse when we entered the yard. His gaze went around the buildings that enclose it, from the stables and sheds to the smokehouse, the brewery, the kitchen, the bathhouse, the god shrine, and thence to the hall. And Thorgunna was standing in the doorway.

Their gazes locked for a little, and I saw her color but thought nothing of it then. Our shoes rang on the flagging as we crossed the yard and kicked the dogs aside. My two thralls halted in cleaning the stables to gawp, until I got them back to work with the remark that a man good for naught else was always a pleasing sacrifice. That's one use-ful practice you Christians lack; I've never made a human offering myself, but you know not how helpful is the fact that I could do so.

We entered the hall, and I told the folk Gerald's name and how we had found him. Ragnhild set her maids hop-ping, to stoke up the fire in the middle trench and fetch beer, while I led Gerald to the high seat and sat down by him. Thorgunna brought us the filled horns. His standing was not like yours, for whom we use our outland cups.

Gerald tasted the brew and made a face. I felt somewhat offended, for my beer is reckoned good, and asked him if aught was wrong. He laughed with a harsh note and said no, but he was used to beer that foamed and was not sour.

"And where might they make such?" I wondered testily.

"Everywhere," he said. "Iceland, too—no. . . ." He stared before him in an empty wise. "Let's say . . . in Vinland."

"Where is Vinland?" I asked.

"The country to the west whence I came. I thought you knew. . . . Wait a bit." He frowned. "Maybe I can find out something. Have you heard of Leif Eiriksson?"

"No," I said. Since then it has struck me that this was one proof of his tale, for Leif Eiriksson is now a well-known chief; and I also take more seriously those yarns of land seen by Bjarni Herjulfsson.

"His father, Erik the Red?" went on Gerald.

"Oh yes," I said. "If you mean the Norseman who came hither because of a manslaughter, and left Iceland in turn for the same reason, and has now settled with his friends in Greenland."

"Then this is . . . a little before Leif's voyage," he muttered. "The late tenth century."

"See here," broke in Helgi, "we've been forbearing with you, but now is no time for riddles. We save those for feasts and drinking bouts. Can you not say plainly whence you come and how you got here?"

Gerald looked down at the floor, shaking.

"Let the man alone, Helgi," said Thorgunna. "Can you not see he's troubled?"

He raised his head and gave her the look of a hurt dog that someone has patted. The hall was dim; enough light seeped in the loft windows that no candles were lit, but not enough to see well by. Nevertheless, I marked a reddening in both their faces.

Gerald drew a long breath and fumbled about. His clothes were made with pockets. He brought out a small parchment box and from it took a little white stick that he put in his mouth. Then he took out another box, and a wooden stick therefrom which burst into flame when he scratched. With the fire he kindled the stick in his mouth, and sucked in the smoke.

We stared. "Is that a Christian rite?" asked Helgi.

"No . . . not just so." A wry, disappointed smile twisted his lips. "I thought you'd be more surprised, even terrified."

"It's something new," I admitted, "but we're a sober folk on Iceland. Those fire sticks could be useful. Did you come to trade in them?"

"Hardly." He sighed. The smoke he breathed in seemed to steady him, which was odd, because the smoke in the hall had made him cough and water at the eyes. "The truth is, well, something you will not believe. I can hardly believe it myself."

We waited. Thorgunna stood leaning forward, her lips parted.

"That lightning bolt—" Gerald nodded wearily. "I was out in the storm, and somehow the lightning must have smitten me in just the right way, a way that happens only once in many thousands of times. It threw me back into the past."

Those were his words, priest. I did not understand, and told him so.

"It's hard to grasp," he agreed. "God give that I'm merely dreaming. But if this is a dream I must endure till I awaken. . . . Well, look. I was born one thousand, nine hundred, and thirty-three years after Christ, in a land to the west which you have not yet found. In the twenty-fourth year of my life, I was in Iceland with my country's war host. The light-ning struck me, and now, now it is less than one thousand years after Christ, and yet I am here—almost a thousand years before I was born, I am here!"

We sat very still. I signed myself with the Hammer and took a long pull from my horn. One of the maids whim-pered, and Ragnhild whispered so fiercely I could hear: "Be still. The poor fellow's out of his head. There's no harm in him."

I thought she was right, unless maybe in the last part. The gods can speak through a madman, and the gods are not always to be trusted. Or he could turn berserker, or he could be under a heavy curse that would also touch us.

He slumped, gazing before him. I caught a few fleas and cracked them while I pondered. Gerald noticed and asked with some horror if we had many fleas here.

"Why, of course," said Thorgunna. "Have you none?"

"No." He smiled crookedly. "Not yet."

"Ah," she sighed, "then you *must* be sick."

She was a level-headed girl. I saw her thought, and so did Ragnhild and Helgi. Clearly, a man so sick that he had no fleas could be expected to rave. We might still fret about whether we could catch the illness, but I deemed this un-likely; his woe was in the head, maybe from a blow he had taken. In any case, the matter was come down to earth now, something we could deal with.

I being a godi, a chief who holds sacrifices, it behooved me not to turn a stranger out. Moreover, if he could fetch in many of those fire-kindling sticks, a profitable trade might be built up. So I said Gerald should go to rest. He protested, but we manhandled him into the shut-bed, and there he lay tired and was soon asleep. Thorgunna said she would take care of him.

*　*　*

The next eventide I meant to sacrifice a horse, both because of the timber we had found and to take away any curse that might be on Gerald. Furthermore, the beast I picked was old and useless, and we were short of fresh meat. Gerald had spent the morning lounging moodily around the garth, but when I came in at noon to eat I found him and my daughter laughing.

"You seem to be on the road to health," I said.

"Oh yes. It ... could be worse for me." He sat down at my side as the carles set up the trestle table and the maids brought in the food. "I was ever much taken with the age of the vikings, and I have some skills."

"Well," I said, "if you have no home, we can keep you here for a while."

"I can work," he said eagerly. "I'll be worth my pay."

Now I knew he was from afar, because what chief would work on any land but his own, and for hire at that? Yet he had the easy manner of the high-born, and had clearly eaten well throughout his life. I overlooked that he had made me no gifts; after all, he was shipwrecked.

"Maybe you can get passage back to your United States," said Helgi. "We could hire a ship. I'm fain to see that realm."

"No," said Gerald bleakly. "There is no such place. Not yet."

"So you still hold to that idea you came from tomorrow?" grunted Sigurd. "Crazy notion. Pass the pork."

"I do," said Gerald. Calm had come upon him. "And I can prove it."

"I don't see how you speak our tongue, if you hail from so far away," I said. I would not call a man a liar to his face, unless we were swapping friendly brags, but—

"They speak otherwise in my land and time," he said, "but it happens that in Iceland the tongue changed little

since the old days, and because my work had me often talking with the folk, I learned it when I came here."

"If you are a Christian," I said, "you must bear with us
while we sacrifice tonight."

"I've naught against that," he said. "I fear I never was
a very good Christian. I'd like to watch. How is it done?"

I told him how I would smite the horse with a hammer
before the god, and cut its throat, and sprinkle the blood
about with willow twigs; thereafter we would butcher the
carcass and feast. He said hastily:

"Here's my chance to prove what I am. I have a weapon
that will kill the horse with, with a flash of lightning."

"What is it?" I wondered. We crowded around while he
took the metal club out of its sheath and showed it to us. I
had my doubts; it looked well enough for hitting a man, I
reckoned, but had no edge, though a wondrously skillful
smith had forged it. "Well, we can try," I said. You have
seen how on Iceland we are less concerned to follow the
rites exactly than they are in the older countries.

Gerald showed us what else he had in his pockets. There
were some coins of remarkable roundness and sharpness,
though neither gold nor true silver; a tiny key; a stick with
lead in it for writing; a flat purse holding many bits of
marked paper. When he told us gravely that some of this
paper was money, Thorgunna herself had to laugh. Best was
a knife whose blade folded into the handle. When he saw
me admiring that, he gave it to me, which was well done
for a shipwrecked man. I said I would give him clothes and
a good ax, as well as lodging for as long as needful.

No, I don't have the knife now. You shall hear why. It's
a pity, for that was a good knife, though rather small.

"What were you ere the war arrow went out in your
land?" asked Helgi. "A merchant?"

"No," said Gerald. "I was an . . . *endjinur* . . . that is, I was learning how to be one. A man who builds things, bridges and roads and tools ... more than just an artisan. So I think my knowledge could be of great value here." I saw a fever in his eyes. "Yes, give me time and I'll be a king."

"We have no king on Iceland," I grunted. "Our forefathers came hither to get away from kings. Now we meet at the Things to try suits and pass new laws, but each man must get his own redress as best he can."

"But suppose the one in the wrong won't yield?" he asked.

"Then there can be a fine feud," said Helgi, and went on to relate some of the killings in past years. Gerald looked unhappy and fingered his *gun*. That is what he called his fire-spitting club. He tried to rally himself with a joke about now, at last, being free to call it a gun instead of something else. That disquieted me, smacked of witchcraft, so to change the talk I told Helgi to stop his chattering of manslaughter as if it were sport. With law shall the land be built.

"Your clothing is rich," said Thorgunna softly. "Your folk must own broad acres at home."

"No," he said, "our ... our king gives each man in the host clothes like these. As for my family, we owned no farm, we rented our home in a building where many other families also dwelt."

I am not purse-proud, but it seemed to me he had not been honest, a landless man sharing my high seat like a chief. Thorgunna covered my huffiness by saying, "You will gain a farm later."

After sunset we went out to the shrine. The carles had built a fire before it, and as I opened the door the wooden Odin appeared to leap forth. My house has long invoked him above the others. Gerald muttered to my daughter that it was a clumsy bit of carving, and since my father had made it I was still more angry with him. Some folks have no understanding of the fine arts.

Nevertheless, I let him help me lead the horse forth to the altar stone. I took the blood bowl in my hands and said he could now slay the beast if he would. He drew his gun, put the end behind the horse's ear, and squeezed. We heard a crack, and the beast jerked and dropped with a hole blown through its skull, wasting the brains. A clumsy weapon. I caught a whiff, sharp and bitter like that around a volcano. We all jumped, one of the women screamed, and Gerald looked happy. I gathered my wits and finished the rest of the sacrifice as was right. Gerald did not like having blood sprinkled over him, but then he was a Christian. Nor would he take more than a little of the soup and flesh.

Afterward Helgi questioned him about the gun, and he said it could kill a man at bowshot distance but had no witchcraft in it, only use of some tricks we did not know. Having heard of the Greek fire, I believed him. A gun could be useful in a fight, as indeed I was to learn, but it did not seem very practical—iron costing what it does, and months of forging needed for each one.

I fretted more about the man himself.

And the next morning I found him telling Thorgunna a great deal of foolishness about his home—buildings as tall as mountains, and wagons that flew, or went without horses. He said there were eight or nine thousand thousands of folk in his town, a burgh called New Jorvik or the like. I enjoy a good brag as well as the next man, but this was too much, and I told him gruffly to come along and help me get in some strayed cattle.

After a day scrambling around the hills I saw that Gerald could hardly tell a cow's bow from her stern. We almost had the strays once, but he ran stupidly across their path and turned them, so the whole work was to do again. I asked him with strained courtesy if he could milk, shear, wield scythe or flail, and he said no, he had never lived on a farm.

"That's a shame," I remarked, "for everyone on Iceland does, unless he be outlawed."

He flushed at my tone. "I can do enough else," he answered. "Give me some tools and I'll show you good metal-work."

That brightened me, for truth to tell, none of our household was a gifted smith. "That's an honorable trade," I said, "and you can be of great help. I have a broken sword and several bent spearheads to be mended, and it were no bad idea to shoe the horses." His admission that he did not know how to put on a shoe was not very dampening to me then.

We had returned home as we talked, and Thorgunna came angrily forward. "That's no way to treat a guest, Father," she said. "Making him work like a carle, indeed!"

Gerald smiled. "I'll be glad to work," he said. "I need a ... a stake ... something to start me afresh. Also, I want to repay a little of your kindness."

Those words made me mild toward him, and I said it was not his fault they had different ways in the United States. On the morrow he could begin in the smithy, and I would pay him, yet he would be treated as an equal since craftsmen are valued. This earned him black looks from the housefolk.

That evening he entertained us well with stories of his home; true or not, they made good listening. However, he had no real polish, being unable to compose a line of verse. They must be a raw and backward lot in the United States. He said his task in the war host had been to keep order among the troops. Helgi said this was unheard of, and he must be bold who durst offend so many men, but Gerald said folk obeyed him out of fear of the king. When he added that the term of a levy in the United States was two years, and that men could be called to war even in harvest time, I said he was well out of a country with so ruthless and powerful a lord.

"No," he answered wistfully, "we are a free folk, who say what we please."

"But it seems you may not do as you please," said Helgi.

"Well," Gerald said, "we may not murder a man just because he aggrieves us."

"Not even if he has slain your own kin?" asked Helgi.

"No. It is for the . . . the king to take vengeance, on behalf of the whole folk whose peace has been broken."

I chuckled. "Your yarns are cunningly wrought," I said, "but there you've hit a snag. How could the king so much as keep count of the slaughters, let alone avenge them? Why, he'd not have time to beget an heir!"

Gerald could say no more for the laughter that followed.

The next day he went to the smithy, with a thrall to pump the bellows for him. I was gone that day and night, down to Reykjavik to dicker with Hjalmar Broadnose about some sheep. I invited him back for an overnight stay, and we rode into my steading with his son Ketill, a red-haired sulky youth of twenty winters who had been refused by Thorgunna.

I found Gerald sitting gloomily on a bench in the hall. He wore the clothes I had given him, his own having been spoilt by ash and sparks; what had he awaited, the fool? He talked in a low voice with my daughter.

"Well," I said as I trod in, "how went the tasks?"

My man Grim snickered. "He ruined two spearheads, but we put out the fire he stared ere the whole smithy burned."

"How's this?" I cried. "You said you were a smith."

Gerald stood up, defiant. "I worked with different tools, and better ones, at home," he replied. "You do it otherwise here."

They told me he had built up the fire too hot; his hammer had struck everywhere but the place it should; he had wrecked the temper of the steel through not knowing when to quench it. Smithcraft takes years to learn, of course, but he might have owned to being not so much as an apprentice.

"Well," I snapped, "what can you do, then, to earn your bread?" It irked me to be made a ninny of before Hjalmar and Ketill, whom I had told about the stranger.

"Odin alone knows," said Grim. "I took him with me to ride after your goats, and never have I seen a worse horseman. I asked him if maybe he could spin or weave, and he said no."

"That was no question to ask a man!" flared Thorgunna. "He should have slain you for it."

"He should indeed," laughed Grim. "But let me carry on the tale. I thought we would also repair your bridge over the foss. Well, he *can* barely handle a saw, but he nigh took his own foot off with the adze."

"We don't use those tools, I tell you!" Gerald doubled his fists and looked close to tears.

I motioned my guests to sit down. "I don't suppose you can butcher or smoke a hog, either," I said, "or salt a fish or turf a roof."

"No." I could hardly hear him.

"Well, then, man, whatever can you do?"

"I–" He could get no words out.

"You were a warrior," said Thorgunna.

"Yes, that I was!" he said, his face kindling.

"Small use on Iceland when you have no other skills,"

I grumbled, "but maybe, if you can get passage to the east-lands, some king will take you in his guard." Myself I doubted it, for a guardsman needs manners that will do credit to his lord; but I had not the heart to say so.

Ketill Hjalmarsson had plainly not liked the way Thorgunna stood close to Gerald and spoke for him. Now he fleered and said: "I might also doubt your skill in fighting."

"That I have been trained for," said Gerald grimly.

"Will you wrestle with me?" asked Ketill.

"Gladly!" spat Gerald.

Priest, what is a man to think? As I grow older, I find life to be less and less the good-and-evil, black-and-white thing you call it; we are each of us some hue of gray. This useless fellow, this spiritless lout who could be asked if he did women's work and not lift ax, went out into the yard with Ketill Hajlmarsson and threw him three times running. He had a trick of grabbing the clothes as Ketill rushed him ... I cried a stop when the youth was nearing murderous rage, praised them both, and filled the beer horns. But Ketill brooded sullen on the bench the whole evening.

Gerald said something about making a gun like his own, but bigger, a *cannon* he called it, which would sink ships and scatter hosts. He would need the help of smiths, and also various stuffs. Charcoal was easy, and sulfur could be found by the volcanoes, I suppose, but what is this saltpeter?

Too, being wary by now, I questioned him closely as to how he would make such a thing. Did he know just how to mix the powder? No, he admitted. What size must the gun be? When he told me—at least as long as a man—I laughed and asked him how a piece that size could be cast or bored, supposing we could scrape together so much iron. This he did not know either.

"You haven't the tools to make the tools to make the

tools," he said. I don't understand what he meant by that. "God help me, I can't run through a thousand years of history by myself."

He took out the last of his little smoke sticks and lit it. Helgi had tried a puff earlier and gotten sick, though he remained a friend of Gerald's. Now my son proposed to take a boat in the morning and go with him and me to Ice Fjord, where I had some money outstanding I wanted to collect. Hjalmar and Ketill said they would come along for the trip, and Thorgunna pleaded so hard that I let her come too.

"An ill thing," mumbled Sigurd. "The land trolls like not a woman aboard a vessel. It's unlucky."

"How did your fathers bring women to this island?" I grinned.

Now I wish I had listened to him. He was not a clever man, but he often knew whereof he spoke.

At this time I owned a half-share in a ship that went to Norway, bartering wadmal for timber. It was a profitable business until she ran afoul of vikings during the uproar while Olaf Tryggvason was overthrowing Jarl Haakon there. Some men will do anything to make a living—thieves, cutthroats, they ought to be hanged, the worthless robbers pouncing on honest merchantmen. Had they any courage or honor they would go to Ireland, which is full of plunder.

Well, anyhow, the ship was abroad, but we had three boats and took one of these. Grim went with us others: myself, Helgi, Hjalmar, Ketill, Gerald, and Thorgunna. I saw how the castaway winced at the cold water as we launched her, yet afterward took off his shoes and stockings to let his feet dry. He had been surprised to learn we had a bathhouse—did he think us savages?—but still, he was dainty as a girl and soon moved upwind of our feet.

We had a favoring breeze, so raised mast and sail. Gerald tried to help, but of course did not know one line from another and got them fouled. Grim snarled at him and Ketill laughed nastily. But erelong we were under weigh, and he came and sat by me where I had the steering oar.

He must have lain long awake thinking, for now he ventured shyly: "In my land they have . . . will have . . . a rig and rudder which are better than these. With them, you can sail so close to the wind that you can crisscross against it."

"Ah, our wise sailor offers us redes," sneered Ketill.

"Be still," said Thorgunna sharply. "Let Gerald speak."

Gerald gave her a look of humble thanks, and I was not unwilling to listen. "This is something which could easily be made," he said. "While not a seaman, I've been on such boats myself and know them well. First, then, the sail should not be square and hung from a yardarm, but three-cornered, with the two bottom corners lashed to a yard swiveling fore and aft from the mast; and there should be one or two smaller headsails of the same shape. Next, your steering oar is in the wrong place. You should have a rudder in the stern, guided by a bar." He grew eager and traced the plan with his fingernail on Thorgunna's cloak. "With these two things, and a deep keel, going down about three feet for a boat this size, a ship can move across the wind . . . thus."

Well, priest, I must say the idea has merits, and were it not for the fear of bad luck—for everything of his was unlucky—I might yet play with it. But the drawbacks were clear, and I pointed them out in a reasonable way.

"First and worst," I said, "this rudder and deep keel would make it impossible to beach the ship or go up a shallow river. Maybe they have many harbors where you hail from, but here a craft must take what landings she can find, and must be speedily launched if there should be an attack."

"The keel can be built to draw up into the hull," he said, "with a box around so that water can't follow."

"How would you keep dry rot out of the box?" I answered. "No, your keel must be fixed, and must be heavy if the ship is not to capsize under so much sail as you have drawn. This means iron or lead, ruinously costly.

"Besides," I said, "this mast of yours would be hard to unstep when the wind dropped and oars came out. Furthermore, the sails are the wrong shape to stretch as an awning when one must sleep at sea."

"The ship could lie out, and you go to land in a small boat," he said. "Also, you could build cabins aboard for shelter."

"The cabins would get in the way of the oars," I said, "unless the ship were hopelessly broad-beamed or else the oarsmen sat below a deck; and while I hear that galley slaves do this in the southlands, free men would never row in such foulness."

"Must you have oars?" he asked like a very child.

Laughter barked along the hull. The gulls themselves, hovering to starboard where the shore rose dark, cried their scorn.

"Do they have tame winds in the place whence you came?" snorted Hjalmar. "What happens if you're becalmed—for days, maybe, with provisions running out—"

"You could build a ship big enough to carry many weeks' provisions," said Gerald.

"If you had the wealth of a king, you might," said Helgi. "And such a king's ship, lying helpless on a flat sea, would be swarmed by every viking from here to Jomsborg. As for leaving her out on the water while you make camp, what would you have for shelter, or for defense if you should be trapped ashore?"

Gerald slumped. Thorgunna said to him gently: "Some folk have no heart to try anything new. I think it's a grand idea."

He smiled at her, a weary smile, and plucked up the will to say something about a means for finding north in cloudy weather; he said a kind of stone always pointed north when hung from a string. I told him mildly that I would be most interested if he could find me some of this stone; or if he knew where it was to be had, I could ask a trader to fetch me a piece. But this he did not know, and fell silent. Ketill opened his mouth, but got such an edged look from Thorgunna that he shut it again. His face declared what a liar he thought Gerald to be.

The wind turned crank after a while, so we lowered the mast and took to the oars. Gerald was strong and willing, though awkward; however, his hands were so soft that erelong they bled. I offered to let him rest, but he kept doggedly at the work.

Watching him sway back and forth, under the dreary creak of the holes, the shaft red and wet where he gripped it, I thought much about him. He had done everything wrong which a man could do—thus I imagined then, not knowing the future—and I did not like the way Thorgunna's eyes strayed to him and rested. He was no man for my daughter, landless and penniless and helpless. Yet I could not keep from liking him. Whether his tale was true or only madness, I felt he was honest about it; and surely whatever way by which he came hither was a strange one. I noticed the cuts on his chin from my razor; he had said he was not used to our kind of shaving and would grow a beard. He had tried hard. I wondered how well I would have done, landing alone in this witch country of his dreams, with a gap of forever between me and my home.

Maybe that same wretchedness was what had turned Thorgunna's heart. Women are a kittle breed, priest, and you who have forsworn them belike understand them as well as I who have slept with half a hundred in six different lands.

I do not think they even understand themselves. Birth and life and death, those are the great mysteries, which none will ever fathom, and a woman is closer to them than a man.

The ill wind stiffened, the sea grew gray and choppy under low, leaden clouds, and our headway was poor. At sunset we could row no more, but must pull in to a small, unpeopled bay, and make camp as well as could be on the strand.

We had brought firewood and timber along. Gerald, though staggering with weariness, made himself useful, his sulfury sticks kindling the blaze more easily than flint and steel. Thorgunna set herself to cook our supper. We were not much warded by the boat from a lean, whining wind; her cloak fluttered like wings and her hair blew wild above the streaming flames. It was the time of light nights, the sky a dim, dusky blue, the sea a wrinkled metal sheet, and the land like something risen out of dream mists. We men huddled in our own cloaks, holding numbed hands to the fire and saying little.

I felt some cheer was needed, and ordered a cask of my best and strongest ale broached. An evil Norn made me do that, but no man escapes his weird. Our bellies seemed the more empty now when our noses drank in the sputter of a spitted joint, and the ale went swiftly to our heads. I remember declaiming the death-song of Ragnar Hairybreeks for no other reason than that I felt like declaiming it.

Thorgunna came to stand over Gerald where he sat. I saw how her fingers brushed his hair, ever so lightly, and Ketill Hjalmarsson did too. "Have they no verses in your land?" she asked.

"Not like yours," he said, glancing up. Neither of them looked away again. "We sing rather than chant. I wish I had my *gittar* here—that's a kind of harp."

"Ah, an Irish bard," said Hjalmar Broadnose.

I remember strangely well how Gerald smiled, and what he said in his own tongue, though I know not the meaning: *"Only on me mither's side, begorra."* I suppose it was magic.

"Well, sing for us," laughed Thorgunna.

"Let me think," he said. "I shall have to put it in Norse words for you." After a little while, still staring at her through the windy gloaming, he began a song. It had a tune I liked, thus:

> *From this valley they tell me you're leaving.*
> *I will miss your bright eyes and sweet smile.*
> *You will carry the sunshine with you*
> *That has brightened my life all the while. . . .*

I don't remember the rest, save that it was not quite seemly.

When he had finished, Hjalmar and Grim went over to see if the meat was done. I spied a glimmer of tears in my daughter's eyes. "That was a lovely thing," she said.

Ketill sat straight. The flames splashed his face with wild, running red. A rawness was in his tone: "Yes, we've found what this fellow can do. Sit about and make pretty songs for the girls. Keep him for that, Ospak."

Thorgunna whitened, and Helgi clapped hand to sword. Gerald's face darkened and his voice grew thick: "That was no way to talk. Take it back."

Ketill rose. "No," he said. "I'll ask no pardon of an idler living off honest yeomen."

He was raging, but had kept sense enough to shift the insult from my family to Gerald alone. Otherwise he and his father would have had the four of us to deal with. As it was, Gerald stood too, fists knotted at his sides, and said: "Will you step away from here and settle this?"

"Gladly!" Ketill turned and walked a few yards down the beach, taking his shield from the boat. Gerald followed. Thorgunna stood stricken, then snatched his ax and ran after him.

"Are you going weaponless?" she shrieked.

Gerald stopped, looking dazed. "I don't want anything like that," he said. "Fists—"

Ketill puffed himself up and drew sword. "No doubt you're used to fighting like thralls in your land," he said. "So if you'll crave my pardon, I'll let this matter rest."

Gerald stood with drooped shoulders. He stared at Thorgunna as if he were blind, as if asking her what to do. She handed him the ax.

"So you want me to kill him?" he whispered.

"Yes," she answered.

Then I knew she loved him, for otherwise why should she have cared if he disgraced himself?

Helgi brought him his helmet. He put it on, took the ax, and went forward.

"Ill is this," said Hjalmar to me. "Do you stand by the stranger, Ospak?"

"No," I said. "He's no kin or oath-brother of mine. This is not my quarrel."

"That's good," said Hjalmar. "I'd not like to fight with you. You were ever a good neighbor."

We stepped forth together and staked out the ground. Thorgunna told me to lend Gerald my sword, so he could use a shield too, but the man looked oddly at me and said he would rather have the ax. They squared off before each other, he and Ketill, and began fighting.

This was no holmgang, with rules and a fixed order of blows and first blood meaning victory. There was death between those two. Drunk though the lot of us were, we saw that and so had not tried to make peace. Ketill stormed in with the sword whistling in his hand. Gerald sprang back, wielding the ax awkwardly. It bounced off Ketill's shield. The youth grinned and cut at Gerald's legs. Blood welled forth to stain the ripped breeches.

What followed was butchery. Gerald had never used a battle-ax before. So it turned in his grasp and he struck with the flat of the head. He would have been hewn down at once had Ketill's sword not been blunted on his helmet and had he not been quick on his feet. Even so, he was erelong lurching with a dozen wounds.

"Stop the fight!" Thorgunna cried, and sped toward them. Helgi caught her arms and forced her back, where she struggled and kicked till Grim must help. I saw grief on my son's face, but a wolfish glee on the carle's.

Ketill's blade came down and slashed Gerald's left hand. He dropped the ax. Ketill snarled and readied to finish him. Gerald drew his gun. It made a flash and a barking noise. Ketill fell. Blood gushed from him. His lower jaw was blown off and the back of his skull was gone.

A stillness came, where only the wind and the sea had voice.

Then Hjalmar trod forth, his mouth working but otherwise a cold steadiness over him. He knelt and closed his son's eyes, as a token that the right of vengeance was his. Rising, he said: "That was an evil deed. For that you shall be outlawed."

"It wasn't witchcraft," said Gerald in a stunned tone. "It was like a . . . a bow. I had no choice. I didn't want to fight with more than my fists."

I got between them and said the Thing must decide this matter, but that I hoped Hjalmar would take weregild for Ketill.

"But I killed him to save my own life!" protested Gerald.

"Nevertheless, weregild must be paid, if Ketill's kin will

take it," I explained. "Because of the weapon, I think it will be doubled, but that is for the Thing to judge."

Hjalmar had many other sons, and it was not as if Gerald belonged to a family at odds with his own, so I felt he would agree. However, he laughed coldly and asked where a man lacking wealth would find the silver.

Thorgunna stepped up with a wintry calm and said we would pay. I opened my mouth, but when I saw her eyes I nodded. "Yes, we will," I said, "in order to keep the peace."

"So you make this quarrel your own?" asked Hjalmar.

"No," I answered. "This man is no blood of mine. But if I choose to make him a gift of money to use as he wishes, what of it?"

Hjalmar smiled. Sorrow stood in his gaze, but he looked on me with old comradeship.

"One day he may be your son-in-law," he said. "I know the signs, Ospak. Then indeed he will be of your folk. Even helping him now in his need will range you on his side."

"And so?" asked Helgi, most softly.

"And so, while I value your friendship, I have sons who will take the death of their brother ill. They'll want revenge on Gerald Samsson, if only for the sake of their good names, and thus our two houses will be sundered and one manslaying will lead to another. It has happened often enough ere now." Hjalmar sighed. "I myself wish peace with you, Ospak, but if you take this killer's side it must be otherwise."

I thought for a moment, thought of Helgi lying with his head cloven, of my other sons on their steads drawn to battle because of a man they had never seen, I thought of having to wear byrnies each time we went down for driftwood and never knowing when we went to bed if we would wake to find the house ringed in by spearmen.

"Yes," I said, "You are right Hjalmar. I withdraw my

offer. Let this be a matter between you and him alone."

We gripped hands on it.

Thorgunna uttered a small cry and flew into Gerald's arms. He held her close. "What does this mean?" he asked slowly.

"I cannot keep you any longer," I said, "but maybe some crofter will give you a roof. Hjalmar is a law-abiding man and will not harm you until the Thing has outlawed you. That will not be before they meet in fall. You can try to get passage out of Iceland ere then."

"A useless one like me?" he replied in bitterness.

Thorgunna whirled free and blazed that I was a coward and a perjurer and all else evil. I let her have it out before I laid my hands on her shoulders.

"I do this for the house," I said. "The house and the blood, which are holy. Men die and women weep, but while the kindred live our names are remembered. Can you ask a score of men to die for your hankerings?"

Long did she stand, and to this day I know not what her answer would have been. But Gerald spoke.

"No," he said. "I suppose you have right, Ospak . . . the right of your time, which is not mine." He took my hand, and Helgi's. His lips brushed Thorgunna's cheek. Then he turned and walked out into the darkness.

I heard, later, that he went to earth with Thorvald Hallsson, the crofter of Humpback Fell, and did not tell his host what had happened. He must have hoped to go unnoticed until he could somehow get berth on an eastbound ship. But of course word spread. I remember his brag that in the United States folk had ways to talk from one end of the land to another. So he must have scoffed at us, sitting in our lonely steads, and not known how fast news would get around.

Thorvald's son Hrolf went to Brand Sealskin-Boots to talk about some matter, and mentioned the guest, and soon the whole western island had the tale.

Now, if Gerald had known he must give notice of a manslaying at the first garth he found, he would have been safe at least till the Thing met, for Hjalmar and his sons are sober men who would not needlessly kill a man still under the wing of the law. But as it was, his keeping the matter secret made him a murderer and therefore at once an outlaw. Hjalmar and his kin rode straight to Humpback Fell and haled him forth. He shot his way past them with the gun and fled into the hills. They followed him, having several hurts and one more death to avenge. I wonder if Gerald thought the strangeness of his weapon would unnerve us. He may not have understood that every man dies when his time comes, neither sooner nor later, so that fear of death is useless.

At the end, when they had him trapped, his weapon gave out on him. Then he took a dead man's sword and defended himself so valiantly that Ulf Hjalmarsson has limped ever since. That was well done, as even his foes admitted. They are an eldritch breed in the United States, but they do not lack manhood.

When he was slain, his body was brought back. For fear of the ghost, he having maybe been a warlock, it was burned, and everything he had owned was laid in the fire with him. Thus I lost the knife he gave me. The barrow stands out on the moor, north of here, and folk shun it, though the ghost has not walked. Today, with so much else happening, he is slowly being forgotten.

And that is the tale, priest, as I saw it and heard it. Most men think Gerald Samsson was crazy, but I myself now believe he did come from out of time, and that his doom was that no man may ripen a field before harvest season.

Yet I look into the future, a thousand years hence, when they fly through the air and ride in horseless wagons and smash whole towns with one blow. I think of this Iceland then, and of the young United States men come to help defend us in a year when the end of the world hovers close. Maybe some of them, walking about on the heaths, will see that barrow and wonder what ancient warrior lies buried there, and they may well wish they had lived long ago in this time, when men were free.

FOREVER TO A HUDSON BAY BLANKET

JAMES TIPTREE, JR.

Tiptree's canon, one of the most intense and intensely compressed (1968–1987) in science fiction, fuses sex and death in ways found by no other science fiction writer; here time travel is used as the engine for that conflation. As Damon Knight wrote of another story, asking its author (not Tiptree) for a rewrite for *Orbit*, "I want this story to hurt. I want to feel a searing at the end." Here it is, the thing itself, as the trapdoor of the story yaws.

James Tiptree, Jr. was one pseudonym (there was another) for most of the science fiction of Alice Sheldon (1915–1987), a research psychologist, CIA operative, child star of her mother the anthropologist's 1927 memoir, *Alice in Jungleland*, and the author of two novels and about 70 short stories, most of canonic worth.

Dov Rapelle was a nice person, personally. He was so nice you didn't notice that he wasn't overpoweringly bright in a survival sense. He also owned a long skier's body and a lonesome dreamy Canuck face that he got from his fifth grandfather who came out to Calgary, Alberta as a dowser. By the time the face got down to Dov a solid chunk of Alberta Hydroelectric came with it. But the Rapelles lived plain; Calgary, Alberta was one of the few places in the twentyfirst century where a young man could be like Dov and not be spoiled silly.

Calgary has the tallest water-tower on the continent, you know, and all that tetra-wheat and snow sports money. And it's a long way from the Boswash and San Frangeles style of life. People from Calgary still do things like going home to see their folks over winter vacation. And in Calgary you aren't used to being phoned up by strange girls in Callao, Peru at 0200 Christmas morning.

The girl was quite emotional. Dov kept asking her name

and she kept crying and sobbing, "Say something, Dovy, Dovy, *please!*" She had a breathy squeak that sounded young and expensive.

"What should I say?" asked Dov reasonably.

"Your voice, Oh, *Dovy!*" she wept, "I'm so far *away!* Please, please talk to me, Dovy!"

"Well, look," Dov began, and the phone went dead.

When his folks asked him what that was he shrugged and grinned his nice grin. He didn't get it.

Christmas was on Monday. Wednesday night the phone rang again. This time the operator was French, but it was clearly the same girl.

"Dovy? Dovy Rapelle?" She was breathing hard.

"Yeah, speaking. Who's this?"

"Oh, Dovy. *Dovy!* Is that really you?"

"Yeah, it's me. Look, did you call me before?"

"Did I?" she said vaguely. And then she started crying "Oh Dovy, Oh Dovy," and it was the same dialog all over again until the line quit.

He did not get it.

By Friday Dov was beginning to feel hemmed in, so he decided to go check on their cabin on Split Mountain. The Rapelles were not jetbuggy types; they liked peace and quiet. Dov took his plain old four-wheeler out behind Bragg Creek into the pass as far as the plows had been and then he put on his pack and skis and started breaking trail. The snow was perfect, dry and fast. In no time he was up past the bare aspens and larches and into the high spruce woods.

He came out on the moraine by the lake at sundown. The snow was heavily wind-drifted here. He cut across bare ice and found the front of the cabin buried under a six-foot overhang of snow. It was about dark by the time he'd shovelled in and got a fire going from the big woodpile in back.

He was bringing in his second bucket of snow to melt when he heard the *chunka-chunka* of a copter coming through the pass.

It zoomed over the clearing and hovered. Dov could see two heads bobbing around inside. Then it settled down twenty yards away sending a wave of white all over and somebody tumbled out.

The first thing Dov thought of was trouble at home. The next thing was his fire. He had just turned to go put it out when he realised the chopper was lifting back up.

It went up like a yak in a feather factory. Through the blizzard Dov saw a small pale body floundering toward him.

"Dovy! Dovy! Is that you?"

It was the girl, or at least her voice.

She was stumbling like crazy, up to her crotch in the snow in the fading light. Just as Dov reached her she went down on all fours and all he could see was her little stark-bare pink ass sticking up with a glittery-green thing on one cheek. And about a yard of silver hair.

"Yo ho," he said involuntarily, which is a Stonie indian phrase meaning "Behold!"

She turned up a pretty-baby face with a green jewelbug on the forehead.

"It's you!" she sneezed. Her teeth were chattering.

"You're really not dressed for snow," Dov observed. "Here." He reached down and scooped her up and toted her indoors, snow and green butterflies and rosy ass and all. His frosty pink Christmas cake with a razor-blade inside.

When he got the lamp going she turned out to be as naked in front as she was in back, and about sixteen at the oldest. A kid, he decided, on some kind of spinout. While he wrapped her in his Hudson Bay blanket he tried to recall where he could have met her. No success. He plonked her on the snowshoe chair and built up the fire. She kept sniffling and chattering, but it wasn't very informational.

"Oh, Dovy, Dovy, it's you! D-Dovy! Speak to me. Say something, please, Dovy!"

"Well, for starters—"

"Do you like me? I'm attractive, am't I?" She opened the blanket to look at herself. "I mean, am I attractive to *you?* Oh, Dovy, s-say something! I've come so *far*, I chartered three jets, I, I,—Oh, Dovy *d-darling!*"

And she exploded out of the blanket into his arms like a monkey trying to climb him, whimpering "Please, Dovy, love me," nuzzling, squirming her little body, shivering and throbbing and pushing cold little fingers into his snow-suit, under his belt. "*Please*, Dovy, please, there isn't much time. *Love me.*"

To which Dov didn't respond quite as you'd expect. Because it so happened that this cabin had been the prime scene of Dov's early fantasy life. Especially the *winter fantasy*, the one where Dovy was snuggled in the blankets watching the fire gutter out and listening to the storm howl . . . and there comes a feeble scratching at the door . . . and it turns out to be a beautiful lost girl, and he has to take off all her clothes and warm her up *all over* and wrap her up in the Hudson Bay blanket . . . and he's very tender and respectful but *she knows* what's going to happen, and later he does all kinds of things to her on the blanket. (When Dov was fourteen he could only say the words *Hudson Bay blanket* in a peculiar hoarse whisper.) The girl in one version was a redhead named Georgiana Ochs, and later on he actually did get Georgiana up to the cabin where they spent a weekend catching terrible colds. Since then the cabin had been the site of several other erotic enactments, but somehow it never came up to the original script.

So now here he was with the original script unrolling around him but it still wasn't quite right. In the script *Dov* undressed the girl, *Dov's* hands did the feeling-out. The girl's part called for trembling appreciation, all right. But it didn't call for shinnying up him like a maniac or grabbing his dick in ice-cold paws.

So he stood for a minute with his hands squeezing her baby buttocks, deliberately holding her away from his crotch until something communicated and she looked up, panting.

"Wait, Oh," she gasped, and frowned crossly, apparently at herself. "Please . . . I'm not crazy, Dovy, I—I—"

He walked stiffly across the hearth with her, trying to keep his snowsuit from falling down, and dumped her on the bunk, where she lay flopped like a puppy, with her knees open and her little flat belly going in and out, in and out. There was an emerald butterfly on her ash-blond muff.

"All right," he said firmly (but nicely). "Now look. Who are you?"

Her mouth worked silently and her eyes sent *Love you, love you, love you* up to him. Her eyes didn't seem wild or druggy, but they had a funny deep-down spark, like something lived in there.

"You name, kid. What's your name?"

"L-Loolie," she whispered.

"Loolie who?" He said patiently.

"Loolie . . . Aerovulpa." Somewhere in his head a couple of neurones twitched, but they didn't connect.

"Why did you come here, Loolie?"

Her eyes glistened, brimmed over. "Oh, no," she sobbed, gulped. "It's been so *long*, such a terribly long, long, way—" her head rolled from side to side, hurtfully. "Oh, Dovy, please, there'll be *time* for all this later, I know you don't remember me—just *please* let me touch you, please—it *hurt* so—"

Soft arms pleading up for him, little breasts pleading

with their puckered noses. This was getting more like the script. When Dov didn't move she suddenly wailed and curled up into a foetal ball.

"I've sp-spoiled everything," she wept, burrowing wetly in the Hudson Bay blanket.

That did it, for a nice person like Dov. One of his hands went down and patted little Tarbaby's back, and then his other hand joined the first and his snow suit fell down. Her back somehow turned into her front and curled up around him, and his knees were feeling the bunk boards while two downy thighs locked around his hips and sucked him in.

And he got a shock.

The shock came a bit late, the shock was wrapped around him and thrusting at him so that he had no choice but to ram on past her squeal—and after that he didn't have time to worry about anything except letting the sun burst in.

But it is a fact that even in Calgary you don't meet many maidenheads. It says something for Dov that he knew the way.

Now, a twentyfirst-century maidenhead isn't a big thing, sociopsychologicalwise. On the other hand, it wasn't a nothing, especially for a nice person like Dov. What it did was to move the episode one step out of the fantasy class— or rather, one step into another fantasy.

Particularly when Loolie said what girls often do, after-ward. Looking at him anxious-humble, stroking his stomach. "Do you mind? I mean, my being a virgin?"

"Well, now," said Dov, trying to think decisively while peeling a squashed green butterfly out of his neck.

"Truly, honestly, did you mind?"

"Honestly, no." He balanced the butterfly on her head.

"It did hurt a *little* . . . Oh, Ooh," she cried distractedly, "Your blanket . . ."

They were deciding the blanket didn't matter when Loolie looked at her little fingernail and started kissing his stomach.

"Dovy dear, don't you think, couldn't we," she mumbled, "I mean, it's only the first time I ever—try again?"

Dov found himself agreeing.

The second time was infinitely better. The second time was something to challenge fantasy. It was so good that the scrap of Dov's mind that wasn't occupied with the electric baby eeling under and over and around him . . . began to wonder. Virginal fucks did not, in his experience, achieve such loin-bursting poetry, such fitting, such flowing surge to velocities sustained beyond escape, such thrust and burn and build with the ex-virgin sobbing rhythmically, "Love you, Dovy, Do-o-ovy," giving everything to it in the best position of all until all the stages went nova together—

". . . Don't sleep yet, Dovy, please wake up a minute?"

He opened one eye and rolled off; he was really a nice person.

Loolie leaned on his chest, worshipping him through her pale damp hair.

"I almost forgot." She grinned, suddenly naughty. He felt her hair, her breasts move down his belly, down his thighs and shins to his feet. Sleepily he noted a warm wetness closing over his big toe. Her mouth? Some kind of toe joy, he thought—and then the signal made it six feet back to his brain.

"Hey-y-y!" He smacked her butt. "That hurt! You *bit* me!"

Her face came around laughing. She was really great-looking.

"I bit your big toe." She nodded solemnly. "That's *very important.* It means you're my true love." Her eyes suddenly got wet again. "I love you so, Dovy. Will you remember, I bit your toe?"

"Well, sure I'll remember," he grinned uneasily. The neurones that had twitched sometime back, boosted by stimulation from his toe finally made connection.

"Hey, Loolie. What you said ... Is your name *Aerovulpa?*"

She nodded slowly.

"*The* Aerovulpa?"

Another nod, her eyes glowing at him.

"Oh god." He tried to remember what he'd seen about it. Aerovulpa ... The Family ... Mr. Aerovulpa, he gathered, was not in tune with the twentyfirst century—maybe not the twentieth, even. And this was an Aerovulpa virgin all over his legs. Ex-virgin.

"By any chance is your father sending a private army up here after you, Loolie?"

"Poor Daddy," she smiled. "He's dead." The far beacon in her eyes was coming closer. "Dovy. You didn't ask me my whole name."

"Your what?"

"I'm Loolie Aerovulpa ... Rapelle."

He stared. He didn't get it at all.

"I don't—are you some kind of relative?"

She nodded, her eyes enormous, weird.

"A very close relative." Her lips feathered his cheek.

"I never met you. I swear."

He felt her swallow. Loolie drew back and looked at him for a couple of long breaths and then glanced down at her little finger. He saw she had a tiny timer implanted in the nail.

"You haven't asked me how old I am either," she said quietly.

"So?"

"I'm seventy-five."

"Huh?" Dov stared. No geriatrics imaginable could—

"Seventy-five years old. I am. Inside, I mean, me, now."

Then he got it.

"You—you—"

"Yes. I'm time-jumping."

"Time-jumper . . . !" He'd heard about it, but he didn't believe it. Now he looked and saw . . . seventy-five years looking out of her baby eyes. Old. The spark in there was old.

Loolie checked the nail again. "I have to tell you something, Dovy." She took hold of his face solemnly. "I have to warn you. It's very important. Darling, don't ever ig-g-g—*eugh-gh*—"

Her jaws jabbered, her head flopped—and her whole body slumped on him, dead girl.

He scrambled out and had just got his ear on her heart-beat when Loolie's mouth gulped air. He turned his head and saw her eyes open, widen, wander to his body, her body, and back to his.

"Who're you?" she asked, clear and cool. Asking for information.

He drew back.

"Uh. Dov Rapelle." He saw her face, her eyes were so different. She sat up. A stranger teenager was sitting in his bunk, studying him so clinically he reached for the blankets.

"Hey, look!" She pointed at the window. "Snow! Oh, great! Where am I? Where is this?"

"It's my cabin. In Calgary, Alberta. Listen, are you all right? You were time-jumping, I think."

"Yeah," said Loolie absently, smiling at the snow. "I don't remember anything, you never do." She squirmed, looking around and then suddenly squirmed again and said

"Oh, my," and stopped looking around. She put her hand under herself and her eyes locked on his.

"Uh . . . Hey—what *happened?*"

"Well," Dov began, "You, I mean we . . ." He was too nice to blame it all on her.

She bugged her eyes, still feeling herself.

"But that's *impossible!*"

Dov shook his head, no. Then he changed it to yes.

"No," she insisted bewilderedly. "I mean, I've been *hyped.* Daddy had me fixed so I couldn't. I mean, men are *repulsive* to me." She nodded. "Girls too. Sex, it's a nothing. All I do, all I do is *sailing* races. Star class, yick. I'm *so* bored!"

Dov couldn't find a thing to say, he just sat there on the bunk holding the blanket. Loolie put out her hand and touched his shoulder tentatively.

"H'mh." She frowned. "That's funny. You don't *feel* repulsive." She put her other hand on him. "You feel all right. Maybe nice. Hey this is weird. You mean, we *did it?*"

He nodded.

"Did I, like, *enjoy* it?"

"You seemed to, yes."

She shook her head wonderingly, grinning. "Oh, ho, ho. Hey, Daddy will be wild!"

"Your father?" said Dov. "Isn't he—you said he was dead."

"Daddy? Of course he's not dead." She stared at him. "I don't remember a thing about it. All I remember is being in some big old house, being *seventy-five.* It was awful." She shuddered. "All stringy and creepy. I felt, bleeah. And those weird old people. I just said I was sick and went and lay down and watched the shows. And slept. For two days, I guess. Hey, when is this? I'm hungry!"

"December twenty-ninth," Dov told her dazedly. "Do you do this a lot, time-jumping?"

"Oh no." She pushed her hair back, "Just a few times, I mean, Daddy just *installed* it. I was so bored, I thought, well, it would be nice to give myself a treat. I mean, when I'm *old*, I'll enjoy being sixteen again for a little while, don't you think?"

"I wouldn't know. We don't have anything like that here. In fact, I never believed they existed."

"Oh, they exist." She nodded importantly, frowning at him. "Of course they're *very expensive*. There's only a few in the *world* I guess. Hey, you know, I saw your picture there. By the mirror. I am *so* hungry. There has to be food here. Sex is supposed to make you hungry, right?"

She scrambled off the bunk, trailing blanket. "I'm starved! Can I help you cook? Oh, my glitterbugs. Oh dear. Is that the *moon?* We're up in real *mountains?*" She ran around to the windows. "Daddy never lets me go anywhere. Oh, mountains are fantastic! Hey, you really do look nice. I mean, being a man isn't so hideous." She spun back to him, nose to nose. "Look, you have to *tell* me all about it." Her eyes slid around, suddenly shy. "I mean, *everything*, God, I'm hungry. Listen, since we, I mean, I don't *remember*, you know. Can't we sort of *try* it over again? Hey, I forgot your name, I'm *sorry—*"

"Loolie," Dov said. He closed his eyes. "Will you please just shut up one minute? I have to think."

But all he could think was that she had a good idea: Food.

So he fried up some corned beef hash, with Loolie all over the cabin like a mongoose, opening the door, smooshing snow on her face, admiring the moon and the mountains, running over to poke him with a spruce twig. When she turned her attention to the fire he was pleased to see that she put the wood on right. They sat down to eat. Dov wanted very much to ask about her father. But he couldn't— being a nice person—break through Loolie's excitement about him, and the mountains, and him, and the cabin, and him, and—

It began to dawn on Dov that this little Aerovulpa had a pretty sad locked-up sliver of the twentyfirst century.

"You ought to see this place when the ice goes out," he told her. "The big melt. And the avalanches."

"Oh, Dovy, I'm so bitched with *people*—places. I mean, nobody *cares* about anything real. Like this is beautiful. Dovy, will you, when I—"

That was when her father's private army came *chunga-chunga* out of the night sky.

Dov scrambled into his suit and discovered that the army consisted of one small hysterical man and one large hairless man.

"Uncle Vic!" cried Loolie. She ran up and patted the small man while the large man showed Dov several embossed badges.

"Your father, your father!" Uncle Vic spluttered, thrusting Loolie away and glaring round the cabin. His eyes focussed on the bunk. The big man stood stolidly by the door.

"Angry, yes!" moaned Uncle Vic. He took off his hat and put it on again and grabbed Dov's snowsuit.

"Do you know who this girl is?" he hissed.

"She says she's Loolie Aerovulpa. She was time-jumping," Dov said, being reasonable.

"I know, I know! Terrible!" The little man's eyes rolled. "Louis—Mr. Aerovulpa—turned it off. How could you do this to him, girl?"

"I haven't done a thing to Daddy, Uncle Vic."

Her uncle marched over to the bunk, grabbed up the blanket, hissed, and threw it on the floor.

"You—you—"

"Daddy had no right to *do* that!" Loolie cried. "It's *my* life. It didn't work, anyway. I—I love it here, I mean, I think I—"

"No!" the little man shrieked. He scuttled back to Loolie and started shaking her. "Your father!" he yelled. "He will have you psyched, he will have you deleted! Puta! Pffah! and as for you, you—" He whirled on Dov and began to spray old-world discourtesies.

At which point, Dov, although a nice person, was starting to get considerably browned. He recalled coming up here for some peace and quiet. Now he looked at the little man, and the big man, and Loolie, and finished lacing up his boots.

"Getup! Move!" the little man screamed. "You are coming with us!"

"My folks will wonder where I am," Dov objected reasonably, thinking the two men looked like urban types.

"On your feet, felo!" Uncle Vic flapped his hands at the big man, who came away from the door and jerked his head at Dov.

"Get moving, boy." He had one hand in his pocket like an old movie.

Dov got up.

"Okay, but you need some clothes for Miss Aerovulpa, don't you think? Maybe her father won't be so wild if you bring her back dressed."

Uncle Vic glared distractedly at Loolie who was sticking out of her blanket.

"I'll get a snowsuit in the closet," Dov said. He moved carefully toward the woodshed door by the fireplace, wondering if urban types would buy the idea of a closet in a mountain cabin. The big man took his hand out his pocket with something in it pointed at Dov's back, but he didn't move.

Just as Dov's hand reached the latch he heard Loolie's mouth pop open and held his breath. She didn't say anything.

Then he was twisting through the door and yanking out the main brace of the woodpile. Cordwood crashed down against the door while Dov assisted matters by leaping up the pile, grabbing the axe as he went. He scrambled around the eaves onto the lean-to and whipped around the chimney, hearing bangings from below.

From the chimney he launched himself up to the roof-ridge. The big front drift was still there. He rode a snowslide down over the front door, slamming the bar-latch as he landed, grabbed up his skis and was galloping through the drifts to the far side of the helicopter.

The first shots came through the cabin window as he swung his axe at the main rotor bearings. His body was behind the copter and the cabin windows were too small for the big man. When his axe achieved an unhealthy effect on the rotors Dov gave the gas tank a couple of whacks, decided not to bother igniting it, buried the axe in the tail vane and scuttled down the morraine into a private ravine. Glass was crashing, voices bellowing behind him.

The ravine became a long narrow tunnel under the snowbowed spruces. Dov frog-crawled down it until the noise was faint, like coyote pups. Presently the ravine widened and debouched into a steep snowfield. Dov buckled on his skis. The moon rode out of a cloudrack. Dov straightened up and took off down the glittering white slopes. As he flew along gulping in the peace and quiet, he hoped Loolie would be all right. Vic was her uncle, it had to be okay.

In an hour he had reached the parked snowbus and was

headed back to Calgary where *his* uncle, Ben Rapelle, was chief of the RCM mountain patrol.

He felt free.

But he wasn't. Because Loolie—Loolie Number One, that is—had said her last name was Rapelle. And his toe swelled up.

That turned out to be, as she'd also said, very important.

Next morning, after the patrol brought Loolie and Uncle Vic and his enforcer all safe and sound down to Headquarters, Loolie insisted on phoning her psychomed. So when her father, Mr. Aerovulpa, arrived in his private VTO the psychomed was with him.

Mr. Aerovulpa turned out to be quite unlike Uncle Vic, who was actually, it seemed, only a third cousin. For too many generations swarthy Aerovulpa sperm had been frisking into blond Scandinavian-type wombs; the current Mr. Aerovulpa was a tall yellow-grey glacier with a worried, lumpy Swedish face. If he was wild he didn't show it. He appeared only very weary.

"Eulalia," he sighed depletedly in Ben Rapelle's office. That was Loolie's real name and he always called her by it, having no talent for fatherhood. He looked from his only child to the psychomed whom he had employed to ensure a marriageable product.

Now it had all blown up in his face.

"But how . . . ?" asked Mr. Aerovulpa. "You assured me, Doctor . . ." His voice was quiet but not warm. "Uncle" Vic shied nervously. They were all standing around the Patrol office, Dov with a socmoc on one foot.

"The time-jump," shrugged the psychomed. He was plump and slightly wall-eyed, which gave him an air of manic cheer. "It was the older Loolie who was in this body, Louis. This older persona was no longer conditioned. You really should have been more careful. What on earth did you want with a thing like that, time-jumping at your age? And the cost, my god."

Mr. Aerovulpa sighed.

"I acquired it for a particular purpose." He frowned abstractedly at the Rapelles. "A very small trip. I wished to observe . . ."

"To see if you had a *grandson*, eh! Eh, eh?" The psycher chortled. "Of course. Well, did you?"

For some reason Mr. Aerovulpa chose to continue this intimate topic. "I found myself at my desk," he said. "On it was a portrait." His bleak eyes searched his daughter, froze onto Dov.

Dov blinked. It had just occurred to him that a securely hyped and guarded virgin might not be otherwise defended from maternity. Loolie sucked in her lower lip, made a face.

The psychomed eyed them both, head cocked.

"Tell me, Loolie, when you came back to yourself, did you find this young man, ah, disgusting? Repellent? The situation was traumatic?"

Loolie smiled at him, wider and wider, swinging her head slowly from side to side. "Oh, no . . . Oh, *no!* It was fantastic, *he*'s fantastic, he's beautiful. Only—"

"Only what?"

Her smile turned to Dov, melted. "Well, we never, I mean, I wish—"

"All right!" The psychomed held up his hand. "I see. Now, tell me, Loolie. Think. Did you by any chance bite his toe?"

"Uncle" Vic made a noise. Loolie looked incredulous. "Bite his toe?" she echoed. "Of course not."

The psychomed turned to Dov and let his gaze sink to the socmoc. "Did she, young man?"

"Why?" asked Dov cautiously. Everybody began looking at the socmoc.

"Did she?"

"I never!" said Loolie indignantly.

"You don't know," Dov told her. "You did, before. When you were seventy-five."

"Bite your toe? What for?"

"Because that was the key cue," said the psychomed. He pulled his ear. "Oh bother. You remember, Louis. I told you."

Mr. Aerovulpa's expression had retreated further into the ice age.

"The idea was not to make you sexless for life, my dear," the psycher told Loolie. "There had to be a cue, a key to undo the conditioning. Something easy but improbable, which couldn't possibly happen by accident. I considered several possibilities. Yes. All things considered, the toe-bite seemed best." He nodded benevolently. "You recall, Louis, you wanted no matrimonial scandals."

Mr. Aerovulpa said nothing.

"A beautiful job of imprinting, if I do say so myself." The psycher beamed. "Absolutely irreversible, I guarantee it. The man whose toe she bites—" he pointed at Dov, one eye rolling playfully "—or rather, *bit*, she will love that man and that man only so long as she lives. Guaranteed!"

In the silence Mr. Aerovulpa passed one hand over his Dag Hammarskjold forehead and breathed out carefully. His gaze lingered from Loolie to Dov to Ben Rapelle like a python inspecting inexplicably inedible rabbits.

"It is . . . possible . . . that we shall see more of each other," he observed coldly. "At the moment I trust it is . . . agreeable to you that my daughter return to her schooling. Victor."

"Right here, Louis!"

"You will remain to provide our . . . apologies to these gentlemen and to accomplish any necessary, ah, restorations. I am . . . not pleased. Come, Eulalia."

"Oh, Dovy!" Loolie cried as she was hustled out. Dov's uncle Ben grunted warningly. And the Aerovulpas departed.

But not, of course, permanently.

Came Springtime in the Rockies and with it a very round-bellied and lovelorn teenager, escorted this time by a matron of unmistakable character and hardihood. Dov got out the ponies and they rode up into the singing forests and rainbow torrents and all the shy, free, super-delights of the wild country Dov loved. And he saw that Loolie truly wanted to live there and share his kind of life in addition to being wildly in love with him, and anyone could see that Loolie herself was luscious and radiant and eager and potentially sensible in spots, especially when it came to getting rid of the matron. *And* Dov really was a nice person, in spite of his distrust of the Aerovulpa ambiance. (The ambiance was now making itself felt in the form of a phoney demographic survey team snooping all over Calgary.)

So when summer ripened Dov journeyed warily to the Aerovulpa island off Pulpit Harbor, where he soon discovered that the ambiance didn't repel him half as much as Loolie attracted him. Even the nicest young man is not immune to the notion of a beautiful semi-virginal ever-adoring child-bride of great fortune.

"What, ah, career do you plan for yourself?" Mr. Aerovulpa asked Dov on one of his rare appearances on the island.

"Avalanche research," Dov told him, thus confirming the survey team's report. Mr. Aerovulpa's eyelids drooped minutely. The alliances he had contemplated for Loolie had featured interests of a far more seismic type.

"Basically, sir, I'm a geo-ecologist. It's a great field."

"Oh, it's wonderful, Daddy!" sang Loolie. "I'm going to do all his records!"

Mr. Aerovulpa's eyes drifted from his daughter's face to

her belly. The Lump was now known to be male. Mr. Aerovulpa had not arrived where he was by ignoring facts, and he was really not a twenty-first-century man. "Ah," he said drearily, and departed.

But the wedding itself was far from dreary. It was magnificently simple, out on the lawn above the sea with a forcefield keeping off the Maine weather and an acre of imported wildflowers. The guest list was small, dominated by a number of complicated old ladies of exotic title and entourage among whom the Alberta contingent stood out like friendly grin-silos.

And then everybody went away and left Dov and Loolie for a week to themselves in paradise.

"Oh, Dovy," sighed Loolie on the third day, "I wish I could stay like this the rest of my life!"

This not very remarkable sentiment was uttered as they lay on the sauna solarium glowing like fresh boiled shrimps.

"You just say that because you bit my toe," said Dov. He was thinking about sailing, to which he had recently been introduced.

"I never!" Loolie protested. She turned over. "Hey, you know, I wonder. When did I *actually* meet you?"

"Last Christmas."

"No, that's what I mean. I mean, I came there because I already loved you, didn't I? And that's where I met you. It's funny."

"Yeah."

"I *love* you so, Dovy."

"I love you too. Listen, let's take your big boat out today, should we?"

And they had a wonderful sail on the dancing trimaran all the way around Acadia Park Island and back to a great clam dinner. That night in bed afterwards Loolie brought it up again.

"Unh," said Dov sleepily.

She traced his spine with her nose.

"*Listen*, Dovy. Wouldn't it be fantastic to live this day over again? I mean like when we're *old*."

"Hunk-unh."

"Daddy has the jumper right here, you know. I was here over Christmas when I *did* it. That's what the big power plant over by the cove is for, I told you."

"Hunh-unh."

"Why don't we do it tomorrow?"

"Unh," said Dovy. "Hey, what did you say?"

"We could time-jump tomorrow, *together*," Loolie smiled dreamily. "Then when we're old we could be *young* like we are for awhile. Together."

"Absolutely not," said Dov. And he told her why it was an insane idea. And he told her and told her.

"It's dangerous. What if one of us turned out to be dead?"

"Oh, if you're dead nothing *happens*, I mean, you can only switch places with *yourself*. The, the persona something symmetry, I mean, if you're not *there* nothing happens. You just stay here. The book says so, it's perfectly safe."

"It's insane anyway. What about the Lump?"

Loolie giggled. "It would be a great experience for him."

"What do you mean? What if he finds himself with the mind of a six-months embryo while he's driving a jet?"

"Oh, he *couldn't*! I mean, he'd know it was going to happen, because it *did*, you know? So when he got that old he'd sit down or something. Like when *I* get to be seventy-five I'll know I'll be jumped back here and go and meet you."

"No, Loolie. It's insane. Forget it."

So she forgot it. For several hours.

"Dovy, I *worry* so. Isn't it awful we have to get *old*?

Think how great it would be, having a day to look forward to. Being young again, just for a day. For half an hour, even. Isn't it *dreary*, thinking about getting old?"

Dov opened one eye. He had felt thoughts like that himself.

"I mean, we wouldn't miss a few hours now. We have so much time. But think when you're, oh, like sixty, maybe you'll be sick or *degenerating*—and you'll know you're going to jump back and feel great and, and go sailing and be like we are!"

Loolie was being crafty with that "sailing," she was gripped by the primal dream. Pay now, play later.

"You can't be sure it's safe, Loolie."

"Well, *I* did it, didn't I? Three times. Nothing goes wrong 'cause you *know* it's going to happen," she repeated patiently. "I mean, when you get there you *expect* it. I found a note I'd written to myself telling me what to do. Like the butler's name was Johan. And my friends. And to say I was sick."

"You could see the future?" Dov frowned. "What happened? I mean, the news?"

"Oh, well, I don't know, I mean I wasn't very *curious*. All I saw was some old house. Like it was partly underground, I guess. But Dovy, you *know* about things, you could sell all the news, even in just like half an hour you could find out what was going on. You could even read your own research, maybe!"

"Hmh . . ."

That wasn't quite the end of it of course. It was the evening of the sixth day when Dov and Loolie came in from the moonlight on the shore and went hand in hand into Mr. Aerovulpa's quiet corridors. (Which were found unlocked, an out-of-character fact unless it is recalled that Mr. Aerovulpa had glimpsed the future too.) There was a handle set on standby. Loolie threw it and power hummed up beyond a gleaming wall in which was set a kind of air-lock. She swung the lockport and revealed a cubicle inside the wall.

"It's just big enough for all three of us," she giggled, pulling him in. "What do you suppose we'll do, I mean, the old usses who came back here? I mean, we aren't giving them very *long*."

"Ask your son," said Dov fondly, mentally reviewing the exciting things he wanted to find out about THE FUTURE.

So they set the dials that would exchange their young psyches with their older selves forty years ahead, when Dov would be—good god, *sixty-two*. Loolie let Dov be cautious (this first time, she told herself secretly) and he selected thirty minutes, no more. They clasped hands. And Loolie tipped the silent tumblers of the activator circuit, which unleashed the titanic capacitators waiting to cup the chamber in a temporal anomaly, OOOMM!

—And which by a million-to-one chance shot young Dov Rapelle uptime into the lethal half-hour when a coronary artery ballooned and ruptured as he lay alone in a strange city.

And little Loolie Aerovulpa Rapelle returned from a meaningless stroll in a shopping arcade in Pernambuco to find herself holding Dov's dead body on the control room floor.

Because dying any time is an experience you don't survive.

Not even—as Loolie later pointed out to the numerous temporal engineers her father had to hire—not even when it involves a paradox. For how could Dov have died at *twenty-two* if he actually died at *sixty-two*? Something was terribly wrong. Something that had to be fixed, that *must be fixed*, if it took the whole Aerovulpa fortune, Loolie insisted. She went right on saying it because the psychomed had been quite right. Dovy was the only man she ever loved and she loved him all her life.

The temporal engineers shrugged, and so did the mathematicians. They told her that paradoxes were accumulating elsewhere in the society by that time, too, even though only a few su-pra-legal heavy persons owned jumpers. Alternate time-tracks, perhaps? Or maybe time-independent hysteresis? Paradoxes of course were wrong. They shouldn't happen.

But when one does—*who do you complain to*?

Which wasn't much help to a loving little girl facing fifty-nine long grey empty years ... *twenty-one thousand, five hundred and forty-five* blighted days and lonely nights to wait ... for her hour in the arms of her man on a Hudson Bay blanket.

ANACHRON

DAMON KNIGHT

What science fiction has so often illuminated is this: time travel, that power fantasy is, paradoxically entrapping rather than liberating. "Anachron," which extends that prank to a distant place and then slams it into that small, enclosed space which is Knight's most obsessive landscape, is exceptional, barbarous, ungiving. Like Cornell Woolrich's greatest stories, it closes on protagonist and reader like a coffin (this is not necessarily a winning endorsement). The starkness of this story strips the concept of time travel to the colder jurisdiction of that core.

Damon Knight, a Grand Master (1995) of the Science Fiction and Fantasy Writers of America, sold his first stories in the early 1940s, but it was through the lucid and biting short stories of the late 1940s and 1950s that he achieved lasting effect; the stories have been gathered into many collections, of which *The Best of Damon Knight* (1976) is probably the best. Knight edited the 21 volumes of the influential original anthology, *Orbit*, from 1965 through the late 1970's. He is the author of many novels; *A for Anything The People Market* is arguably the best but a 1990s novel, *Humpty-Dumpty: An Oval*, shows no failure of skill. Knight lives in Oregon with his wife, the equally distinguished writer, Kate Wilhelm.

The body was never found. And for that reason alone, there was no body to find.

It sounds like inverted logic—which, in a sense, it is—but there's no paradox involved. It was a perfectly orderly and explicable event, even though it could only have happened to a Castellare.

Odd fish, the Castellare brothers. Sons of a Scots-Englishwoman and an expatriate Italian, born in England, educated on the Continent, they were at ease anywhere in the world and at home nowhere.

Nevertheless, in their middle years, they had become settled men. Expatriates like their father, they lived on the island of Ischia, off the Neapolitan coast, in a palace—*quattrocento*, very fine, with peeling cupids on the walls, a multitude of rats, no central heating and no neighbors.

They went nowhere; no one except their agents and their lawyers came to them. Neither had ever married. Each, at about the age of thirty, had given up the world of people for an inner world of more precise and more enduring pleasures. Each was an amateur—a fanatical, compulsive amateur.

They had been born out of their time.

Peter's passion was virtu. He collected relentlessly, it would not be too much to say savagely; he collected as some men hunt big game. His taste was catholic, and his acquisitions filled the huge rooms of the palace and half the vaults under them—paintings, statuary, enamels, porcelain, glass, crystal, metalwork. At fifty, he was a round little man with small, sardonic eyes and a careless patch of pinkish goatee.

Harold Castellare, Peter's talented brother, was a scientist. An amateur scientist. He belonged in the nineteenth century, as Peter was a throwback to a still earlier epoch. Modern science is largely a matter of teamwork and drudgery, both impossible concepts to a Castellare. But Harold's intelligence was in its own way as penetrating and original as a Newton's or a Franklin's. He had done respectable work in physics and electronics, and had even, at his lawyer's insistence, taken out a few patents. The income from these, when his own purchases of instruments and equipment did not consume it, he gave to his brother, who accepted it without gratitude or rancor.

Harold, at fifty-three, was spare and shrunken, sallow and spotted, with a bloodless, melancholy countenance; on his upper lip grew a neat hedge of pink-and-salt mustache, the companion piece and antithesis of his brother's goatee.

On a certain May morning, Harold had an accident.

Goodyear dropped rubber on a hot stove; Archimedes took a bath; Becquerel left a piece of uranium ore in a drawer with a photographic plate. Harold Castellare, working patiently with an apparatus which had so far consumed a great deal of current without producing anything more spectacular than some rather unusual corona effects, sneezed convulsively and dropped an ordinary bar magnet across two charged terminals.

Above the apparatus a huge, cloudy bubble sprang into being.

Harold, getting up from his instinctive crouch, blinked at it in profound astonishment. As he watched, the cloudiness abruptly disappeared and he was looking *through* the bubble at a section of tessellated flooring that seemed to be about three feet above the real floor. He could also see the corner of a carved wooden bench, and on the bench a small, oddly shaped stringed instrument.

Harold swore fervently to himself, made agitated notes, and then began to experiment. He tested the sphere cautiously with an electroscope, with a magnet, with a Geiger counter. Negative. He tore a tiny bit of paper from his notepad and dropped it toward the sphere. The paper disappeared; he couldn't see where it went.

Speechless, Harold picked up a meter stick and thrust it delicately forward. There was no feeling of contact; the rule went into and through the bubble as if the latter did not exist. Then it touched the stringed instrument, with a solid click. Harold pushed. The instrument slid over the edge of the bench and struck the floor with a hollow thump and jangle.

Staring at it, Harold suddenly recognized its tantalizingly familiar shape.

Recklessly he let go the meter stick, reached in and picked the fragile thing out of the bubble. It was solid and cool in his fingers. The varnish was clear, the color of the wood glowing through it. It looked as if it might have been made yesterday.

Peter owned one almost exactly like it, except for preservation—a viola d'amore of the seventeenth century.

Harold stooped to look through the bubble horizontally. Gold and rust tapestries hid the wall, fifty feet away, except for an ornate door in the center. The door began to open; Harold saw a flicker of umber.

Then the sphere went cloudy again. His hands were empty; the viola d'amore was gone. And the meter stick, which he had dropped inside the sphere, lay on the floor at his feet.

"Look at that," said Harold simply.

Peter's eyebrows went up slightly. "What is it, a new kind of television?"

"No, no. Look here." The viola d'amore lay on the bench, precisely where it had been before. Harold reached into the sphere and drew it out.

Peter started. "Give me that." He took it in his hands, rubbed the smoothly finished wood. He stared at his brother. "By God and all the saints," he said. "Time travel."

Harold snorted impatiently. "My dear Peter, 'time' is a meaningless word taken by itself, just as 'space' is."

"But, barring that, time travel."

"If you like, yes."

"You'll be quite famous."

"I expect so."

Peter looked down at the instrument in his hands. "I'd like to keep this, if I may."

"I'd be very happy to let you, but you can't."

As he spoke the bubble went cloudy; the viola d'amore was gone like smoke.

"There, you see?"

"What sort of devil's trick is that?"

"It goes back ... Later you'll see. I had that thing out once before, and this happened. When the sphere became transparent again, the viol was where I had found it."

"And your explanation for this?"

Harold hesitated. "None. Until I can work out the appropriate mathematics—"

"Which may take you some time. Meanwhile, in layman's language—"

Harold's face creased with the effort and interest of translation. "Very roughly, then—I should say it means that events are conserved. Two or three centuries ago—"

"Three. Notice the sound holes."

"Three centuries ago, then, at this particular time of day, someone was in that room. If the viola were gone, he or she would have noticed the fact. That would constitute an alteration of events already fixed; therefore it doesn't happen. For the same reason, I conjecture, we can't see into the sphere, or—" he probed at it with a fountain pen—"I thought not—or reach into it to touch anything; that would also constitute an alteration. And anything we put into the sphere while it is transparent comes out again when it becomes opaque. To put it very crudely, we cannot alter the past."

"But it seems to me that we did alter it. Just now, when you took the viol out, even if no one of that time saw it happen."

"This," said Harold, "is the difficulty of using language as a means of exact communication. If you had not forgotten all your calculus . . . However. It may be postulated (remembering of course that everything I say is a lie, because I say it in English) that an event which doesn't influence other events is not an event. In other words—"

"That, since no one saw you take it, it doesn't matter whether you took it or not. A rather dangerous precept, Harold; you would have been burned at the stake for that at one time."

"Very likely. But it can be stated in another way or,

indeed, in an infinity of ways which only seem to be different. If someone, let us say God, were to remove the moon as I am talking to you, using zero duration, and substitute an exact replica made of concrete and plaster of Paris, with the same mass, albedo and so on as the genuine moon, it would make no measurable difference in the universe as we perceive it—and therefore we cannot certainly say that it hasn't happened. Nor, I may add, does it make any difference whether it has or not."

" 'When there's no one about on the quad,' " said Peter.

"Yes. A basic and, as a natural consequence, a meaningless problem of philosophy. Except," he added, "in this one particular manifestation."

He stared at the cloudy sphere. "You'll excuse me, won't you, Peter? I've got to work on this."

"When will you publish, do you suppose?"

"Immediately. That's to say, in a week or two."

"Don't do it till you've talked it over with me, will you? I have a notion about it."

Harold looked at him sharply. "Commercial?"

"In a way."

"No," said Harold. "This is not the sort of thing one patents or keeps secret, Peter."

"Of course. I'll see you at dinner, I hope?"

"I think so. If I forget, knock on the door, will you?"

"Yes. Until then."

"Until then."

At dinner, Peter asked only two questions.

"Have you found any possibility of changing the time your thing reaches—from the seventeenth century to the eighteenth, for example, or from Monday to Tuesday?"

"Yes, as a matter of fact. Amazing. It's lucky that I had a rheostat already in the circuit; I wouldn't dare turn the current off. Varying the amperage varies the time set. I've had it up to what I think was Wednesday of last week—at any rate, my smock was lying over the workbench where I left it, I remember, Wednesday afternoon. I pulled it out. A curious sensation, Peter—I was wearing the same smock at the time. And then the sphere went opaque and of course the smock vanished. That must have been myself, coming into the room."

"And the future?"

"Yes. Another funny thing. I've had it forward to various times in the near future, and the machine itself is still there, but nothing's been done to it—none of the things I'm thinking I might do. That might be because of the conservation of events, again, but I rather think not. Still farther forward there are cloudy areas, blanks; I can't see anything that isn't in existence now, apparently, but here, in the next few days, there's nothing of that.

"It's as if I were going away. Where do you suppose I'm going?"

Harold's abrupt departure took place between midnight and morning. He packed his own grip, it would seem, left unattended, and was seen no more. It was extraordinary, of course, that he should have left at all, but the details were in no way odd. Harold had always detested what he called "the tyranny of the valet." He was, as everyone knew, a most independent man.

On the following day Peter made some trifling experiments with the time-sphere. From the sixteenth century he picked up a scent bottle of Venetian glass; from the eighteenth, a crucifix of carved rosewood; from the nineteenth, when the palace had been the residence of an Austrian count and his Italian mistress, a hand-illuminated copy of

De Sade's *La Nouvelle Justine*, very curiously bound in human skin.

They all vanished, naturally, within minutes or hours— all but the scent bottle. This gave Peter matter for reflection. There had been half a dozen flickers of cloudiness in the sphere just futureward of the bottle; it ought to have vanished, but it hadn't. But then, he had found it on the floor near a wall with quite a large rat hole in it.

When objects disappeared unaccountably, he asked himself, was it because they had rolled into rat holes, or because some time fisher had picked them up when they were in a position to do so?

He did not make any attempt to explore the future. That afternoon he telephoned his lawyers in Naples and gave them instructions for a new will. His estate, including his half of the jointly owned Ischia property, was to go to the Italian government on two conditions: (1) that Harold Castellare should make a similar bequest of the remaining half of the property and (2) that the Italian government should turn the palace into a national museum to house Peter's collection, using the income from his estate for its administration and for further acquisitions. His surviving relatives—two cousins in Scotland—he cut off with a shilling each.

He did nothing more until after the document had been brought out to him, signed and witnessed. Only then did he venture to look into his own future.

Events were conserved, Harold had said—meaning, Peter very well understood, events of the present and future as well as of the past. But was there only one pattern in which the future could be fixed? Could a result exist before its cause had occurred?

The Castellare motto was *Audentes fortuna juvat*—into

which Peter, at the age of fourteen, had interpolated the word *"prudentesque"*: "Fortune favors the bold—and the prudent."

Tomorrow: no change; the room he was looking at was so exactly like this one that the time sphere seemed to vanish. The next day: a cloudy blur. And the next, and the next . . .

Opacity, straight through to what Peter judged, by the distance he had moved the rheostat handle, to be ten years ahead. Then, suddenly, the room was a long marble hall filled with display cases.

Peter smiled wryly. If you were Harold, obviously you could not look ahead and see Peter working in your laboratory. And if you were Peter, equally obviously, you could not look ahead and know whether the room you saw was an improvement you yourself were going to make, or part of a museum established after your death, eight or nine years from now, or . . .

No. Eight years was little enough, but he could not even be sure of that. It would, after all, be seven years before Harold could be declared legally dead. . . .

Peter turned the vernier knob slowly forward. A flicker, another, a long series. Forward faster. Now the flickering melted into a grayness; objects winked out of existence and were replaced by others in the showcases; the marble darkened and lightened again, darkened and lightened, darkened and remained dark. He was, Peter judged, looking at the hall as it would be some five hundred years in the future. There was a thick film of dust on every exposed surface; rubbish and the carcass of some small animal had been swept carelessly into a corner.

The sphere clouded.

When it cleared, there was an intricate trail of footprints in the dust, and two of the showcases were empty.

The footprints were splayed, trifurcate, and thirty inches long.

After a moment's deliberation Peter walked around the workbench and leaned down to look through the sphere from the opposite direction. Framed in the nearest of the four tall windows was a scene of picture-postcard banality: the sun-silvered bay and the foreshortened arc of the city, with Vesuvio faintly fuming in the background. But there was something wrong about the colors, even grayed as they were by distance.

Peter went and got his binoculars.

The trouble was, of course, that Naples was green. Where the city ought to have been, a rankness had sprouted. Between the clumps of foliage he could catch occasional glimpses of gray-white that might equally well have been boulders or the wreckage of buildings. There was no movement. There was no shipping in the harbor.

But something rather odd was crawling up the side of the volcano. A rust-orange pipe, it appeared to be, supported on hairline struts like the legs of a centipede, and ending without rhyme or reason just short of the top.

While Peter watched, it turned slowly blue.

One day further forward: now all the display cases had been looted; the museum, it would seem, was empty.

Given, that in five centuries the world, or at any rate the department of Campania, has been overrun by a race of Somethings, the human population being killed or driven out in the process; and that the conquerors take an interest in the museum's contents, which they have accordingly removed.

Removed where, and why?

This question, Peter conceded, might have a thousand answers, nine hundred and ninety-nine of which would mean that he had lost his gamble. The remaining answer was: to the vaults, for safety.

With his own hands Peter built a hood to cover the apparatus on the workbench and the sphere above it. It was unaccustomed labor; it took him the better part of two days. Then he called in workmen to break a hole in the stone flooring next to the interior wall, rig a hoist, and cut the power cable that supplied the time-sphere loose from its supports all the way back to the fuse box, leaving him a single flexible length of cable more than a hundred feet long. They unbolted the workbench from the floor, attached casters to its legs, lowered it into the empty vault below, and went away.

Peter unfastened and removed the hood. He looked into the sphere.

Treasure.

Crates, large and small, racked in rows into dimness.

With pudgy fingers that did not tremble, he advanced the rheostat. A cloudy flicker, another, a leaping blur of them as he moved the vernier faster—and then there were no more, to the limit of the time-sphere's range.

Two hundred years, Peter guessed—A.D. 2700 to 2900 or thereabout—in which no one would enter the vault. Two hundred years of "unliquidated time."

He put the rheostat back to the beginning of that uninterrupted period. He drew out a small crate and prized it open.

Chessmen, ivory with gold inlay, Florentine, fourteenth century. Superb.

Another, from the opposite rack.

T'ang figurines, horses and men, ten to fourteen inches high. Priceless.

*　　*　　*

The crates would not burn, Tomaso told him. He went down to the kitchen to see, and it was true. The pieces lay in the roaring stove untouched. He fished one out with a poker; even the feathery splinters of the unplaned wood had not ignited.

It made a certain extraordinary kind of sense. When the moment came for the crates to go back, any physical scrambling that had occurred in the meantime would have no effect; they would simply put themselves together as they had been before, like Thor's goats. But burning was another matter; burning would have released energy which could not be replaced.

That settled one paradox, at any rate. There was another that nagged at Peter's orderly mind. If the things he took out of that vault, seven hundred-odd years in the future, were to become part of the collection bequeathed by him to the museum, preserved by it, and eventually stored in the vault for him to find—then precisely where had they come from in the first place?

It worried him. Peter had learned in life, as his brother had in physics, that one never gets anything for nothing.

Moreover, this riddle was only one of his perplexities, and that not among the greatest. For another example, there was the obstinate opacity of the time-sphere whenever he attempted to examine the immediate future. However often he tried it, the result was always the same: a cloudy blank, all the way forward to the sudden unveiling of the marble gallery.

It was reasonable to expect the sphere to show nothing at times when he himself was going to be in the vault, but this accounted for only five or six hours out of every twenty-four. Again, presumably, it would show him no changes to be made by himself, since foreknowledge would make it possible for him to alter his actions. But he laboriously cleared one end of the vault, put up a screen to hide the rest and made a vow—which he kept—not to alter the clear space or move the screen for a week. Then he tried again—with the same result.

The only remaining explanation was that sometime during the next ten years something was going to happen which he would prevent if he could; and the clue to it was there, buried in that frustrating, unbroken blankness.

As a corollary, it was going to be something which he *could* prevent if only he knew what it was . . . or even when it was supposed to happen.

The event in question, in all probability, was his own death. Peter therefore hired nine men to guard him, three to a shift—because one man alone could not be trusted, two might conspire against him, whereas three, with the very minimum of effort, could be kept in a state of mutual suspicion. He also underwent a thorough medical examination, had new locks installed on every door and window, and took every other precaution ingenuity could suggest. When he had done all these things, the next ten years were as blank as before.

Peter had more than half expected it. He checked through his list of safeguards once more, found it good, and thereafter let the matter rest. He had done all he could; either he would survive the crisis or he would not. In either case, events were conserved; the time-sphere could give him no forewarning.

Another man might have found his pleasure blunted by guilt and fear; Peter's was whetted to a keener edge. If he had been a recluse before, now he was an eremite; he grudged every hour that was not given to his work. Mornings he spent in the vault, unpacking his acquisitions; afternoons and evenings, sorting, cataloguing, examining and—the word is not too strong—gloating. When three weeks had passed in this way, the shelves were bare as far as the power cable would allow him to reach in every direction, except for crates whose contents were undoubtedly too large to pass through the sphere. These, with heroic self-control, Peter had left untouched.

And still he had looted only a hundredth part of that incredible treasure house. With grappling hooks he could have extended his reach by perhaps three or four yards, but at the risk of damaging his prizes; and in any case this would have been no solution but only a postponement of the problem. There was nothing for it but to go through the sphere himself and unpack the crates while on the other "side" of it.

Peter thought about it in a fury of concentration for the rest of the day. So far as he was concerned, there was no question that the gain would be worth any calculated risk; the problem was how to measure the risk and if possible reduce it.

Item: He felt a definite uneasiness at the thought of venturing through that insubstantial bubble. Intuition was supported, if not by logic, at least by a sense of the dramatically appropriate. Now, if ever, would be the time for his crisis.

Item: Common sense did not concur. The uneasiness had two symbols. One was the white face of his brother Harold just before the water closed over it; the other was a phantasm born of those gigantic, splayed footprints in the dust of the gallery. In spite of himself, Peter had often found himself trying to imagine what the creatures that made them must look like, until his visualization was so clear that he could almost swear he had seen them.

Towering monsters they were, with crested ophidian heads and great unwinking eyes; and they moved in a strutting glide, nodding their heads, like fantastic barnyard fowl.

But, taking these premonitory images in turn: first, it was impossible that he should ever be seriously inconvenienced by Harold's death. There were no witnesses, he was sure; he had struck the blow with a stone; stones also were the weights that had dragged the body down, and the rope was an odd length Peter had picked up on the shore. Second, the three-toed Somethings might be as fearful as all the world's bogies put together; it made no difference, he could never meet them.

Nevertheless, the uneasiness persisted. Peter was not satisfied; he wanted a lifeline. When he found it, he wondered that he had not thought of it before.

He would set the time-sphere for a period just before one of the intervals of blankness. That would take care of accidents, sudden illnesses, and other unforeseeable contingencies. It would also insure him against one very real and not at all irrational dread: the fear that the mechanism which generated the time-sphere might fail while he was on the other side. For the conservation of events was not a condition created by the sphere but one which limited its operation. No matter what happened, it was impossible for him to occupy the same place-time as any future or past observer; therefore, when the monster entered that vault, Peter would not be there any more.

There was, of course, the scent bottle to remember. Every rule has its exception; but in this case, Peter thought, the example did not apply. A scent bottle could roll into a rat hole; a man could not.

He turned the rheostat carefully back to the last flicker of grayness; past that to the next, still more carefully. The interval between the two, he judged, was something under an hour: excellent.

His pulse seemed a trifle rapid, but his brain was clear

and cool. He thrust his head into the sphere and sniffed cautiously. The air was stale and had a faint, unpleasant odor, but it was breathable.

Using a crate as a stepping stool, he climbed to the top of the workbench. He arranged another crate close to the sphere to make a platform level with its equator. And seven and a half centuries in the future, a third crate stood on the floor directly under the sphere.

Peter stepped into the sphere, dropped, and landed easily, legs bending to take the shock. When he straightened, he was standing in what to all appearances was a large circular hole in the workbench; his chin was just above the top of the sphere.

He lowered himself, half squatting, until he had drawn his head through and stepped down from the crate.

He was in the future vault. The sphere was a brightly luminous thing that hung unsupported in the air behind him, its midpoint just higher than his head. The shadows it cast spread black and wedge-shaped in every direction, melting into obscurity.

Peter's heart was pounding miserably. He had an illusory stifling sensation, coupled with the idiotic notion that he ought to be wearing a diver's helmet. The silence was like the pause before a shout.

But down the aisles marched the crated treasures in their hundreds.

Peter set to work. It was difficult, exacting labor, opening the crates where they lay, removing the contents and nailing the crates up again, all without disturbing the positions of the crates themselves, but it was the price he had to pay for his lifeline. Each crate was in a sense a microcosm, like the vault itself—a capsule of unliquidated time. But the vault's term would end some fifty minutes from now, when crested heads nodded down these aisles; those of the crates' interiors, for all that Peter knew to the contrary, went on forever.

The first crate contained lacework porcelain; the second, shakudō sword hilts; the third, an exquisite fourth-century Greek ornament in *repoussé* bronze, the equal in every way of the Siris bronzes.

Peter found it almost physically difficult to set the thing down, but he did so; standing on his platform crate in the future with his head projecting above the sphere in the present—like (again the absurd thought!) a diver rising from the ocean—he laid it carefully beside the others on the workbench.

Then down again, into the fragile silence and the gloom. The next crates were too large, and those just beyond were doubtful. Peter followed his shadow down the aisle. He had almost twenty minutes left: enough for one more crate, chosen with care, and an ample margin.

Glancing to his right at the end of the row, he saw a door. It was a heavy door, rivet-studded, with a single iron step below it. There had been no door there in Peter's time; the whole plan of the building must have been altered. *Of course!* he realized suddenly. If it had not, if so much as a single tile or lintel had remained of the palace as he knew it, then the sphere could never have let him see or enter this particular here-and-now, this—what would Harold have called it?—this nexus in spacetime.

For if you saw any now-existing thing as it was going to appear in the future, you could alter it in the present—carve your initials in it, break it apart, chop it down—which was manifestly impossible, and therefore . . .

And therefore the first ten years were necessarily blank when he looked into the sphere, not because anything unpleasant was going to happen to him, but because in that

time the last traces of the old palace had not yet been erad-
icated.

There was no crisis.

Wait a moment, though! Harold had been able to look
into the near future.... But—of course—Harold had been
about to die.

In the dimness between himself and the door he saw a
rack of crates that looked promising. The way was uneven;
one of the untidy accumulations of refuse that seemed to
be characteristic of the Somethings lay in windrows across
the floor. Peter stepped forward carefully—but not carefully
enough.

Harold Castellare had had another accident—and again, if
you choose to look at it in that way, a lucky one. The blow
stunned him; the old rope slipped from the stones; flaccid,
he floated where a struggling man might have drowned. A
fishing boat nearly ran him down, and picked him up instead. He was suffering from a concussion, shock, exposure,
asphyxiation and was more than three quarters dead. But
he was still alive when he was delivered, an hour later, to
a hospital in Naples.

There were, of course, no identifying papers, labels or
monograms in his clothing—Peter had seen to that—and for
the first week after his rescue Harold was quite genuinely
unable to give any account of himself. During the second
week he was mending but uncommunicative, and at the end
of the third, finding that there was some difficulty about
gaining his release in spite of his physical recovery, he affected to regain his memory, gave a circumstantial but entirely fictitious identification and was discharged.

To understand this as well as all his subsequent actions,
it is only necessary to remember that Harold was a Castel-

lare. In Naples, not wishing to give Peter any unnecessary anxiety, he did not approach his bank for funds but cashed a check with an incurious acquaintance, and predated it by four weeks. With part of the money so acquired he paid his hospital bill and rewarded his rescuers. Another part went for new clothing and for four days' residence in an inconspicuous hotel, while he grew used to walking and dressing himself again. The rest, on his last day, he spent in the purchase of a discreetly small revolver and a box of cartridges.

He took the last boat to Ischia and arrived at his own front door a few minutes before eleven. It was a cool evening, and a most cheerful fire was burning in the central hall.

"Signor Peter is well, I suppose," said Harold, removing his coat.

"Yes, Signor Harold. He is very well, very busy with his collection."

"Where is he? I should like to speak to him."

"He is in the vaults, Signor Harold. But . . ."

"Yes?"

"Signor Peter sees no one when he is in the vaults. He has given strict orders that no one is to bother him, Signor Harold, when he is in the vaults."

"Oh, well," said Harold. "I daresay he'll see me."

It was a thing something like a bear trap, apparently, except that instead of two semicircular jaws it had four segments that snapped together in the middle, each with a shallow, sharp tooth. The pain was quite unendurable.

Each segment moved at the end of a thin arm, cunningly hinged so that the ghastly thing would close over whichever of the four triggers you stepped on. Each arm had a spring too powerful for Peter's muscles. The whole affair was connected by a chain to a staple solidly embedded in the concrete floor; it left Peter free to move some ten inches in any direction. Short of gnawing off his own leg, he thought sickly, there was very little he could do about it.

The riddle was, what could the thing possibly be doing here? There were rats in the vaults, no doubt, now as in his own time, but surely nothing larger. Was it conceivable that even the three-toed Somethings would set an engine like this to catch a rat?

Lost inventions, Peter thought irrelevantly, had a way of being rediscovered. Even if he suppressed the time-sphere during his lifetime and it did not happen to survive him, still there might be other time-fishers in the remote future— not here, perhaps, but in other treasure houses of the world. And that might account for the existence of this metal-jawed horror. Indeed, it might account for the vault itself—a better man-trap—except that it was all nonsense; the trap could only be full until the trapper came to look at it. Events, and the lives of prudent time-travelers, were conserved.

And he had been in the vault for almost forty minutes. Twenty minutes to go, twenty-five, thirty at the most, then the Somethings would enter and their entrance would free him. He had his lifeline; the knowledge was the only thing that made it possible to live with the pain that was the center of his universe just now. It was like going to the dentist, in the bad old days before procaine; it was very bad, sometimes, but you knew that it would end.

He cocked his head toward the door, holding his breath. A distant thud, another, then a curiously unpleasant squeaking, then silence.

But he had heard them. He knew they were there. It couldn't be much longer now.

* * *

Three men, two stocky, one lean, were playing cards in the passageway in front of the closed door that led to the vault staircase. They got up slowly.

"Who is he?" demanded the shortest one.

Tomaso clattered at him in furious Sicilian; the man's face darkened, but he looked at Harold with respect.

"I am now," stated Harold, "going down to see my brother."

"No, Signor," said the shortest one positively.

"You are impertinent," Harold told him.

"Yes, Signor."

Harold frowned. "You will not let me pass?"

"No, Signor."

"Then go and tell my brother I am here."

The shortest one said apologetically but firmly that there were strict orders against this also; it would have astonished Harold very much if he had said anything else.

"Well, at least I suppose you can tell me how long it will be before he comes out?"

"Not long, Signor. One hour, no more."

"Oh, very well, then," said Harold pettishly, turning half away. He paused. "One thing more," he said, taking the gun out of his pocket as he turned, "put your hands up and stand against the wall there, will you?"

The first two complied slowly. The third, the lean one, fired through his coat pocket, just like the gangsters in the American movies.

It was not a sharp sensation at all, Harold was surprised to find; it was more as if someone had hit him in the side with a cricket bat. The racket seemed to bounce interminably from the walls. He felt the gun jolt in his hand as he fired back, but couldn't tell if he had hit anybody. Everything seemed to be happening very slowly, and yet it was astonishingly hard to keep his balance. As he swung around he saw the two stocky ones with their hands half inside their jackets, and the lean one with his mouth open, and Tomaso with bulging eyes. Then the wall came at him and he began to swim along it, paying particular attention to the problem of not dropping one's gun.

As he weathered the first turn in the passageway the roar broke out afresh. A fountain of plaster stung his eyes; then he was running clumsily, and there was a bedlam of shouting behind him.

Without thinking about it he seemed to have selected the laboratory as his destination; it was an instinctive choice, without much to recommend it logically. In any case, he realized halfway across the central hall, he was not going to get there.

He turned and squinted at the passageway entrance; saw a blur move and fired at it. It disappeared. He turned again awkwardly, and had taken two steps nearer an armchair which offered the nearest shelter, when something clubbed him between the shoulderblades. One step more, knees buckling, and the wall struck him a second, softer blow. He toppled, clutching at the tapestry that hung near the fireplace.

When the three guards, whose names were Enrico, Alberto and Luca, emerged cautiously from the passage and approached Harold's body, it was already flaming like a Viking's in its impromptu shroud; the dim horses and men and falcons of the tapestry were writhing and crisping into brilliance. A moment later an uncertain ring of fire wavered toward them across the carpet.

Although the servants came with fire extinguishers and with buckets of water from the kitchen, and although the fire department was called, it was all quite useless. In five minutes the whole room was ablaze; in ten, as windows burst and walls buckled, the fire engulfed the second story. In twenty a mass of flaming timbers dropped into the vault through the hole Peter had made in the floor of the laboratory, utterly destroying the time-sphere apparatus and reaching shortly thereafter, as the authorities concerned were later to agree, an intensity of heat entirely sufficient to consume a human body without leaving any identifiable trace. For that reason alone, there was no trace of Peter's body to be found.

The sounds had just begun again when Peter saw the light from the time-sphere turn ruddy and then wink out like a snuffed candle.

In the darkness, he heard the door open.

ON THE NATURE
OF TIME

BILL PRONZINI

Here, what appears to be a time loop is not: time travel—contrary to how it might have been originally envisioned—is not necessarily broadening. If this is Tuesday, it must Carthage. If this is Thursday, can Constantinople be far behind?

Bill Pronzini, an acclaimed mystery writer whose thirty-five year career and more than 25 series novels of his Nameless detective (who has lasted and evolved as few series characters: he is comparable to Simenon's Maigret) have brought him awards and increasing audience. He has published forty or fifty science fiction stories alone or in collaboration (most of the collaborations with the editor), and one collaborative (again with the editor) science-fiction novel, *Prose Bowl*. He is a native and continuing Californian.

When I was six I dreamed that my father was murdered. That I sleepwalked into his workroom in the middle of the night and found him on the floor, bleeding from a gunshot wound in the temple. That at the edge of my vision I had a fleeting glimpse of an intruder but could not identify him. I screamed in my sleep and awoke in my bed, my father bending over me, his face fearful in the dull glow from the hallway.

"You scream all the time in your sleep, Bobby," he said. "You've got to stop it; I can't take it anymore, I can't concentrate on my work." Then he pulled the covers over my head and went away and left me lying there, trembling.

When I was sixteen I wished that the dream of my father's murder had not been a dream at all. And when I was thirty-six I stood over his coffin in the rectory of St. Joseph's, weeping bitter tears because it had taken him three decades more of my life to die.

Every one of the moments of that time had been extracted from me, extracted in pain and guilt, and now he

was dead and there was no way to reach him, to make rep-
aration. He died peacefully, it was said; of emphysema, in
deep coma in a hospital room. I was summoned by long
distance telephone—there were no other relatives, no
friends—and I buried him properly, the bitter tears falling
along with clumps of sod on that $700 silk-lined coffin.

It is true that early on my father exerted a great deal of
influence over me, that in some ways I was his surrogate.
But I did not want it that way. Please understand: I did not
want it that way.

My father was a backyard physicist, a tinkerer, an in-
ventor, an engineering school dropout who was a minor
civil servant in the United States Patent Office most of his
adult life. He had, as all backyard tinkering dropouts do, big
plans, big ideas (as I did once, before he bled them out of
me). He worked on perpetual motion, on a universal solvent,
on a time machine. He read science fiction magazines, he
earned a correspondence Doctor of Divine Metaphysics, he
wrote letters to the editors of scientific journals (under a
pseudonym, so as not to jeopardize his GS-5 rating), railing
against the "hypocrisy of organized science." The true big
ideas were happening in the cellars and basements of private citizens like himself, he said, but the men with degrees
and government contracts were in conspiracy to suppress
them. No one listened to him, of course; no one ever listens
to Doctors of Divine Metaphysics. They did not even publish
his letters.

My mother died early (and in my dreams again, often)
and there were only my father and me in the large house
his parents had willed him, plus a faceless succession of
housekeepers. In the night my father would slam around the
basement and speak loudly of his plans to no one at all, in
counterpoint to the sounds of metal on metal.

When I was ten . . . no, it must have been eight . . . as

soon as I had mastered the bare tools of literacy, he enlisted me to carry on his life's work. "The two of us, Bobby," he said. "You'll be my disciple; we'll be the father and son, the Dumas *pere et fils* of scientific research." And he showed me blueprints for the universal solvent; explained how the proper time machine would short-circuit temporal paradox; put me to work hammering and cutting and shaping with the tools in his workshop.

I dreamed of him dead, murdered, but he lived on and taught me all that he knew. All that he knew was nothing. I understood very early on (children understand everything very early on; growth is a matter of unlearning), but it is always best to humor tinkerers and divine metaphysicians. A father has terrific power, after all, the son only the cachet of vulnerability. In the nights, while I worked with him, he spoke to me of joints, creaks in time, balls of force that would circumvent the second law of thermodynamics. My sleep, once wrecked by dreams of his murder or my mother's death, perished in these years. We had so many plans. We worked together. We forged the fire.

We did, of course, nothing at all.

In time my father's department at the patent office was subsumed under a larger one and both his duties and his hours changed. Our experiments decreased; my life broadened slightly. I was a brilliant student, a National Merit Scholar; I obtained a scholarship to the Massachusetts Institute of Technology which included room and board, and I enrolled there at the age of seventeen. After which, not once did I set foot in my father's house nor he in any place which I occupied.

I was a brilliant student in college as well, if somewhat antisocial (but then, so were a number of my classmates). I learned to play the bassoon. I had three dates with two girls. I did original research on the temporal question. I graduated with honors, took a graduate degree, assumed more honors, took a doctorate, remained in academia. My career flattened out, it may be said, at the age of twenty-eight; I went to a small midwestern university and became chairman of its three-member Department of Physics. I never married: I could not get past the idea of my dead mother being mounted by my unmurdered father.

My researches into temporal paradox continued. And these researches, to my own amazement, did not fail; three months after my father's death from emphysema, I invented a time machine.

Small experiments with watches and rodents proved that the machine worked. Detector sweeps through hours, weeks, months, years made recoveries; it had effective compass; it could be controlled for time and place. There remained only the supreme test of sending a human being, sending myself (the only true experiment is the one of risk) back into the mists of time.

The question of where I would go and what I would do was no question at all: I would return to a night before I was conceived, a night in the year 1943, and I would murder my father as I had seen him murdered in my dream.

As a student of temporal paradox, I postulated that this would result in my obliteration—a not inelegant way to commit suicide. One must understand the depths of my unhappiness, my self-destructiveness. It is not easy being a failed prodigy, not easy to come from a childhood populated by an unmurdered father and a dead mother.

Thus I made my calculations, set the controls, and found myself, the instant after I had activated the machine, in my father's workshop on the night of February 6, 1943. In my hand was a .38 caliber revolver. My father, hunched over his blueprints, looked up, his mad eyes glinting with strange lights. Quite calmly, before he could speak, I shot him in the temple and watched him fall, all clutter and spectacles, over his workbench.

At that very instant something exceptional happened: the room shimmered and faded and there was a snapping sensation, as of a rubber band releasing. In the time it took me to blink, the workshop stopped shimmering, stopped fading—and was different than it had been moments ago. Subtly different, as if it were not the same workshop at all. Or the same workshop at a different point in time.

Then, to my further astonishment, my six-year-old self burst into the room. I stared at him/me, but he/I seemed only vaguely aware of my presence. I was a fat unlovable child with many facial tics, complicated now by fear and grief. He/I pointed at my father's body. "He's dead!" I/he screamed. After which my six-year-old self rushed out of the workshop, leaving me there alone.

But that was not all. When I looked back at the workbench, my father's corpse had disappeared. My time machine, too.

It was then that I understood the laws of temporality for the first time in all their futility and decency. There is no temporal paradox. What could not happen simply cannot and must not happen. As soon as I had shot my father, Time had snapped me forward a full seven years to the year 1950, the the sixth year of my life, to the night I had dreamed I saw him murdered. And to further seal the apparent rent in its fabric, it had unmurdered my father and made *me* assume his place; *I* had ceased to exist at the age of thirty-six so that I could become—truly—my father's surrogate.

Consider my horror as I surmised all of this. Consider it as I was compelled in the next second to rush into the room where my six-year-old self lay weeping under the blankets and say to him, "You scream all the time in your sleep, Bobby. You've got to stop it; I can't take it anymore, I can't concentrate on my work." Consider it as I saw how Time would be served, what I would do to myself in order that I, as my father, could live three more decades and die of emphysema; in order that my six-year-old self could grow up as I had grown up, and invent a time machine, and come back to the year 1943 to murder my father, and be snapped forward into the year 1950 . . . over and over again, the perpetual reenactment.

The message of my story, then, is as simple as it is terrible: you must make no researches into temporal paradox, invent no time machine, plan no temporal crimes. For if you do you will suffer the same fate as I.

To become oneself; to destroy oneself.

To make all deaths one's own.

A LITTLE SOMETHING
FOR US TEMPUNAUTS

PHILIP K. DICK

Here again is the time loop (see Harness's "Time Trap"), the perpetual recurrence; the trigger for this one as could be expected in a work of Phillip K. Dick is not malice but human error. "I felt such sadness when I finished this story," (for the 1974 original anthology *Final Stage*) Dick wrote, "there is just an awful loss coming from this." Dick, best known for the exquisite paranoia and reality flux of his plots, was less noted (an injustice) for the compassion with which he portrayed his usually lonely and struggling characters, struggling to do better, almost always doing worse.

Dick (1928–1982) has had a brilliant and lucrative posthumous Hollywood career which would have accorded with his worldview; dead, he has become a star. *Blade Runner, Total Recall, Imposter* were based on his work; a Steven Spielberg film based on his 1956 *Fantastic Universe* novelette, *Minority Report*, was released in 2002. Dick, a native Californian, rarely left the State, let alone the country, and never saw New York City.

Wearily, Addison Doug plodded up the long path of synthetic redwood rounds, step by step, his head down a little, moving as if he were in actual physical pain. The girl watched him, wanting to help him, hurt within her to see how worn and unhappy he was, but at the same time she rejoiced that he was there at all. On and on, toward her, without glancing up, going by feel . . . like he's done this many times, she thought suddenly. Knows the way too well. Why?

"Addi," she called, and ran toward him. "They said on the TV you were dead. All of you were killed!"

He paused, wiping back his dark hair which was no longer long; just before launch they had cropped it. But he had evidently forgotten. "You believe everything you see on TV?" he said, and came on again, haltingly, but smiling now. And reaching up for her.

God, it felt good to hold him, and to have him clutch at her again, with more strength than she had expected. "I was going to find somebody else," she gasped. "To replace you."

"I'll knock your head off if you do," he said. "Anyhow, that isn't possible; nobody could replace me."

"But what about the implosion?" she said. "On reentry; they said—"

"I forget," Addison said, in the tone he used when he meant, I'm not going to discuss it. The tone had always angered her before, but not now. This time she sensed how awful the memory was. "I'm going to stay at your place a couple days," he said, as together they moved up the path toward the open front door of the tilted A-frame house. "If that's okay. And Benz and Crayne will be joining me, later on; maybe even as soon as tonight. We've got a lot to talk over and figure out."

"Then all three of you survived." She gazed up into his careworn face. "Everything they said on TV . . ." She understood, then. Or believed she did. "It was a cover story. For—political purposes, to fool the Russians. Right? I mean, the Soviet Union'll think the launch was a failure because on re-entry—"

"No," he said. "A chrononaut will be joining us, most likely. To help figure out what happened. General Toad said one of them is already on his way here; they got clearance already. Because of the gravity of the situation."

"Jesus," the girl said, stricken. "Then who's the cover story for?"

"Let's have something to drink," Addison said. "And then I'll outline it all for you."

"Only thing I've got at the moment is California brandy."

Addison Doug said, "I'd drink anything right now, the way I feel." He dropped to the couch, leaned back, and sighed a ragged, distressed sigh, as the girl hurriedly began fixing both of them a drink.

The FM radio in the car yammered, "... grieves at the stricken turn of events precipitating out of an unheralded ..."

"Official nonsense babble," Crayne said, shutting off the radio. He and Benz were having trouble finding the house, having only been there once before. It struck Crayne that this was somewhat informal a way of convening a conference of this importance, meeting at Addison's chick's pad out here in the boondocks of Ojai. On the other hand, they wouldn't be pestered by the curious. And they probably didn't have much time. But that was hard to say; about that no one knew for sure.

The hills on both sides of the road had once been forests, Crayne observed. Now housing tracts and their melted, irregular, plastic roads marred every rise in sight. "I'll bet this was nice once," he said to Benz, who was driving.

"The Los Padres National Forest is near here," Benz said. "I got lost in there when I was eight. For hours I was sure a rattler would get me. Every stick was a snake."

"The rattler's got you now," Crayne said.

"All of us," Benz said.

"You know," Crayne said, "it's a hell of an experience to be dead."

"Speak for yourself."

"But technically—"

"If you listen to the radio and TV." Benz turned toward him, his big gnome face bleak with admonishing sternness. "We're no more dead than anyone else on the planet. The difference for us is that our death date is in the past, whereas everyone else's is set somewhere at an uncertain time in the future. Actually, some people have it pretty damn well set, like people in cancer wards; they're as certain as we are. More so. For example, how long can we stay here before we go back? We have a margin, a latitude that a terminal cancer victim doesn't have."

Crayne said caustically, "The next thing you'll be telling us to cheer us up is that we're in no pain."

"Addi is. I watched him lurch off earlier today. He's got it psychosomatically—made it into a physical complaint. Like God's kneeling on his neck; you know, carrying a much-too-great burden that's unfair, only he won't complain out loud . . . just points now and then at the nail hole in his hand." He grinned.

"Addi has got more to live for than we do."

"Every man has more to live for than any other man. I don't have a cute chick to sleep with, but I'd like to see the semi's rolling along the Riverside Freeway at sunset a few more times. It's not what you have to live for; it's that you want to live to see it, to be there—that's what is so damn sad."

They rode on in silence.

In the quiet living room of the girl's house the three tempunauts sat around smoking, taking it easy; Addison Doug thought to himself that the girl looked unusually foxy and desirable in her stretched-tight white sweater and microskirt and he wished, wistfully, that she looked a little less interesting. He could not really afford to get embroiled in such stuff, at this point. He was too tired. "Does she know," Benz said, indicating the girl, "what this is all about? I mean, can we talk openly? It won't wipe her out?"

"I haven't explained it to her yet," Addison said.

"You goddam well better," Crayne said.

"What is it?" the girl said, stricken, sitting upright with one hand directly between her breasts. As if clutching at a religious artifact that isn't there, Addison thought.

"We got snuffed on re-entry," Benz said. He was, really, the cruelest of the three. Or at least the most blunt. "You see, Miss . . ."

"Hawkins," the girl whispered.

"Glad to meet you, Miss Hawkins." Benz surveyed her in his cold, lazy fashion. "You have a first name?"

"Merry Lou."

"Okay, Merry Lou," Benz said. To the other two men he observed, "Sounds like the name a waitress has stitched on her blouse. Merry Lou's my name and I'll be serving you dinner and breakfast and lunch and dinner and breakfast for the next few days or however long it is before you all give up and go back to your own time; that'll be fifty-three dollars and eight cents, please, not including tip. And I hope y'all never come back, y'hear?" His voice had begun to shake; his cigarette, too. "Sorry, Miss Hawkins," he said, then. "We're all screwed up by the implosion at re-entry time. As soon as we got here in ETA we learned about it. We've known longer than anyone else; we knew as soon as we hit Emergence Time."

"But there's nothing we could do," Crayne said.

"There's nothing anyone can do," Addison said to her, and put his arm around her. It felt like a déjà vu thing but then it hit him. We're in a closed time loop, he thought, we keep going through this again and again, trying to solve the re-entry problem, each time imagining it's the first time, the only time . . . and never succeeding. Which attempt is this? Maybe the millionth; we have sat here a million times, raking the same facts over and over again and getting nowhere. He felt bone-weary, thinking that. And he felt a sort of vast philosophical hate toward all other men, who did not have this enigma to deal with. We all go to one place, he thought, as the Bible says. But . . . for the three of us, we have been there already. Are lying there now. So it's wrong to ask us to stand around on the surface of Earth afterward and argue and worry about it and try to figure out what malfunctioned. That should be, rightly, for our heirs to do. We've had enough already.

He did not say this aloud, though—for their sake.

"Maybe you bumped into something," the girl said.

Glancing at the others, Benz said sardonically, "Maybe we 'bumped into something.'"

"The TV commentators keep saying that," Merry Lou said, "about the hazard in re-entry of being out of phase spatially and colliding right down to the molecular level with tangent objects, any one of which—" She gestured. "You know. 'No two objects can occupy the same space at the same time.' So everything blew up, for that reason." She glanced around questioningly.

"That is the major risk factor," Crayne acknowledged. "At least theoretically, as Doctor Fein at Planning calculated when they got into the hazard question. But we had a variety of safety locking devices provided that functioned automatically. Re-entry couldn't occur unless these assists had stabilized us spatially so we would not overlap. Of course, all those devices, in sequence, might have failed. One after the other. I was watching my feedback 'metric scopes on launch, and they agreed, every one of them, that we were phased properly at that time. And I heard no warning tones. Saw none, neither." He grimaced. "At least it didn't happen then."

Suddenly Benz said, "Do you realize that our next-of-kin are now rich? All our Federal and commercial life insurance payoff. Our 'next of kin'—God forbid, that's us, I guess. We can apply for tens of thousands of dollars, cash on the line. Walk into our brokers' offices and say, 'I'm dead; lay the heavy bread on me.'"

Addison Doug was thinking, the public memorial services. That they have planned, after the autopsies. That long line of black-draped Cads going down Pennsylvania Avenue, with all the government dignitaries and double-domed scientist types—*and we'll be there.* Not once but twice. Once in the oak hand-rubbed brass-fitted flag-draped caskets, but also . . . maybe riding in open limos, waving at the crowds of mourners.

"The ceremonies," he said aloud.

The others stared at him, angrily, not comprehending. And then, one by one, they understood; he saw it on their faces.

"No," Benz grated. "That's—impossible."

Crayne shook his head emphatically. "They'll order us to be there, and we will be. Obeying orders."

"Will we have to *smile*?" Addison said. "To fucking *smile*?"

"No," General Toad said slowly, his great wattled head shivering about on his broomstick neck, the color of his skin dirty and mottled, as if the mass of decorations on his stiffboard collar had started part of him decaying away. "You are not to smile, but on the contrary are to adopt a properly grief-stricken manner. In keeping with the national mood of sorrow at this time."

"That'll be hard to do," Crayne said.

The Russian chrononaut showed no response; his thin beaked face, narrow within his translating earphones, remained strained with concern.

"The nation," General Toad said, "will become aware of your presence among us once more for this brief interval; cameras of all major TV networks will pan up on you without warning, and at the same time, the various commentators have been instructed to tell their audiences something like the following." He got out a piece of typed material, put on his glasses, cleared his throat and said, " 'We seem to be focusing on three figures riding together. Can't quite make them out. Can you?' " General Toad lowered the paper. "At this point they'll interrogate their colleagues extempore. Finally they'll exclaim, 'Why Roger,' or Walter or Ned, as the case may be, according to the individual network—"

"Or Bill," Crayne said. "In case it's the Bufonidae network, down there in the swamp."

General Toad ignored him. "They will severally exclaim, 'Why Roger, I believe we're seeing the three tempunauts themselves! Does this indeed mean that somehow the difficulty—?' And then the colleague commentator says in his somewhat more somber voice, 'What we're seeing at this time I think, David,' or Henry or Pete or Ralph, whichever it is, 'consists of mankind's first verified glimpse of what the technical people refer to as Emergence Time Activity or ETA. Contrary to what might seem to be the case at first sight, these are *not*—repeat not—our three valiant tempunauts as such, as we would ordinarily experience them, but more likely picked up by our cameras as the three of them are temporarily suspended in their voyage to the future, which we initially had reason to hope would take place in a time continuum roughly a hundred years from now . . . but it would seem that they somehow undershot and are here now, at this moment, which of course is, as we know, our present.' "

Addison Doug closed his eyes and thought, Crayne will ask him if he can be panned up on by the TV cameras holding a balloon and eating cotton candy. I think we're all going nuts from this, all of us. And then he wondered, How many times have we gone through this idiotic exchange?

I can't prove it, he thought wearily. But I know it's true. We've sat here, done this miniscule scrabbling, listened to and said all this crap, many times. He shuddered. Each rinky dink word . . .

"What's the matter?" Benz said acutely.

The Soviet chrononaut spoke up for the first time.

"What is the maximum interval of ETA possible to your three-man team? And how large a percent has been exhausted by now?"

After a pause Crayne said, "They briefed us on that before we came in here today. We've consumed approximately one-half of our maximum total ETA interval."

"However," General Toad rumbled, "we have scheduled the Day of National Mourning to fall within the expected period remaining to them of ETA time. This required us to speed up the autopsy and other forensic findings, but in view of public sentiment, it was felt . . ."

The autopsy, Addison Doug thought, and again he shuddered; this time he could not keep his thoughts within himself and he said, "Why don't we adjourn this nonsense meeting and drop down to Pathology and view a few tissue sections enlarged and in color, and maybe we'll brainstorm a couple of vital concepts that'll aid medical science in its quest for explanations? Explanations—that's what we need. Explanations for problems that don't exist yet; we can develop the problems later." He paused. "Who agrees?"

"I'm not looking at my spleen up there on the screen," Benz said. "I'll ride in the parade but I won't participate in my own autopsy."

"You could distribute microscopic purple-stained slices of your own gut to the mourners along the way," Crayne said. "They could provide each of us with a doggy bag; right, General? We can strew tissue sections like confetti. I still think we should smile."

"I have researched all the memoranda about smiling," General Toad said, riffling the pages stacked before him, "and the consensus at policy is that smiling is not in accord with national sentiment. So that issue must be ruled closed. As far as your participating in the autopsical procedures which are now in progress—"

"We're missing out as we sit here," Crayne said to Addison Doug. "I always miss out."

Ignoring him, Addison addressed the Soviet chrononaut. "Officer N. Gauki," he said into his microphone, dangling on his chest, "what in your mind is the greatest terror facing a time traveler? That there will be an implosion due to coincidence on re-entry, such as has occurred in our launch? Or did other traumatic obsessions bother you and your comrade during your own brief but highly successful time flight?"

N. Gauki after a pause answered, "R. Plenya and I exchanged views at several informal times. I believe I can speak for us both when I respond to your question by emphasizing our perpetual fear that we had inadvertently entered a closed time loop and would never break out."

"You'd repeat it forever?" Addison Doug asked.

"Yes, Mr. A. Doug," the chrononaut said, nodding somberly.

A fear that he had never experienced before overcame Addison Doug. He turned helplessly to Benz and muttered, "Shit." They gazed at each other.

"I really don't believe this is what happened," Benz said to him in a low voice, putting his hand on Doug's shoulder; he gripped hard, the grip of friendship. "We just imploded on re-entry, that's all. Take it easy."

"Could we adjourn soon?" Addison Doug said in a hoarse, strangling voice, half-rising from his chair. He felt the room and the people in it rushing in at him, suffocating him. Claustrophobia, he realized. Like when I was in grade school, when they flashed a surprise test on our teaching machines, and I saw I couldn't pass it. "Please," he said simply, standing. They were all looking at him, with different expressions. The Russian's face was especially sympathetic, and deeply lined with care. Addison wished—"I want to go home," he said to them all, and felt stupid.

He was drunk. It was late at night, at a bar on Hollywood Boulevard; fortunately Merry Lou was with him, and he was having a good time. Everyone was telling him so, anyhow. He clung to Merry Lou and said, "The great unity in life, the supreme unity and meaning, is man and woman. Their absolute unity; right?"

"I know," Merry Lou said. "We studied that in class." Tonight, at his request, Merry Lou was a small blonde girl, wearing purple bellbottoms and high heels and an open midriff blouse. Earlier she had had a lapis lazuli in her navel, but during dinner at Ting Ho's it had popped out and been lost. The owner of the restaurant had promised to keep on searching for it, but Merry Lou had been gloomy ever since. It was, she said, symbolic. But of what she did not say. Or anyhow he could not remember; maybe that was it. She had told him what it meant, and he had forgotten.

An elegant young black at a nearby table, with an Afro and striped vest and overstuffed red tie, had been staring at Addison for some time. He obviously wanted to come over to their table but was afraid to; meanwhile, he kept on staring.

"Did you ever get the sensation," Addison said to Merry Lou, "that you knew exactly what was about to happen? What someone was going to say? Word for word? Down to the slightest detail? As if you had already lived through it once before?"

"Everybody gets into that space," Merry Lou said. She sipped a Bloody Mary.

The black rose and walked toward them. He stood by Addison. "I'm sorry to bother you, sir."

Addison said to Merry Lou, "He's going to say, 'Don't I know you from somewhere? Didn't I see you on TV?' "

"That was precisely what I intended to say," the black said.

Addison said, "You undoubtedly saw my picture on page forty-six of the current issue of *Time*, the section on new medical discoveries. I'm the G.P. from a small town in Iowa catapulted to fame by my invention of a widespread, easily available cure for eternal life. Several of the big pharmaceutical houses are already bidding on my vaccine."

"That might have been where I saw your picture," the black said, but he did not appear convinced. Nor did he appear drunk; he eyed Addison Doug intensely. "May I seat myself with you and the lady?"

"Sure," Addison Doug said. He now saw, in the man's hand, the ID of the U.S. security agency that had ridden herd on the project from the start.

"Mr. Doug," the security agent said as he seated himself beside Addison, "you really shouldn't be here shooting off your mouth like this. If I recognized you some other dude might and freak out. It's all classified until the Day of Mourning. Technically, you're in violation of a Federal Statute by being here; did you realize that? I should haul you in. But this is a difficult situation; we don't want to do something uncool and make a scene. Where are your two colleagues?"

"At my place," Merry Lou said. She had obviously not seen the ID. "Listen," she said sharply to the agent, "why don't you get lost? My husband here has been through a grueling ordeal, and this is his only chance to unwind."

Addison looked at the man. "I knew what you were going to say before you came over here." Word for word, he thought. I am right, and Benz is wrong and this will keep happening, this replay.

"Maybe," the security agent said, "I can induce you to go back to Miss Hawkins' place voluntarily. Some info arrived—" he tapped the tiny earphone in his right ear—"just a few minutes ago, to all of us, to deliver to you, marked urgent, if we located you. At the launch site ruins . . . they've been combing through the rubble, you know?"

"I know," Addison said.

"They think they have their first clue. Something was brought back by one of you. From ETA, over and above what you took, in violation of all your pre-launch training."

"Let me ask you this," Addison Doug said, "Suppose somebody does see me? Suppose somebody does recognize me? So what?"

"The public believes that even though re-entry failed, the flight into time, the first American time-travel launch, was successful. Three U.S. tempunauts were thrust a hundred years into the future—roughly twice as far as the Soviet launch of last year. That you only went a *week* will be less of a shock if it's believed that you three chose deliberately to remanifest at this continuum because you wished to attend, in fact felt compelled to attend—"

"We wanted to be in the parade," Addison interrupted. "Twice."

"You were drawn to the dramatic and somber spectacle of your own funeral procession, and will be glimpsed there by the alert camera crews of all major networks. Mr. Doug, really, an awful lot of high level planning and expense have gone into this to help correct a dreadful situation; trust us, believe me. It'll be easier on the public, and that's vital, if there's ever to be another U.S. time shot. And that is, after all, what we all want."

Addison Doug stared at him. "We want what?"

Uneasily, the security agent said, "To take further trips into time. As you have done. Unfortunately, you yourself cannot ever do so again, because of the tragic implosion and death of the three of you. But other tempunauts—"

"We want what? Is that what we want?" Addison's voice rose; people at nearby tables were watching, now. Nervously.

"Certainly," the agent said. "And keep your voice down."

"I don't want that," Addison said. "I want to stop. To stop forever. To just lie in the ground, in the dust, with everyone else. To see no more summers—the *same* summer."

"Seen one you've seen them all," Merry Lou said hysterically. "I think he's right, Addi; we should get out of here. You've had too many drinks, and it's late, and this news about the—"

Addison broke in, "What was brought back? How much extra mass?"

The security agent said, "Preliminary analysis shows that machinery weighing about one hundred pounds was lugged back into the time-field of the module and picked up along with you. This much mass—" The agent gestured. "That blew up the pad right on the spot. It couldn't begin to compensate for that much more than had occupied its open area at launch time."

"Wow!" Merry Lou said, eyes wide. "Maybe somebody sold one of you a quadraphonic phono for a dollar ninety-eight including fifteen-inch air-suspension speakers and a lifetime supply of Neil Diamond records." She tried to laugh, but failed; her eyes dimmed over. "Addi," she whispered, "I'm sorry. But it's sort of—weird. I mean, it's absurd; you all were briefed, weren't you, about your return weight? You weren't even to add so much as a piece of paper to what you took. I even saw Doctor Fein demonstrating the reasons on TV. And one of you hoisted a hundred pounds of machinery into the field? You must have been trying to self-destruct, to do that!" Tears slid from her eyes; one tear rolled out onto her nose and hung there. He reached reflexively to wipe it away, as if helping a little girl rather than a grown one.

"I'll fly you to the analysis site," the security agent said, standing up. He and Addison helped Merry Lou to her feet; she trembled as she stood a moment, finishing her Bloody Mary. Addison felt acute sorrow for her, but then, almost at once, it passed. He wondered why. One can weary even of that, he conjectured. Of caring for someone. If it goes on too long—on and on. Forever. And, at last, even after that, into something no one before, not God Himself, maybe, had ever had to suffer and in the end, for all His great heart, succumb to.

As they walked through the crowded bar toward the street, Addison Doug said to the security agent, "Which one of us—"

"They know which one," the agent said as he held the door to the street open for Merry Lou. The agent stood, now, behind Addison, signalling for a gray Federal car to land at the red parking area. Two other security agents, in uniform, hurried toward them.

"Was it me?" Addison Doug asked.

"You better believe it," the security agent said.

The funeral procession moved with aching solemnity down Pennsylvania Avenue, three flag-draped caskets and dozens of black limousines passing between rows of heavily coated, shivering mourners. A low haze hung over the day, gray outlines of buildings faded into the rain-drenched murk of the Washington March day.

Scrutinizing the lead Cadillac through prismatic binoculars, TV's top news and public events commentator Henry Cassidy droned on at his vast unseen audience, "... sad recollections of that earlier train among the wheatfields carrying the coffin of Abraham Lincoln back to burial and the nation's capital. And what a sad day this is, and what appropriate weather, with its dour overcast and sprinkles!" In his monitor he saw the Zoomar lens pan up on the fourth Cadillac, as it followed those with the caskets of the dead tempunauts.

His engineer tapped him on the arm.

"We appear to be focussing on three unfamiliar figures so far not identified, riding together," Henry Cassidy said into his neck mike, nodding agreement. "So far I'm unable to quite make them out. Are your location and vision any better from where you're placed, Everett?" he inquired of his colleague and pressed the button that notified Everett Branton to replace him on the air.

"Why Henry," Branton said in a voice of growing excitement, "I believe we're actually eyewitness to the three American tempunauts as they remanifest themselves on their historic journey into the future!"

"Does this signify," Cassidy said, "that somehow they have managed to solve and overcome the—"

"Afraid not, Henry," Branton said in his slow, regretful voice. "What we're eyewitnessing to our complete surprise consists of the Western world's first verified glimpse of what the technical people refer to as Emergence Time Activity."

"Ah yes, ETA," Cassidy said brightly, reading it off the official script the Federal authorities had handed him before air time.

"Right, Henry. Contrary to what *might* seem to be the case at first sight, these are not—repeat *not*—our three brave tempunauts as such, as we would ordinarily experience them—"

"I grasp it now, Everett," Cassidy broke in excitedly, since his authorized script read CASS BREAKS IN EXCITEDLY. "Our three tempunauts have momentarily suspended in their historic voyage to the future, which we believe will span across to a time-continuum roughly a century from now ... It would seem that the overwhelming grief and drama of this unanticipated day of mourning has caused them to ..."

"Sorry to interrupt, Henry," Everett Branton said, "but I think, since the procession has momentarily halted on its slow march forward, that we might be able to ..."

"No!" Cassidy said, as a note was handed him in a swift scribble, reading: *Do not interview 'nauts. Urgent. Dis. previous inst.* "I don't think we're going to be able to ..." he continued, "... to speak briefly with tempunauts Benz, Crayne, and Doug, as you had hoped, Everett. As we had all briefly hoped to." He wildly waved the boom-mike back; it had already begun to swing out expectantly toward the stopped Cadillac. Cassidy shook his head violently at the mike technician and his engineer.

Perceiving the boom-mike swinging at them, Addison Doug stood up in the back of the open Cadillac. Cassidy groaned. He wants to speak, he realized. Didn't they reinstruct *him*? Why am I the only one they get across to? Other boom-mikes representing other networks plus radio station interviewers on foot now were rushing out to thrust up their microphones into the faces of the three tempunauts, especially Addison Doug's. Doug was already beginning to speak, in response to a question shouted up to him by a reporter. With his boom-mike off, Cassidy couldn't hear the question, nor Doug's answer. With reluctance, he signalled for his own boom-mike to trigger on.

"... before," Doug was saying loudly.

"In what manner, 'All this has happened before'?" the radio reporter, standing close to the car, was saying.

"I mean," U.S. tempunaut Addison Doug declared, his face red and strained, "that I have stood here in this spot and said again and again, and all of you have viewed this parade and our deaths at re-entry endless times, a closed cycle of trapped time which must be broken."

"Are you seeking," another reporter jabbered up at Addison Doug, "for a solution to the re-entry implosion disaster which can be applied in retrospect so that when you do return to the past you will be able to correct the malfunction and avoid the tragedy which cost—or for you three, will cost—your lives?"

Tempunaut Benz said, "We are doing that, yes."

"Trying to ascertain the cause of the violent implosion and eliminate the cause before we return," tempunaut Crayne added, nodding. "We have learned already that for reasons unknown, a mass of nearly one hundred pounds of miscellaneous Volkswagen motor parts, including cylinders, the head . . ."

This is awful, Cassidy thought. "This is amazing!" he said aloud, into his neck mike. "The already tragically deceased U.S. tempunauts, with a determination that could emerge only from the rigorous training and discipline to which they were subjected—and we wondered why at the time but can clearly see why now—have already analyzed the mechanical slip-up responsible, evidently, for their own deaths, and have begun the laborious process of sifting through and eliminating causes of that slip-up so that they can return to their original launch site and re-enter without mishap."

"One wonders," Branton mumbled onto the air and into his feedback earphone, "what the consequences of this alteration of the near past will be. If in re-entry they do *not* implode and are *not* killed, then they will not—well, it's too complex for me, Henry, these time paradoxes that Doctor

Fein at the Time Extrusion Labs in Pasadena has so frequently and eloquently brought to our attention."

Into all the microphones available, of all sorts, tempunaut Addison Doug was saying, more quietly now, "We must not eliminate the cause of re-entry implosion. The only way out of this trap is for us to die. Death is the only solution for this. For the three of us." He was interrupted as the procession of Cadillacs began to move forward.

Shutting off his mike momentarily, Henry Cassidy said to his engineer, "Is he nuts?"

"Only time will tell," his engineer said in a hard-to-hear voice.

"An extraordinary moment in the history of the United States involvement in time travel," Cassidy said, then, into his now live mike. "Only time will tell—if you will pardon the inadvertent pun—whether tempunaut Doug's cryptic remarks, uttered impromptu at this moment of supreme suffering for him, as in a sense to a lesser degree it is for all of us, are the words of a man deranged by grief or an accurate insight into the macabre dilemma that in theoretical terms we knew all along might eventually confront—confront and strike down with its lethal blow—a time-travel launch, either ours or the Russians'."

He segued, then, to a commercial.

"You know," Branton's voice muttered in his ear, not on the air but just to the control room and to him, "if he's right they ought to let the poor bastards die."

"They ought to release them," Cassidy agreed. "My God, the way Doug looked and talked, you'd imagine he'd gone through this for a thousand years and then some! I wouldn't be in his shoes for anything."

"I'll bet you fifty bucks," Branton said, "they have gone through this before. Many times."

"Then we have, too," Cassidy said.

Rain fell now, making all the lined-up mourners shiny. Their faces, their eyes, even their clothes—everything glistened in wet reflections of broken, fractured light, bent and sparkling, as, from gathering gray formless layers above them, the day darkened.

"Are we on the air?" Branton asked.

Who knows? Cassidy thought. He wished the day would end.

The Soviet chrononaut N. Gauki lifted both hands impassionedly and spoke to the Americans across the table from him in a voice of extreme urgency. "It is the opinion of myself and my colleague R. Plenya, who for his pioneering achievements in time travel has been certified a Hero of the Soviet People, and rightly so, that based on our own experience and on theoretical material developed both in your own academic circles and in the Soviet Academy of Sciences of the USSR, we believe that tempunaut A. Doug's fears may be justified. And his deliberate destruction of himself and his team mates at re-entry, by hauling a huge mass of auto parts back with him from ETA, in violation of his orders, should be regarded as the act of a desperate man with no other means of escape. Of course, the decision is up to you. We have only advisory position in this matter."

Addison Doug played with his cigarette lighter on the table and did not look up. His ears hummed, and he wondered what that meant. It had an electronic quality. Maybe we're within the module again, he thought. But he did not perceive it; he felt the reality of the people around him, the table, the blue plastic lighter between his fingers. No smoking in the module during re-entry, he thought. He put the lighter carefully away in his pocket.

"We've developed no concrete evidence whatsoever," General Toad said, "that a closed-time loop has been set up.

There's only the subjective feelings of fatigue on the part of Mr. Doug. Just his belief that he's done all this repeatedly. As he says, it is very probably psychological in nature." He rooted pig-like among the papers before him. "I have a report, not disclosed to the media, from four psychiatrists at Yale on his psychological make-up. Although unusually stable, there is a tendency toward cyclothymia on his part, culminating in acute depression. This naturally was taken into account long before the launch, but it was calculated that the joyful qualities of the two others in the team would offset this functionally. Anyhow that depressive tendency in him is exceptionally high, now." He held the paper out, but no one at the table accepted it. "Isn't it true, Doctor Fein," he said, "that an acutely depressed person experiences time in a peculiar way, that is, circular time, time repeating itself, getting nowhere, around and around? The person gets so psychotic that he refuses to let go of the past. Re-runs it in his head constantly."

"But you see," Dr. Fein said, "this subjective sensation of being trapped is perhaps all we would have." This was the research physicist whose basic work had laid the theoretical foundation for the project. "If a closed loop did unfortunately lock into being."

"The general," Addison Doug said, "is using words he doesn't understand."

"I researched the ones I was unfamiliar with," General Toad said. "The technical psychiatric terms . . . I know what they mean."

To Addison Doug, Benz said, "Where'd you get all those VW parts, Addi?"

"I don't have them yet," Addison Doug said.

"Probably picked up the first junk he could lay his hands on," Crayne said. "Whatever was available, just before we started back."

"Will start back," Addison Doug corrected.

"Here are my instructions to the three of you," General Toad said. "You are not in any way to attempt to cause damage or implosion or malfunction during re-entry, either by lugging back extra mass or by any other method that enters your mind. You are to return as scheduled and in replica of the prior simulations. This especially applies to you, Mr. Doug." The phone by his right arm buzzed. He frowned, picked up the receiver. An interval passed, and then he scowled deeply and set the receiver back down, loudly.

"You've been overruled," Dr. Fein said.

"Yes, I have," General Toad said. "And I must say at this time that I am personally glad because my decision was an unpleasant one."

"Then we can arrange for implosion at re-entry." Benz said after a pause.

"The three of you are to make the decision," General Toad said. "Since it involves your lives. It's been entirely left up to you. Whichever way you want it. If you're convinced you're in a closed time loop, and you believe a massive implosion at re-entry will abolish it—" He ceased talking, as tempunaut Doug rose to his feet. "Are you going to make another speech, Doug?" he said.

"I just want to thank everyone involved," Addison Doug said. "For letting us decide." He gazed haggard-faced and wearily around at all the individuals seated at the table. "I really appreciate it."

"You know," Benz said slowly, "blowing us up at re-entry could add nothing to the chances of abolishing a closed loop. In fact that could do it, Doug."

"Not if it kills us all," Crayne said.

"You agree with Addi?" Benz said.

"Dead is dead," Crayne said. "I've been pondering it.

What other way is more likely to get us out of this? Than if we're dead? What possible other way?"

"You may be in no loop," Dr. Fein pointed out.

"But we may be," Crayne said.

Doug, still on his feet, said to Crayne and Benz, "Could we include Merry Lou in our decision-making?"

"Why?" Benz said.

"I can't think too clearly any more," Doug said. "Merry Lou can help me; I depend on her."

"Sure," Crayne said. Benz, too, nodded.

General Toad examined his wristwatch stoically and said, "Gentlemen, this concludes our discussion."

Soviet chrononaut Gauki removed his headphones and neck mike and hurried toward the three U.S. tempunauts, his hand extended; he was apparently saying something in Russian, but none of them could understand it. They moved away somberly, clustering close.

"In my opinion you're nuts, Addi," Benz said. "But it would appear that I'm the minority now."

"If he *is* right," Crayne said, "if—one chance in a billion—if we are going back again and again forever, that would justify it."

"Could we go see Merry Lou?" Addison Doug said. "Drive over to her place now?"

"She's waiting outside," Crayne said.

Striding up to stand beside the three tempunauts, General Toad said, "You know, what made the determination go the way it did was the public reaction to how you, Doug, looked and behaved during the funeral procession. The NSC advisors came to the conclusion that the public would, like you, rather be certain it's over for all of you. That it's more of a relief to them to know you're free of your mission than to save the project and obtain a perfect re-entry. I guess you really made a lasting impression on them, Doug. That whining you did." He walked away, then, leaving the three of them standing there alone.

"Forget him," Crayne said to Addison Doug. "Forget everyone like him. We've got to do what we have to."

"Merry Lou will explain it to me," Doug said. She would know what to do, what would be right.

"I'll go get her," Crayne said, "and after that the four of us can drive somewhere, maybe to her place, and decide what to do. Okay?"

"Thank you," Addison Doug said, nodding; he glanced around for her hopefully, wondering where she was. In the next room, perhaps, somewhere close. "I appreciate that," he said.

Benz and Crayne eyed each other. He saw that, but did not know what it meant. He knew only that he needed someone, Merry Lou most of all, to help him understand what the situation was. And what to finalize on to get them out of it.

Merry Lou drove them north from Los Angeles in the su-perfast lane of the freeway toward Ventura, and after that inland to Ojai. The four of them said very little. Merry Lou drove well, as always; leaning against her, Addison Doug felt himself relax into a temporary sort of peace.

"There's nothing like having a chick drive you," Crayne said, after many miles had passed in silence.

"It's an aristocratic sensation," Benz murmured. "To have a woman do the driving. Like you're nobility being chauffeured."

Merry Lou said, "Until she runs into something. Some big slow object."

Addison Doug said, "When you saw me trudging up to your place . . . up the redwood round path the other day. What did you think? Tell me honestly."

"You looked," the girl said, "as if you'd done it many times. You looked worn and tired and—ready to die. At the end." She hesitated. "I'm sorry, but that's how you looked, Addi. I thought to myself, he knows the way too well."

"Like I'd done it too many times."

"Yes," she said.

"Then you vote for implosion," Addison Doug said.

"Well—"

"Be honest with me," he said.

Merry Lou said, "Look in the back seat. The box on the floor."

With a flashlight from the glove compartment the three men examined the box. Addison Doug, with fear, saw its contents. VW motor parts, rusty and worn. Still oily.

"I got them from behind a foreign car garage near my place," Merry Lou said. "On the way to Pasadena. The first junk I saw that seemed as if it'd be heavy enough. I had heard them say on TV at launch time that anything over fifty pounds up to—"

"It'll do it," Addison Doug said. "It did do it."

"So there's no point in going to your place," Crayne said. "It's decided. We might as well head south toward the module. And initiate the procedure for getting out of ETA. And back to re-entry." His voice was heavy but evenly pitched. "Thanks for your vote, Miss Hawkins."

She said, "You are all so tired."

"I'm not," Benz said. "I'm mad. Mad as hell."

"At me?" Addison Doug said.

"I don't know," Benz said. "It just—Hell." He lapsed into brooding silence then. Hunched over, baffled and inert. Withdrawn as far as possible from the others in the car.

At the next freeway junction she turned the car south. A sense of freedom seemed now to fill her, and Addison Doug felt some of the weight, the fatigue, ebbing already.

On the wrist of each of the three men the emergency alert receiver buzzed its warning tone; they all started.

"What's that mean?" Merry Lou said, slowing the car.

"We're to contact General Toad by phone as soon as possible," Crayne said. He pointed. "There's a Standard Station over there; take the next exit, Miss Hawkins. We can phone in from there."

A few minutes later Merry Lou brought her car to a halt beside the outdoor phone booth. "I hope it's not bad news," she said.

"I'll talk first," Doug said, getting out. Bad news, he thought with labored amusement. Like what? He crunched stiffly across to the phone booth, entered, shut the door behind him, dropped in a dime and dialed the toll-free number.

"Well, do I have news!" General Toad said when the operator had put him on the line. "It's a good thing we got hold of you. Just a minute—I'm going to let Doctor Fein tell you this himself. You're more apt to believe him than me." Several clicks, and then Doctor Fein's reedy, precise, scholarly voice, but intensified by urgency.

"What's the bad news?" Addison Doug said.

"Not bad, necessarily," Dr. Fein said. "I've had computations run since our discussion, and it would appear—by that I mean it is statistically probable but still unverified for a certainty—that you are right, Addison. You are in a closed time loop."

Addison Doug exhaled raggedly. You nowhere autocratic mother, he thought. You probably knew all along.

"However," Dr. Fein said excitedly, stammering a little, "I also calculate—we jointly do, largely through Cal Tech—that the greatest likelihood of maintaining the loop is to implode on re-entry. Do you understand, Addison? If you lug all those rusty VW parts back and implode, then your statistical chances of closing the loop forever is greater than if you simply re-enter and all goes well."

Addison Doug said nothing.

"In fact, Addi—and this is the severe part that I have to stress—implosion at re-entry, especially a massive, calculated one of the sort we seem to see shaping up—do you grasp all this, Addi? Am I getting through to you? For Chrissake, Addi? Virtually *guarantees* the locking in of an absolutely unyielding loop such as you've got in mind. Such as we've all been worried about from the start." A pause. "Addi? Are you there?"

Addison Doug said, "I want to die."

"That's your exhaustion from the loop. God knows how many repetitions there've been already of the three of you—"

"No," he said and started to hang up.

"Let me speak with Benz and Crayne," Dr. Fein said rapidly. "Please, before you go ahead with re-entry. Especially Benz; I'd like to speak with him in particular. Please, Addison. For their sake; your almost total exhaustion has—"

He hung up. Left the phone booth, step by step.

As he climbed back into the car, he heard their two alert receivers still buzzing. "General Toad said the automatic call for us would keep your two receivers doing that for a while," he said. And shut the car door after him. "Let's take off."

"Doesn't he want to talk to us?" Benz said.

Addison Doug said, "General Toad wanted to inform us that they have a little something for us. We've been voted a special Congressional Citation for valor or some damn thing like that. A special medal they never voted anyone before. To be awarded posthumously."

"Well, hell—that's about the only way it can be awarded," Crayne said.

Merry Lou, as she started up the engine, began to cry.

"It'll be a relief," Crayne said presently, as they returned bumpily to the freeway, "when it's over."

It won't be long now, Addison Doug's mind declared.

On their wrists the emergency alert receivers continued to put out their combined buzzing.

"They will nibble you to death," Addison Doug said. "The endless wearing down by various bureaucratic voices."

The others in the car turned to gaze at him inquiringly, with uneasiness mixed with perplexity.

"Yeah," Crayne said. "These automatic alerts are really a nuisance." He sounded tired. As tired as I am, Addison Doug thought. And, realizing this, he felt better. It showed how right he was.

Great drops of water struck the windshield; it had now begun to rain. That pleased him too. It reminded him of that most exalted of all experiences within the shortness of his life: the funeral procession moving slowly down Pennsylvania Avenue, the flag-draped caskets. Closing his eyes he leaned back and felt good at last. And heard, all around him once again, the sorrow-bent people. And, in his head, dreamed of the special Congressional Medal. For weariness, he thought. A medal for being tired.

He saw, in his head, himself in other parades too, and in the deaths of many. But really it was one death and one parade. Slow cars moving along the street in Dallas, and with Dr. King as well . . . He saw himself return again and again, in his closed cycle of life, to the national mourning that he could not and they could not forget. He would be there; they would always be there; it would always be, and every one of them would return together again and again forever. To the place, the moment, they wanted to be. The event which meant the most to all of them.

This was his gift to them, the people, his country. He had bestowed upon the world a wonderful burden. The dreadful and weary miracle of eternal life.

RIPPLES IN THE DIRAC SEA

GEOFFREY A. LANDIS

O f course the concept of time travel can be seen as solip-
sistic; all event, all chronological effect as the outcome of
desire. Metaphysics and physics can be put in service of
wish fulfillment or overwhelming anxiety. That noted as perhaps the
lever of this story, "Ripples in the Dirac Sea" is nonetheless the most
virtuosic treatment of time paradox known to me and deserved its
Nebula Award in the late 1980s, more perhaps than any other winner competing in the category of short story; it was far ahead of its
competition that year, and would have been in any year.

Landis, a physicist, is the author of a novel, *Mars Crossing* and
recent collection, *Impact Parameter*; he lives with his wife, Mary
Terzillo, also a Nebula Award winner in Ohio. He and his wife
therefore share with Nancy Kress/Charles Sheffield the distinction of
the only marriages in which both partners have won that award.

My death looms over me like a tidal wave, rushing toward me with an inexorable slow-motion majesty. And yet I flee, pointless though it may be.

I depart, and my ripples diverge to infinity, like waves smoothing out the footprints of forgotten travellers.

We were so careful to avoid any paradox, the day we first tested my machine. We pasted a duct-tape cross onto the concrete floor of a windowless lab, placed an alarm clock on the mark, and locked the door. An hour later we came back, removed the clock, and put the experimental machine in the room with a super-eight camera set in the coils. I aimed the camera at the X, and one of my grad students programmed the machine to send the camera back half an hour, stay in the past five minutes, then return. It left and returned without even a flicker. When we developed the film, the time on the clock was half an hour before we loaded the camera. We'd succeeded in opening the door into the past. We celebrated with coffee and champagne.

Now that I know a lot more about time, I understand our mistake, that we had not thought to put a movie camera in the room with the clock to photograph the machine as it arrived from the future. But what is obvious to me now was not obvious then.

I arrive, and the ripples converge to the instant *now* from the vastness of the infinite sea.

To San Francisco, June 8, 1965. A warm breeze riffles across dandelion-speckled grass, while puffy white clouds form strange and wondrous shapes for our entertainment. Yet so very few people pause to enjoy it. They scurry about, diligently preoccupied, believing that if they act busy enough, they must be important. "They hurry so," I say. "Why can't they slow down, sit back, enjoy the day?"

"They're trapped in the illusion of time," says Dancer. He lies on his back and blows a soap bubble, his hair flopping back long and brown in a time when "long" hair meant anything below the ear. A puff of breeze takes the bubble down the hill and into the stream of pedestrians. They uniformly ignore it. "They're caught in the belief that what they do is important to some future goal." The bubble pops against a briefcase, and Dancer blows another. "You and I, we know how false an illusion that is. There is no past, no future, only the now, eternal."

He was right, more right than he could have possibly imagined. Once I, too, was preoccupied and self-important. Once I was brilliant and ambitious. I was twenty-eight years old, and I made the greatest discovery in the world.

From my hiding place I watched him come up the service elevator. He was thin almost to the point of starvation, a nervous man with stringy blond hair and an armless white T-shirt. He looked up and down the hall, but failed to see me hidden in the janitor's closet. Under each arm was a two-gallon can of gasoline, in each hand another. He put down three of the cans and turned the last one upside down, then walked down the hall, spreading a pungent trail of gasoline. His face was blank. When he started on the second can, I figured it was about enough. As he passed my hiding spot, I walloped him over the head with a wrench, and called hotel security. Then I went back to the closet and let the ripples of time converge.

I arrived in a burning room, flames licking forth at me, the heat almost too much to bear. I gasped for breath—a mistake—and punched at the keypad.

Notes on the Theory and Practice of Time Travel:

1. Travel is possible only into the past.
2. The object transported will return to exactly the time and place of departure.
3. It is not possible to bring objects from the past to the present.
4. Actions in the past cannot change the present.

One time I tried jumping back a hundred million years, to the Cretaceous, to see dinosaurs. All the picture books show the landscape as being covered with dinosaurs. I spent three days wandering around a swamp—in my new tweed suit—before catching even a glimpse of any dinosaur larger than a basset hound. That one—a theropod of some sort, I don't know which—skittered away as soon as it caught a whiff of me. Quite a disappointment.

My professor in transfinite math used to tell stories about a hotel with an infinite number of rooms. One day all the rooms are full, and another guest arrives. "No problem," says the desk clerk. He moves the person in room one into room two, the person in room two into room three, and so on. Presto! A vacant room.

A little later, an infinite number of guests arrive. "No problem," says the dauntless desk clerk. He moves the person in room one into room two, the person in room two into room four, the person in room three into room six, and so on. Presto! An infinite number of rooms vacant.

My time machine works on just that principle.

Again I return to 1965, the fixed point, the strange attractor to my chaotic trajectory. In years of wandering I've met countless people, but Daniel Ranien—Dancer—was the only one who truly had his head together. He had a soft, easy smile, a battered secondhand guitar, and as much wisdom as it has taken me a hundred lifetimes to learn. I've known him in good times and bad, in summer days with blue skies that we swore would last a thousand years, in days of winter blizzards with drifted snow piled high over our heads. In happier times we have laid roses into the barrels of rifles; we have laid our bodies across the city streets in the midst of riots, and not been hurt. And I have been with him when he died, once, twice, a hundred times over.

He died on February 8, 1969, a month into the reign of King Richard the Trickster and his court fool Spiro, a year before Kent State and Altamont and the secret war in Cambodia slowly strangled the summer of dreams. He died, and there was—is—nothing I can do. The last time he died I dragged him to a hospital, where I screamed and ranted until finally I convinced them to admit him for observation, though nothing seemed wrong with him. With X rays and arteriograms and radioactive tracers, they found the incipient bubble in his brain; they drugged him, shaved his beautiful long brown hair, and operated on him, cutting out the offending capillary and tying it off neatly. When the anesthetic wore off, I sat in the hospital room and held his hand. There were big purple blotches under his eyes. He gripped my hand and stared, silent, into space. Visiting hours or no, I didn't let them throw me out of the room. He just stared. In the gray hours just before dawn he sighed softly and died. There was nothing at all that I could do.

Time travel is subject to two constraints: conservation of energy, and causality. The energy to appear in the past is only borrowed from the Dirac sea, and since ripples in the Dirac sea propagate in the negative t direction, transport is only into the past. Energy is conserved in the present as long as the object transported returns with zero time delay, and the principle of causality assures that actions in the past cannot change the present. For example, what if you went into the past and killed your father? Who, then, would invent the time machine?

Once I tried to commit suicide by murdering my father, before he met my mother, twenty-three years before I was born. It changed nothing, of course, and even when I did it, I knew it would change nothing. But you have to try these things. How else could I know for sure?

Next we tried sending a rat back. It made the trip through the Dirac sea and back undamaged. Then we tried a trained rat, one we borrowed from the psychology lab across the green without telling them what we wanted it for. Before its little trip it had been taught to run through a maze to get a piece of bacon. Afterwards, it ran the maze as fast as ever.

We still had to try it on a human. I volunteered myself and didn't allow anyone to talk me out of it. By trying it on myself, I dodged the university regulations about experimenting on humans.

The dive into the negative-energy sea felt like nothing at all. One moment I stood in the center of the loop of Renselz coils, watched by my two grad students and a technician; the next I was alone, and the clock had jumped back exactly one hour. Alone in a locked room with nothing but a camera and a clock, that moment was the high point of my life.

The moment when I first met Dancer was the low point. I was in Berkeley, a bar called Trishia's, slowly getting trashed. I'd been doing that a lot, caught between omnipotence and despair. It was 1967. 'Frisco then—it was the middle of the hippy era—seemed somehow appropriate.

There was a girl, sitting at a table with a group from the university. I walked over to her table and invited myself to sit down. I told her she didn't exist, that her whole world didn't exist, it was all created by the fact that I was watching, and would disappear back into the sea of unreality as soon as I stopped looking. Her name was Lisa, and she argued back. Her friends, bored, wandered off, and in a while Lisa realized just how drunk I was. She dropped a bill on the table and walked out into the foggy night.

I followed her out. When she saw me following, she clutched her purse and bolted.

He was suddenly there under the streetlight. For a second I thought he was a girl. He had bright blue eyes and straight brown hair down to his shoulders. He wore an embroidered Indian shirt, with a silver and turquoise medallion around his neck and a guitar slung across his back. He was lean, almost stringy, and moved like a dancer or a karate master. But it didn't occur to me to be afraid of him.

He looked me over. "That won't solve your problem, you know," he said.

And instantly I was ashamed. I was no longer sure exactly what I'd had in mind or why I'd followed her. It had been years since I'd first fled my death, and I had come to think of others as unreal, since nothing I could do would permanently affect them. My head was spinning. I slid down the wall and sat down, hard, on the sidewalk. What had I come to?

He helped me back into the bar, fed me orange juice and pretzels, and got me to talk. I told him everything. Why not, since I could unsay anything I said, undo anything I did? But I had no urge to. He listened to it all, saying nothing. No one else had ever listened to the whole story before. I can't explain the effect it had on me. For uncountable years I'd been alone, and then, if only for a moment . . . It hit me with the intensity of a tab of acid. If only for a moment, I was not alone.

We left arm in arm. Half a block away, Dancer stopped, in front of an alley. It was dark.

"Something not quite right here." His voice had a puzzled tone.

I pulled him back. "Hold on. You don't want to go down there—" He pulled free and walked in. After a slight hesitation, I followed.

The alley smelled of old beer, mixed with garbage and stale vomit. In a moment, my eyes became adjusted to the dark.

Lisa was cringing in a corner behind some trash cans. Her clothes had been cut away with a knife, and lay scattered around. Blood showed dark on her thighs and one arm. She didn't seem to see us. Dancer squatted down next to her and said something soft. She didn't respond. He pulled off his shirt, and wrapped it around her, then cradled her in his arms and picked her up. "Help me get her to my apartment."

"Apartment, hell. We'd better call the police," I said.

"Call the pigs? Are you crazy? You want them to rape her, too?"

I'd forgotten; this was the sixties. Between the two of us, we got her to Dancer's VW bug and took her to his apartment in The Hashbury. He explained it to me quietly as we drove, a dark side of the summer of love that I'd not seen before. It was greasers, he said. They come down to Berkeley because they heard that hippie chicks gave it away free, and get nasty when they met one who thought otherwise.

Her wounds were mostly superficial. Dancer cleaned her, put her in bed, and stayed up all night beside her, talking and crooning and making little reassuring noises. I slept on one of the mattresses in the hall. When I woke up in the morning, they were both in his bed. She was sleeping quietly. Dancer was awake, holding her. I was aware enough to realize that that was all he was doing, holding her, but still I felt a sharp pang of jealousy, and didn't know which one of them it was that I was jealous of.

Notes for a Lecture on Time Travel

The beginning of the twentieth century was a time of intellectual giants, whose likes will perhaps never again be equaled. Einstein had just invented relativity, Heisenberg and Schrödinger quantum mechanics, but nobody yet knew how to make the two theories consistent with each other. In 1930, a new person tackled the problem. His name was Paul Dirac. He was twenty-eight years old. He succeeded where the others had failed.

His theory was an unprecedented success, except for one small detail. According to Dirac's theory, a particle could have either positive or negative energy. What did this mean, a particle of negative energy? How could something have negative energy? And why don't ordinary—positive energy— particles fall down into these negative energy states, releasing a lot of free energy in the process?

You or I might have merely stipulated that it was impossible for an ordinary positive energy particle to make a transition to negative energy. But Dirac was not an ordinary man. He was a genius, the greatest physicist of all, and he had an answer. If every possible negative energy state was already occupied, a particle couldn't drop into a negative energy state. Ah ha! So Dirac postulated that the entire universe is entirely filled with negative energy particles. They surround us, permeate us, in the vacuum of outer space and in the center of the earth, every possible place a particle could be. An infinitely dense "sea" of negative energy particles. The Dirac sea.

His argument had holes in it, but that comes later.

Once I went to visit the crucifixion. I took a jet from Santa Cruz to Tel Aviv, and a bus from Tel Aviv to Jerusalem. On a hill outside the city, I dove through the Dirac sea.

I arrived in my three-piece suit. No way to help that, unless I wanted to travel naked. The land was surprisingly green and fertile, more so than I'd expected. The hill was now a farm, covered with grape arbors and olive trees. I hid the coils behind some rocks and walked down to the road. I didn't get far. Five minutes on the road, I ran into a group of people. They had dark hair, dark skin, and wore clean white tunics. Romans? Jews? Egyptians? How could I tell? They spoke to me, but I couldn't understand a word. After a while two of them held me, while a third searched me. Were they robbers, searching for money? Romans, searching for some kind of identity papers? I realized how naive I'd been to think I could just find appropriate dress and somehow blend in with the crowds. Finding nothing, the one who'd done the search carefully and methodically beat me up. At last he pushed me face down in the dirt. While the other two held me down, he pulled out a dagger and slashed through the tendons on the back of each leg. They were merciful, I guess. They left me with my life. Laughing and talking incomprehensibly among themselves, they walked away.

My legs were useless. One of my arms was broken. It took me four hours to crawl back up the hill, dragging myself with my good arm. Occasionally people would pass by on the road, studiously ignoring me. Once I reached the hiding place, pulling out the Renselz coils and wrapping them around me was pure agony. By the time I entered return on the keypad I was wavering in and out of consciousness. I finally managed to get it entered. From the Dirac sea the ripples converged

and I was in my hotel room in Santa Cruz. The ceiling had started to fall in where the girders had burned through. Fire alarms shrieked and wailed, but there was no place to run. The room was filled with dense, acrid smoke. Trying not to breathe, I punched out a code on the keypad, somewhen, anywhen other than that one instant

and I was in the hotel room, five days before. I gasped for breath. The woman in the hotel bed shrieked and tried to pull the covers up. The man screwing her was too busy to pay any mind. They weren't real anyway. I ignored them and paid a little more attention to where to go next. Back to '65, I figured. I punched in the combo

and was standing in an empty room on the thirtieth floor of a hotel just under construction. A full moon gleamed on the silhouettes of silent construction cranes. I flexed my legs experimentally. Already the memory of the pain was beginning to fade. That was reasonable, because it had never happened. Time travel. It's not immortality, but it's got to be the next best thing.

You can't change the past, no matter how you try.

In the morning I explored Dancer's pad. It was crazy, a small third-floor apartment a block off Haight Ashbury that had been converted into something from another planet. The floor of the apartment had been completely covered with old mattresses, on top of which was a jumbled confusion of quilts, pillows, Indian blankets, stuffed animals. You took off your shoes before coming in—Dancer always wore sandals, leather ones from Mexico with soles cut from old tires. The radiators, which didn't work anyway, were spray painted in Day-Glo colors. The walls were plastered with posters: Peter Max prints, brightly colored Eschers, poems by Allen Ginsberg, record album covers, peace-rally posters, a "Haight Is Love" sign, FBI ten-most-wanted posters torn down from a post office with the photos of famous antiwar activists circled in magic marker, a huge peace symbol in passion-pink. Some of the posters were illuminated with black light and luminesced in impossible colors. The air was musty with incense and the banana-sweet smell of dope. In one corner a record player played *Sergeant Pepper's Lonely Hearts Club Band* on infinite repeat. Whenever one copy of the album got too scratchy, inevitably one of Dancer's friends would bring in another.

He never locked the door. "Somebody wants to rip me off, well, hey, they probably need it more than I do anyway, okay? It's cool." People dropped by any time of day or night.

I let my hair grow long. Dancer and Lisa and I spent that summer together, laughing, playing guitar, making love, writing silly poems and sillier songs, experimenting with drugs. That was when LSD was blooming onto the scene like sunflowers, when people were still unafraid of the strange and beautiful world on the other side of reality. That was a time to live. I knew that it was Dancer that Lisa truly loved, not me, but in those days free love was in the air like the scent of poppies, and it didn't matter. Not much, anyway.

Notes for a Lecture on Time Travel (continued)

Having postulated that all of space was filled with an infinitely dense sea of negative energy particles, Dirac went further and asked if we, in the positive-energy universe, could interact with this negative-energy sea. What would happen, say, if you added enough energy to an electron to take it out of the negative-energy sea? Two things: first, you would create an electron, seemingly out of nowhere. Second, you would leave behind a "hole" in the sea. The hole, Dirac realized, would act as if it were a particle itself, a particle exactly like an electron except for one thing: it would have the opposite charge. But if the hole ever encountered an electron, the electron would fall back into the Dirac sea, annihilating both electron and hole in a bright burst of energy. Eventually they gave the hole in the Dirac sea a name of its own: "positron." When Anderson discovered the positron two years later to vindicate Dirac's theory, it was almost an anticlimax.

And over the next fifty years, the reality of the Dirac sea was almost ignored by physicists. Antimatter, the holes in the sea, was the important feature of the theory; the rest was merely a mathematical artifact.

Seventy years later, I remembered the story my transfinite math teacher told and put it together with Dirac's theory. Like putting an extra guest into a hotel with an infinite number of rooms, I figured out how to borrow energy from the Dirac sea. Or, to put it another way: I learned how to make waves.

And waves on the Dirac sea travel backward in time.

Next we had to try something more ambitious. We had to send a human back farther into history, and obtain proof of the trip. Still we were afraid to make alterations in the past, even though the mathematics stated that the present could not be changed.

We pulled out our movie camera and chose our destinations carefully.

In September of 1853 a traveler named William Hapland and his family crossed the Sierra Nevadas to reach the California coast. His daughter Sarah kept a journal, and in it she recorded how, as they reached the crest of Parker's Ridge, she caught her first glimpse of the distant Pacific ocean exactly as the sun touched the horizon, "in a blays of cryms'n glorie," as she wrote. The journal still exists. It was easy enough for us to conceal ourselves and a movie camera in a cleft of rocks above the pass, to photograph the weary travelers in their ox-drawn wagon as they crossed.

The second target was the great San Francisco earthquake of 1906. From a deserted warehouse that would survive the quake—but not the following fire—we watched and took movies as buildings tumbled down around us and embattled firemen in horse-drawn fire-trucks strove in vain to quench a hundred blazes. Moments before the fire reached our building, we fled into the present.

The films were spectacular.

We were ready to tell the world.

There was a meeting of the AAAS in Santa Cruz in a month. I called the program chairman and wangled a spot as an invited speaker without revealing just what we'd accomplished to date. I planned to show those films at the talk. They were to make us instantly famous.

The day that Dancer died we had a going-away party, just Lisa and Dancer and I. He knew he was going to die; I'd told him and somehow he believed me. He always believed me. We stayed up all night, playing Dancer's secondhand guitar, painting psychedelic designs on each other's bodies with greasepaint, competing against each other in a marathon game of cutthroat Monopoly, doing a hundred silly, ordinary things that took meaning only from the fact that it was the last time. About four in the morning, as the glimmer of false-dawn began to show in the sky, we went down to the bay and, huddling together for warmth, went tripping. Dancer took the largest dose, since he wasn't going to return. The last thing he said, he told us not to let our dreams die; to stay together.

We buried Dancer, at city expense, in a welfare grave. We split up three days later.

I kept in touch with Lisa, vaguely. In the late seventies she went back to school, first for an MBA, then law school. I think she was married for a while. We wrote each other cards on Christmas for a while, then I lost track of her. Years later, I got a letter from her. She said that she was finally able to forgive me for causing Dan's death.

It was a cold and foggy February day, but I knew I could find warmth in 1965. The ripples converged.

Anticipated questions from the audience:

Q (old, stodgy professor): It seems to me this proposed temporal jump of yours violates the law of conservation of mass/energy. For example, when a transported object is transported into the past, a quantity of mass will appear to vanish from the present, in clear violation of the conservation law.

A (me): Since the return is to the exact time of departure, the mass present is constant.

Q: Very well, but what about the arrival in the past? Doesn't this violate the conservation law?

A: No. The energy needed is taken from the Dirac sea, by the mechanism I explain in detail in the *Phys Rev* paper. When the object returns to the "future," the energy is restored to the sea.

Q (intense young physicist): Then doesn't Heisenberg uncertainty limit the amount of time that can be spent in the past?

A: A good question. The answer is yes, but because we borrow an infinitesimal amount of energy from an infinite number of particles, the amount of time spent in the past can be arbitrarily large. The only limitation is that you must leave the past an instant before you depart from the present.

In half an hour I was scheduled to present the paper that would rank my name with Newton's and Galileo's—and Dirac's. I was twenty-eight years old, the same age as Dirac when he announced his theory. I was a firebrand, preparing to set the world aflame. I was nervous, rehearsing the speech in my hotel room. I took a swig out of an old Coke that one of my grad students had left sitting on top of the television. The evening news team was babbling on, but I wasn't listening.

I never delivered that talk. The hotel had already started to burn; my death was already foreordained. Tie neat, I inspected myself in the mirror, then walked to the door. The doorknob was warm. I opened it onto a sheet of fire. Flame burst through the opened door like a ravening dragon. I stumbled backward, staring at the flames in amazed fascination.

Somewhere in the hotel I heard a scream, and all at once I broke free of my spell. I was on the thirtieth story; there was no way out. My thought was for my machine. I rushed across the room and threw open the case holding the time machine. With swift, sure fingers I pulled out the Renselz coils and wrapped them around my body. The carpet had caught on fire, a sheet of flame between me and any possible escape. Holding my breath to avoid suffocation, I punched an entry into the keyboard and dove into time.

I return to that moment again and again. When I hit the final key, the air was already nearly unbreathable with smoke. I had about thirty seconds left to live, then. Over the years I've nibbled away my time down to ten seconds or less.

I live on borrowed time. So do we all, perhaps. But I know when and where my debt will fall due.

Dancer died on February 9, 1969. It was a dim, foggy day. In the morning he said he had a headache. That was unusual, for Dancer. He never had headaches. We decided to go for a walk through the fog. It was beautiful, as if we were alone in a strange, formless world. I'd forgotten about his headache altogether, until, looking out across the sea of fog from the park over the bay, he fell over. He was dead before the ambulance came. He died with a secret smile on his face. I've never understood that smile. Maybe he was smiling because the pain was gone.

Lisa committed suicide two days later.

You ordinary people, you have the chance to change the future. You can father children, write novels, sign petitions, invent new machines, go to cocktail parties, run for president. You affect the future with everything you do. No matter what I do, I cannot. It is too late for that, for me. My actions are written in flowing water. And having no effect, I have no responsibilities. It makes no difference what I do, not at all.

When I first fled the fire into the past, I tried everything I could to change it. I stopped the arsonist, I argued with mayors, I even went to my own house and told myself not to go to the conference.

But that's not how time works. No matter what I do, talk to a governor or dynamite the hotel, when I reach that critical moment—the present, my destiny, the moment I left—I vanish from whenever I was, and return to the hotel room, the fire approaching ever closer. I have about ten seconds left. Every time I dive through the Dirac sea, everything I changed in the past vanishes. Sometimes I pretend that the changes I make in the past create new futures, though I know this is not the case. When I return to the present, all the changes are wiped out by the ripples of the converging wave, like erasing a blackboard after a class.

Someday I will return and meet my destiny. But for now, I live in the past. It's a good life, I suppose. You get used to the fact that nothing you do will ever have any effect on the world. It gives you a feeling of freedom. I've been places no one has ever been, seen things no one alive has ever seen. I've given up physics, of course. Nothing I discover could endure past that fatal night in Santa Cruz. Maybe some people would continue for the sheer joy of knowledge. For me, the point is missing.

But there are compensations. Whenever I return to the hotel room, nothing is changed but my memories. I am again twenty-eight, again wearing the same three-piece suit, again have the fuzzy taste of stale cola in my mouth. Every time I return, I use up a little bit of time. One day I will have no time left.

Dancer, too, will never die. I won't let him. Every time I get to that final February morning, the day he died, I return to 1965, to that perfect day in June. He doesn't know me, he never knows me. But we meet on that hill, the only two willing to enjoy the day doing nothing. He lies on his back, idly fingering chords on his guitar, blowing bubbles and staring into the clouded blue sky. Later I will introduce him to Lisa. She won't know us either, but that's okay. We've got plenty of time.

"Time," I say to Dancer, lying in the park on the hill. "There's so much time."

"All the time there is," he says.

HALL OF MIRRORS

FREDRIC BROWN

In this brief, savage short story, time travel is not an instrument (as is usually the case) for power but instead of victimization. What comes from the work is an intense loneliness, a signal entrapment which goes beyond the closed room, the silence of revelation.

Fredric Brown (1906–1972) is probably the only writer to have achieved equal achievement and prominence in both science fiction and mystery. *The Fabulous Clipjoint* (1947) won the first MWA Edgar Award for best first novel, his first science-fiction novel, *What Mad Universe* (1948) has never been out of print. He was probably science fiction's best practitioner of the short-short story. A recent complete collection of his short science fiction, *From These Ashes* (Nesfa Press), proves that judgment.

For an instant you think it is temporary blindness, this sudden dark that comes in the middle of a bright afternoon.

It *must* be blindness, you think; could the sun that was tanning you have gone out instantaneously, leaving you in utter blackness?

Then the nerves of your body tell you that you are *standing*, whereas only a second ago you were sitting comfortably, almost reclining, in a canvas chair. In the patio of a friend's house in Beverly Hills. Talking to Barbara, your fiancée. Looking at Barbara—Barbara in a swim suit—her skin golden tan in the brilliant sunshine, beautiful.

You wore swimming trunks. Now you do not feel them on you; the slight pressure of the elastic waistband is no longer there against your waist. You touch your hands to your hips. You are naked. And standing.

Whatever has happened to you is more than a change to sudden darkness or to sudden blindness.

You raise your hands gropingly before you. They touch

a plain smooth surface, a wall. You spread them apart and each hand reaches a corner. You pivot slowly. A second wall, then a third, then a door. You are in a closet about four feet square.

Your hand finds the knob of the door. It turns and you push the door open.

There is light now. The door has opened to a lighted room . . . a room that you have never seen before.

It is not large, but it is pleasantly furnished—although the furniture is of a style that is strange to you. Modesty makes you open the door cautiously the rest of the way. But the room is empty of people.

You step into the room, turning to look behind you into the closet, which is now illuminated by light from the room. The closet is and is not a closet; it is the size and shape of one, but it contains nothing, not a single hook, no rod for hanging clothes, no shelf. It is an empty, blank-walled, four-by-four-foot space.

You close the door to it and stand looking around the room. It is about twelve by sixteen feet. There is one door, but it is closed. There are no windows. Five pieces of furniture. Four of them you recognize—more or less. One looks like a very functional desk. One is obviously a chair . . . a comfortable-looking one. There is a table, although its top is on several levels instead of only one. Another is a bed, or couch. Something shimmering is lying across it and you walk over and pick the shimmering something up and examine it. It is a garment.

You are naked, so you put it on. Slippers are part way under the bed (or couch) and you slide your feet into them. They fit, and they feel warm and comfortable as nothing you have ever worn on your feet has felt. Like lamb's wool, but softer.

You are dressed now. You look at the door—the only

door of the room except that of the closet (closet?) from which you entered it. You walk to the door and before you try the knob, you see the small typewritten sign pasted just above it that reads:

This door has a time lock set to open in one hour. For reasons you will soon understand, it is better that you do not leave this room before then. There is a letter for you on the desk. Please read it.

It is not signed. You look at the desk and see that there is an envelope lying on it.

You do not yet go to take that envelope from the desk and read the letter that must be in it.

Why not? Because you are frightened.

You see other things about the room. The lighting has no source that you can discover. It comes from nowhere. It is not indirect lighting; the ceiling and the walls are not reflecting it at all.

They didn't have lighting like that, back where you came from. What did you mean by *back where you came from?*

You close your eyes. You tell yourself: *I am Norman Hastings. I am an associate professor of mathematics at the University of Southern California. I am twenty-five years old, and this is the year nineteen hundred and fifty-four.*

You open your eyes and look again.

They didn't use that style of furniture in Los Angeles— or anywhere else that you know of—in 1954. That thing over in the corner—you can't even guess what it is. So might your grandfather, at your age, have looked at a television set.

You look down at yourself, at the shimmering garment that you found waiting for you. With thumb and forefinger you feel its texture.

It's like nothing you've ever touched before.

I am Norman Hastings. This is nineteen hundred and fifty-four.

Suddenly you must know, and at once.

You go to the desk and pick up the envelope that lies upon it. Your name is typed on the outside. *Norman Hastings.*

Your hands shake a little as you open it. Do you blame them?

There are several pages, typewritten. Dear Norman, it starts. You turn quickly to the end to look for the signature. It is unsigned.

You turn back and start reading.

"Do not be afraid. There is nothing to fear, but much to explain. Much that you must understand before the time lock opens that door. Much that you must accept and—obey.

"You have already guessed that you are in the future—in what, to you, seems to be the future. The clothes and the room must have told you that. I planned it that way so the shock would not be too sudden, so you would realize it over the course of several minutes rather than read it here—and quite probably disbelieve what you read.

"The 'closet' from which you have just stepped is, as you have by now realized, a time machine. From it you stepped into the world of 2004. The date is April 7th, just fifty years from the time you last remember.

"You cannot return.

"I did this to you and you may hate me for it; I do not know. That is up to you to decide, but it does not matter. What does matter, and not to you alone, is another decision which you must make. I am incapable of making it.

"Who is writing this to you? I would rather not tell you just yet. By the time you have finished reading this, even though it is not signed (for I knew you would look first for a signature), I will not need to tell you who I am. You will know.

"I am seventy-five years of age. I have, in this year 2004, been studying 'time' for thirty of those years. I have completed the first time machine ever built—and thus far, its construction, even the fact that it has been constructed, is my own secret.

"You have just participated in the first major experiment. It will be your responsibility to decide whether there shall ever be any more experiments with it, whether it should be given to the world, or whether it should be destroyed and never used again."

End of the first page. You look up for a moment, hesitating to turn the next page. Already you suspect what is coming.

You turn the page.

"I constructed the first time machine a week ago. My calculations had told me that it would work, but not how it would work. I had expected it to send an object back in time—it works backward in time only, not forward—physically unchanged and intact.

"My first experiment showed me my error. I placed a cube of metal in the machine—it was a miniature of the one you just walked out of—and set the machine to go backward ten years. I flicked the switch and opened the door, expecting to find the cube vanished. Instead I found it had crumbled to powder.

"I put in another cube and sent it two years back. The second cube came back unchanged, except that it was newer, shiner.

"That gave me the answer. I had been expecting the cubes to go back in time, and they had done so, but not in the sense I had expected them to. Those metal cubes had been fabricated about three years previously. I had sent the first one back years before it had existed in its fabricated form. Ten years ago it had been ore. The machine returned it to that state.

"Do you see how our previous theories of time travel have been wrong? We expected to be able to step into a time machine in, say, 2004, set it for fifty years back, and then step out in the year 1954 ... but it does not work that way. The machine does not move in time. Only whatever is within the machine is affected, and then just with relation to itself and not to the rest of the Universe."

"I confirmed this with guinea pigs by sending one six weeks old five weeks back and it came out a baby.

"I need not outline all my experiments here. You will find a record of them in the desk and you can study it later.

"Do you understand now what has happened to you, Norman?"

You begin to understand. And you begin to sweat.

The *I* who wrote that letter you are now reading is *you*, yourself at the age of seventy-five, in the year of 2004. You are that seventy-five-year-old man, with your body returned to what it had been fifty years ago, with all the memories of fifty years of living wiped out.

You invented the time machine.

And before you used it on yourself, you made these arrangements to help you orient yourself. You wrote yourself the letter which you are now reading.

But if those fifty years are—to you—gone, what of all your friends, those you loved? What of your parents? What of the girl you are going—were going—to marry?

You read on:

"Yes, you will want to know what has happened. Mom died in 1963, Dad in 1968. You married Barbara in 1956. I am sorry to tell you that she died only three years later, in a plane crash. You have one son. He is still living; his name is Walter; he is now forty-six years old and is an accountant in Kansas City."

Tears come into your eyes and for a moment you can no longer read. Barbara dead—dead for forty-five years. And only minutes ago, in subjective time, you were sitting next to her, sitting in the bright sun in a Beverly Hills patio . . .

You force yourself to read again.

"But back to the discovery. You begin to see some of its implications. You will need time to think to see all of them.

"It does not permit time travel as we have thought of time travel, but it gives us immortality of a sort. Immortality of the kind I have temporarily given us.

"*Is it good?* Is it worth while to lose the memory of fifty years of one's life in order to return one's body to relative youth? The only way I can find out is to try, as soon as I have finished writing this and made my other preparations.

"You will know the answer.

"But before you decide, remember that there is another problem, more important than the psychological one. I mean overpopulation.

"If our discovery is given to the world, if all who are old or dying can make themselves young again, the population will almost double every generation. Nor would the world—not even our own relatively enlightened country—be willing to accept compulsory birth control as a solution.

"Give this to the world, as the world is today in 2004, and within a generation there will be famine, suffering, war. Perhaps a complete collapse of civilization.

"Yes, we have reached other planets, but they are not suitable for colonizing. The stars may be our answer, but we are a long way from reaching them. When we do, some-day, the billions of habitable planets that must be out there will be our answer . . . our living room. But until then, what is the answer?

"Destroy the machine? But think of the countless lives it can save, the suffering it can prevent. Think of what it would mean to a man dying of cancer. Think . . ."

Think. You finish the letter and put it down.

You think of Barbara dead for forty-five years. And of the fact that you were married to her for three years and that those years are lost to you.

Fifty years lost. You damn the old man of seventy-five whom you became and who has done this to you . . . who has given you this decision to make.

Bitterly, you know what the decision must be. You think that *he* knew, too, and realize that he could safely leave it in your hands. Damn him, he *should* have known.

Too valuable to destroy, too dangerous to give.

The other answer is painfully obvious.

You must be custodian of this discovery and keep it secret until it is safe to give, until mankind has expanded to the stars and has new worlds to populate, or until, even without that, he has reached a state of civilization where he can avoid overpopulation by rationing births to the number of accidental—or voluntary—deaths.

If neither of those things has happened in another fifty years (and are they likely so soon?), then you, at seventy-five, will be writing another letter like this one. You will be undergoing another experience similar to the one you're going through now. And making the same decision, of course.

Why not? You'll be the same person again.

Time and again, to preserve this secret until Man is ready for it.

How often will you again sit at a desk like this one, thinking the thoughts you are thinking now, feeling the grief you now feel?

There is a click at the door and you know that the time lock has opened, that you are now free to leave this room, free to start a new life for yourself in place of the one you have already lived and lost.

But you are in no hurry now to walk directly through that door.

You sit there, staring straight ahead of you blindly, seeing in your mind's eye the vista of a set of facing mirrors, like those in an old-fashioned barber shop, reflecting the same thing over and over again, diminishing into far distance.

3 RMS GOOD VUE

KAREN HABER

Contiguous with the literature of time travel are—let us admit this—our own fantasies of change. Get back there, do it right, take back the words that broke the spirit, the choice that led to disaster. Bet the right horse instead of the wrong one, kiss the right person this time and leave the wrong one. Despair not annealed but corrected. "3 RMS GOOD VUE," which links this wish to the lost flowers of the Berkeley (non-) Revolution, is a poignant exemplification of an inescapably poignant theme.

Karen Haber is the author of several accomplished novels (*The Mutant Season*) and a greater number of short stories, many of which, like this, are truly elegant. She is married to Robert Silverberg, co-edited with him the revived *Universe* series, and now the best of the year anthology for this publisher, reviews for *Locus*, and has an extensive background in magazine journalism.

A partment for rent," said the net ad. "3 rms, gd view. Potrero Hill area, $1200 a month, utilities pd."

It sounded like a dream. Every San Francisco apartment I had seen in the last six months had waiting lists for their waiting lists.

"Southern exp. Pets OK."

Better and better.

Then I found the catch. The apartment was available, all right. In 1968.

Don't misunderstand me. I'm not one of those with a temporal bias. And God knows, I've always wanted to live in San Francisco.

I first came north in '07 on a family expedition to the Retro-Pan-Pacific Exposition. The fair was fun, but what I loved even better was San Francisco: the sunswept hillsides, the streets lined with bright flower boxes, the digitalized ding-a-ling of the street car bells floating in the cool air, the fog creeping in at dusk. Heaven, especially after thirteen summers spent baking in the San Fernando Valley. I vowed to come back.

It took me seventeen years and a divorce, but I did it. Right after I graduated from Boalt and passed the bar.

Unfortunately, housing was tight—in fact, strangulated. The city had instituted severe building restrictions back in '03 and got what it asked for: all residential construction not only stopped but vanished, gone eastward to the greener pastures of Contra Costa County.

I got on the waiting list of every real estate agent in the Bay Area, but the best digs I would find was a studio apartment—more like a large walk-in closet with plumbing—in a renovated duplex in Yuba City. Add on a three-hour commute to my job in San Francisco's financial district, and we're not exactly talking about positive quality of life.

So when I saw the net ad, I jumped. And stopped in midair. As I said, I have no temporal biases. But I'm not one of those sentimental history nuts just dying to travel back to the Crucifixion, either. I like realtime just fine, thank you. Always have. It's a peculiar trait, considering my family.

My grandmother lives in 1962, and has for the last ten years. She said it was the last time that America believed in itself as a country. And it's safe. She likes the peace and quiet of the pre-computer era. "Loosen up, Chrissy," she said to me before she left. "You should be more flexible. There's nothing wrong with living in the past."

My brother lives in 1997 where he's pierced his nose, lip, eyebrows, and had his scalp tattooed in concentric circles of red and black. Every now and then I get a note from him through e-mail: "Come visit. We'll hit the clubs. Don't you ever take a vacation? I thought girls wanted to have fun."

As for Mom, well, she likes 1984. But then, she always did have an odd sense of humor.

Pardon me if I like realtime best. I've always had my feet planted firmly in the present. Practical, sturdy Christine. In the lofty hierachy of Mount Olympus, I'd be placed just to the left of Zeus in the marble frieze, in the Athena position. Yes, I even have the gray eyes and brown hair to go with the no-nonsense attitude. I'm tall and muscular, as befits your basic warrior goddess/business attorney type. My stature is useful, too—who wants a lawyer who doesn't look intimidating?

And I've never wanted to go backward. We all remember the first reports of time travel glitches. Shari, one of my prelaw classmates at Berkeley, wanted to spend her Christmas break in the village where her French great-great-great grandmother lived. But a power surge from Sacramento sent her to the fourteenth century instead. Talk about your bad neighborhoods. If she hadn't gotten her shots before she left—complaining all the way—she'd probably have come back sporting buboes the size and color of rotten nectarines.

After Shari's brush with the Black Death, I told myself I was immune to the allure of era-hopping. I ignored the net ads for Grand Tours: the Crucifixion and sack of Rome package, $1,598. Dark Ages through the Enlightenment, two weeks for $2,100, all meals and tips included. (These packages are especially popular with the Japanese, who have become time-travel junkies. And why not? They can go away and come back without losing any realtime at work.)

Even when the Koreans made portable transport units for home or office, I shrugged and stuck by realtime. But when I saw the listing in the paper, I looked around the stucco walls of my apartment/cell and threw all my sturdy, practical notions to the wind. An apartment on Portrero

Hill? In a nanosecond, Pallas Athena transmuted into impulsive Mercury.

My hands trembled with excitement and impatience as I sent my credit history to Jerry Raskin, the real estate agent listed on the ad. Almost immediately I received an appointment to view the apartment. This Raskin sure didn't waste any time.

We met at his office in the Tenderloin. He was a short man, barely reaching my shoulder, with thinning dark hair and a doughy nose that looked like a half-baked biscuit. A matte black Mitsubishi temp transport unit sat behind his desk. I stared at it uneasily.

"Want to look over the premises?" he asked. He gestured toward the unit.

"Uh, yes. Of course." I took a deep breath and stepped over the threshold of the transport.

There was a sudden fragmentation of color, of sound. I was in a high white space, falling. I was stepping into an apartment on Potrero Hill, shaking my head in wonder.

Even before the shimmering transport effect had diminished, Jerry had launched into his sales pitch. "It's a gem," he said proudly. "I hardly ever get this kind of listing." He flicked an invisible piece of lint from the shoulder of his green silk suit. "Once every five years."

It was perfect. Big sunny rooms paneled in pine, full of light, ready for plants. Hardwood floors. There was even a little balcony off the bedroom where I could watch the fog drift in over Twin Peaks in the summer afternoons.

All wound up and oblivious to my rapture, Raskin rattled on. "You can install a transport unit in the closet for your morning and evening commute to realtime. It's a steal. What's your rail commute cost from Yuba City?"

I didn't need much convincing. "I'll take it."

"Two year lease," he said. "Sign here." Then he brandished an additional piece of paper. "This too."

"What is it?" I was Pallas Athena again, staring down suspiciously onto the sweaty center of his bald spot. "If this is a pet restriction clause, I'm going to protest. Your ad didn't say anything about it. I've got a cat." I didn't bother to mention that I kept MacHeath at work—there was more room for him there than at home. But wherever—and whenever—I went, he went.

"Sure, sure," Raskin said. "You can keep your kitty as long as you pay a deposit. This is just your standard noninterference contract."

"Noninterference contract?"

He looked at me like I was stupid. It rarely happens. When it does, I don't like it.

"You know," he said, and recited in a sing-song voice: "Don't change the past or the past will change you. The time laws. You lawyers understand this kind of thing. You, and you alone, are responsible for any dislocation of past events, persons or things, et cetera et cetera. Read the small print and sign."

A sudden chill teased my upper vertebrae. Noninterference? Well, why would I interfere with the past? The morning sunlight streamed in through the big window in the front room. High clouds scudded over the hillside. I shook off the shivers and signed.

A week later, I took up residence, hanging my tiny collection of photos, putting down rugs, and glorying in my privacy. MacHeath didn't care much for the transport effect but he approved of his new improved situation. After sniffing every corner of the place, he made an appointment with the sun and spent the rest of the day following it from window to window.

Life's pendulum swung me between work and home,

uptime and downtime, in an easy arc. Thanks to the transport I could leave the house at any time of day and return a moment later. This made for a great deal of quality time, spent snuggled up with MacHeath on the red corduroy sofa, and on my own in the heart of a smaller, cozier city. I wandered gratefully along the waterfront, bought sourdough bread and lingered over coffee in North Beach jazz clubs. Everywhere was color and life and music: garish psychedelic posters printed in what I think were called Day-Glo inks, announcing musical groups with odd names like the Jackson's Airplane. Shaggy-haired, brightly dressed, childishly friendly people piled in casual groups on the street, in buses, and in the old houses lining Haight Street and Asbury. I fell in love with the past—at least with San Francisco's past.

Uptime, at work, they asked me how I could stand to watch history go by without comment.

"Don't you ever want to warn somebody?" said Bill Hawthorne, the senior partner. "Don't you ever want to call up Martin Luther King or Robert Kennedy and say, 'Stay away from hotel balconies,' or 'Don't go in the kitchen'?"

"Shame on you, Bill," I said. "You know that's against the law."

In fact, I watched, agog, as the alarming parade of assassinations and demonstrations took place. History on the hoof. I began to see why people got hooked on the past. It's a much realer form of video.

And during the year I lived in 1968, Martin Luther King was assassinated in Memphis, and Robert Kennedy in Los Angeles. And somebody moved into the downstairs apartment.

It had remained empty for so long that I'd begun to think of it as part of my domain. Oh, I knew that some uptime renter would probably appear one morning, strangely dressed, keeping to him or herself. I'd seen one or two folks in the neighborhood whom I suspected of being residential refugees from uptime like me, but I had avoided them, and they, me. We all played the game with discretion.

I was out of town, uptime, when the people downstairs moved in. The first sign I had of their presence was the primal beat of rock music reverberating through my lovingly stained floorboards, occasionally punctuated by the high manic whine of amplified electric guitars. Boom-boom-bah. Boom-boom-bah. For five hours I considered various legal strategies showing just cause for murder. Sorry, Your Honor, but it was self-defense. Their music made me psychotic and if I hadn't stopped it, the entire neighborhood would have been at risk and all of history would have been changed so I had to do it, don't you see?

About three in the morning, somebody turned off the music.

The next day, as I was blearily putting out my garbage, I met my neighbor. He was sitting in the backyard, smoking a sweet-smelling cigarette. The pungent smoke curled up above his head in lazy circles. Long wavy blond hair fell to the middle of his back. He was wearing jeans and a brown suede vest but aside from that his interest in clothing seemed minimal. His toenails were black with grime.

"Name's Duffy," he said. He jerked his head at a hefty woman in a long muslin skirt and peasant blouse who stood in the doorway, smiling spacily at me. "That's Parvati." Parvati's strawberry-blond hair was gathered into two fat braids that fell past her knees. She was wearing metal-rimmed eyeglasses whose lenses flashed prismatic reflections on the grass. I stared, fascinated. I'd forgotten that in this era people used external devices to correct their vision.

The head jerked again, this time toward an urchin with

a dirty face, stringy blond hair, and big blue eyes. "Our kid, Rainbow."

Rainbow wiped her nose against the back of her hand and stared at me. All three of them stared at me, at my burr haircut, severe business suit, dark shoes, glossy briefcase. I realized that, to my new hippie neighbors, I must have looked like some kind of strange male impersonator.

"Hi," I said. "Nice to meet you." I began to climb the stairs to my apartment.

"Far out," Duffy said. He was staring at my briefcase. "You some kind of secretary or actress or something?"

"Something." I was through my door and had closed it behind me before he could ask anything else.

Weekends I took long walks through Golden Gate Park. It was green, beautiful, and filled with people who were probably Duffy's relatives.

"Peace," they said, and I nodded.

"Love."

I smiled.

"Could you lay a little bread on me, please?"

I shook my head and walked away, confused—did I look like a baker?

For trips to the grocery store I bought a lime-green Volkswagen Beetle—the classic—with a dented purple fender, third-hand, and after some abrupt bucking rides down the block, mastered the quaint antique stick shift and clutch.

As for clothing, well, I found used jeans in the neighborhood Army-Navy store and a loose-fitting top of muslin tie-dyed pink and red. The shirt itched a bit when I wore it and turned my underwear gray-pink in the washer, but it was good camouflage. With a red bandana wrapped around my head to cover my short hair, I almost managed to look inconspicuous.

I quickly learned my neighbors' schedule: they stayed up all night vibrating my apartment with their music and slept all day. Apparently Rainbow didn't go to school. Once, I glanced out my window to see her staring up hungrily at my place. I tried not to see her. I really tried.

One night, late, as the guitars whined and I was about to switch on my noise dampers, there was a knock at the door.

"Who is it?"

"Duffy."

I opened the door a crack. "What's up?"

Lids at half-mast, he peered at me and smiled muzzily. "Thought you might want to come to a party." He smiled muzzily.

"No thanks. I need my sleep."

"C'mon, don't be such a hard lady," he said. "Parvati's gone to see her folks. Just you 'n me."

I almost laughed. Men rarely looked at me the way he was looking at me now. While I might have welcomed it from one or two of the attorneys I knew in realtime, I was not interested in this dirty, lazy, antediluvian jerk.

"That's too small a party for me. No thanks."

"Hey, Parvati won't mind. Whatever goes down is cool with her."

"Congratulations. Hope she knows a good lawyer when things start to warm up." I shut the door.

The apartment was blissfully quiet after that—in fact, I didn't hear Duffy's music for at least a week. Didn't see him or Rainbow, or any of their friends except for once, when I was putting out the garbage, Rainbow appeared at the front window, pressed her little hands against the pane, and stared out at me. I smiled. She didn't smile back. When she turned to walk away, I saw that her hands had left dirty smudges on the glass.

I spent a week in realtime on an important case, and when I got back, discovered that I had new neighbors.

Duffy and his family were gone. In their place were two skinny guys in their twenties with long dark hair, beards, and the same interest in the same kind of loud guitar music. They barely acknowledged my presence, which was fine.

One night, late, after my noise dampers had cycled and shut down, I heard a child crying. It was the high, keening, hopeless sound of one who doesn't expect to be comforted. The kind of sound no child should ever have to make, any time or place.

I got out of bed, listened, heard it again, opened the front door. Then I couldn't hear it any more. The night was silent save for the creaking floorboards under my feet. Was I imagining things? MacHeath yawned elaborately as I got back into bed and made a sleepy inquisitive sound.

"It's nothing," I said. "Bad dream."

The next night I heard it again—the sound of a child crying hopelessly, long after everybody else in the world was asleep.

Two days later, I saw her.

Rainbow was standing in the backyard, weaving back and forth. Her eyes were half-closed as though she were stoned.

I took a step toward her. "Honey, are you all right?"

She opened her eyes. The pupils were massive, almost engulfing the blue irises.

"Rainbow, where's your mommy?"

"Mommy?" She looked at me, her face crumpled into tears, and she ran into the house.

I didn't hear the crying again after that.

But I did meet one of Rainbow's babysitters. He was waiting outside one morning as I brought out the garbage.

"Hey, sister."

I ignored him, thinking about torts, about deed restrictions. About Rainbow.

Suddenly there was a hand on my shoulder. "Hey. You deaf?" Another hand attached itself to my ass.

I leaned toward him. He came closer. I grabbed his arm and, ducking, pulled hard. He landed headfirst, sprawled among the garbage cans. For a moment, I thought that I'd killed him. Then he groaned and rolled over onto his side. He lay there, stunned, peering up at me.

"Hands off," I said, enunciating carefully. "I don't know you. I don't want to." I kicked the can beside his head to emphasize the point. He winced and nodded.

After that, he left me alone. But I came home one night to find that the door to my apartment had been vandalized: somebody had tried to force the lock. Good thing I'd brought a security sealer from uptime and installed it. Whoever had attempted the deed had contented themselves with carving the word "bitch" into the wood just above the doorknob.

Don't you forget it.

I left the graffito exactly where it was.

The crying at night resumed. I began to wonder if I should call somebody. But who? Where were Duffy and Parvati? Were they really even her parents? And what kind of child welfare agencies were available in the 1960s in San Francisco? Could Rainbow hope for anything better than what she had right now? Besides, the time laws were explicit: No interference.

I didn't know what to do, so I waited. She who hesitates, loses.

I transported home one night at eleven o'clock into a dark smoke-filled apartment. Fire. Where? I couldn't find the source. I felt the floor—hot, too hot. No time to waste. I called the fire department, grabbed MacHeath, and was halfway out the door before I remembered the transport unit.

Cursing, I disconnected it, threw it into my briefcase, and ran down the stairs, arms full of squirming orange cat.

By the time I got to the pavement, the lower apartment was completely engulfed, the flames roaring. As the upper story caught I watched the flames dance up the curtains and part my front window. Imagined them licking and consuming my rugs, quilts, clothing. My life. I could hear the deafening screams of sirens as firetrucks raced down the street.

Lights came on in houses up and down the block and sleepy faces peered through windows, through open doors. Tears—from smoke or fear, I don't know which—ran down my face to soak MacHeath's fur. He struggled furiously, trying to get away from the strange sounds, the people, the dark. Finally I stowed him in my Beetle.

Firemen kicked in the door downstairs and played water from a rubber hose into the inferno. It might have all been interestingly antique if it hadn't been happening to me.

Those firemen did good work. Within an hour the flames had subsided. The charred timbers sent plumes of smoke high into the air, but the fire was dead.

Shivering, I watched as the bodies were carried out: blackened beyond recognition, more like burned logs than people. Nine corpses, nine flaking, reeking corpses. And one more, smaller than the rest. The last to be brought out. Rainbow.

"Found her by the back window." The fireman's face was blackened, his voice hoarse. "I think she was trying to open it and get out. But the damned thing was painted shut." Gently he set her down. "Jesus, I've got two at home around her age. Damned shame."

"Yeah." I didn't trust myself to say more. Quickly as I could, I turned around and got out of there. I spent the night at a neighbor's house. The next morning, I waited until my Good Samaritan had left for work at the shipyards, then I plugged in the transport, set it for autoretrieve, and took MacHeath back to realtime, right into Jerry Raskin's office.

"You son of a bitch!" I grabbed him by the lapel of his cheap silver coat. "You knew that place was going to burn down when you rented it to me."

"What?" He stared at my soot-stained face and there was real fear in his eyes. "I had no idea. Chrissy, you've got to believe me."

"I shook him until his teeth chattered. "You are required by law to do a time sweep in order to alert tenants to potential dangers."

"I did. I did. The records came up clean. The former owner must have lied to the insurance company."

"Reckless endangerment," I said. "How does that sound, for starters? How would you like to be charged with a felony?"

Raskin's eyes were huge with terror now. I put him down and he backed away from me until the desk separated us. "Now let's just calm down," he said. "You look okay to me. You got out all right, didn't you? I'll refund your deposit. I swear, I didn't know."

I decided not to waste my energy. Raskin wasn't worth it. Back I went to Yuba City. Found a studio apartment that almost had room for me and MacHeath. Tried to forget.

By day it was easy. San Francisco put on her best show for me: The Golden Gate Bridge glistened in the sunlight. The bay was dotted by solar-powered sailboats. The cable cars' recorded bells rang. The scent of coffee and chocolate wafted up from the power-blowers installed at Ghiradelli Square. My work was blessedly absorbing.

But at night my dreams were filled with little girls with dirty faces and large blue eyes, terrified little girls with their hands and faces pressed against a wall of unyielding glass as flames raced up behind them.

"Help," they cried. "Help me, Mommy!".

"Help me, Daddy!"

"Help me, Christine!."

On my way to work one morning, I glanced through the window as we pulled into Powell Station. Another train had come in on the parallel track, and in it a small girl with big blue eyes stared at me with great seriousness. Her hands were pressed against the window. I looked down at my net paper. When I looked up again, she was gone. But two small handprints smudged the glass where she had been.

That night I went back.

I went back to 1968 and stood outside the house and watched as the fire gained strength. Watched, paralyzed, as choking smoke billowed upward. Saw a woman—me—peer out the upstairs window with fierce, frightened eyes as she held an orange cat in her arms. Was that severe face really mine? I didn't have time to wonder.

I saw a flash at the downstairs window. A small face, eyes huge. Rainbow, struggling with the latch. The smoke filled the room behind her. She beat against the window, coughing.

I moved, then. Picked up a rock.

The fire engines howled in the distance.

I saw myself coming down the stairs and darted to the side, out of sight, quickly, quickly, until I knew that I was putting MacHeath in the car with my back to the house.

Awkwardly, then, I changed history. Smashed the window. Reached through jagged glass that scratched my hands and arms, grabbed the child, and pulled her through. The flames chased her right up to the edge of the sill, but they couldn't have her. No. Not this time.

Rainbow clung to me, sobbing, and I rocked her gently.

"It's okay, honey," I whispered. My hands smeared blood and soot on her face. I didn't care. She was alive.

When she had calmed enough to fall into an exhausted sleep, I handed her to a neighbor and crept away. I didn't want anybody to notice that there were two of me there.

Back in realtime, I took along shower, bandaged my wounds, and had two glasses of smooth old scotch, vintage 1991.

The next morning, I called in a favor from Jimmy Wu, keeper of the SFPD database.

"Her name's Rainbow."

Good old Jimmy searched for her, beginning in late 1968. He looked and looked for Rainbow. He never found a trace of her.

"Shit, Chrissy," he said. "They were all called Rainbow that year. "Or Morning Star or Peacelove. I need a real name, like Tammy or Katie or Sarah, and a social security number. A last name would be really nice."

So the trail fizzled out in the backyard of a smoldering house on Potrero Hill, fifty-six years ago. And nothing anomalous ever happened that I could detect—not one ripple of difference in the timeline. MacHeath didn't turn green, I didn't grow wings. San Francisco glittered as always in the chilly summer sunlight. I guess some people are just throwaway people. They don't make any difference at all, in any time.

Did she survive to adulthood? Or did she overdose in some gas station bathroom near Reseda when she was twelve? Did I break every time law on the books merely to postpone her fate? I don't know—but I do know one thing. I sleep better now.

The rhythms of routine distracted me. My cuts healed. My memories receded to a comfortable distance.

About three days ago, I got a call from a real estate agent in the Castro.

"Christine? I got your name from Jerry Raskin."

"I'm not interested in downtime apartments."

She laughed a breathy laugh. "Oh, I only deal in real-time estate. And he got two places I want to show you. The first is a beauty: a three-bedroom apartment in the Potrero Hill area. Upstairs and down. Used to be a two-family unit. You've got to see it to believe it."

Everything inside me stilled to a whisper. I could see the window again, that window with its small dirty fingerprints.

"Hello? Hello?"

Somehow I found my voice. "I've seen it."

"But that's impossible. This apartment just came on the market."

"Believe me, I've seen it. In fact, you might say that I've spent way too much time on it already." And then I hung up.

TIME TRAP

CHARLES HARNESS

The maddening concept of the time loop, an individual or world trapped in eternal recurrence probably finds its earliest example in Heinlein's (1941) *By His Bootstraps* but achieves a kind of intricacy and bewildering force in this 1948 story, Charles L. Harness's first published work. This is perhaps the most rigorous and testing treatment of the theme and has been enormously influential, not only in literary terms (see the Phillip K. Dick story in this volume), but in film. *Groundhog Day* or *Being John Malkovich* owe plenty to this one.

Harness, a patent attorney, retired about 15 years ago and, writing prolifically in retirement, published a small and influential body of work early; his novel *The Rose* is much admired. He wrote virtually no fiction from the early 1950s until the late 1960s, but his body of work now comprises several novels and long short stories, and is much admired. "TIME TRAP" and his first novel, *The Paradox Men* (1949), Harness has written, were the consequence of his need for money at the time; having money he had no real impetus for too long. Alas.

*T*he Great Ones themselves never agreed whether the events constituting Troy's cry for help had a beginning. But the warning signal did have an end. The Great Ones saw to that. Those of the Great Ones who claim a beginning for the story date it with the expulsion of the evil Sathanas from the Place of Suns, when he fled, horribly wounded, spiraling evasively inward, through sterechronia without number, until, exhausted, he sank and lay hidden in the crystallizing magma of a tiny new planet at the galactic rim.

General Blade sometimes felt that leading a resistance movement was far exceeding his debt to decent society and that one day soon he would allow his peaceful nature to override his indignant pursuit of justice. Killing a man, even a very bad man, without a trial, went against his grain. He sighed and rapped on the table.

"As a result of Blogshak's misappropriation of funds voted to fight the epidemic," he announced, "the death toll this morning reached over one hundred thousand. Does the

Assassination Subcommittee have a recommendation?"

A thin-lipped man rose from the gathering. "The Provinarch ignored our warning," he said rapidly. "This subcommittee, as you all know, some days ago set an arbitrary limit of one hundred thousand deaths. Therefore this subcommittee now recommends that its plan for killing the Provinarch be adopted at once. Tonight is very favorable for our plan, which, incidentally, requires a married couple. We have thoroughly catasynthesized the four bodyguards who will be with him on this shift and have provided irresistible scent and sensory stimuli for the woman. The probability for its success insofar as assassination is concerned is about seventy-eight per cent; the probability of escape of our killers is sixty-two per cent. We regard these probabilities as favorable. The Legal Subcommittee will take it from there."

Another man arose. "We have retained Mr. Poole, who is with us tonight." He nodded gravely to a withered little man beside him. "Although Mr. Poole has been a member of the bar but a short time, and although his pre-legal life—some seventy years of it—remains a mystery which he does not explain, our catasynthesis laboratory indicates that his legal knowledge is profound. More important, his persuasive powers, tested with a trial group of twelve professional evaluators, sort of a rehearsal for a possible trial, border on hypnosis. He has also suggested an excellent method of disposing of the corpse to render identification difficult. According to Mr. Poole, if the assassinators are caught, the probability of escaping the devitalizing chamber is fifty-three per cent."

"Mr. Chairman!"

General Blade turned toward the new speaker, who stood quietly several rows away. The man seemed to reflect a gray inconspicuousness, relieved only by a gorgeous rosebud in his lapel. Gray suit, gray eyes, graying temples. On closer examination, one detected an edge of flashing blue in the grayness. The eyes no longer seemed softly unobtrusive, but icy, and the firm mouth and jutting chin seemed polished steel. General Blade had observed this phenomenon dozens of times, but he never-tired of it.

"You have the floor, Major Troy," he said.

"I, and perhaps other League officers, would like to know more about Mr. Poole," came the quiet, faintly metallic voice. "He is not a member of the League, and yet Legal and Assassination welcome him in their councils. I think we should be provided some assurance that he has no associations with the Provinarch's administration. One traitor could sell the lives of all of us."

The Legal spokesman arose again. "Major Troy's objections are in some degree merited. We don't know who Mr. Poole is. His mind is absolutely impenetrable to telepathic probes. His fingerprint and eye vein patterns are a little obscure. Our attempts at identification"—he laughed sheepishly—"always key out to yourself, major. An obvious impossibility. So far as the world is concerned, Mr. Poole is an old man who might have been born yesterday! All we know of him is his willingness to co-operate with us to the best of his ability—which, I can assure you, is tremendous. The catasynthesizer has established his sympathetic attitude beyond doubt. Don't forget, too, that he could be charged as a principal in this assassination and devitalized himself. On the whole, he is our man. If our killers are caught, we must use him."

Troy turned and studied the little lawyer with narrowing eyes; Poole's face seemed oddly familiar. The old man returned the gaze sardonically, with a faint suggestion of a smile.

"Time is growing short, major," urged the Assassination chairman. "The Poole matter has already received the attention of qualified League investigators. It is not a proper matter for discussion at this time. If you are satisfied with the arrangements, will you and Mrs. Troy please assemble the childless married couples on your list? The men can draw lots from the fish bowl on the side table. The red ball decides." He eyed Troy expectantly.

Still standing, Troy looked down at the woman in the adjacent seat. Her lips were half-parted, her black eyes somber pools as she looked up at her husband.

"Well, Ann?" he telepathed.

Her eyes seemed to look through him and far beyond. "He will make you draw the red ball, Jon," she murmured, trancelike. "Then he will die, and I will die. But Jon Troy will never die. Never die. Never die. Nev—"

"Wake up, Ann!" Troy shook her by the shoulder. To the puzzled faces about them, he explained quickly, "My wife is something of a seeress." He 'pathed again: "Who is *he?*"

Ann Troy brushed the black hair from her brow slowly. "It's all confused. *He* is someone in this room—" She started to get up.

"Sit down, dear," said Troy gently. "If I'm to draw the red ball, I may as well cut this short." He slid past her into the aisle, strode to the side table, and thrust his hand into the hole in the box sitting there.

Every eye was on him.

His hand hit the invisible fish bowl with its dozen-odd plastic balls. Inside the bowl, he touched the little spheres at random while he studied the people in the room. All old friends, except—Poole. That tantalizing face. Poole was now staring like the rest, except that beads of sweat were forming on his forehead.

Troy swirled the balls around the bowl; the muffled clatter was audible throughout the room. He felt his fingers

CHARLES HARNESS

close on one. His hands were perspiring freely. With an effort he forced himself to drop it. He chose another, and
looked at Poole. The latter was frowning. Troy could not
bring his hand out of the bowl. His right arm seemed par-
tially paralyzed. He dropped the ball and rolled the mass
around again. Poole was now smiling. Troy hesitated a moment, then picked a ball from the center of the bowl. It felt
slightly moist. He pulled it out, looked at it grimly, and held
it up for all to see.

"Just 'path that!" whispered the jail warden reverently to
the night custodian.

"You know I can't telepath," said the latter grumpily.
"What are they saying?"

"Not a word all night. They seem to be taking a sym-
posium of the best piano concertos since maybe the twentieth century. Was Chopin twentieth or twenty-first?
Anyhow, they're up to the twenty-third now, with Darnoval.
Troy reproduces the orchestra and his wife does the piano.
You'd think she had fifty years to live instead of five
minutes."

"Both seem nice people," ruminated the custodian. "If
they hadn't killed the Provinarch, maybe they'd have become famous 'pathic musicians. She had a lousy lawyer. She
could have got off with ten years sleep if he'd half tried."
He pushed some papers across the desk. "I've had the chamber checked. Want to look over the readings?"

The warden scanned them rapidly. "Potential difference,
eight million; drain rate, ninety vital units/minute; estimated period of consciousness, thirty seconds; estimated
durance to nonrecovery point, four minutes; estimated durance to legal death, five minutes." He initialed the front
sheet. "That's fine. When I was younger they called it the
'vitality drain chamber.' Drain rate was only two v.u./min.

Took an hour to drain them to unconsciousness. Pretty hard on the condemned people. Well, I'd better go officiate."

When Jon and Ann Troy finished the Darnoval concerto they were silent for a few moments, exchanging simply a flow of wordless, unfathomable perceptions between their cells. Troy was unable to disguise a steady beat of gloom. "We'll have to go along with Poole's plan," he 'pathed, "though I confess I don't know what his idea is. Take your capsule now."

His mind registered the motor impulses of her medulla as she removed the pill from its concealment under her arm-pit and swallowed it. Troy then perceived her awareness of her cell door opening, of grim men and women about her. Motion down corridors. Then the room. A clanging of doors. A titanic effort to hold their fading contact. One last de-spairing communion, loving, tender.

Then nothing.

He was still sitting with his face buried in his hands, when the guards came to take him to his own trial that morning.

"This murder," announced the Peoples' advocate to the twelve evaluators, "this crime of taking the life of our be-loved Provinarch Blogshak, this heinous deed—is the most horrible thing that has happened in Niork in my lifetime. The creature charged with this crime"—he pointed an ac-cusing finger at the prisoner's box—"Jon Troy has been psyched and has been adjudged integrated at a preliminary hearing. Even his attorney"—here bowing ironically to a beady-eyed little man at counsels' table—"waived the de-fense of nonintegration."

Poole continued to regard the Peoples' advocate with bitter weariness, as though he had gone through this a thou-sand times and knew every word that each of them was going to say. The prisoner seemed oblivious to the advocate, the twelve evaluators, the judge, and the crowded courtroom. Troy's mind was blanked out. The dozen or so educated telepaths in the room could detect only a deep beat of sadness.

"I shall prove," continued the inexorable advocate, "that this monster engaged our late Provinarch in conversation in a downtown bar, surreptitiously placed a lethal dose of *skon* in the Provinarch's glass, and that Troy and his wife—who, incidentally, paid the extreme penalty herself early this—"

"Objection!" cried Poole, springing to his feet. The defendant, not his wife, is now on trial."

"Sustained," declared the judge. "The advocate may not imply to the evaluators that the possible guilt of the present defendant is in any way determined by the proven guilt of any past defendant. The evaluators must ignore that implication. Proceed, advocate."

"Thank you, your honor." He turned again to the evaluators' box and scanned them with a critical eye. "I shall prove that the prisoner and the late Mrs. Troy, after poisoning Provinarch Blogshak, carried his corpse into their sedan, and that they proceeded then to a deserted area on the outskirts of the city. Unknown to them they were pursued by four of the mayor's bodyguards, who, alas, had been lured aside at the bar by Mrs. Troy. Psychometric determinations taken by the police laboratory will be offered to prove it was the prisoner's intention to dismember the corpse and burn it to hinder the work of the police in tracing the crime to him. He had got only as far as severing the head when the guards' ship swooped up and hovered overhead. He tried to run back to his own ship, where his wife was waiting, but the guards blanketed the area with a low-voltage stun."

The advocate paused. He was not getting the reaction

in the evaluators he deserved, but he knew the fault was not his. He was puzzled; he would have to conclude quickly.

"Gentlemen," he continued gravely; "for this terrible thing, the Province demands the life of Jon Troy. The monster must enter the chamber tonight." He bowled to the judge and returned to counsels' table.

The judge acknowledged the retirement and turned to Poole. "Does the defense wish to make an opening statement?"

"The defense reiterates its plea of 'not guilty' and makes no other statement," grated the old man.

There was a buzz around the advocates' end of the table. An alert defense with a weak case always opened to the evaluators. Who was this Poole? What did he have? Had they missed a point? The prosecution was committed now. They'd have to start with their witnesses.

The advocate arose. "The prosecution offers as witness Mr. Fonstile."

"Mr. Fonstile!" called the clerk.

A burly, resentful-looking man blundered his way from the benches and walked up to the witness box and was sworn in.

Poole was on his feet. "May it please the court!" he croaked.

The judge eyed him in surprise. "Have you an objection, Mr. Poole?"

"No objection, your honor," rasped the little man, without expression. "I would only like to say that the testimony of this witness, the bartender in the Shawn Hotel, is probably offered by my opponent to prove facts which the defense readily admits, namely, that the witness observed Mrs. Troy entice the four bodyguards of the deceased to another part of the room, that the present defendant surreptitiously placed a powder in the wine of the deceased, that the deceased drank the wine and collapsed, and was carried out of the room by the defendant, followed by his wife." He bowed to the judge and sat down.

The judge was nonplussed. "Mr. Poole, do you understand that you are responsible for the defense of this prisoner, and that he is charged with a capital offense?"

"That is my understanding, your honor."

"Then if prosecution is agreeable, and wishes to elicit no further evidence from the witness, he will be excused."

The advocate looked puzzled, but called the next witness, Dr. Warkon, of the Provincial Police Laboratory. Again Poole was on his feet. This time the whole court eyed him expectantly. Even Troy stared at him in fascination.

"May it please the court," came the now-familiar monotone, "the witness called by the opposition probably expects to testify that the deceased's finger prints were found on the wineglass in question, that traces of deceased's saliva were identified in the liquid content of the glass, and that a certain quantity of *skon* was found in the wine remaining in the glass."

"And one other point, Mr. Poole," added the Peoples' advocate. "Dr. Warkon was going to testify that death from *skon* poisoning normally occurs within thirty seconds, owing to syncope. Does the defense concede that?"

"Yes."

"The witness is then excused," ordered the judge.

The prisoner straightened up. Troy studied his attorney curiously. The mysterious Poole with the tantalizing face, the man so highly recommended by the League, had let Ann go to her death with the merest shadow of a defense. And now he seemed even to state the prosecution's case rather than defend the prisoner.

Nowhere in the courtroom did Troy see a League member. But then, it would be folly for General Blade to attempt his rescue. That would attract unwelcome attention to the League.

He had been abandoned, and was on his own. Many League officers had been killed by Blogshak's men, but rarely in the devitalizing chamber. It was a point of honor to die weapon in hand. His first step would be to seize a blaster from one of the guards, use the judge as a shield, and try to escape through the judge's chambers. He would wait until he was put on the stand. It shouldn't be long, considering how Poole was cutting corners.

The advocate was conferring with his assistants. "What's Poole up to?" one of them asked, "If he is going on this far, why not get him to admit all the facts constituting a prima facie case: Malice, intent to kill, and all that?"

The advocate's eyes gleamed. "I think I know what he's up to now," he exulted. "I believe he's forgotten an elementary theorem of criminal law. He's going to admit everything, then demand we produce Blogshak's corpse. He must know it was stolen from the bodyguards when their ship landed at the port. No corpse, no murder, he'll say. But you don't need a corpse to prove murder. We'll hang him with his own rope!" He arose and addressed the judge.

"May it please the court, the prosecution would like to ask if the defense will admit certain other facts which I stand ready to prove."

The judge frowned. "The prisoner pleaded not guilty. Therefore the court will not permit any admission of the defense to the effect that the prisoner did kill the deceased, unless he wants to change his plea." He looked inquiringly at Poole.

"I understand, your honor," said Poole. "May I hear

what facts the learned prosecutor wishes me to accede to?"

For a moment the prosecutor studied his enigmatic antagonist like a master swordsman.

"First, the prisoner administered a lethal dose of *skon* to the deceased with malice aforethought, and with intent to kill. Do you concede that?"

"Yes."

"And that the deceased collapsed within a few seconds and was carried from the room by the defendant and his wife?"

"We agree to that."

"And that the prisoner carried the body to the city outskirts and there decapitated it?"

"I have already admitted that."

The twelve evaluators, a selected group of trained experts in the estimation of probabilities, followed this unusual procedure silently.

"Then your honor, the prosecution rests." The advocate felt dizzy, out of his depth. He felt he had done all that was necessary to condemn the prisoner. Yet Poole seemed absolutely confident, almost bored.

"Do you have any witnesses, Mr. Poole," queried the judge.

"I will ask the loan of Dr. Warkon, if the Peoples' advocate will be so kind," replied the little man.

"I'm willing." The advocate was beginning to look harassed. Dr. Warkon was sworn in.

"Dr. Warkon, did not the psychometer show that the prisoner intended to kill Blogshak in the tavern and decapitate him at the edge of the city?"

"Yes, sir."

"Was, in fact, the deceased dead when he was carried from the hotel?"

"He had enough *skon* in him to have killed forty people."

"Please answer the question."

"Well, I don't know. I presume he was dead. As an expert, looking at all the evidence, I should say he was dead. If he didn't die in the room, he was certainly dead a few seconds later."

"Did you feel his pulse at any time, or make any examination to determine the time of death?"

"Well, no."

Now, thought the advocate, comes the no corpse, no murder. If he tries that, I've got him.

But Poole was not to be pushed.

"Would you say the deceased was dead when the prisoner's ship reached the city limits?"

"Absolutely!"

"When you, as police investigator, examined the scene of the decapitation, what did you find?"

"The place where the corpse had lain was easily identified. Depressions in the sand marked the back, head, arms, and legs. The knife was lying where the prisoner dropped it. Marks of landing gear of the prisoner's ship were about forty feet away. Lots of blood, of course."

"Where was the blood?"

"About four feet away from the head, straight out."

Poole let the statement sink in, then:

"Dr. Warkon, as a doctor of medicine, do you realize the significance of what you have just said?"

The witness gazed at his inquisitor as though hypnotized. "Four feet . . . jugular spurt—" he muttered to no one. He stared in wonder, first at the withered, masklike face before him, then at the advocate, then at the judge. "Your honor, the deceased's heart was still beating when the prisoner first applied the knife. The poison didn't kill him!"

An excited buzz resounded through the courtroom.

Poole turned to the judge. "Your honor, I move for a summary judgment of acquittal."

The advocate sprang to his feet, wordless.

"Mr. Poole," remonstrated the judge, "your behavior this morning has been extraordinary, to say the least. On the bare fact that the prisoner killed with a knife instead of with poison, as the evidence at first indicated, you ask summary acquittal. The court will require an explanation."

"Your honor"—there was a ghost of a smile flitting about the prim, tired mouth—"to be guilty of a crime, a man must intend to commit a crime. There must be a *mens rea*, as the classic expression goes. The act and the intent must coincide. Here they did not. Jon Troy intended to kill the Provinarch in the bar of the Shawn Hotel. He gave him poison, but Blogshak didn't die of it. Certainly up to the time the knife was thrust into Blogshak's throat, Troy may have been guilty of assault and kidnapping, but not murder. If there was any murder, it must have been at the instant he decapitated the deceased. Yet what was his intent on the city outskirts? He wanted to mutilate a corpse. His intent was not to murder, but to mutilate. We have the act, but not the intent—no *mens rea*. Therefore the act was not murder, but simply mutilation of a corpse—a crime punishable by fine or imprisonment, but not death."

Troy's mind was whirling. This incredible, dusty little man had freed him.

"But Troy's a murderer!" shouted the advocate, his face white. "Sophisms can't restore a life!"

"The court does not recognize the advocate!" said the judge harshly. "Cut those remarks from the record," he directed the scanning clerk. "This court is guided by the principles of common law descended from ancient England. The learned counsel for the defense has stated those principles correctly. Homicide is not murder if there is no intent to kill. And mere intent to kill is not murder if the poison doesn't take effect. This is a strange, an unusual case, and it is revolting for me to do what I have to do. I acquit the prisoner."

"Your honor!" cried the advocate. Receiving recognition, he proceeded. "This . . . this felon should not escape completely. He should not be permitted to make a travesty of the law. His own counsel admits he has broken the statutes on kidnaping, assault, and mutilation. The evaluators can at least return a verdict of guilty on those counts."

"I am just as sorry as you are," replied the judge, "but I don't find those counts in the indictment. You should have included them."

"If you release him, your honor, I'll re-arrest him and frame a new indictment."

"This court will not act on it. It is contrary to the Constitution of this Province for a person to be prosecuted twice on the same charge or on a charge which should have been included in the original indictment. The Peoples' advocate is estopped from taking further action on this case. This is the final ruling of this court." He took a drink of water, wrapped his robes about him, and strode through the rear of the courtroom to his chambers.

Troy and Poole, the saved and the savior, eyed one another with the same speculative look of their first meeting.

Poole opened the door of the 'copter parked outside the Judiciary Building and motioned for Troy to enter. Troy froze in the act of climbing in.

A man inside the cab, with a face like a claw, was pointing a blaster at his chest.

The man was Blogshak!

Two men recognizable as the Provinarch's bodyguards suddenly materialized behind Troy.

"Don't give us any trouble, major," murmured Poole easily. "Better get in."

The moment Troy was pushed into the subterranean suite he sensed Ann was alive—drugged insensate still, but alive, and near. This knowledge suppressed momentarily Blogshak's incredible existence and Poole's betrayal. Concealing his elation, he turned to Poole.

"I should like to see my wife."

Poole motioned silently to one of the guards, who pulled back sliding doors. Beyond a glass panel, which was actually a transparent wall of a tile room, Ann lay on a high white metal bed. A nurse was on the far side of the bed, exchanging glances with Poole. At some unseen signal from him the nurse swabbed Ann's left arm and thrust a syringe into it.

A shadow crossed Troy's face. "What is the nurse doing?"

"In a moment Mrs. Troy will awaken. Whether she stays awake depends on you."

"On me? What do you mean?"

"Major, what you are about to learn can best be demonstrated rather than described. Sharg, the rabbit!"

The bettle-browed man opened a large enamel pan on the table. A white rabbit eased its way out, wrinkling its nose gingerly. Sharg lifted a cleaver from the table. There was a flash of metal, a spurt of blood, and the rabbit's head fell to the floor. Sharg picked it up by the ears and held it up expectantly. The eyes were glazed almost shut. The rabbit's body lay limp in the pan. At a word from Poole, Sharg carefully replaced the severed head, pressing it gently to the bloody neck stub. Within seconds the nose twitched, the eyes blinked, and the ears perked up. The animal shook itself vigorously, scratched once or twice at the bloody ring around its neck, then began nibbling at a head of lettuce in the pan.

Troy's mind was racing. The facts were falling in line. All at once everything made sense. With knowledge came utmost wariness. The next move was up to Poole, who was examining with keen eyes the effect of his demonstration on Troy.

"Major, I don't know how much you have surmised, but at least you cannot help realizing that life, even highly organized vertebrate life, is resistant to death in your presence."

Troy folded his arms but volunteered nothing. He was finally getting a glimpse of the vast and secret power supporting the Provinarch's tyranny, long suspected by the League but never verified.

"You could not be expected to discover this marvelous property in yourself except by the wildest chance," continued Poole. "As a matter of fact, our staff discovered it only when Blogshak and his hysterical guards reported to us, after your little escapade. But we have been on the lookout for your type for years. Several mutants with this chacteristic have been predicted by our probability geneticists for this century, but you are the first known to us—really perhaps the only one in existence. One is all we need.

"As a second and final test of your power, we decided to try the effect of your aura on a person in the devitalizing chamber. For that reason we permitted Mrs. Troy to be condemned, when we could easily have prevented it. As you now know, your power sustained your wife's life against a strong drain of potential. At my instruction she drugged herself in her cell simply to satisfy the doctor who checked her pulse and reflexes afterwards. When the staff—my employers—examined her here, they were convinced that you had the mutation they were looking for, and we put the finishing touches on our plans to save you from the chamber."

Granting I have some strange biotic influence, thought Troy, still, something's wrong. He says his bunch became interested in me *after* my attempt on Blogshak. *But Poole was at the assassination meeting!* What is his independent interest?

Poole studied him curiously. "I doubt that you realize what tremendous efforts have been made to insure your presence here. For the past two weeks the staff has hired several thousand persons to undermine the critical faculties of the four possible judges and nine hundred evaluators who might have heard your case. Judge Gallon, for example, was not in an analytical mood this morning because we saw to it that he won the Province Chess Championship with his Inner Gambit—a prize he has sought for thirty years. But if he had fooled us and given your case to the evaluators, we were fairly certain of a favorable decision. You noticed how they were not concentrating on the advocate's opening statement? They couldn't; they were too full of the incredible good fortune they had encountered the previous week. Sommers had been promoted to a full professorship at the Provincial University. Gunnard's obviously faulty thesis on space strains had been accepted by the *Steric Quarterly*— after we bought the magazine. But why go on? Still, if the improbable had occurred, and you had been declared guilty by the evaluators, we would simply have spirited you away from the courtroom. With a few unavoidable exceptions, every spectator in the room was a trained staff agent, ready to use his weapons—though in the presence of your aura, I doubt they could have hurt anyone.

"Troy, the staff had to get you here, but we preferred to do it quietly. Now, why are you here? I'll tell you. Your aura, we think, will keep—" Poole hesitated. "Your aura will keep ... It ... from dying during an approaching crisis in its life stream."

"It? What is this 'it'? And what makes you so sure I'll stay?"

"The staff has not authorized me to tell you more concerning the nature of the entity you are to protect. Suffice to say that It is a living, sentient being. And I think you'll stay, because the hypo just given Mrs. Troy was pure *skon*."

Troy had already surmised as much. The move was perfect. If he stayed near her, Ann, though steeped in the deadliest known poison, would not die. But why had they been so sure he would not stay willingly, without Ann as hostage? He 'pathed the thought to Poole, who curtly refused to answer.

"Now, major, I'm going to turn this wing of the City Building over to you. For your information, your aura is effective for a certain distance within the building, but just how far I'm not going to tell you. However, you are not permitted to leave your apartment at all. The staff has demoted the Provinarch, and he's now the corporal of your bodyguard. He would be exceedingly embarrassed if you succeeded in leaving. Meals will be brought to you regularly. The cinematic and micro library is well stocked on your favorite subjects. Special concessions may even be made as to things you want in town. But you can never touch your wife again. That pane of glass will always be between you. A psychic receptor tuned to your personality integration is fixed within Mrs. Troy's room. If you break the glass panel, or in any other way attempt to enter the room, the receptor will automatically actuate a bomb mechanism imbedded beneath Mrs. Troy's cerebellum. She would be blown to little bits—each of them alive as long as you were around. It grieves us to be crude, but the situation requires some such safeguard."

"When will my wife recover consciousness?"

"Within an hour or so. But what's your hurry? You'll be here longer than you think."

The little lawyer seemed lost in thought for a moment. Then he signaled Blogshak and the guards, and the four left. Blogshak favored Troy with a venemous scowl as he closed and locked the door.

There was complete and utter silence. Even the rabbit sat quietly on the table, blinking its eyes at Troy.

Left alone, the man surveyed the room, his perceptions palping every square foot rapidly but carefully. He found nothing unusual. He debated whether to explore the wing further or to wait until Ann awakened. He decided on the latter course. The nurse had left. They were together, with just a sheet of glass between. He explored Ann's room mentally, found nothing.

Then he walked to the center table and picked up the rabbit. There was the merest suggestion of a cicatrix encircling the neck.

Wonderful, but frightful, thought Troy. Who, what, am I?

He put the rabbit back in the box pulled a comfortable armchair against the wall opposite the glass panel, where he had a clear view of Ann's room, and began a methodical attempt to rationalize the events of the day.

He was jolted from his reverie by an urgent 'pathic call from Ann. After a flurry of tender perceptions each unlocked his mind to the other.

Poole had planted an incredible message in Ann's ESP lobe.

"Jon," she warned, "it's coded to the Dar— . . . I mean, it's coded to the notes and frequencies of our last concerto, in the death house. You'll have to synchronize. I'll start."

How did Poole know we were familiar with the concerto? thought Troy.

"Think on this carefully, Jon Troy, and guard it well," urged Poole's message. "I cannot risk my identity, but I am your friend. It—the Outcast—has shaped the destinies of vertebrate life on earth for millions of years, for two purposes. One is a peculiar kind of food. The other is . . . you. You have been brought here to preserve an evil life. But I urge you, develop your latent powers and destroy that life!

"Jon Troy, the evil this entity has wreaked upon the earth, entirely through his human agents thus far, is incalculable. It will grow even worse. You thought a sub-electronic virus caused the hundred thousand deaths which launched you on your assassination junket. Not so! The monster in the earth directly beneath you simply drained them of vital force, in their homes, on the street, in the theater, anywhere and everywhere. Your puny League has been fighting the Outcast for a generation without the faintest conception of the real enemy. If you have any love for humanity, search Blogshak's mind today. The staff physicians will be in this wing of the building today, too. Probe them. This evening, if I am still alive, I shall explain more, in person, free from Blogshak's crew."

"You have been wondering about the nature of the being whose life you are protecting," said Poole in a low voice, as he looked about the room. "As you learned when you searched the minds of the physicians this morning, he is nothing human. I believe him to have been wounded in a battle with his own kind, and that he has lain in his present pit for millions of years, possibly since pre-Cambrian times.

He probably has extraordinary powers even in his weakened state, but to my knowledge he has never used them."

"Why not?" asked Troy.

"He must be afraid of attracting the unwelcome attention of those who look for him. But he has maintained his life somehow. The waste products of his organic metabolism are fed into our sewers daily. He has a group of physicians and physicists—a curious mixture!—who keep in repair his three-dimensional neural cortex and run a huge administrative organization designed for his protection."

"Seems harmless enough, so far," said Troy.

"He's harmless except for one venemous habit. I thought I told you about it in the message I left with Ann. You must have verified it if you probed Blogshak thoroughly."

"But I couldn't understand such near cannibalism in so advanced—"

"Certainly not cannibalism! Do we think of ourselves as cannibals when we eat steaks? Still, that's my main objection to him. His vitality must be maintained by the absorption of other vitalities, preferably as high up the evolutionary scale as possible. Our thousands of deaths monthly can be traced to his frantic hunger for vital fluid. The devitalizing department, which Blogshak used to run, is the largest section of the staff."

"But what about the people who attend him? Does he snap up any of them?"

"He hasn't yet. They all have a pact with him. Help him, and he helps them. Every one of his band dies old, rich, evil, and envied by their ignorant neighbors. He gives them everything they want. Sometimes they forget, like Blogshak, that society can stand just so much of their evil."

"Assuming all you say is true—how does it concern my own problem, getting Ann out of here and notifying the League?"

Poole shook his head dubiously. "You probably have some tentative plans to hypnotize Blogshak and make him turn off the screen. But no one on the staff understands the screen. None of them can turn it off, because none of them turned it on. The chief surgeon believes it to be a direct, focused emanation from a radiator made long ago and known now only to the Outcast. But don't think of escaping just yet. You can strike a tremendous, fatal blow without leaving this room!

"This afternoon," Poole continued with growing nervousness, "there culminates a project initiated by the Outcast millennia ago. Just ninety years ago the staff began the blueprints of a surgical operation on the Outcast on a scale which would dwarf the erection of the Mechanical Integrator. Indeed, you won't be surprised to learn that the Integrator, capable of planar sterechronic analysis, was but a preliminary practice project, a rehearsal for the main event."

"Go on," said Troy absently. His sensitive hearing detected heavy breathing from beyond the door.

"To perform this colossal surgery, the staff must disconnect for a few seconds all of the essential neural trunks. When this is done, but for your aura, the Outcast would forever after remain a mass of senseless protoplasm and electronic equipment. With your aura they can make the most dangerous repairs in perfect safety. When the last neural is down, you simply suppress your aura and the Outcast is dead. Then you could force your way out. From then on, the earth could go its merry way unhampered. Your League would eventually gain ascendancy and—"

"What about Ann?" asked Troy curtly. "Wouldn't she die along with the Outcast?"

"Didn't both of you take an oath to sacrifice each other before you'd injure the League or abandon an assignment?"

"That's a nice legal point," replied Troy, watching the

corridor door behind Poole open a quarter of an inch. "I met Ann three years ago in a madhouse, where I had hidden away after a League assignment. She wasn't mad, but the stupid overseer didn't know it. She had the ability to project herself to other probability worlds. I married her to obtain a warning instrument of extreme delicacy and accuracy. Until that night in the death house, I'd have abided by League rules and abandoned her if necessary. But no longer. Any plan which includes her death is out. Suffering humanity can go climb a tree."

Poole's voice was dry and cracking. "I presumed you'd say that. You leave me no recourse. After I tell you who I am you will be willing to turn off your aura even at the cost of Ann's life. I am your . . . agh—"

A knife whistled through the open door and sank in Poole's neck. Blogshak and Sharg rushed in. Each man carried an ax.

"You dirty traitor!" screamed Blogshak. His ax crashed through the skull of the little old man even as Troy sprang forward. Sharg caught Troy under the chin with his ax handle. For some minutes afterward Troy was dimly aware of chopping, chopping, chopping.

Troy's aching jaw finally awoke him. He was lying on the sofa, where his keepers had evidently placed him. There was an undefinable raw odor about the room.

The carpet had been changed.

Troy's stomach muscles tensed. What had this done to Ann? He was unable to catch her ESP lobe. Probably out wandering through the past, or future.

While he tried to touch her mind, there was a knock on the door, and Blogshak entered with a man dressed in surgeon's white.

"Our operation apparently was a success, despite your little mishap," 'pathed the latter to Troy. "The next thirty years will tell us definitely whether we did this correctly. I'm afraid you'll have to stick around until then. I understand you're great chums with the Provinarch—ex-Provinarch, should I say? I'm sure he'll entertain you. I'm sorry about Poole. Poor fellow! Muffed his opportunities. Might have risen very high on the staff. But everything works out for the best, doesn't it?"

Troy glared at him wordlessly.

"Once we're out of here," 'pathed Troy in music code that afternoon, "we'll get General Blade to drop a plute fission on this building. It all revolves around the bomb under your cerebellum. If we can deactivate either the screen or the bomb, we're out. It's child's play to scatter Blogshak's bunch."

"If I had a razor," replied Ann, "I could cut the thing out. I can feel it under my neck muscles."

"Don't talk nonsense. What can you give me on Poole?"

"He definitely forced you to choose the red ball at the League meeting. Also, he knew he was going to be killed in your room. That made him nervous."

"Did he *know* he was going to be killed, or simply anticipated the possibility?"

"He knew. *He had seen it before!*"

Troy began pacing restlessly up and down before the glass panel, but never looking at Ann, who lay quietly in the bed apparently reading a book. The nurse sat in a chair at the foot of Ann's bed, arms folded, implacably staring at her ward.

"Puzzling, very puzzling," mused Troy. "Any idea what he was going to tell me about me aura?"

"No."

"Anything on his identity?"

"I don't know—I had a feeling that I . . . we—No, it's all

too vague. I noticed just one thing for certain."

"What was that?" asked Troy. He stopped pacing and appeared to be examining titles on the bookshelves.

"He was wearing your rosebud!"

"But that's crazy! I had it on all day. You must have been mistaken."

"You know I can't make errors on such matters."

"That's so." Troy resuming his pacing. "Yet, I refuse to accept the proposition that both of us were wearing my rosebud at the same instant. Well, never mind. While we're figuring a way to deactivate your bomb, we'd also better give a little thought to solving my aura.

"The solution is known—we have to assume that our unfortunate friend knew it. Great Galaxy! What our League biologists wouldn't give for a chance at this! We must change our whole concept of living matter. Have you ever heard of the immortal heart created by Alexis Carrel?" he asked abruptly.

"No."

"At some time during the Second Renaissance, early twentieth century, I believe, Dr. Carrel removed a bit of heart tissue from an embryo chick and put it in a nutrient solution. The tissue began to expand and contract rhythmically. Every two days the nutrient solution was renewed and excess growth cut away. Despite the catastrophe that had overwhelmed the chick—as a chick—the individual tissue lived on independently because the requirements of its cells were met. This section of heart tissue beat for nearly three centuries, until it was finally lost in the Second Atomic War."

"Are you suggesting that the king's men can put Humpty Dumpty together again if due care has been taken to nourish each part?"

"It's a possibility. Don't forget the skills developed by

the Muscovites in grafting skin, ears, corneas, and so on."

"But that's a long process—it takes weeks."

"Then let's try another line. Consider this: The amoeba lives in a fluid medium. He bumps into his food, which is generally bacteria or bits of decaying protein, flows around it, digests it at leisure, excretes his waste matter, and moves on. Now go on up the evolutionary scale past the coelenterates and flatworms, until we reach the first truly three-dimensional animals—the coelomates. The flatworm had to be flat because he had no blood vessels. His food simply soaked into him. But cousin roundworm, one of the coelomates, grew plump and solid, because his blood vessels fed his specialized interior cells, which would otherwise have no access to food.

"Now consider a specialized cell—say a nice long muscle cell in the rabbit's neck. It can't run around in stagnant water looking for a meal. It has to have its breakfast brought to it, and its excrement carried out by special messenger, or it soon dies."

Troy picked a book from the shelf and leafed through it idly.

Ann wondered mutely whether her nurse had been weaned on a lemon.

"This messenger," continued Troy, "is the blood. It eventually reaches the muscle cell by means of a capillary—a minute blood vessel about the size of a red corpuscle. The blood in the capillary gives the cell everything it needs and absorbs the cell waste matter. The muscle cell needs a continuously fresh supply of oxygen, sugar, amino-acids, fats, vitamins, sodium, calcium, and potassium salts, hormones, water and maybe other things. It gets these from the hemoglobin and plasma, and it sheds carbon dioxide, ammonium compounds, and so on. Our cell can store up a little food within its own boundaries to tide it over for a number of hours. But oxygen it must have, every instant."

"You're just making the problem worse," interposed Ann. "If you prove that blood must circulate oxygen continuously to preserve life, you'll have yourself out on a limb. If you'll excuse the term, the rabbit's circulation was decisively cut off."

"That's the poser," agreed Troy. "The blood didn't circulate, but the cells didn't die. And think of this a moment: Blood is normally alkaline, with a pH of 7.4. When it absorbs carbon dioxide as a cell excretion, blood becomes acid, and this steps up respiration to void the excess carbon dioxide, via the lungs. But so far as I could see, the rabbit didn't even sigh after he got his head back. There was certainly no heavy breathing."

"I'll have to take your word for it; I was out cold."

"Yes, I know." Troy began pacing the room again. "It isn't feasible to suppose the rabbit's plasma was buffered to an unusual degree. That would mean an added concentration of sodium bicarbonate and an increased solids content. The cellular water would dialyze into the blood and kill the creature by simple dehydration."

"Maybe he had unusual reserves of hemoglobin," suggested Ann. "That would take care of your oxygen problem."

Troy rubbed his chin. "I doubt it. There are about five million red cells in a cubic millimeter of blood. If there are very many more, the cells would oxidize muscle tissue at a tremendous rate, and the blood would grow hot, literally cooking the brain. Our rabbit would die of a raging fever. Hemoglobin dissolves about fifty times as much oxygen as plasma, so it doesn't take much hemoglobin to start an internal conflagration."

"Yet the secret must lie in the hemoglobin. You just

admitted that the cells could get along for long periods with only oxygen," persisted Ann.

"It's worth thinking about. We must learn more about the chemistry of the cell. You take it easy for a few days while I go through Poole's library."

"Could I do otherwise?" murmured Ann.

". . . thus the effect of confinement varies from person to person. The claustrophobe deteriorates rapidly, but the agoraphobe mellows, and may find excuses to avoid the escape attempt. The person of high mental and physical attainments can avoid atrophy by directing his every thought to the destruction of the confining force. In this case, the increment in mental prowess is 3.1 times the logarithm of the duration of confinement measured in years. The intelligent and determined prisoner can escape if he lives long enough."—J. and A. T., An Introduction to Prison Escape, 4th Edition, League Publishers, p. 14.

In 1811 Avogadro, in answer to the confusing problems of combining chemical weights, invented the molecule. In 1902 Einstein resolved an endless array of incompatible facts by suggesting a mass-energy relation. Three centuries later, in the tenth year of his imprisonment, Jon Troy was driven in near-despair to a similar stand. In one sure step of dazzling intuition, he hypothesized the viton.

"The secret goes back to our old talks on cell preservation," he explained with ill-concealed excitement to Ann. "The cell can live for hours without proteins and salts, because it has means of storing these nutrients from past meals. But oxygen it must have. The hemoglobin takes up molecular oxygen in the lung capillaries, ozonizes it, and, since hemin is easily reduced, the red cells give up oxygen to the muscle cells that need it, in return for carbon dioxide. After it takes up the carbon dioxide, hemin turns purple and enters the vein system on the way back to the lungs, and we can forget it.

"Now, what is hemin? We can break it down into etio-pyrophorin, which, like chlorophyll, contains four pyrrole groups. The secret of chlorophyll has been known for years. Under a photon catalyst of extremely short wave length, such as ultraviolet light, chlorophyll seizes molecule after molecule of carbon dioxide and synthesizes starches and sugars, giving off oxygen. Hemin, with its etiopyrophorin, works quite similarly, except that it doesn't need ultraviolet light. Now—"

"But animal cell metabolism works the other way," objected Ann. "Our cells take up oxygen and excrete carbon dioxide."

"It depends which cells you are talking about," reminded Troy. "The red corpuscle takes up carbon dioxide just as its plant cousin, chlorophyll, does, and they both excrete oxygen. Oxygen is just as much an excrement of the red cell as carbon dioxide is of the muscle cell."

"That's true," admitted Ann.

"And that's where the viton comes in," continued Troy. "It preserves the status quo of cell chemistry. Suppose that an oxygen atom has just been taken up by an amino-acid molecule within the cell protoplasm. The amino-acid immediately becomes unstable, and starts to split out carbon dioxide. In the red corpuscle, a mass of hemin stands by to seize the carbon dioxide and offer more oxygen. But the exchange never takes place. Just as the amino-acid and the hemin reach toward one another, their electronic attractions are suddenly neutralized by a bolt of pure energy from me: The viton! Again and again the cells try to exchange, with the same result. They can't die from lack of oxygen, because their individual molecules never attain an oxygen deficit. The viton gives a very close approach to immortality!"

"But *we* seem to be getting older. Perhaps your vitons don't reach every cell?"

"Probably not," admitted Troy. "They must stream radially from some central point within me, and of course they would decrease in concentration according to the inverse square law of light. Even so, they would keep enough cells alive to preserve life as a whole. In the case of the rabbit, after the cut cell surfaces were rejoined, there were still enough of them alive to start the business of living again. One might suppose, too, that the viton accelerates the reestablishment of cell boundaries in the damaged areas. That would be particularly important with the nerve cells."

"All right," said Ann. "You've got the viton. What are you going to do with it?"

"That's another puzzler. First, what part of my body does it come from? There must be some sort of a globular discharge area fed by a relatively small but impenetrable duct. If we suppose a muscle controlling the duct—"

"What you need is an old Geiger-Müller," suggested Ann. "Locate your discharge globe first, then the blind spot on it caused by the duct entry. The muscle has to be at that point."

"I wonder—" mused Troy. "We have a burnt-out cinema projection bulb around here somewhere. The vacuum ought to be just about soft enough by now to ionize readily. The severed filament can be the two electron poles." He laughed mirthlessly: "I don't know why I should be in a hurry. I won't be able to turn off the viton stream even if I should discover the duct-muscle."

Weeks later, Troy found his viton sphere, just below the cerebral frontal lobe. The duct led somewhere into the pineal region. Very gingerly he investigated the duct environment.

A small but dense muscle mass surrounded the entry of the duct to the bulk of radiation.

On the morning of the first day of the thirty-first year of their imprisonment, a few minutes before the nurse was due with the *skon* hypo, Ann 'pathed to Troy that she thought the screen was down. A joint search of the glass panel affirmed this.

Ann was stunned, like a caged canary that suddenly notices the door is open—she fears to stay, yet is afraid to fly away.

"Get your clothes on, dear," urged Troy. "Quickly now! If we don't contact the League in the next ten minutes, we never shall."

She dressed like an automaton.

Troy picked the lock on the corridor door noiselessly, with a key he had long ago made for this day, and opened the portal a quarter of an inch. The corridor seemed empty for its whole half-mile length. There was a preternatural pall of silence hanging over everything. Ordinarily, someone was always stirring about the corridor at this hour. He peered closely at the guard's cubicle down the hall. His eyes were not what they once were, and old Blogshak had never permitted him to be fitted with contacts.

He sucked in his breath sharply. The door of the cubicle was open, and two bodies were visible on the floor. One of the bodies had been a guard. The green of his uniform was plainly visible. The other corpse had white hair and a face like a wrinkled, arthritic claw. It was Blogshak.

Two mental processes occurred within Troy. To the cold, objective Troy, the thought occurred that the viton flow was ineffective beyond one hundred yards. Troy the human being wondered why the Outcast had not immediately remedied this weak point in the guard system. Heart pounding, he stepped back within the suite. He seized a chair, warned

Ann out of the way, and hurled it through the glass panel.
Ann stepped gingerly through the jagged gap. He held her
for a moment in his arms. Her hair was a pure white, her
face furrowed. Her body seemed weak and infirm. But it was
Ann. Her eyes were shut and she seemed to be floating
through time and space.

"No time for a trance now!" He shook her harshly, pulling her out of the room and down the corridor. He looked
for a stair. There was none.

"We'll have to chance an autovator!" he panted, thinking he should have taken some sort of bludgeon with him.
If several of the staff should come down with the 'vator, he
doubted his ability to hypnotize them all.

He was greatly relieved when he saw an empty 'vator
already on the subterranean floor. He leaped in, pulling Ann
behind him, and pushed the bottom to close the door. The
door closed quietly, and he pushed the button for the first
floor.

"We'll try the street floor first," he said, breathing heavily. "Don't look around when we leave the 'vator. Just chat-
ter quietly and act as though we owned the place."

The street floor was empty.

An icy thought began to grow in Troy's mind. He
stepped into a neighboring 'vator, carrying Ann with him
almost bodily, closed the door, and pressed the last button.
Ann was mentally out, but was trying to tell him something.
Her thoughts were vague, unfocused.

If they were pursued, wouldn't the pursuer assume they
had left the building? He hoped so.

A malicious laughter seemed to follow them up the
shaft.

He gulped air frantically to ease the roar in his ears.
Ann had sunk into a semi-stupor. He eased her to the floor.
The 'vator continued to climb. It was now in the two hun-

dreds. Minutes later it stopped gently at the top floor, the door opened, and Troy managed to pull Ann out into a little plaza.

They were nearly a mile above the city.

The penthouse roof of the City Building was really a miniature country club, with a small golf course, swimming pool, and club house for informal administrative functions. A cold wind now blew across the closely cut green. The swimming pool was empty. Troy shivered as he dragged Ann near the dangerously low guard rail and looked over the city in the early morning sunlight.

As far as he could see, nothing was moving. There were no cars gliding at any of the authorized traffic levels, no 'copters or transocean ships in the skies.

For the first time, Troy's mind sagged, and he felt like the old man he was.

As he stared, gradually understanding, yet half-unbelieving, the rosebud in his lapel began to speak.

Mai-kel condensed the thin waste of cosmic gas into several suns and peered again down into the sterechron. There could be no mistake—there was a standing wave of recurrent time emanating from the tiny planet. The Great One made himself small and approached the little world with cautious curiosity. Sathanas had been badly wounded, but it was hard to believe his integration had deteriorated to the point of permitting oscillation in time. And no intelligent life capable of time travel was scheduled for this galaxy. Who, then? Mai-kel synchronized himself with the oscillation so that the events constituting it seemed to move at their normal pace. His excitement multiplied as he followed the cycle.

It would be safest, of course, to volatilize the whole planet. But then, that courageous mite, that microscopic human being who had created the time trap would be lost.

Extirpation was indicated—a clean, fast incision done at just the right point of the cycle.

Mai-kel called his brothers.

Troy suppressed an impulse of revulsion. Instead of tearing the flower from his coat, he pulled it out gently and held it at arm's length, where he could watch the petals join and part again, in perfect mimicry of the human mouth.

"Yes, little man, I am what you call the Outcast. There are no other little men to bring my message to you, so I take this means of—"

"You mean you devitalized every man, woman, and child in the province . . . in the whole world?" croaked Troy.

"Yes. Within the past few months, my appetite has been astonishingly good, and I have succeeded in storing within my neurals enough vital fluid to carry me into the next sterechron. There I can do the same, and continue my journey. There's an excellent little planet waiting for me, just bursting with genial bipedal life. I can almost feel their vital fluid within me, now. And I'm taking you along, of course, in case I meet some . . . old friends. We'll leave now."

"Jon! Jon!" cried Ann, from behind him. She was standing, but weaving dizzily. Troy was at her side in an instant. "Even *he* doesn't know who Poole is!"

"Too late for any negative information now, dear," said Troy dully.

"But it isn't negative. If *he* doesn't know, then he won't stop you from going back." Her voice broke off in a wild cackle.

Troy looked at her in sad wonder.

"Jon," she went on feverishly, "your vitons help preserve the status quo of cells by preventing chemical change, but that is only part of the reason they preserve life. Each viton must also contain a quantum of time flow, which dissolves the vital fluid of the cell and reprecipitates it into the next instant. This is the only hypothesis which explains the preservation of the giant neurals of the Outcast. There was no chemical change going on in them which required stabilization, but something had to keep the vital fluid alive. Now, if you close the duct suddenly, the impact of unreleased vitons will send you back through time in your present body, as an old man. Don't you understand about Poole, now, Jon? You will go back thirty years through time, establish yourself in the confidence of both the League and the staff, attend the assassination conference, make young Troy choose the red ball again, defend him at the trial, and then you will die in that horrible room again. You have no choice about doing this, *because it has already happened!* Good-by, darling! You are Poole!"

There was an abrupt swish. Ann had leaped over the guard rail into space.

A gurgle of horror died in Troy's throat. Still clutching the now silent rose in his hand, he jammed the viton muscle with all his will power. There was a sickening shock, then a flutter of passing days and nights. As he fell through time, cold fingers seemed to snatch frantically at him. But he knew he was safe.

As he spiraled inward, Troy-Poole blinked his eyes involuntarily, as though reluctant to abandon a languorous escape from reality. He was like a dreamer awakened by having his bedclothes blown off in an icy gale.

He slowly realized that this was not the first time he had suddenly been bludgeoned into reality. Every seventy years the cycle began for him once more. He knew now that seventy years ago he had completed another identical circle in time. And the lifetime before that, and the one prior.

There was no beginning and no ending. The only reality was this brief lucid interval between cycles, waiting for the loose ends of time to cement. He had the choice at this instant to vary the life stream, to fall far beyond Troy's era, if he liked, and thus to end this existence as the despairing toy of time. What had he accomplished? Nothing, except retain, at the cost of almost unbearable monotony and pain, a weapon pointed at the heart of the Outcast, a weapon he could never persuade the young Troy to use, on account of Ann. Troy old had no influence over Troy young. Poole could never persuade Troy.

Peering down through the hoary wastes of time he perceived how he had hoped to set up a cycle in the time stream, a standing wave noticeable to the entities who searched for the Outcast. Surely with their incredible intellects and perceptions this discrepancy in the ordered universe would not go unnoticed. He had hoped that this trap in the time flow would hold the Outcast until relief came. But as his memory returned he realized that he had gradually given up hope. Somehow he had gone on from a sense of duty to the race from which he had sprung. From the depths of his aura-fed nervous system he had always found the will to try again. But now his nervous exhaustion, increasing from cycle to cycle by infinitesimal amounts, seemed overpowering.

A curious thought occurred to him. There must have been, at one time, a Troy without a Poole to guide—or entangle—him. There must have been a beginning—some prototype Troy who selected the red ball by pure accident, and who was informed by a prototype staff of his tremendous power. After that, it was easy to assume that the first Troy "went back" as the prototype Poole to scheme against the life of the Outcast.

But searching down time, Troy-Poole now found only

the old combination of Troy and Poole he knew so well. Hundreds, thousands, millions of them, each preceding the other. As far back as he could sense, there was always a Poole hovering over a Troy. Now he would become the next Poole, enmesh the next Troy in the web of time, and go his own way to bloody death. He could not even plan a comfortable suicide. No, to maintain perfect oscillation of the time trap, all Pooles must always die in the same manner as the first Poole. There must be no invariance. He suppressed a twinge of impatience at the lack of foresight in the prototype Poole.

"Just this once more," he promised himself wearily, "then I'm through. Next time I'll keep on falling."

General Blade sometimes felt that leading a resistance movement was far exceeding his debt to decent society and that one day soon he would allow his peaceful nature to override his indignant pursuit of justice. Killing a man, even a very bad man, without a trial, went against his grain. He sighed and rapped on the table.

"As a result of Blogshak's misappropriation of funds to fight the epidemic," he announced, "the death toll this morning reached over one hundred thousand. Does the Assassination Subcommittee have a recommendation?"

A thin-lipped man rose from the gathering. "The Provinarch ignored our warning," he said rapidly. "This subcommittee, as you all know, some days ago set an arbitrary limit of one hundred thousand deaths. Therefore this subcommittee now recommends that its plan for killing the Provinarch be adopted at once. Tonight is very favorable for our—"

A man entered the room quietly and handed General Blade an envelope. The latter read it quickly, then stood up.

"I beg your pardon, but I must break in," he announced. "Information I have just received may change our plans completely. This report from our intelligence service is so incredible that I won't read it to you. Let's verify it over the video."

He switched on the instrument. The beam of a local newscasting agency was focused tridimensionally before the group. It showed a huge pit or excavation which appeared to move as the scanning newscaster moved. The news comments were heard in snatches. "No explosion . . . no sign of any force . . . just complete disappearance. An hour ago the City Building was the largest structure in . . . now nothing but a gaping hole a mile deep . . . the Provinarch and his entire council were believed in conference . . . no trace—"

General Blade turned an uncomprehending face to the committee. "Gentlemen, I move that we adjourn this session pending an investigation."

Jon Troy and Ann left through the secret alleyway. As he buttoned his topcoat against the chill night air, he sensed that they were being followed. "Oh, hello?"

"I beg your pardon, Major Troy, and yours, madam. My name is Poole, Legal Subcommittee. You don't know me—yet, but I feel that I know you both very well. Your textbook on prison escape has inspired and sustained me many times in the past. I was just admiring your boutonniere, major. It seems so lifelike for an artificial rosebud. I wonder if you could tell me where I might buy one?"

Troy laughed metallicly. "It's not artificial. I've worn it for weeks, but it's a real flower, from my own garden. It just won't die."

"Extraordinary," murmured Poole, fingering the red blossom in his own lapel. "Could we run in here for a cocktail? Bartender Fonstile will fix us something special, and we can discuss a certain matter you really ought to know about."

The doorman of the Shawn Hotel bowed to the three as they went inside.

BROOKLYN PROJECT

WILLIAM TENN

Time travel as transgressive effect, author of chaos: This savage
story, a mocking parody of Ray Bradbury's more famous "A
Sound of Thunder," was, remarkably, published four years before the Bradbury, thus being one of the very few works of art which
responds devastatingly to that which has yet to occur. (Surely the
symphonies of Mahler or the works of Kafka would also fall into
that category.) Rejected by all of the better-paying markets, this fear-
making story, a brutal anticipation not only of Bradbury but "Tail
Gunner" Joe McCarthy, sold for a half a cent a word or less to
Malcolm Reis of *Planet Stories*. Reis said in taking the story not
without trepidation, "This one is for God," Tenn recalls in the af-
terword in his recent collection, *Immodest Proposals*. "We're allowed one for God."

"Tenn" has always been the pseudonym of Phillip Klass whose
first story, "Alexander the Bait" appeared in *Astounding*'s 2/46 issue,
there were subsequently about 50 stories, the best of which—all
available in *Immodest Proposals* and its companion volume, *Here
Comes Civilization* published by NESFA Press in 2001—comprise
the finest body of satire and social criticism in the literature of science fiction. Many of them—such as "Party of the Two Parts"—are
also overwhelmingly comic. Klass was a Professor of English at Penn

State University for about three decades, retiring about ten years ago. There were only one or two stories during his academic career, there have been a few more since then. Late in the unusual case of this writer, have been as good as early or middle.

The gleaming bowls of light set in the creamy ceiling dulled when the huge, circular door at the back of the booth opened. They returned to white brilliance as the chubby man in the severe black jumper swung the door shut behind him and dogged it down again.

Twelve reporters of both sexes exhaled very loudly as he sauntered to the front of the booth and turned his back to the semi-opaque screen stretching across it. Then they all rose in deference to the cheerful custom of standing whenever a security official of the government was in the room.

He smiled pleasantly, waved at them and scratched his nose with a wad of mimeographed papers. His nose was large and it seemed to give added presence to his person. "Sit down, ladies and gentlemen, do sit down. We have no official fol-de-rol in the Brooklyn Project. I am your guide, as you might say, for the duration of this experiment—the acting secretary to the executive assistant on press relations. My name is not important. Please pass these among you."

They each took one of the mimeographed sheets and

passed the rest on. Leaning back in the metal bucket seats, they tried to make themselves comfortable. Their host squinted through the heavy screen and up at the wall clock, which had one slowly revolving hand. He patted his black garment jovially where it was tight around the middle.

"To business. In a few moments, man's first large-scale excursion into time will begin. Not by humans, but with the aid of a photographic and recording device which will bring us incalculably rich data on the past. With this experiment, the Brooklyn Project justifies ten billion dollars and over eight years of scientific development; it shows the validity not merely of a new method of investigation, but of a weapon which will make our glorious country even more secure, a weapon which our enemies may justifiably dread.

"Let me caution you, first, not to attempt the taking of notes even if you have been able to smuggle pens and pencils through Security. Your stories will be written entirely from memory. You all have a copy of the Security Code with the latest additions as well as a pamphlet referring specifically to Brooklyn Project regulations. The sheets you have just received provide you with the required lead for your story; they also contain suggestions as to treatment and coloring. Beyond that—so long as you stay within the framework of the documents mentioned—you are entirely free to write your stories in your own variously original ways. The press, ladies and gentlemen, must remain untouched and uncontaminated by government control. Now, any questions?"

The twelve reporters looked at the floor. Five of them began reading from their sheets. The paper rustled noisily.

"What, no questions? Surely there must be more interest than this in a project which has broken the last possible frontier—the fourth dimension, time. Come now, you are the representatives of the nation's curiosity—you must have questions. Bradley, you look doubtful. What's bothering you? I assure you, Bradley, that I don't bite."

They all laughed and grinned at each other.

Bradley half-rose and pointed at the screen. "Why does it have to be so thick? I'm not the slightest bit interested in finding out how chronar works, but all we can see from here is a grayed and blurry picture of men dragging apparatus around on the floor. And why does the clock only have one hand?"

"A good question," the acting secretary said. His large nose seemed to glow. "A very good question. First, the clock has but one hand, because, after all, Bradley, this is an experiment in time, and Security feels that the time of the experiment itself may, through some unfortunate combination of information leakage and foreign correlation—in short, a clue might be needlessly exposed. It is sufficient to know that when the hand points to the red dot, the experiment will begin. The screen is translucent and the scene below somewhat blurry for the same reason—camouflage of detail and adjustment. I *am* empowered to inform you that the details of the apparatus are—uh, very significant. Any other questions? Culpepper? Culpepper of Consolidated, isn't it?"

"Yes, sir. Consolidated News Service. Our readers are very curious about that incident of the Federation of Chronar Scientists. Of course, they have no respect or pity for them—the way they acted and all—but just what did they mean by saying that this experiment was dangerous because of insufficient data? And that fellow, Dr. Shayson, their president, do you know if he'll be shot?"

The man in black pulled at his nose and paraded before them thoughtfully. "I must confess that I find the views of the Federation of Chronar Scientists—or the federation of chronic *sighers*, as we at Pike's Peak prefer to call them—

are a trifle too exotic for my tastes; I rarely bother with weighing the opinions of a traitor in any case. Shayson himself may or may not have incurred the death penalty for revealing the nature of the work with which he was entrusted. On the other hand, he—uh, *may not* or *may* have. That is all I can say about him for reasons of security."

Reasons of security. At the mention of the dread phrase, every reporter straightened against the hard back of his chair. Culpepper's face lost its pinkness in favor of a glossy white. They can't consider the part about Shayson a leading question, he thought desperately. But I shouldn't have cracked about that damned federation!

Culpepper lowered his eyes and tried to look as ashamed of the vicious idiots as he possibly could. He hoped the acting secretary to the executive assistant on press relations would notice his horror.

The clock began ticking very loudly. Its hand was now only one-fourth of an arc from the red dot at the top. Down on the floor of the immense laboratory, activity had stopped. All of the seemingly tiny men were clustered around two great spheres of shining metal resting against each other. Most of them were watching dials and switchboards intently; a few, their tasks completed, chatted with the circle of black-jumpered Security guards.

"We are almost ready to begin Operation Periscope. Operation Periscope, of course, because we are, in a sense, extending a periscope into the past—a periscope which will take pictures and record events of various periods ranging from fifteen thousand years to four billion years ago. We felt that in view of the various critical circumstances attending this experiment—international, scientific—a more fitting title would be Operation Crossroads. Unfortunately, that title has been—uh, preempted."

Everyone tried to look as innocent of the nature of that

other experiment as years of staring at locked library shelves would permit.

"No matter. I will now give you a brief background in chronar practice as cleared by Brooklyn Project Security. Yes, Bradley?"

Bradley again got partly out of his seat. "I was wondering—we know there has been a Manhattan Project, a Long Island Project, a Westchester Project and now a Brooklyn Project. Has there ever been a Bronx Project? I come from the Bronx; you know, civic pride."

"Quite. Very understandable. However, if there is a Bronx Project you may be assured that until its work has been successfully completed, the only individuals outside of it who will know of its existence are the President and the Secretary of Security. If—*if*, I say—there is such an institution, the world will learn of it with the same shattering suddenness that it learned of the Westchester Project. I don't think that the world will soon forget *that*."

He chuckled in recollection and Culpepper echoed him a bit louder than the rest. The clock's hand was close to the red mark.

"Yes, the Westchester Project and now this; our nation shall yet be secure! Do you realize what a magnificent weapon chronar places in our democratic hands? To examine only one aspect—consider what happened to the Coney Island and Flatbush Subprojects (the events are mentioned in those sheets you've received) before the uses of chronar were fully appreciated.

"It was not yet known in those first experiments that Newton's third law of motion—action equalling reaction—held for time as well as it did for the other three dimensions of space. When the first chronar was excited backward into time for the length of a ninth of a second, the entire laboratory was propelled into the future for a like period and returned in an—uh, unrecognizable condition. That fact, by the way, has prevented excursions into the future. The equipment seems to suffer amazing alterations and no human could survive them. But do you realize what we could do to an enemy by virtue of that property alone? Sending an adequate mass of chronar into the past while it is adjacent to a hostile nation would force that nation into the future—all of it simultaneously—a future from which it would return populated only with corpses!"

He glanced down, placed his hands behind his back and teetered on his heels. "That is why you see two spheres on the floor. Only one of them, the ball on the right, is equipped with chronar. The other is a dummy, matching the other's mass perfectly and serving as a counterbalance. When the chronar is excited, it will plunge four billion years into our past and take photographs of an Earth that was still a half-liquid, partly gaseous mass solidifying rapidly in a somewhat inchoate solar system.

"At the same time, the dummy will be propelled four billion years into the future, from whence it will return much changed but for reasons we don't completely understand. They will strike each other at what is to us *now* and bounce off again to approximately half the chronological distance of the first trip, where our chronar apparatus will record data of an almost solid planet, plagued by earthquakes and possibly holding forms of sublife in the manner of certain complex molecules.

"After each collision, the chronar will return roughly half the number of years covered before, automatically gathering information each time. The geological and historical periods we expect it to touch are listed from I to XXV in your sheets; there will be more than twenty-five, naturally, before both balls come to rest, but scientists feel that all periods after that number will be touched for such a short while as to be unproductive of photographs and other material. Remember, at the end, the balls will be doing little more than throbbing in place before coming to rest, so that even though they still ricochet centuries on either side of the present, it will be almost unnoticeable. A question, I see."

The thin woman in gray tweeds beside Culpepper got to her feet. "I—I know this is irrelevant," she began, "but I haven't been able to introduce my question into the discussion at any pertinent moment. Mr. Secretary—"

"Acting secretary," the chubby little man in the black suit told her genially. "I'm only the acting secretary. Go on."

"Well, I want to say—Mr. Secretary, is there any way at all that our post-experimental examination time may be reduced? Two years is a very long time to spend inside Pike's Peak simply out of fear that one of us may have seen enough and be unpatriotic enough to be dangerous to the nation. Once our stories have passed the censors, it seems to me that we could be allowed to return to our homes after a safety period of, say, three months. I have two small children and there are others here—"

"Speak for yourself, Mrs. Bryant!" the man from Security roared. "It is Mrs. Bryant, isn't it? Mrs. Bryant of the Women's Magazine Syndicate? Mrs. *Alexis* Bryant." He seemed to be making minute pencil notes across his brain.

Mrs. Bryant sat down beside Culpepper again, clutching her copy of the amended Security Code, the special pamphlet on the Brooklyn Project and the thin mimeographed sheet of paper very close to her breast. Culpepper moved hard against the opposite arm of his chair. Why did everything have to happen to him? Then, to make matters worse, the crazy woman looked tearfully at him as if expecting sympathy. Culpepper stared across the booth and crossed his legs.

"You must remain within the jurisdiction of the Brooklyn Project because that is the only way that Security can be *certain* that no important information leakage will occur before the apparatus has changed beyond your present recognition of it. You didn't have to come, Mrs. Bryant—you volunteered. You all volunteered. After your editors had designated you as their choices for covering this experiment, you all had the peculiarly democratic privilege of refusing. None of you did. You recognized that to refuse this unusual honor would have shown you incapable of thinking in terms of National Security, would have, in fact implied a criticism of the Security Code itself from the standpoint of the usual two-year examination time. And now this! For someone who had hitherto been thought as able and trustworthy as yourself, Mrs. Bryant, to emerge at this late hour with such a request makes me, why it," the little man's voice dropped to a whisper, "—it almost makes me doubt the effectiveness of our Security screening methods."

Culpepper nodded angry affirmation at Mrs. Bryant, who was biting her lips and trying to show a tremendous interest in the activities on the laboratory floor.

"The question *was* irrelevant. Highly irrelevant. It took up time which I had intended to devote to a more detailed discussion of the popular aspects of chronar and its possible uses in industry. But Mrs. Bryant must have her little feminine outburst. It makes no difference to Mrs. Bryant that our nation is daily surrounded by more and more hostility, more and more danger. These things matter not in the slightest to Mrs. Bryant. All she is concerned with are the two years of her life that her country asks her to surrender so that the future of her own children may be more secure."

The acting secretary smoothed his black jumper and became calmer. Tension in the booth decreased.

"Activation will occur at any moment now, so I will

briefly touch upon those most interesting periods which the chronar will record for us and from which we expect the most useful data. I and II, of course, since they are the periods at which the Earth was forming into its present shape. Then III, the Pre-Cambrian Period of the Proterozoic, one billion years ago, the first era in which we find distinct records of life—crustaceans and algae for the most part. VI, a hundred twenty-five million years in the past, covers the Middle Jurassic of the Mesozoic. This excursion into the so-called 'Age of Reptiles' may provide us with photographs of dinosaurs and solve the old riddle of their coloring, as well as photographs, if we are fortunate, of the first appearance of mammals and birds. Finally, VIII and IX, the Oligocene and Miocene Epochs of the Tertiary Period, mark the emergence of man's earliest ancestors. Unfortunately, the chronar will be oscillating back and forth so rapidly by that time that the chance of any decent recording—"

A gong sounded. The hand of the clock touched the red mark. Five of the technicians below pulled switches and, almost before the journalists could lean forward, the two spheres were no longer visible through the heavy plastic screen. Their places were empty.

"The chronar has begun its journey to four billion years in the past! Ladies and gentlemen, an historic moment—a profoundly historic moment! It will not return for a little while; I shall use the time in pointing up and exposing the fallacies of the—ah, *federation of chronic sighers!*"

Nervous laughter rippled at the acting secretary to the executive assistant on press relations. The twelve journalists settled down to hearing the ridiculous ideas torn apart.

"As you know, one of the fears entertained about travel to the past was that the most innocent-seeming acts would cause cataclysmic changes in the present. You are probably familiar with the fantasy in its most currently popular form—if Hitler had been killed in 1930, he would not have forced scientists in Germany and later occupied countries to emigrate, this nation might not have had the atomic bomb, thus no third atomic war, and Venezuela would still be part of the South American continent.

"The traitorous Shayson and his illegal federation extended this hypothesis to include much more detailed and minor acts such as shifting a molecule of hydrogen that in our past really was never shifted.

"At the time of the first experiment at the Coney Island Subproject, when the chronar was sent back for one-ninth of a second, a dozen different laboratories checked through every device imaginable, searched carefully for any conceivable change. There were none! Government officials concluded that the time stream was a rigid affair, past, present, and future, and nothing in it could be altered. But Shayson and his cohorts were not satisfied: they—"

I. Four billion years ago. The chronar floated in a cloudlet of silicon dioxide above the boiling Earth and languidly collected its data with automatically operating instruments. The vapor it had displaced condensed and fell in great, shining drops.

"—insisted that we should do no further experimenting until we had checked the mathematical aspects of the problem yet again. They went so far as to state that it was possible that if changes occurred we would not notice them, that no instruments imaginable could detect them. They claimed we would accept these changes as things that had always existed. Well! This at a time when our country—and theirs, ladies and gentlemen of the press, *theirs*, too—was in greater danger than ever. Can you—"

Words failed him. He walked up and down the booth,

shaking his head. All the reporters on the long, wooden bench shook their heads with him in sympathy.

There was another gong. The two dull spheres appeared briefly, clanged against each other and ricocheted off into opposite chronological directions.

"There you are." The government official waved his arms at the transparent laboratory floor above them. "The first oscillation has been completed; has anything changed? Isn't everything the same? But the dissidents would maintain that alterations have occurred and we haven't noticed them. With such faith-based, unscientific viewpoints, there can be no argument. People like these—"

II. Two billion years ago. The great ball clicked its photographs of the fiery, erupting ground below. Some red-hot crusts rattled off its sides. Five or six thousand complex molecules lost their basic structure as they impinged against it. A hundred didn't.

"—will labor thirty hours a day out of thirty-three to convince you that black isn't white, that we have seven moons instead of two. They are especially dangerous—"

A long, muted note as the apparatus collided with itself. The warm orange of the corner lights brightened as it started out again.

"—because of their learning, because they are sought for guidance in better ways of vegetation." The government official was slithering up and down rapidly now, gesturing with all of his pseudopods. "We are faced with a very difficult problem, at present—"

III. One billion years ago. The primitive triple trilobite the machine had destroyed when it materialized began drifting down wetly.

"—a very difficult problem. The question before us: should we *shllk* or shouldn't we *shllk*?" He was hardly speaking English now; in fact, for some time, he hadn't been speaking at all. He had been stating his thoughts by slapping one pseudopod against the other—as he always had . . .

IV. A half-billion years ago. Many different kinds of bacteria died as the water changed temperature slightly.

"This, then, is no time for half measures. If we can reproduce well enough—"

V. Two hundred fifty million years ago. VI. A hundred twenty-five million years ago.

"—to satisfy the Five Who Spiral, we have—"

VII. Sixty-two million years. VIII. Thirty-one million. IX. Fifteen million. X. Seven and a half million.

"—spared all attainable virtue. Then—"

XI. XII. XIII. XIV. XV. XVI. XVII. XVIII. XIX. Bong—bong—bong bongbong-bongongongngngngggg . . .

"—we are indeed ready for refraction. And that, I tell you, is good enough for those who billow and those who snap. But those who billow will be proven wrong as always, for in the snapping is the rolling and in the rolling is only truth. There need be no change merely because of a sodden cilium. The apparatus has rested at last in the fractional conveyance; shall we view it subtly?"

They all agreed, and their bloated purpled bodies dissolved into liquid and flowed up and around to the apparatus. When they reached its four square blocks, now no longer shrilling mechanically, they rose, solidified, and regained their slime-washed forms.

"See," cried the thing that had been the acting secretary to the executive assistant on press relations. "See, no matter how subtly! Those who billow were wrong: we haven't changed." He extended fifteen purple blobs triumphantly. "Nothing has changed!"

TIMETIPPING

JACK M. DANN

I wish that I had said this but it was Robert Silverberg (the editor of the original anthology *Epoch*, in which this story first appeared in 1975), who noted on rereading this story recently that " 'Timetipping' is the work that Bernard Malamud would have written for The Magazine of Fantasy & Science Fiction if Boucher had been able to tease a story out of him." This is both amazingly perceptive and somehow a little short of my own extravagant admiration for a story which takes the voice of, say, Malamud's TALKING HORSE to places that Malamud, that sensible realist with occasional flashes of surrealism, could not have conceived. Time here is seen as neither epochal or transitory, compartmentalized or disassembled but rather as utterly fluid. In this Chagall painting of a story woe, desire and Chassids on broomsticks tumble into that river without banks.

Jack Dann is the author of several science fiction novels alone (*The Man Who Melted, Junction* or in collaboration (HIGH STEEL, with the late Jack Haldeman). His novel of a re-imagined Da Vinci, *The Memory Cathedral* was highly praised and *Da Vinci Rising*, a novella excerpt won the Nebula Award for 1997. A subsequent historical novel, *The Silent* re-imagined the Civil War. Dann, a native of central New York State has lived in Australia for the last decade.

Since timetipping, everything moved differently. Nothing was for certain, anything could change (depending on your point of view), and almost anything could happen, especially to forgetful old men who often found themselves in the wrong century rather than on the wrong street.

Take Moishe Hodel, who was too old and fat to be climbing ladders; yet he insisted on climbing to the roof of his suburban house so that he could sit on the top of a stone-tuff church in Goreme six hundred years in the past. Instead of praying, he would sit and watch monks. He claimed that since time and space were *meshuggeh* (what's crazy in any other language?), he would search for a quick and godly way to travel to synagogue. Let the goyim take the trains.

Of course, Paley Litwak, who was old enough to know something, knew from nothing when the world changed and everything went blip. His wife disappeared, and a new one returned in her place. A new Golde, one with fewer lines and dimples, one with starchy white hair and missing teeth.

Upon arrival, all she said was, "This is almost right. You're almost the same, Paley. Still, you always go to shul?"

"Shul?" Litwak asked, resolving not to jump and scream and ask God for help. With all the changing, Litwak would stand straight and wait for God. "What's a shul?"

"You mean you don't know from shul, and yet you wear such a yarmulke on your head?" She pulled her babushka through her fingers. "A shul. A synagogue, a temple. Do you pray?"

Litwak was not a holy man, but he could hold up his head and not be afraid to wink at God. Certainly he prayed. And in the following weeks Litwak found himself in shul more often than not—so she had an effect on him; after all, she was his wife. Where else was there to be? With God he had a one-way conversation—from Litwak's mouth to God's ears—but at home it was turned around. There, Litwak had no mouth, only ears. How can you talk with a woman who thinks fornicating with other men is holy?

But Litwak was a survivor; with the rest of the world turned over and doing flip-flops, he remained the same. Not once did he trip into a different time, not even an hour did he lose or gain; and the only places he went were those he could walk to. He was the exception to the rule. The rest of the world was adrift; everyone was swimming by, blipping out of the past or future and into the present here or who-knows-where.

It was a new world. Every street was filled with commerce, every night was carnival. Days were built out of strange faces, and nights went by so fast that Litwak remained in the synagogue just to smooth out time. But there was no time for Litwak, just services and prayers and holy smells.

Yet the world went on. Business almost as usual. There were still rabbis and chasids and grocers and cabalists; fat

Hoffa, a congregant with a beard that would make a Baal Shem jealous, even claimed that he knew a cabalist that had invented a new gematria for foretelling everything concerning money.

"So who needs gematria?" Litwak asked. "Go trip tomorrow and find out what's doing."

"Wrong," said Hoffa as he draped his prayer shawl over his arm, waiting for a lull in the conversation to say the holy words before putting on the tallis. "It does no good to go there if you can't get back. And when you come back, everything is changed, anyway. Who do you know that's really returned? Look at you, you didn't have gray hair and earlocks yesterday."

"Then, that wasn't *me* you saw. Anyway, if everybody but me is tripping and tipping back and forth, in and out of the devil's mouth, so to speak, then what time do you have to use this new gematria?"

Hoffa paused and said, "So the world must go on. You think it stops because heaven shakes it. . . ."

"You're so sure it's heaven?"

". . . but *you* can go see the cabalist; you're stuck in the present, you sit on one line. Go talk to him; he speaks a passable Yiddish, and his wife walks around with a bare behind."

"So how do you know he's there now?" asked Litwak. "They come and go. Perhaps a Neanderthal or a *klezmer* from the future will take his place."

"So? If he isn't there, what matter? At least you know he's somewhere else. No? Everything goes on. Nothing gets lost. Everything fits, somehow. That's what's important."

It took Litwak quite some time to learn the new logic of the times, but once learned, it became an advantage—especially when his pension checks didn't arrive. Litwak became a fair second-story man, but he robbed only according to society's logic and his own ethical system: one half for the shul and the rest for Litwak.

Litwak found himself spending more time on the streets than in the synagogue, but by standing still on one line he could not help but learn. He was putting the world together, seeing where it was, would be, might be, might not be. When he became confused, he used logic.

And the days passed faster, even with praying and sleeping nights in the shul for more time. Everything whirled around him. The city was a moving kaleidoscope of colors from every period of history, all melting into different costumes as the thieves and diplomats and princes and merchants strolled down the cobbled streets of Brooklyn.

With prisms for eyes, Litwak would make his way home through the crowds of slaves and serfs and commuters. Staking out fiefdoms in Brooklyn was difficult, so the slaves momentarily ran free, only to trip somewhere else, where they would be again grabbed and raped and worked until they could trip again, and again and again until old logic fell apart. King's Highway was a bad part of town. The Boys' Club had been turned into a slave market and gallows room.

Litwak's tiny apartment was the familiar knot at the end of the rope. Golde had changed again, but it was only a slight change. Golde kept changing as her different time lines met in Litwak's kitchen, and bedroom. A few Goldes he liked, but change was gradual, and Goldes tended to run down. So for every sizzling Golde with blond-dyed hair, he suffered fifty or a thousand Goldes with missing teeth and croaking voices.

The latest Golde had somehow managed to buy a parakeet, which turned into a bluejay, a parrot with red feathers, and an ostrich, which provided supper. Litwak had discovered that smaller animals usually timetipped at a faster rate than men and larger animals; perhaps, he thought, it was a question of metabolism. Golde killed the ostrich before something else could take its place. Using logic and compassion, Litwak blessed it to make it kosher—the rabbi was not to be found, and he was a new chasid (imagine) who didn't know Talmud from soap opera; worse yet, he read Hebrew with a Brooklyn twang, not unheard of with such new rabbis. Better that Litwak bless his own meat; let the rabbi bless goyish food.

Another meal with another Golde, this one dark-skinned and pimply, overweight and sagging, but her eyes were the color of the ocean seen from an airplane on a sunny day. Litwak could not concentrate on food. There was a pitched battle going on two streets away, and he was worried about getting to shul.

"More soup?" Golde asked.

She had pretty hands, too, Litwak thought. "No, thank you," he said before she disappeared.

In her place stood a squat peasant woman, hands and ragged dress still stained with rich, black soil. She didn't scream or dash around or attack Litwak; she just wrung her hands and scratched her crotch. She spoke the same language, in the same low tones, that Litwak had listened to for several nights in shul. An Egyptian named Rhampsinitus had found his way into the synagogue, thinking it was a barbarian temple for Baiti, the clown god.

"Baiti?" she asked, her voice rising. "Baiti," she answered, convinced.

So here it ends, thought Litwak, just beginning to recognize the rancid odor in the room as sweat.

Litwak ran out of the apartment before she turned into something more terrible. Changes, he had expected. Things change and shift—that's logic. But not so fast. He had slowed down natural processes in the past (he thought), but now he was slipping, sinking like the rest of them. A bald Samson adrift on a raft.

Time isn't a river, Litwak thought as he pushed his way through larger crowds, all adrift, shouting, laughing, blipping in and out, as old men were replaced by ancient monsters and fears; but dinosaurs occupied too much space, always slipped, and could enter the present world only in torn pieces—a great ornithischian wing, a stegosaurian tail with two pairs of bony spikes, or, perhaps, a four-foot-long tyrannosaurus' head.

Time is a hole, Litwak thought. He could feel its pull.

Whenever Litwak touched a stranger—someone who had come too many miles and minutes to recognize where he was—there was a pop and a skip, and the person disappeared. Litwak had disposed of three gilded ladies, an archdeacon, a birdman, a knight with Norman casque, and several Sumerian serfs, in this manner. He almost tripped over a young boy who was doggedly trying to extract a tooth from the neatly severed head of a tyrannosaurus.

The boy grabbed Litwak's leg, racing a few steps on his knees to do so, and bit him. Screaming in pain, Litwak pulled his leg away, felt an unfamiliar pop, and found the synagogue closer than he had remembered. But this wasn't his shul; it was a cathedral, a caricature of his beloved synagogue.

"Catch him," shouted the boy with an accent so thick that Litwak could barely make out what he said. "He's the thief who steals from the shul."

"*Gevalt*, this is the wrong place," Litwak said, running toward the cathedral.

A few hands reached for him, but then he was inside. There, in God's salon, everything was, would be, and had to be the same: large clerestory windows; double aisles for

Thursday processions; radiating chapels modeled after Amiens 1247; and nave, choir, and towers, all styled to fit the stringent requirements of halakic law.

Over the altar, just above the holy ark, hung a bronze plate representing the egg of Khumu, who created the substance of the world on a potter's wheel. And standing on the plush pulpit, his square face buried in a prayer book, was Rabbi Rhampsinitus.

"Holy, holy, holy," he intoned. Twenty-five old men sang and wailed and prayed on cue. They all had beards and earlocks and wore conical caps and prayer garments.

"That's him," shouted the boy.

Litwak ran to the pulpit and kissed the holy book.

"Thief, robber, purloiner, depredator."

"Enough," Rhampsinitus said. "The service is concluded. God has not winked his eye. Make it good," he told the boy.

"Well, look who it is."

Rhampsinitus recognized Litwak at once. "So it is the thief. Stealer from God's coffers, you have been excommunicated as a second-story man."

"But I haven't stolen from the shul. This is not even my time or place."

"He speaks a barbarian tongue," said Rhampsinitus. "What's shul?"

"This Paley Litwak is twice, or thrice, removed," interrupted Moishe Hodel, who could timetip at will to any synagogue God chose to place around him. "He's new. Look and listen. *This* Paley Litwak probably does not steal from the synagogue. Can you blame him for what someone else does?"

"Moishe Hodel?" asked Litwak. "Are you the same one I knew from Beth David on King's Highway?"

"Who knows?" said Hodel. "I know a Beth David, but not on King's Highway, and I know a Paley Litwak who was stuck in time and had a wife named Golde who raised hamsters."

"That's close, but—"

"So don't worry. I'll speak for you. It takes a few hours to pick up the slang, but it's like Yinglish, only drawled out and spiced with too many Egyptisms."

"Stop blaspheming," said Rhampsinitus. "Philosophy and logic are very fine indeed," he said to Hodel. "But this is a society of law, not philosophers, and law demands reparations."

"But I have money," said Litwak.

"There's your logic," said Rhampsinitus. "Money, especially such barbarian tender as yours, cannot replace the deed. Private immorality and public indecency are one and the same."

"He's right," said Hodel with a slight drawl.

"Jail the tergiversator," said the boy.

"Done," answered Rhampsinitus. He made a holy sign and gave Litwak a quick blessing. Then the boy's sheriffs dragged him away.

"Don't worry, Paley," shouted Moishe Hodel. "Things change."

Litwak tried to escape from the sheriffs, but he could not change times. It's only a question of will, he told himself. With God's help, he could initiate a change and walk, or slip, into another century, a friendlier time.

But not yet. Nothing shifted; they walked a straight line to the jail, a large pyramid still showing traces of its original limestone casing.

"Here we are," said one of the sheriffs. "This is a humble town. We don't need ragabrash and riffraff—it's enough we have foreigners. So timetip or slip or flit somewhere else. There's no other way out of this depository."

They deposited him in a narrow passageway and dropped the entrance stone behind him.

It was hard to breathe, and the damp air stank. It was completely dark. Litwak could not see his hands before his eyes.

Gotenyu, he thought as he huddled on the cold stone floor. For a penny they plan to incarcerate me. He recited the Shma Yisroel and kept repeating it to himself, ticking off the long seconds with each syllable.

For two days he prayed; at least it seemed like two days. Perhaps it was four hours. When he was tired of praying, he cursed Moishe Hodel, wishing him hell and broken fingers. Litwak sneezed, developed a nervous cough, and his eyes became rheumy. "It's God's will," he said aloud.

Almost in reply, a thin faraway voice sang, "Oh, my goddess, oh, my goddess, oh, my goddess, Clem-en-tine!"

It was a familiar folk tune, sung in an odd Spanish dialect. But Litwak could understand it, for his mother's side of the family spoke in Ladino, the vernacular of Spanioli Jews.

So there, he thought. He felt the change. Once he had gained God's patience, he could slip, tip, and stumble away.

Litwak followed the voice. The floor began to slope upward as he walked through torchlit corridors and courtyards and rooms. In some places, not yet hewn into living quarters, stalactite and stalagmite remained. Some of the rooms were decorated with wall paintings of clouds, lightning, the sun, and masked dancers. In one room was a frieze of a great plumed serpent; in another were life-size mountain lions carved from lava. But none of the rooms were occupied.

He soon found the mouth of the cave. The bright sunlight blinded him for an instant.

"I've been waiting for you," said Castillo Moldanado in

a variation of Castilian Spanish. "You're the third. A girl arrived yesterday, but she likes to keep to herself."

"Who are you?" asked Litwak.

"A visitor, like you." Moldanado picked at a black mole under his eye and smoothed his dark, thinning hair.

Litwak's eyes became accustomed to the sunlight. Before him was desert. Hills of cedar and piñon were mirages in the sunshine. In the far distance, mesa and butte overlooked red creeks and dry washes. This was a thirsty land of dust and sand and dirt and sun, broken only by a few brown fields, a ranch, or an occasional trading post and mission. But to his right and left, and hidden behind him, pueblos thrived on the faces of sheer cliffs. Cliff dwellings and cities made of smooth-hewn stone commanded valley and desert.

"It looks dead," Moldanado said. "But all around you is life. The Indians are all over the cliffs and desert. Their home is the rock itself. Behind you is Cliff Palace, which contains one hundred and fifty rooms. And they have rock cities in Cañon del Muerto and, farther south, in Walnut Canyon."

"I see no one here but us," Litwak said.

"They're hiding," said Moldanado. "They see the change and think we're gods. They're afraid of another black kachina, an, evil spirit."

"Ah," Litwak said. "A dybbuk."

"You'll see natives soon enough. Ayoyewe will be here shortly to rekindle the torches, and for the occasion, he'll dress in his finest furs and turkey feathers. They call this cave Keet Seel, mouth of the gods. It was given to me. And I give it to you.

"Soon there will be more natives about, and more visitors. We'll change the face of their rocks and force them out. With greed."

"And logic," said Litwak.

Moldanado was right. More visitors came every day and

settled in the desert and caves and pueblos. Romans, Serbs, Egyptians, Americans, Skymen, Mormons, Baalists, and Trackers brought culture and religion and weapons. They built better buildings, farmed, bartered, stole, prayed, invented, and fought until they were finally visited by governors and diplomats. But that changed too, when everyone else began to timetip.

Jews also came to the pueblos and caves. They came from various places and times, bringing their conventions, babel, tragedies, and hopes. Litwak hoped for a Maimonides, a Moses ben Nachman, a Luria, even a Schwartz, but there were no great sages to be found, only Jews. And Litwak was the first. He directed, instigated, ordered, soothed, and founded a minyan for prayer. When they grew into a full-time congregation, built a shul and elected a rabbi, they gave Litwak the honor of sitting on the pulpit in a plush-velvet chair.

Litwak was happy. He had prayer, friends, and authority.

Nighttime was no longer dark. It was a circus of laughter and trade. Everything sparkled with electric light and prayer. The Indians joined the others, merged, blended, were wiped out. Even a few Jews disappeared. It became faddish to wear Indian clothes and feathers.

Moldanado was always about now, teaching and leading, for he knew the land and native customs. He was a natural politico; when Litwak's shul was finished, he even attended a maariv service. It was then that he told Litwak about "Forty-nine" and Clementine.

"What about that song?" Litwak had asked.

"You know the tune."

"But not the words."

"Clementine was the goddess of Los Alamos," Moldanado said. "She was the first nuclear reactor in the world to utilize fissionable material. It blew up, of course. 'Forty-nine' was the code name for the project that exploded the first atom bomb. But I haven't felt right about incorporating 'Forty-nine' into the song."

"I don't think this is a proper subject to discuss in God's house," Litwak said. "This is a place of prayer, not bombs."

"But this is also Los Alamos."

"Then we must pray harder," Litwak said.

"Have you ever heard of the atom bomb?" asked Moldanado.

"No," said Litwak, turning the pages in his prayer book.

Moldanado found time to introduce Litwak to Baptista Founce, the second visitor to arrive in Los Alamos. She was dark and fragile and reminded Litwak of his first Golde. But she was also a shikse who wore a gold cross around her neck. She teased, chased, and taunted Litwak until he had her behind the shul in daylight.

Thereafter, he did nothing but pray. He starved himself, beat his chest, tore his clothes, and waited on God's patience. The shul was being rebuilt, so Litwak took to praying in the desert. When he returned to town for food and rest, he could not even find the shul. Everything was changing.

Litwak spent most of his time in the desert, praying. He prayed for a sign and tripped over a trachodon's head that was stuck in the sand.

So it changes, he thought as he stared at the rockscape before him. He found himself atop a ridge, looking down on an endless field of rocks, a stone tableau of waves in a gray sea. To his right was a field of cones. Each cone cast a flat black shadow. But behind him, cliffs of soft tuff rose out of the stone sea. A closer look at the rock revealed hermitages and monasteries cut into the living stone.

Litwak sighed as he watched a group of monks waiting their turn to climb a rope ladder into a monastic compound.

They spoke in a strange tongue and crossed themselves before they took to the ladder.

There'll be no shul here, he said to himself. This is my punishment. A dry, goyish place. But there was no thick, rich patina of sophisticated culture here. This was a simple place, a rough, real hinterland, not yet invaded by dybbuks and kachinas.

Litwak made peace with the monks and spent his time sitting on the top of a stone-tuff church in Goreme six hundred years in the past. He prayed, and sat, and watched the monks. Slowly he regained his will, and the scenery changed.

There was a monk that looked like Rhampsinitus.

Another looked like Moldanado.

At least, Litwak thought, there could be no Baptista Founce here. With that (and by an act of unconscious will), he found himself in his shul on King's Highway.

"Welcome back, Moishe," said Hoffa. "You should visit this synagogue more often."

"Moishe?" asked Litwak.

"Well, aren't you Moishe Hodel, who timetips to synagogue?"

"I'm Paley Litwak. No one else." Litwak looked at his hands. They were his own.

But he was in another synagogue. "Holy, holy, holy," Rabbi Rhampsinitus intoned. Twenty-five old men sang and wailed and prayed on cue. They all had beards and earlocks and wore conical caps and prayer garments.

"So, Moishe," said Rhampsinitus, "you still return. You really have mastered God's chariot."

Litwak stood still, decided, and then nodded his head and smiled. He thought of the shul he had built and found himself sitting in his plush chair. But Baptista Founce was sitting in the first row, praying.

Before she could say, "Paley," he was sitting on a stone-tuff church six hundred years in the past.

Perhaps tomorrow he'd go to shul. Today he'd sit and watch monks.

THE CHRONOLOGY PROTECTION CASE

PAUL LEVINSON

The inalterable nature of time, that clamp which resists paradox, is an anomaly at the center of many (perhaps most) of the stories on this theme (and not coincidentally most of the stories in this book). Here is a recent and strong example which could be also seen as an extension of and commentary on Fritz Leiber's remarkable "Try and Change the Past" (1958); in both, the humor and superficial geniality mask some much darker material.

Paul Levinson, who holds a doctorate in Media Studies and chairs its department at the New School, has published several stories and two novels starring his NYC police investigator Phil D'Amato. This 1995 *Analog* novelette was auspiciously the first of them, and a Nebula finalist. Levinson is the former President of the Science Fiction and Fantasy Writers of America.

C arl put the call through just as I was packing up for the day. "She says she's some kind of physicist," he said, and although I rarely took calls from the public, I jumped on this one.

"Dr. D'Amato?" she asked.

"Yes?"

"I saw you on television last week—on that cable talk show. You said you had a passion for physics." Her voice had a breathy elegance.

"True," I said. Forensic science was my profession, but cutting edge physics was my love. Too bad there wasn't a way to nab rapist murderers with spectral traces. "And you're a physicist?" I asked.

"Oh yes, sorry," she said. "I should introduce myself. I'm Lauren Goldring. Do you know my work?"

"Ahm . . ." The name did sound familiar. I ran through the Rolodex in my head, though these days my computer was becoming more reliable than my brain. "Yes!" I snapped my fingers. "You had an article in *Scientific American* last month about some Hubble data."

"That's right," she said, and I could hear her relax just a bit. "Look, I'm calling you about my husband—he's disappeared. I haven't heard from him in two days."

"Oh," I said. "Well, that's really not my department. I can connect you to—"

"No, please," she said. "It's not what you think. I'm sure his disappearance has something to do with his work. He's a physicist, too."

Forty minutes later I was in my car on my way to her house, when I should have been home with pizza and the cat. No contest: a physicist in distress always wins.

Her Bronxville address wasn't too far from mine in Yonkers.

"Dr. D'Amato?" She opened the door.

I nodded. "Phil."

"Thank you so much for coming," she said, and ushered me in. Her eyes looked red, like she suffered from allergies or had been crying. But few people have allergies in March.

The house had a quiet appealing beauty. As did she.

"I know the usual expectations in these things," she said. "He has another woman, we've been fighting. And I'm sure that most women whose vanished husbands *have* been having affairs are quick to profess their certainty that that's not what's going on in *their* cases."

I smiled. "OK, I'm willing to start with the assumption that your case is different. Tell me how."

"Would you like a drink, some wine?" She walked over to a cabinet, must've been turn of the century.

"Just ginger ale, if you have it," I said, leaning back in the plush Morris chair she'd shown me to.

She returned with the ginger ale, and some sort of spar-kling water for herself. "Well, as I told you on the phone, Ian and I are physicists—"

"Is his last name Goldring, like yours?"

Lauren nodded. "And, well, I'm sure this has something to do with his project."

"You two don't do the same work?" I asked.

"No," she said. "My area's the cosmos at large—big bang theory, black holes in space, the big picture. Ian's was, is, on the other end of the spectrum. Literally. His area's quan-tum mechanics." She started to sob.

"It's OK," I said. I got up and put my hand on her shoul-der. Quantum mechanics could be frustrating, I know, but not *that* bad.

"No," she said. "It isn't OK. Why am I using the past tense for Ian?"

"You think some harm's come to him?"

"I don't know," her lips quivered. She did know, or thought she knew.

"And you feel this had something to do with his work with tiny particles? Was he exposed to dangerous radia-tion?"

"No," she said. "That's not it. He was working on some-thing called quantum signaling. He always told me every-thing about his work—and I told him everything about mine—we had that kind of relationship. And then a few months ago, he suddenly got silent. At first I thought maybe he *was* having an affair—"

And the thought popped into my head: if I had a woman with your class, an affair with someone else would be the last thing on my mind.

"But then I realized it was deeper than that. It was some-thing, something that frightened him, in his work. Some-thing that I think he wanted to shield me from."

"I'm pretty much of an amiable amateur when it comes to quantum mechanics," I said, "but I know something about it. Suppose you tell me all you know about Ian's work, and why it could be dangerous."

What I, in fact, fully grasped about quantum mechanics I could write on a postcard to my sister in Boston and it would likely fit. It had to do with light and particles so small that they were often indistinguishable in their behavior and prone to paradox at every turn. A particularly vexing aspect that even Einstein and his colleagues tried to tackle in the 1930s involved two particles that at first collided and then traveled at sublight speeds in opposite directions: would observation of one have an instantaneous effect on the other? Did the two particles, having once collided, now exist ever after in some sort of mysterious relationship or field, a bond between them so potent that just to measure one was to influence the other, regardless of how far away? Einstein wondered about this in a thought experiment. Did interaction of subatomic particles tie their futures together forever, even if one stayed on Earth and the other wound up beyond Pluto? Real experiments in the 1960s and after suggested that's just what was happening, at least in local areas, and this supported Heisenberg's and Bohr's classic "Copenhagen" interpretation that quantum mechanics was some kind of mind-over-matter deal—that just looking at a quantum or tiny particle, maybe even thinking about it, could affect not only it but related particles. Einstein would've preferred to find another cause—nonmental—for such phenomena. But that could lead to an interpretation of quantum mechanics as faster-than-light action—the particle on Earth somehow sent an instant signal to the particle in space—which of course ran counter to Einstein's relativity theories.

Well, I guess that would fill more than your average

postcard. The truth is, blood and semen and DNA evidence were a lot easier to make sense of than quantum mechanics, which was one reason that kind of esoteric science was just a hobby with me. Of course, one way that QM had it over forensics is that it rarely had to do with dead bodies. But Lauren Goldring was wanting to tell me that maybe it did in at least one case, her husband's.

"Ian was part of a small group of physicists working to demonstrate that QM was evidence of faster-than-light travel, time travel, maybe both," she said.

"Not a product of the mind?" I asked.

"No," she said, "not as in the traditional interpretation."

"But doesn't faster-than-light travel contradict Einstein?" I asked.

"Not necessarily," Lauren said. "It seems to contradict the simplest interpretations, but there may be some loopholes."

"Go on," I said.

"Well, there's a lot of disagreement even among the small group of people Ian was working with. Some think the data supports both faster-than-light *and* time travel. Others are sure that time travel is impossible even though—"

"You're not saying that you think some crazy envious scientist killed him?" I asked.

"No," Lauren said. "It's much deeper than that."

A favorite phrase of hers. "I don't understand," I said.

"Well, Stephen Hawking, for one, says that although the equations suggest that time travel might be possible on the quantum level, the Universe wouldn't let this happen..." She paused and looked at me. "You've heard about Hawking's work in this area?"

"I know about Hawking in general," I said. "I'm not that much of an amateur. But not about his work in time travel."

"You're very unusual for a forensic scientist," she said,

with an admiring edge I very much liked. "Anyway, Hawking thinks that whatever quantum mechanics may permit, the Universe just won't allow time travel—because the level of paradox time travel would create would just unravel the whole Universe."

"You mean like if I could get a message back to JFK that he would be killed, and he believed me and acted upon that information and didn't go to Dallas and wasn't killed, this would create a world in which I would grow up with no knowledge that JFK had ever been killed, which would mean I would have no motive to send the message that saved JFK, but if I didn't send that message then JFK would be killed—"

"That's it," Lauren said. "Except on the quantum level you might achieve that paradox by sending back information just a few seconds in time—say, in the form of a command that would shut down the generating circuit and prevent the information from being sent in the first place—"

"I see," I said.

"And, well, because things like that, if they could happen, if they happened all the time, would lead to a constantly remade, inside-out, self-effacing universe. Hawking promulgated his 'chronology protection conjecture'—the Universe protects the existing time line, whatever the theoretical possibilities of time travel."

"How does your husband fit into this?" I asked.

"He was working on a device, an experiment, to disprove Hawking's conjecture," she said. "He was trying to create a local wormhole with temporal effects."

"And you think he somehow disappeared into this?" Jeez, this was beginning to sound like a bad episode of *Star Trek* already. But she seemed rational, everything she'd outlined made sense, and something in her manner continued to compel my attention.

"I don't know." She looked like she was close to tears again.

"All right," I said. "Here's what I think we should do. I'm going to call in Ian's disappearance to a friend in the Department. He's a precinct captain, and he'll take this seriously. He'll contact all the airports, get Ian's picture out to cops on the beat—"

"But I don't think—"

"I know," I said. "You've got a gut feeling that something more profound is going on. And maybe you're right. But we've got to cover all the bases."

"OK," she said quietly, and I noticed that her lips were quivering again.

"Will you be all right tonight? I'll be back to you tomorrow morning." I took her hand.

"I guess so," she said huskily, and squeezed my hand.

I didn't feel like letting go, but I did.

The news the next morning was terrible. I don't care what the shrinks say: flat-out confirmed death is always worse than ambiguous unresolved disappearance.

I couldn't bring myself to just call her on the phone. I drove to her home, hoping she was in.

She opened the door. I tried to keep a calm face, but I'm not that good an actor.

She understood immediately. "Oh no!" she cried out. She staggered and collapsed in my arms. "Please no."

"I'm sorry," I said, and touched her hair. I felt like kissing her forehead, but didn't. I hardly knew her, yet I felt very close to her, a part of her world. "They found him a few hours ago near Columbia University. Looks like another stupid, senseless, god damned random drive-by shooting. That's the kind of world we live in." I didn't know whether this would in any way lessen her pain. At least his death had nothing to do with his work.

"No, not random," she said, sobbing. "Not random."

"OK," I said, "you need to rest, I'm going to call someone over here to give you a sedative. I'll stay with you till then."

The medic was over in fifteen minutes. He gave her a shot, and she was asleep a few minutes later. "Not random. Not random," she mumbled.

I called the captain, and asked if he could send a uniform over to stay with Lauren for the afternoon. He wasn't happy—his people were overworked, like everyone—but he owed me. Many's the time I'd saved his butt with some piece of evidence I'd uncovered in the back of an orifice.

I dropped by the autopsy. Nothing unusual there. Three bullets from a cheap punk's gun, one shattered the heart, did all the damage, Ian Goldring's dead. No sign of radiation damage, no strange chemistry in the body. No possible connection that I could see to anything Lauren had told me. Still, the coroner was a friend. I explained to him that the victim was the husband of a friend and asked if he could run any and every conceivable test at his disposal to determine if there was anything different about this corpse. He said sure. I knew he wouldn't find anything, though.

I went back to my office. I thought of calling Lauren and telling her about the autopsy, but she'd be better off if I let her rest. I was tired of looking at dead bodies. I turned on my computer and looked at its screen instead. I was on a few physics lists on the Internet. I logged on and did some reading about Hawking and his chronology protection conjecture.

"Lady physicist on the phone for you again," Carl called out. It was late afternoon already. I logged off and rubbed my eyes.

"Hi," Lauren said.

"You OK?" I asked.

"Yeah," she said. "I just got off the phone with one of the other researchers in Ian's group, and I think I've got part of this figured out." She sounded less tentative than yesterday—like she was indeed more on top of what was actually going on, or thought she was—but more worried.

I started to tell her, as gently as I could, about the autopsy.

"Doesn't matter," she interrupted me. "I mean, I don't think the *way* that Ian was killed has any relevance to this. It's the fact that he *was* killed that counts—the reason he was killed."

The reason—everyone wants reasons in this irrational society. Science in the laboratory deals with reason. In the outside world, you're lucky if you can find a reason. "I know it's painful," I said. "But Ian's death had no reason—his killer was likely just a high-flying kid with a gun. Happens all the time. Ian was just in the wrong place. A random victim in the murder lottery."

"No, not random," Lauren said.

She'd said the same thing this morning. I could hear her starting to sob again.

"Look, Phil," she continued. "I really think I'm close to understanding this. I'm going to make a few more calls. I, uh, we hardly know each other, but I feel good talking this out with you. Our conversation last night helped me a lot. Can I call you back in an hour? Or maybe—I don't know, if you're not busy tonight—could you come over again?"

She didn't have to ask twice. "I'll see you at seven. I'll also bring some food in case you're hungry—you have to eat."

*   *   *

I knew even before I drove up that something was wrong. I guess my eyes, after all these years of looking around crime scenes, are especially sensitive to the weak flicker of police lights on the evening sky at a distance. The flicker still turns my stomach.

"What's going on here?" I got out of my car, Chinese food in hand, and asked the uniform.

"Who the hell are you?" he replied.

I fumbled for my ID.

"He's OK." Janny Murphy, the uniform who'd come to stay with Lauren in the afternoon, walked over. "He's forensics."

The food dropped from my hand when I saw the expression on her face. Brown moo-shoo pork juice dribbled down the driveway.

"It's crazy," Janny said. "Doc says it's less than one in ten thousand. Some rare allergy to the shot the medic gave her. It wasn't his fault. It somehow brings out an asthma attack hours later. Fifty percent fatality."

"And Lauren—Dr. Goldring—was in the unlucky part of the curve."

Janny nodded.

"I don't believe this," I said, shaking my head.

"I know," Janny said. "Helluva coincidence. Physicist and his wife, also a physicist, both dying like that."

"Maybe it's not a coincidence," I said.

"What do you mean?" Janny said.

"I don't know what I mean," I said. "Is Lauren—is the body—still here? I'd like to have a look at her."

"Help yourself," Janny gestured inside the house.

I can't say Lauren looked at peace in death. I could almost still see her lips quivering, straining to tell me something, though they were as sealed as the deadest night now.

I had an urge to kiss her face. I'd known her all of two days, wanted as many times to kiss her. Now I never would.

I was aware of Janny standing beside me.

"I'm going home now," I said.

"Sure," Janny said. "The captain says he'd like to talk to you tomorrow morning. Just to wrap this whole mess up. Bad karma."

Yeah, karma, like in Fritz Capra's *Tao of Physics*. Like in two entities crossing each other's paths and then nevermore touching each other's destinies. Like me and this soul with the soft, still lips. Except I had no power to influence Lauren, to make things better for her anymore. And the truth is, I hadn't done much for her when she was alive.

I was awake all night. I logged on to a few more fringy physics lists with my computer and did more reading. Finally it was light outside. I thought about calling Stephen Hawking. He was where? California? Cambridge, England? I wasn't sure. I knew he'd be able to talk to me if I could reach him—I'd seen a video of him talking through a special device—but he'd probably think I was crazy when I told him what I had to say. So I called Jack Donovan instead. He was another friend who owed me. I had lots of friends like that in the city. Jack was a science reporter for *Newsday*, and I'd come through for him with off-the-record background on murder investigations in my bailiwick lots of times. I hoped he'd come through for me now. I was starting to get worried. He had lots of connections in the field—he could talk to scientists who'd shy away from me, my being in the Department and all.

It was seven in the morning. I expected to get his answering machine, but I got him. I told him my story.

"OK," he said. "Why don't you go see the captain at the

precinct, and then come over to see me? I'll do some checking around in the meantime."

I did what Jack said. I kept strictly to the facts with the
captain—no suppositions, no chronological or any other
protection schemes—and he took it all in with his customary
frown. "Damn shame," he muttered. "Nice lady like that.
They oughta take that sedative off the market. Damn drug
companies are too greedy."

"Right," I said.

"You look exhausted," he said. "You oughta take the
rest of the day off."

"More or less what I had in mind," I said, and left for
Jack's.

I thought *my* office was high-tech, but Jack's Hempstead
newsroom looked like something well into the next century.
Computer screens everywhere you looked, sounds of modems chirping on and off like the patter of tiny raindrops.

Jack looked concerned. "You're not going to like this,"
he said.

"What else is new?" I said. "Try me."

"Well, you were right about my having better entrée to
these physicists than you. I did a lot of checking," Jack said.
"There were six people working actively in conjunction with
Ian on this project. A few more, of course, if you take into
account the usual complement of graduate student assistants. But outside of that, the project was sealed up pretty
tightly—not by the government or any agency, but by the
researchers themselves. Sometimes they do that when the
research gets really flaky—like they don't want anyone to
know what they're really doing until they're sure they have
a reliable effect. You wouldn't believe some of the wild
things people have been getting into in the past few years—

especially the physicists—now that they have the Internet to yammer at each other."

"I'm tired, Jack. Please get to the point."

"Well, four of the seven—that includes Ian Goldring—are now dead. One had a heart attack—the day after his doctor told him his cholesterol was in the bottom 10 percent. I guess that's not so strange. Another fell off his roof—he was cleaning out his gutters—and severed his carotid artery on a sharp piece of flagstone that was sticking up on his walk. He bled to death before anyone found him. Another was struck by a car—DOA. And then there's Ian. I could write a story on this even without your conjecture—"

"Please don't," I said.

"It's a weird situation, all right. Four out of seven dying like that—and also Goldring's wife."

"How are the spouses of the other fatalities?" I asked.

"All OK," Jack said. "But none are physicists. None knew anything at all about their husbands' work—all of the dead were men. Lauren Goldring is the only one who had any idea what her husband was up to."

"She wasn't sure," I said. "But I think she figured it out just before she died."

"Maybe they all picked up some virus at a conference they attended—something which threw off their sense of balance, caused their heart rate to speed up." Sam Abrahmson, Jack's editor, strolled by and jumped in. Clearly he'd been listening on the periphery of our conversation. "That could explain the two accidents and the heart attack," he added. "Maybe even the sedative death."

"But not the drive-by shooting of Goldring," I said.

"No," Abrahmson admitted. "But it could be an interesting story anyway. Think about it," he said to Jack and strolled away.

I looked at Jack. "Please, I'm begging you. If I'm right—"

"It's likely something completely different," Jack said. "Some completely different hidden variable."

Hidden variables. I'd been reading about them all night. "What about the other three? Have you been able to get in touch with them?" I asked.

"Nope," Jack said. "Hays and Strauss refused to talk to me about it. Both had their secretaries tell me they were aware of some of the deaths, had decided not to do any more work on the local wormhole project, had no plans to publish what they'd already done, didn't want to talk to me about it or hear from me again. Each claimed to be involved now in something completely different."

"Does that sound to you like the usual behavior of research scientists?" I asked.

"No," Jack said. "The ones I know eat up publicity, and they'd hang on to a project like this for decades, like a dog worrying a bone."

I nodded. "And the third physicist?"

"Fenwick? She's in small plane somewhere in the outback of Australia. I couldn't reach her at all."

"Call me immediately if you hear the plane crashes," I said. I really meant "when" not "if," but I didn't want Jack to think I was even more far gone than I was. "Please try to hold off on any story for now," I said, and made to leave.

"I'll do what I can," Jack said. "Try to get some rest. I think there's something going on here all right, but not what you think."

The drive back to Westchester was harrowing. Two cars nearly side-swiped me, and one big-ass truck stopped so suddenly in front of me that I had all I could do to swerve out of crashing into it and becoming an instant Long Island Expressway pancake.

Let's say the QM time-travel people were right. Particles

are able to influence each other traveling away from each other at huge distances, because they're actually traveling back in time to an earlier position when they were in immediate physical contact. So time travel on the quantum mechanical level is possible—technically.

But let's say Hawking was also right. The Universe can't allow time travel—for to do so would unravel its very being. So it protects itself from dissemination of information backward in time.

That wouldn't be so crazy. People are saying the Universe can be considered one huge organism—a Gaia writ large. Makes sense then, that this organism, like all other organisms, would have tendencies to act on behalf of its own survival—would act to prevent its dissolution via time travel.

But how would such protection express itself? A physicist figures out a way of creating a local wormhole that can send some information back in time—back to his earlier self and equipment—in some non-blatantly paradoxical way. It doesn't shut off the circuit that sent it. So this information is in fact sent and in fact received—by the scientist. But the Universe can't allow that information transfer to stand. So what happens?

Hawking says the Universe's first line of defense is to create energy disturbances severe enough at the mouths of the wormhole to destroy it and its time-channeling ability. OK. But let's say the physicist is smart or lucky enough to create a wormhole that can withstand these self-disruptive forces. What does the Universe do then?

Maybe it makes the scientist forget this information. Maybe causes a minor stroke in the scientist's brain. Maybe causes the equipment to irreparably break down. Maybe the lucky physicist is really unlucky. Maybe this already happened lots of times.

But what happens when a group of scientists around the world who achieve this time travel transfer reach a critical mass—a mass that will soon publish its findings and make them known, irrevocably, to the world?

Jeez!—I jammed the heel of my hand into my car horn and swerved. The damn Volkswagen driver must be drunk out of his mind—

So what happens when this group of scientists gets information from its own future? Has proof of time travel, information that can't be? The Universe regulates itself, polices its time line, in a more drastic way. All existence is equilibrium—a stronger threat to existence evokes a stronger reaction. A freak fatal accident. A sudden massive heart attack. Another no-motive drive-by shooting that the Universe already dishes out to all too many people in this hapless world of ours. Except in this case, the Universe's motive is quite clear and strong: it must protect its chronology, conserve its current existence.

Maybe this already-happened, too. How many physicists on the cutting edges of this science died too young in recent years? Feynman, others... Jeez, here was a story for Jack all right.

But why Lauren? Why did she have to die?

Maybe because the Universe's protection level went beyond just those who received illicit future information. Maybe it extended to those who understood just what it was doing, just—

Whamp! Something big had smashed into the rear of my car, and I was skidding way out of control toward the edge of the Throgs Neck Bridge, toward where some workers had removed the barriers to fix some corrosion or something. I was strangely calm, above it all. I told myself to go easy on the brakes, but my leg clamped down anyway and my speed increased. I wrenched my wheel around, but all that did was spin me into a backward skid off the bridge. My car sailed way the hell out over the black-and-blue Long Island Sound.

The way down took a long time. They'd say I was over-wrought, overtired, that I lost control. But I knew the truth, knew exactly why this was happening. I knew too much, just like Lauren.

Or maybe there was a way out, a weird little corner of my brain piped up.

Maybe I didn't know the truth. Maybe I was wrong.

Maybe if I could convince myself of that, the Universe wouldn't have to protect itself from me. Maybe it would give me a second chance.

My car hit the water.

I was still alive.

I was a pretty fair swimmer.

If only I could force myself never to think of certain things, maybe I had a shot.

Maybe the deaths of the physicists were coincidental after all. . . .

I lost consciousness thinking no, I couldn't just forget what I already knew so well. . . . How could I will myself not to think of that very thing I was trying to will myself not to think about . . . that blared in my mind now like a broken car horn. . . . But if I died, what I knew wouldn't matter any-more. . . .

I awoke fighting sheets . . . of water. No, these were too white. Maybe hospital sheets. Yeah, white hospital sheets. They smelled like that, too.

I opened my eyes. Hospital rooms were hell—I knew bet-ter than most the truth of that—but this was just a hospital room. I was sure of that. I was alive.

And I remembered everything. With a spasm that both

energized and frightened me, I realized that I recalled every-thing I'd been thinking about the Universe and its protective clutch. . . .

But I was still alive.

So maybe my reasoning was not completely right.

"Dr. D'Amato," a female voice, soft but very much in command, said to me. "Good to see you awake."

"Good to *be* awake, Nurse, ah, Johnson." I squinted at her name tag, then her face. "Uhm, what's my situation? How long have I been here?"

She looked at the chart next to my bed. "Just a day and a half," she said. "They fished you out of the Sound. You were suffering from shock. Here." She gave me a cup of water. "Now that you're awake, you can take these orally." She gave me three pills, and turned off the intravenous that I'd just realized was attached to me. She disconnected the tubing from my vein.

I held the pills in my hand. I thought about the Universe again. I envisioned it, rightly or wrongly, as a personal an-tagonist now. Let's say I was right about the reach of its chronology protection after all? Let's say it had spared me in the water because I was on the verge of willing myself to forget? Let's say it had allowed me to get medicine and nutrition intravenously while I was unconscious because while I was unconscious I posed no threat? But let's say now that I was awake, and remembered, it would—

"Dr. D'Amato. Are you falling back asleep on me?" She smiled. "Come on now, be a good boy and take your pills."

They burned in my palm. Maybe they were poison. Maybe something I had a lethal allergy to. Like Lauren. "No," I said. "I'm OK, now, really. I don't need them." I put the pills on the table and swung my legs out of bed.

"I don't believe this," Johnson said. "It's true—you doc-tors make the worst god-awful patients. You just stay put now—hear me?" She gave me a look of exasperation and stalked out the door, likely to get the resident on duty, or— who knew?—security.

I looked around for my clothes. They were on a chair, a dried-out crumpled mess. They stank of oil and saltwater. At least my wallet was still inside my jacket pocket, money damp but intact. Good to see there was still some honesty left in this town.

I dressed quickly and opened the door. The corridor was clear. God damn it, I could leave if I wanted to. I was a patient, not a prisoner.

At least insofar as the hospital was concerned. As for the larger realm of being, I couldn't say anymore.

I took a cab straight home.

The most important new piece of evidence—to this whole case, as well as to me personally—was that I was alive. This meant that my assessment of the Universe's vindictiveness was missing something. Or maybe the Universe was just a less effective assassin of forensic scientists than quantum physicists and their knowing wives.

I called Jack to see if there was anything new.

"Oh, just a second, please," the *Newsday* receptionist said. I didn't like the tone of her voice.

"Hello, can I help you?" This was a man's voice, but not Jack's. He sounded familiar, but I couldn't place him.

"Yes, I'm Dr. Phil D'Amato of NYPD Forensics calling Jack Donovan."

Silence. Then, "Hello, Phil. I'm Sam Abrahmson. You still in the hospital?"

Right. Abrahmson. That was the voice. "No. I'm out. Where's Jack?"

Abrahmson cleared his throat. "He was killed with Dave

Strauss this morning. He'd talked Strauss into going public with this; Strauss supported your story. He'd picked Strauss up at his summer cottage in Ellenville—Strauss had been hiding out there—and was driving him back to the city. They got blown off a small bridge. Freak accident."

"No freakin' accident," I said. "You know that as well as I do." Another particle who'd danced this sick quantum twist with me. Another particle dead. But this one was completely my fault—I'd brought Jack into this.

"I don't know what I know," Abrahmson said. "Except that at this point the story's on hold. Until we find out more."

I was glad to hear he sounded scared. "That's a good idea," I said. "I'll be back to you."

"Take care of yourself," Abrahmson said. "God knows what that subatomic radiation can do to the body and mind. Or maybe it's all just coincidence. God only knows. Take care of yourself."

"Right." Subatomic radiation. Abrahmson's latest culprit. First it was a virus, now it was radiation. I'd said the same stupid thing to Lauren, hadn't I? People like to latch on to something they know when faced with something they don't know—especially something that kills some physicists here, a reporter there, who knew who else? But radiation had nothing to do with this. Stopping it would take a lot more than lead shields.

I tracked down Richard Hays. I was beginning to get a further inkling of what might be going on, and I needed to talk it out with one of the principals. One of the last remaining principals. It could save both our lives.

I used my NYPD clout to intimidate enough secretaries and assistants to get directly through to him.

"Look, I don't care if you're the bleeding head of the FBI," he said. He was British. "I'm going to talk to you about this just once, now, and then never again."

"Thank you, Doctor. So please tell me what you think is happening here. Then I'll tell you what I know, or think I know."

"What's happening is this," Hays said. "I was working on a project with my colleagues. That's true. But I came to realize the project was a dead end—that the phenomena we were investigating weren't real. So I ceased my involvement in that research. I have no intention of ever picking up that research again—of ever publishing about it, or even talking about it, except to indicate that it was a waste of time. I'd strongly advise you to do the same."

I had no idea how he talked ordinarily, but his words on the phone sounded like each had been chosen with the utmost care. "Why do I feel like you're reading from a script, Dr. Hays?"

"I assure you everything I'm saying is real. As you no doubt already have evidence of yourself," Hays said.

"Now you look," I raised my voice. "You can't just sweep this under the rug. If the Universe is at work here in some way, you think you can just avoid it by pretending you don't know about it? The Universe would know about your pretense, too—it's after all still part of the Universe. And word of this will get out anyway—someone will sooner or later publish something. If you want to live, you've got to face this, find out what's really happening here, and—"

"I believe you are seriously mistaken, my friend. And that, I'm afraid, concludes our interview, now and forever." He hung up.

I held on to the disconnected phone, which beeped like a seal, for a long time. I realized that the left side of my body hurt, from my chest up through my shoulder and down my arm. The pain had come on, I thought, at the end of my futile lecture to Hays. Right when I'd talked about publishing. Maybe publishing was the key—maybe talk about dissemination of this information, as opposed to just thinking about it, is what triggered the Universe's backlash. But I was also sure I was right in what I'd said to Hays about the need to confront this, about not running away. . . .

I put the phone back in its receiver and lay down. I was bone tired. Maybe I was getting a heart attack, maybe I wasn't. Maybe I was still in shock from my dip in the Sound. I couldn't fight this all on my own much longer.

The phone rang. I fumbled with the receiver. How long had I been sleeping? "Hello?"

"Dr. D'Amato?" A female voice, maybe Lauren's, maybe Nurse Johnson's. No, someone else.

"Yes?"

"I'm Jennifer Fenwick."

Fenwick, Fenwick—yes, Jennifer Fenwick, the last quantum physicist on this project. I'd wheedled her number from Abrahmson's secretary and left a message for her in Australia—the girl at the hotel wasn't sure if she'd already left. "Dr. Fenwick, I'm glad you called. I, uhm, had some ideas I wanted to talk to you about—regarding the quantum signaling project." I wasn't sure how much she knew and didn't want to scare her off.

She laughed, oddly. "Well, I'm wide open for ideas. I'll take help wherever I can get it. I'm the only damn person left alive from our research group."

"Only person?" So she knew—apparently more than I.

I looked at the clock. It was tomorrow morning already—I'd slept right through the afternoon and night. Good thing I'd called my office and gotten the week off, the absurd part of me that kept track of such trivia noted.

"Richard Hays committed suicide last night," Fenwick's voice cracked. "He left a note saying he couldn't pull it off any longer—couldn't surmount the paradox of deliberately not thinking of something—couldn't overcome his lifelong urge as a scientist to tell the world what he'd discovered. He'd prepared a paper for publication—begged his wife to have it published posthumously if he didn't make it. I spoke to her this morning. I told her to destroy it. And the note, too. Fortunately for her, she had no idea what the paper was about. She's a simple woman—Richard didn't marry her for her brains."

"I see," I said slowly. "Where are you now?"

"I'm in New York," she said. "I wanted to come home—I didn't want to die in Australia."

"Look, you're still alive," I said. "That means you've still got a chance. How about meeting me for lunch"—I looked at the clock again—"in about an hour. The Trattoria II Bambino on 12th Street in the Village is good. As far as I know, no one there has died from the food as yet." How I could bring myself to make a crack like that at a time like this, I didn't know.

"OK," Fenwick said.

She was waiting for me when I arrived. On the way down, I'd fantasized that she'd look just like Lauren. But in fact she looked a little older and wiser. And even more frightened.

"All right," I said after we'd ordered and gotten rid of the waiter. "Here's what I have in mind. You tell me as a physicist where this might not add up. First, everyone who's attempted to publish something about your work has died."

Jennifer nodded. "I spoke to Lauren Goldring the afternoon she died. She told me she was going to the press."

I sighed. "I didn't know that—but it supports my point.

In fact, the two times I even toyed with going public about this, I had fleeting interviews with death. The first time in the water, the second with some sort of pre—heart attack, I'm sure."

Jennifer nodded again. "Same for me. Wheeler wrote about cosmic censorship. Maybe he was on to the same thing as Hawking."

"All right, so what does that tell us?" I said. "Even thinking about publishing this is dangerous. But apparently it's not a capital offense—knowing about this is in itself not fatal. We're still alive. It's as if the Universe allows private, crackpot knowledge in this area—'cause no one takes crackpots seriously, even scientific ones. It's the danger of public dissemination that draws the response—the threat of an objectively accepted scientific theory. Our private knowledge isn't the real problem here. Communication is. The definite intention to publish. That's what kills you. Yeah, cosmic censorship is a good way of putting it."

"OK," Jennifer said.

"OK," I said. "But it's also clear that we can't just ignore this—can't expect to suppress it in our minds. Not having any particular plan to publish won't be enough to save us— not in the long run. Sooner or later after a dark silent night we'd get the urge to shout it out. It's human nature. It's inside of us. Hays's suicide proves it—his note spells it out. You can't just not think of something. You can't just will an idea into oblivion. It's self-defeating. It makes you want to get up on the rooftop and scream it to the world even more—like a repressed love."

"Agreed," Jennifer said. "So what do we do, then?"

"Well, we can't go public with this story, and we can't will ourselves to forget it. But maybe there's a third way. Here's what I was thinking. I can tell you—in strict confidence—that we sometimes do this in forensics." I lowered my voice. "Let's say we have someone who was killed in a certain way, but we don't want the murderer to know that we know how the murder took place. We just deliberately at first publicly interpret the evidence in a different way—after all, there's usually more than one trauma that can result in a given fatal injury to a body—more than one plausible explanation of how someone was killed. Slipped and hit your head on a rock, or someone hit you on the head with a rock—sometimes there's not much difference between the results of the two."

"The Universe is murderous, all right, I can see that, but I don't see how what you're saying would work in our situation," Jennifer said.

"Well, you tell me," I said. "Your group thinks it built a wormhole that allows signaling through time. But couldn't you find another phenomenon to attribute those effects to? After all, we only have time travel on the brain because of H. G. Wells and his literary offspring. Let's say Wells had never written *The Time Machine*? Let's say science fiction had taken a different turn? Then your group would likely have come up with another explanation for your findings. And you can do this now anyway!" I took a sip of wine and realized I felt pretty good. "You can publish an article on your work and attribute your findings to something other than time travel. Indicate they're some sort of other physical effect. Come up with the equivalent of a false phlogiston theory, an attractive bogus conception for this tiny sliver of subatomic phenomena, to account for the time-travel effects. The truth is, few if any serious scientists actually believe that time travel is possible anyway, right? Most think it's just science fiction, nothing else. Who would have reason to suspect a time-travel effect here unless you specifically called attention to it?"

Jennifer considered. "The graduate research assistants

worked only on the data acquisition level. Only the project principals, the seven of us"—she caught her breath, winced—"only the seven of us knew this was about time travel. No one else. Ours were supposedly the best minds in this area. Lot of good it did us."

"I know." I tried to be as reassuring as I could. "But then without that time-travel label, all you've got is another of a hundred little experiments in this area per year—jeez, I checked the literature, there are a lot more than that—and your study would likely get lost in the wash. That should shut the Universe up. That should keep it safe from time travel—send the scientific community off on the wrong track, in a different direction—maybe not send them off in any direction at all. Could you do that?"

Jennifer sipped her wine slowly. Her glass was shaking. Her lips clung to the rim. She was no doubt thinking that her life depended on what she decided to do now. She was probably right. Mine, too.

"Exotic matter is what makes the effect possible," she said at last. "Exotic matter keeps the wormhole open long enough. No one knows much about how it works—in fact, as far as I know, our group created this kind of exotic matter, in which weak forces are suspended, for the first time in our project. I guess I could make a case that a peculiar property of this exotic matter is that it creates effects that mimic time travel in artificial wormholes—I could make a persuasive argument that we didn't really see time travel through that wormhole at all, what we have instead is a reversal of processes to earlier stages when they come in contact with our exotic matter, no signaling from the future. You know—we thought the glass was half full, but it was really half empty."

"No," I said. "That's still not going far enough. You've got to be more daring in your deception—come up with something that doesn't invoke time travel at all, even in the negative. Publishing a paper with results that are explicitly said not to demonstrate time travel is akin to someone the police never heard of coming into the station and saying he didn't do it—that only arouses our suspicion. I'm sorry to be so blunt, Jennifer. But you've got to do more. Can't you come up with some effects of exotic matter that have nothing to do with time travel at all?"

She drained her wineglass and put it down, neither half full nor half empty. Completely empty. "This goes against everything in my life and training as a scientist," she said. "I'm supposed to pursue the truth, wherever it takes me."

"Right," I said. "And how much truth will you be able to pursue when you're like Hays and Strauss and the others?"

"Einstein said the Universe wasn't malicious," she said. "This is unbelievable."

"Maybe Einstein was saying the glass was half empty when he knew it was half full. Maybe he knew just what he was doing—knew which side his bread was buttered—maybe he wanted to live past middle age."

"God Almighty!" She slammed her hand on the table. Glasses rattled. "Couldn't I just swear before you and the Universe never to publish anything about this? Wouldn't that be enough?"

"Maybe, maybe not," I said. "From the Universe's point of view, your publishing a paper that explicitly attributes the effects to something other than time travel seems much safer—to you as well as the Universe. Let's say you change your mind, years from now, and try to publish a paper that says you succeeded with time travel after all. You'd already be on record in the literature as attributing those effects to something else—you'd be much less likely to be believed then. Safer for the Universe. Safer for you. A paper with a false lead is not only our best bet now, it's an insurance policy for our future."

Jennifer nodded, very slowly. "I guess I could come up with something—some phenomenon unrelated to time travel—unsuggestive of it. The connection of quantum effects to human thought has always had great appeal, and even though I personally never saw much more than wishful thinking in that direction."

"That's better," I said quietly.

"But how can we be sure no one else will want to look into these effects?" Jennifer asked.

I shrugged. "Guarantees of anything are beyond us in this situation. The best we can hope for are probabilities—that's how the QM realm operates anyway, isn't it—likelihoods of our success, statistics in favor of our survival. As for your effects, well, effects don't have much impact outside of a supportive context of theory. Psalm 51 says 'Purge me with hyssop and I shall be clean'—the penicillin mold was first identified on a piece of decayed hyssop by a Swedish chemist—but none of this led to antibiotics until spores from a mold landed in Fleming's petri dish, and he placed them in the right scientific perspective. Scientists thought they had evidence of spontaneous generation of maggots in old meat until they learned how flies make love. Astronomers saw lots of evidence for a luminiferous ether until Michelson-Morley decisively proved that wrong. You're working on the cutting edge of physics with your wormholes. No one knows what to expect—you said it yourself—yours were the best minds in this area. *You* can create the context. No one's left to contradict you. Let's face it, if you word your paper properly, it will likely go unnoticed. But if not, it will point people in the wrong direction—and once pointed that way, away from time travel, the world could take years, decades, longer, to look at time travel as a real scientific possibility again. The history of science is filled with wrong glittering paths tenaciously taken and defended. That's the path of life for us. I'm not happy about it, but there it is."

Our food arrived. Jennifer looked away from me and down at her veal.

I hadn't completely won her over yet. But she'd stopped objecting. I understood how she felt. To theoretical scientists, pursuit of truth was sometimes more important than life itself. Maybe that's why I went into flesh-and-blood forensics. I pushed on. "The truth is, we've all been getting along quite well without time travel anyway—it could wreak far more havoc in everyone's lives than nuclear weapons ever did. The Universe may not be wrong here."

She looked up at me.

"It's all up to you now," I said. "I'm not a physicist. I can't pull this off. I can take care of the general media, but not the scientific journals." I thought about Abrahmson at *Newsday*. He hadn't a clue which way was up in this thing. He'd just as soon believe this nightmare was all coincidence—the ever popular placeholder for things people didn't want to understand. I could easily pitch it to him in that way.

She gave me a weak smile. "OK, I'll try it. I'll write the article with the mental spin on the exotic effects. *Physics Review D* was given some general info that we were doing something on exotic matter and is waiting for our report. It'll have maximum impact on other physicists there. The human mind in control of matter will be catnip for a lot of them anyway."

"Good." I smiled back. I knew she meant it. I knew because I suddenly felt very hungry and dug into my own veal with a zest I hadn't felt for anything in a while. It tasted great.

.

Two particles of humanity had connected again. Maybe this time the relationship would go somewhere.

It occurred to me, as I took Jennifer's hand and squeezed it with relief, that maybe this was just what the Universe had wanted all along.

As they say in the department, an ongoing string of deaths is a poor way to keep a secret.

HAWKSBILL STATION

ROBERT SILVERBERG

ere, time travel is the lever for human intervention in a landscape which would have been otherwise inaccessible: in this way, the historical novel can be envisioned in an entirely new way, the conflation of time periods. Here is a prehistoric novella; this is a definitive example of its subgenre (Aldiss's "Poor Little Warrior!," DeCamp's "A Gun for Dinosaur" and of course the collaborative novel, *Genus Homo*, by P. Schuyler Miller & L. Sprague DeCamp). It is a story of exile which could not have been written as other than science fiction, meeting Theodore Sturgeon's extant definition of a good science fiction story.

Robert Silverberg's first science fiction story was published two years shy of half a century ago; his inestimable body of work in the genre has claimed virtually every award (and usually more than once). His 1968 novel, *Up the Line*, is probably the best time travel story ever published but, alas, is far too long for this anthology. Silverberg lives with his wife, Karen Haber, in San Francisco. I have a particular and sentimental fondness for "Hawksbill Station." It was the lead novella in the August 1967 issue of *Galaxy*, which also contained my first published science-fiction story.

Barrett was the uncrowned king of Hawksbill Station. He had been there the longest; he had suffered the most; he had the deepest inner resources of strength.

Before his accident, he had been able to whip any man in the place. Now he was a cripple, but he still had that aura of power that gave him command. When there were problems at the Station, they were brought to Barrett. That was axiomatic. He was the king.

He ruled over quite a kingdom, too. In effect it was the whole world, pole to pole, meridian to meridian. For what it was worth. It wasn't worth very much.

Now it was raining again. Barrett shrugged himself to his feet in the quick, easy gesture that cost him an infinite amount of carefully concealed agony and shuffled to the door of his hut. Rain made him impatient; the pounding of those great greasy drops against the corrugated tin roof was enough even to drive a Jim Barrett loony. He nudged the door open. Standing in the doorway, Barrett looked out over his kingdom.

Barren rock, nearly to the horizon. A shield of raw dolomite going on and on. Raindrops danced and bounced on that continental slab of rock. No trees. No grass. Behind Barrett's hut lay the sea, gray and vast. The sky was gray too, even when it wasn't raining.

He hobbled out into the rain. Manipulating his crutch was getting to be a simple matter for him now. He leaned comfortably, letting his crushed left foot dangle. A rockslide had pinned him last year during a trip to the edge of the Inland Sea. Back home, Barrett would have been fitted with prosthetics, and that would have been the end of it: a new ankle, a new instep, refurbished ligaments and tendons. But home was two billion years away; and home, there's no returning.

The rain hit him hard. Barrett was a big man, six and a half feet tall, with hooded dark eyes, a jutting nose, a chin that was a monarch among chins. He had weighed two hundred fifty pounds in his prime, in the good old agitating days when he had carried banners and pounded out manifestos. But now he was past sixty and beginning to shrink a little, the skin getting loose around the places where the mighty muscles used to be. It was hard to keep your weight in Hawksbill Station. The food was nutritious, but it lacked intensity. A man got to miss steak. Eating brachiopod stew and trilobite hash wasn't the same thing at all. Barrett was past all bitterness, though. That was another reason why the men regarded him as the leader. He didn't scowl. He didn't rant. He was resigned to his fate, tolerant of eternal exile, and so he could help the others get over that difficult heart-clawing period of transition.

A figure arrived, jogging through the rain: Norton. The doctrinaire Khrushchevist with the Trotskyite leanings. A small, excitable man who frequently appointed himself messenger whenever there was news at the Station. He sprinted toward Barrett's hut, slipping and sliding over the naked rocks.

Barrett held up a meaty hand.

"Whoa, Charley. Take it easy or you'll break your neck!"

Norton halted in front of the hut. The rain had pasted the widely spaced strands of his brown hair to his skull. His eyes had the fixed, glossy look of fanaticism—or perhaps just astigmatism. He gasped for breath and staggered into the hut, shaking himself like a wet puppy. He obviously had run all the way from the main building of the Station, three hundred yards away—a long dash over rock that slippery.

"Why are you standing around in the rain?" Norton asked.

"To get wet," said Barrett, following him. "What's the news?"

"The Hammer's glowing. We're getting company."

"How do you know it's a live shipment?"

"It's been glowing for half an hour. That means they're taking precautions. They're sending a new prisoner. Anyway, no supply shipment is due."

Barrett nodded. "Okay. I'll come over. If it's a new man, we'll bunk him in with Latimer."

Norton managed a rasping laugh. "Maybe he's a materialist. Latimer will drive him crazy with all that mystic nonsense. We could put him with Altman."

"And he'll be raped in half an hour."

"Altman's off that kick now," said Norton. "He's trying to create a real woman, not looking for second-rate substitutes."

"Maybe our new man doesn't have any spare ribs."

"Very funny, Jim." Norton did not look amused. "You know what I want the new man to be? A conservative, that's

what. A black-souled reactionary straight out of Adam
Smith. God, that's what I want."

"Wouldn't you be happy with a fellow Bolshevik?"

"This place is full of Bolsheviks," said Norton. "Of all
shades from pale pink to flagrant scarlet. Don't you think
I'm sick of them? Sitting around fishing for trilobites and
discussing the relative merits of Kerensky and Malenkov? I
need somebody to *talk* to, Jim. Somebody I can fight with."

"All right," Barret said, slipping into his rain gear. "I'll
see what I can do about hocusing a debating partner out of
the Hammer for you. A rip-roaring objectivist, okay?" He
laughed. "You know something, maybe there's been a revolution Up Front since we got our last man. Maybe the left
is in and the right is out, and they'll start shipping us nothing *but* reactionaries. How would you like that? Fifty or a
hundred storm troopers, Charley? Plenty of material to de-
bate economics with. And the place will fill up with more
and more of them, until we're outnumbered, and then
maybe they'll have a *putsch* and get rid of all the stinking
leftists sent here by the old regime, and—"

Barrett stopped. Norton was staring at him in amazement,
his faded eyes wide, his hand compulsively smoothing his
thinning hair to hide his embarassment.

Barrett realized that he had just committed one of the
most heinous crimes possible at Hawksbill Station: he had
started to run off at the mouth. There hadn't been any call
for his little outburst. What made it more troublesome was
the fact that *he* was the one who had permitted himself such
a luxury. He was supposed to be the strong one of this place,
the stabilizer, the man of absolute integrity and principle
and sanity on whom the others could lean. And suddenly
he had lost control. It was a bad sign. His dead foot was

throbbing again; possibly that was the reason.

In a tight voice he said, "Let's go. Maybe the new man is here already."

They stepped outside. The rain was beginning to let up; the storm was moving out to sea. In the east over what would one day be the Atlantic, the sky was still clotted with gray mist, but to the west a different grayness was emerging, the shade of normal gray that meant dry weather. Before he had come out here, Barrett had expected to find the sky practically black, because there'd be fewer dust particles to bounce the light around and turn things blue. But the sky seemed to be weary beige. So much for advance theories.

Through the thinning rain they walked toward the main building. Norton accommodated himself to Barrett's limping pace, and Barrett, wielding his crutch furiously, did his damndest not to let his infirmity slow them up. He nearly lost his footing twice and fought hard not to let Norton see.

Hawksbill Station spread out before them.

It covered about five hundred acres. In the center of everything was the main building, an ample dome that contained most of their equipment and supplies. At widely spaced intervals, rising from the rock shield like grotesque giant green mushrooms, were the plastic blisters of the individual dwellings. Some, like Barrett's, were shielded by tin sheeting salvaged from shipments from Up Front. Others stood unprotected, just as they had come from the mouth of the extruder.

The huts numbered about eighty. At the moment, there were a hundred forty inmates in Hawksbill Station, pretty close to the all-time high. Up Front hadn't sent back any hut building materials for a long time, and so all the newer arrivals had to double up with bunkmates. Barrett and all those whose exile had begun before 2014 had the privilege of private dwellings, if they wanted them. (Some did not wish to live alone; Barrett, to preserve his own authority, felt that he was required to.) As new exiles arrived, they bunked in with those who currently lived alone, in reverse order of seniority. Most of the 2015 exiles had been forced to take roommates now. Another dozen deportees and the 2014 group would be doubling up. Of course, there were deaths all up and down the line, and there were plenty who were eager to have company in their huts.

Barrett felt, though, that a man who has been sentenced to life imprisonment ought to have the privilege of privacy, if he desires it. One of his biggest problems here was keeping people from cracking up because there was too little privacy. Propinquity could be intolerable in a place like this.

Norton pointed toward the big, shiny-skinned, green dome of the main building. "There's Altman going in now. And Rudiger. And Hutchett. Something's happening!"

Barrett stepped up his pace. Some of the men entering the building saw his bulky figure coming over the rise in the rock and waved to him. Barrett lifted a massive hand in reply. He felt mounting excitement. It was a big event at the Station whenever a new man arrived. Nobody had come for six months, now. That was the longest gap he could remember. It had started to seem as though no one would ever come again.

That would be a catastrophe.

New men were all that stood between the older inmates and insanity. New men brought news from the future, news from the world that was eternally left behind. They contributed new personalities to a group that always was in danger of going stale.

And, Barrett knew, some men—he was not one—lived in the deluded hope that the next arrival might just turn out to be a woman.

That was why they flocked to the main building when the Hammer began to glow. Barrett hobbled down the path. The rain died away just as he reached the entrance.

Within, sixty or seventy Station residents crowded the chamber of the Hammer—just about every man in the place who was able in body and mind and still alert enough to show curiosity about a newcomer. They shouted greetings to Barrett. He nodded, smiled, deflected their questions with amiable gestures.

"Who's it going to be this time, Jim?"

"Maybe a girl, huh? Around nineteen years old, blonde, and built like—"

"I hope he can play stochastic chess, anyway."

"Look at the glow! It's deepening!"

Barrett, like the others, stared at the Hammer. The complex, involuted collection of unfathomable instruments burned a bright cherry red, betokening the surge of who knew how many kilowatts being pumped in at the far end of the line.

The glow was beginning to spread to the Anvil now, that broad aluminum bedplate on which all shipments from the future were dropped. In another moment—

"Condition Crimson!" somebody suddenly yelled. "Here he comes!"

II

Two billion years up the timeline, power was flooding into the real Hammer of which this was only the partial replica. A man—or something else, perhaps a shipment of supplies—

stood in the center of the real Anvil, waiting for the Hawksbill Field to enfold him and kick him back to the early Paleozoic. The effect of time-travel was very much like being hit with a gigantic hammer and driven clear through the walls of the continuum: hence the governing metaphors for the parts of the machine.

Setting up Hawksbill Station had been a long, slow job. The Hammer had knocked a pathway and had sent back the nucleus of the receiving station, first. Since there was no receiving station on hand to receive the receiving station, a certain amount of waste had occurred. It wasn't necessary to have a Hammer and Anvil on the receiving end, except as a fine control to prevent temporal spread; without the equipment, the field wandered a little, and it was possible to scatter consecutive shipments over a span of twenty or thirty years. There was plenty of such temporal garbage all around Hawksbill Station, stuff that had been intended for original installation, but which because of tuning imprecisions in the pre-Hammer days had landed a couple of decades (and a couple of hundred miles) away from the intended site.

Despite such difficulties, they had finally sent through enough components to the master temporal site to allow for the construction of a receiving station. Then the first prisoners had gone through; they were technicians who knew how to put the Hammer and Anvil together. Of course, it was their privilege to refuse to cooperate. But it was to their own advantage to assemble the receiving station, thus making it possible for them to be sure of getting further supplies from Up Front. They had done the job. After that, outfitting Hawksbill Station had been easy.

Now the Hammer glowed, meaning that they had activated the Hawksbill Field on the sending end, somewhere up around 2028 or 2030 A.D. All the sending was done there.

All the receiving was done here. It didn't work the other way. Nobody really knew why, although there was a lot of superficially profound talk about the rules of entropy.

There was a whining, hissing sound as the edges of the Hawksbill Field began to ionize the atmosphere in the room. Then came the expected thunderclap of implosion, caused by an imperfect overlapping of the quantity of air that was subtracted from this era and the quantity that was being thrust into it. And then, abruptly, a man dropped out of the Hammer and lay, stunned and limp, on the gleaming Anvil.

He looked young, which surprised Barrett considerably. He seemed to be well under thirty. Generally, only middleaged men were sent to Hawksbill Station. Incorrigibles, who had to be separated from humanity for the general good. The youngest man in the place now had been close to forty when he arrived. The sight of this lean, cleancut boy drew a hiss of anguish from a couple of the men in the room, and Barrett understood the constellation of emotions that pained them.

The new man sat up. He stirred like a child coming out of a long, deep sleep. He looked around.

His face was very pale. His thin lips seemed bloodless. His blue eyes blinked rapidly. His jaws worked as though he wanted to say something, but could not find the words.

There were no harmful physiological effects to time-travel, but it could be a jolt to the consciousness. The last moments before the Hammer descended were very much like the final moments beneath the guillotine, since exile to Hawksbill Station was tantamount to a sentence of death. The departing prisoner took his last look at the world of rocket transport and artificial organs, at the world in which he had lived and loved and agitated for a political cause, and then he was rammed into the inconceivably remote past on a one-way journey. It was a gloomy business, and it was not very surprising that the newcomers arrived in a state of emotional shock.

Barrett elbowed his way through the crowd. Automatically, the others made way for him. He reached the lip of the Anvil and leaned over it, extending a hand to the new man. His broad smile was met by a look of blank bewilderment.

"I'm Jim Barrett. Welcome to Hawksbill Station. Here— get off that thing before a load of groceries lands on top of you." Wincing a little as he shifted his weight, Barrett pulled the new man down from the Anvil. It was altogether likely for the idiots Up Front to shoot another shipment along a minute after sending a man.

Barrett beckoned to Mel Rudiger, and the plump anarchist handed the new man an alcohol capsule. He took it and pressed it to his arm without a word. Charley Norton offered him a candy bar. The man shook it off. He looked groggy. A real case of temporal shock, Barrett thought, possibly the worst he had ever seen. The newcomer hadn't even spoken yet. Could the effect really be that extreme?

Barrett said, "We'll go to the infirmary and check you out. Then I'll assign you your quarters. There's time for you to find your way around and meet everybody later on. What's your name?"

"Hahn. Lew Hahn."

"I can't hear you."

"Hahn," the man repeated, still only barely audible.

"When are you from, Lew?"

"2029."

"You feel pretty sick?"

"I feel awful. I don't even believe this is happening to me. There's no such place as Hawksbill Station, is there?"

"I'm afraid there is," Barrett said.

"At least, for most of us. A few of the boys think it's all an illusion induced by drugs. But I have my doubts of that. If it's an illusion, it's a damned good one. Look."

He put one arm around Hahn's shoulders and guided him through the press of prisoners, out of the Hammer chamber and toward the nearby infirmary. Although Hahn looked thin, even fragile, Barrett was surprised to feel the rippling muscles in those shoulders. He suspected that this man was a lot less helpless and ineffectual than he seemed to be right now. He *had* to be, in order to merit banishment to Hawksbill Station.

They passed the door of the building. "Look out there," Barrett commanded.

Hahn looked. He passed a hand across his eyes as though to clear away unseen cobwebs and looked again.

"A late Cambrian landscape," said Barrett quietly. "This would be a geologist's dream, except that geologists don't tend to become political prisoners, it seems. Out in front is the Appalachian Geosyncline. It's a strip of rock a few hundred miles wide and a few thousand miles long, from the Gulf of Mexico to Newfoundland. To the east we've got the Atlantic. A little way to the west we've got the Inland Sea. Somewhere two thousand miles to the west there's the Cordilleran Geosyncline, that's going to be California and Washington and Oregon someday. Don't hold your breath. I hope you like seafood."

Hahn stared, and Barrett, standing beside him at the doorway, stared also. You never got used to the alienness of this place, not even after you lived here twenty years, as Barrett had. It was Earth, and yet it was not really Earth at all, because it was somber and empty and unreal. The gray oceans swarmed with life, of course. But there was nothing on land except occasional patches of moss in the occasional patches of soil that had formed on the bare rock. Even a few cockroaches would be welcome; but insects, it seemed, were still a couple of geological periods in the future. To land-dwellers, this was a dead world, a world unborn.

Shaking his head, Hahn moved away from the door. Barrett led him down the corridor and into the small, brightly lit room that served as the infirmary. Doc Quesada was waiting. Quesada wasn't really a doctor, but he had been a medical technician once, and that was good enough. He was a compact, swarthy man with a look of complete self-assurance. He hadn't lost too many patients, all things considered. Barrett had watched him removing appendices with total aplomb. In his white smock, Quesada looked sufficiently medical to fit his role.

Barrett said, "Doc, this is Lew Hahn. He's in temporal shock. Fix him up."

Quesada nudged the newcomer onto a webfoam cradle and unzipped his blue jersey. Then he reached for his medical kit. Hawksbill Station was well equipped for most medical emergencies, now. The people Up Front had no wish to be inhumane, and they sent back all sorts of useful things, like anesthetics and surgical clamps and medicines and dermal probes. Barrett could remember a time at the beginning when there had been nothing much here but the empty huts; and a man who hurt himself was in real trouble.

"He's had a drink already," said Barrett.

"I see that," Quesada murmured. He scratched at his shortcropped, bristly mustache. The little diagnostat in the cradle had gone rapidly to work, flashing information about Hahn's blood pressure, potassium count, dilation index, and much else. Quesada seemed to comprehend the barrage of facts. After a moment he said to Hahn, "You aren't really sick, are you? Just shaken up a little. I don't blame you.

Here—I'll give you a quick jolt to calm your nerves, and you'll be all right as any of us ever are."

He put a tube to Hahn's carotid and thumbed the snout. The subsonic whirred, and a tranquilizing compound slid into the man's bloodstream. Hahn shivered.

Quesada said, "Let him rest for five minutes. Then he'll be over the hump."

They left Hahn in his cradle and went out of the infirmary. In the hall, Barrett looked down at the little medic and said, "What's the report on Valdosto?"

Valdosto had gone into psychotic collapse several weeks before. Quesada was keeping him drugged and trying to bring him slowly back to the reality of Hawksbill Station. Shrugging, he replied, "The status is quo. I let him out from under the dream-juice this morning, and he was the same as he's been."

"You don't think he'll come out of it?"

"I doubt it. He's cracked for keeps. They could paste him together Up Front, but—"

"Yeah," Barrett said. If he could get Up Front at all, Valdosto wouldn't have cracked. "Keep him happy, then. If he can't be sane, he can at least be comfortable. What about Altman? Still got the shakes?"

"He's building a woman."

"That's what Charley Norton told me. What's he using? A rag, a bone—"

"I gave him surplus chemicals. Chosen for their color, mainly. He's got some foul green copper compounds and a little bit of ethyl alcohol and six or seven other things, and he collected some soil and threw in a lot of dead shellfish, and he's sculpting it all into what he claims is female shape and waiting for lightning to strike it."

"In other words, he's gone crazy," Barrett said.

"I think that's a safe assumption. But he's not molesting

his friends any more, anyway. You didn't think his homosexual phase would last much longer, as I recall."

"No, but I didn't think he'd go off the deep end. If a man needs sex and he can find some consenting playmates here, that's quite all right with me. But when he starts putting a woman together out of some dirt and rotten brachiopod meat it means we've lost him. It's really just too bad."

Quesada's dark eyes flickered. "We're all going to go that way sooner or later, Jim."

"I haven't. You haven't."

"Give us time. I've only been here eleven years."

"Altman's been here only eight. Valdosto even less."

"Some shells crack faster than others," said Quesada. "Here's our new friend.

Hahn had come out of the infirmary to join them. He still looked pale, but the fright was gone from his eyes. He was beginning to adjust to the unthinkable.

He said, "I couldn't help overhearing your conversation. Is there a lot of mental illness here?"

"Some of the men haven't been able to find anything meaningful to do here," Barrett said. "It eats them away. Quesada here has his medical work. I've got administrative duties. A couple of the fellows are studying the sea life. We've got a newspaper to keep some busy. But there are always those who just let themselves slide into despair, and they crack up. I'd say we have thirty or forty certifiable maniacs here at the moment, out of a hundred forty residents."

"That's not so bad," Hahn said. "Considering the inherent instability of the men who get sent here and the unusual conditions of life here."

Barrett laughed. "Hey, you're suddenly pretty articulate, aren't you? What was in the stuff Doc Quesada jolted you with?"

"I didn't mean to sound superior," Hahn said quickly. "Maybe that came out a little too smug. I mean—"

"Forget it. What did you do Up Front, anyway?"

"I was sort of an economist."

"Just what we need," said Quesada. "He can help us solve our balance-of-payments problem."

Barrett said, "If you were an economist, you'll have plenty to discuss here. This place is full of economic theorists who'll want to bounce their ideas off you. Some of them are almost sane, too. Come with me and I'll show you where you're going to stay."

III

The path from the main building to the hut of Donald Latimer was mainly downhill, for which Barrett was grateful even though he knew that he'd have to negotiate the uphill return in a little while. Latimer's hut was on the eastern side of the Station, looking out over the ocean. They walked slowly toward it. Hahn was solicitous of Barrett's game leg, and Barrett was irritated by the exagerrated care the younger man took to keep pace with him.

He was puzzled by this Hahn. The man was full of seeming contradictions—showing up here with the worst case of arrival shock Barrett had even seen, then snapping out of it with remarkable quickness; looking frail and shy, but hiding solid muscles inside his jersey; giving an outer appearance of incompetence, but speaking with calm control. Barrett wondered what this young man had done to earn him the trip to Hawksbill Station, but there was time for such inquiries later. All the time in the world.

Hahn said, "Is everything like this? Just rock and ocean?"

"That's all. Land life hasn't evolved yet. Everything's wonderfully simple, isn't it? No clutter. No urban sprawl. There's some moss moving onto land, but not much."

"And in the sea? Swimming dinosaurs?"

Barrett shook his head. "There won't be any vertebrates for half a million years. We don't even have fish yet, let alone reptiles out there. All we can offer is that which cree-peth. Some shellfish, some big fellows that look like squids and trilobites. Seven hundred billion different species of tri-lobites. We've got a man named Rudiger—he's the one who gave you the drink—who's making a collection of them. He's writing the world's definitive text on trilobites."

"But nobody will ever read it in—in the future."

"Up Front, we say."

"Up Front."

"That's the pity of it," said Barrett. "We told Rudiger to inscribe his book on imperishable plates of gold and hope that it's found by paleontologists. But he says the odds are against it. Two billion years of geology will chew his plates to hell before they can be found."

Hahn sniffed. "Why does the air smell so strange?"

"It's a different mix," Barrett said. "We've analyzed it. More nitrogen, a little less oxygen, hardly any CO_2 at all. But that isn't really why it smells odd to you. The thing is, it's pure air, unpolluted by the exhalations of life. Nobody's been respiring into it but us lads, and there aren't enough of us to matter."

Smiling, Hahn said, "I feel a little cheated that it's so empty. I expected lush jungles of weird plants and pterodactyls swooping through the air and maybe a tyrannosaur crashing into a fence around the Station."

"No jungles. No pterodactyls. No tyrannosaurs. No fences. You didn't do your homework."

"Sorry."

"This is the late Cambrian. Sea life exclusively."

"It was very kind of them to pick such a peaceful era as the dumping ground for political prisoners," Hahn said. "I was afraid it would be all teeth and claws."

"Kind, hell! They were looking for an era where we couldn't do any harm. That meant tossing us back before the evolution of mammals, just in case we'd accidentally got hold of the ancestor of all humanity and snuff him out. And while they were at it, they decided to stash us so far in the past that we'd be beyond all land life, on the theory that maybe even if we slaughtered a baby dinosaur it might affect the entire course of the future."

"They don't mind if we catch a few trilobites?"

"Evidently they think it's safe," Barrett said. "It looks as though they were right. Hawksbill Station has been here for twenty-five years, and it doesn't seem as though we've tampered with future history in any measurable way. Of course, they're careful not to send us any women."

"Why is that?"

"So we don't start reproducing and perpetuating ourselves. Wouldn't that mess up the timelines? A successful human outpost in two billion B.C., that's had all that time to evolve and mutate and grow? By the time the twenty-first century came around, our descendants would be in charge, and the other kind of human being would probably be in penal servitude, and there'd be more paradoxes created than you could shake a trilobite at. So they don't send the women here. There's a prison camp for women, too, but it's a few hundred million years up the time-line in the late Silurian, and never the twain shall meet. That's why Ned Altman's trying to build a woman out of dust and garbage."

"God made Adam out of less."

"Altman isn't God," Barrett said. "That's the root of his

whole problem. Look, here's the hut where you're going to stay. I'm rooming you with Don Latimer. He's a very sensitive, interesting, pleasant person. He used to be a physicist before he got into politics, and he's been here about a dozen years, and I might as well warn you that he's developed a strong and somewhat cockeyed mystic streak lately. The fellow he was rooming with killed himself last year, and since then he's been trying to find some way out of here through extrasensory powers."

"Is he serious?"

"I'm afraid he is. And we try to take him seriously. We all humor each other at Hawksbill Station; it's the only way we avoid a mass psychosis. Latimer will probably try to get you to collaborate with him on his project. If you don't like living with him, I can arrange a transfer for you. But I want to see how he reacts to someone new at the Station. I'd like you to give him a chance."

"Maybe I'll even help him find his psionic gateway."

"If you do, take me along," said Barrett. They both laughed. Then he rapped at Latimer's door. There was no answer, and after a moment Barrett pushed the door open. Hawksbill Station had no locks.

Latimer sat in the middle of the bare rock floor, crosslegged, meditating. He was a slender, gentle-faced man just beginning to look old. Right now he seemed a million miles away, ignoring them completely. Hahn shrugged. Barrett put a finger to his lips. They waited in silence for a few minutes, and then Latimer showed signs of coming up from his trance.

He got to his feet in a single flowing motion, without using his hands. In a low, courteous voice he said to Hahn, "Have you just arrived?"

"Within the last hour. I'm Lew Hahn."

"Donald Latimer. I regret that I have to make your acquaintance in these surroundings. But maybe we won't have to tolerate this illegal imprisonment much longer."

Barrett said, "Don, Lew is going to bunk with you. I think you'll get along well. He was an economist in 2029 until they gave him the Hammer."

"Where do you live?" Latimer asked, animation coming into his eyes.

"San Francisco."

The glow faded. Latimer said, "Were you ever in Toronto? I'm from there. I had a daughter—she'd be twenty-three now, Nella Latimer. I wondered if you knew her."

"No. I'm sorry."

"It wasn't very likely. But I'd love to know what kind of a woman she became. She was a little girl when I last saw her. Now I guess she's married. Or perhaps they've sent her to the other Station. Nella Latimer—you're sure you didn't know her?"

Barrett left them together. It looked as though they'd get along. He told Latimer to bring Hahn up to the main building at dinner for introductions and went out. A chilly drizzle had begun again. Barrett made his way slowly, painfully up the hill. It had been sad to see the light flicker from Latimer's eyes when Hahn said he didn't know his daughter. Most of the time, men at Hawksbill Station tried not to speak about their families, preferring to keep those tormenting memories well repressed. But the arrival of newcomers generally stirred old ties. There was never any news of relatives and no way to obtain any, because it was impossible for the Station to communicate with anyone Up Front. No way to ask for the photo of a loved one, no way to request specific medicines, no way to obtain a certain book or a coveted tape. In a mindless, impersonal way, Up Front sent periodic shipments to the Station of things thought useful—reading matter, medical supplies, technical equipment, food. Occasionally they were startling in their generosity, as when they sent a case of Burgundy, or a box of sensory spools, or a recharger for the power pack. Such gifts usually meant a brief thaw in the world situation, which customarily produced a short-lived desire to be kind to the boys in Hawksbill Station. But they had a policy about sending information about relatives. Or about contemporary newspapers. Fine wine, yes; a tridim of a daughter who would never be seen again, no.

For all Up Front knew, there was no one alive in Hawksbill Station. A plague could have killed everyone off ten years ago, but there was no way of telling. That was why the shipments still came back. The government whirred and clicked with predictable continuity. The government, whatever else it might be, was not malicious. There were other kinds of totalitarianism besides bloody repressive tyranny.

Pausing at the top of the hill, Barrett caught his breath. Naturally, the alien air no longer smelled strange to him. He filled his lungs with it. Once again the rain ceased. Through the grayness came the sunshine, making the naked rocks sparkle. Barrett closed his eyes a moment and leaned on his crutch and saw, as though on an inner screen, the creatures with many legs climbing up out of the sea, and the mossy carpets spreading, and the flowerless plants uncoiling and spreading their scaly branches, and the dull hides of eerie amphibians glistening on the shores and the tropic heat of the coal-forming epoch descending like a glove over the world.

All that lay far in the future. Dinosaurs. Little chittering mammals. Pithecanthropus in the forests of Java. Sargon and Hannibal and Attila and Orville Wright and Thomas Edison and Edmond Hawksbill. And finally a benign government that would find the thoughts of some men so intolerable that the only safe place to which they could be banished was a rock at the beginning of time. The government was too civilized to put men to death for subversive activities and too cowardly to let them remain alive. The compromise was the living death of Hawksbill Station. Two billion years of impassable time was suitable insulation even for the most nihilistic idea.

Grimacing a little, Barrett struggled the rest of the way back toward his hut. He had long since come to accept his exile, but accepting his ruined foot was another matter entirely. The idle wish to find a way to regain the freedom of his own time no longer possessed him; but he wished with all his soul that the blank-faced administrators Up Front would send back a kit that would allow him to rebuild his foot.

He entered his hut and flung his crutch aside, sinking down instantly on his cot. There had been no cots when he had come to Hawksbill Station. He had come here in the fourth year of the Station, when there were only a dozen buildings and little in the way of creature comforts. It had been a miserable place, then, but the steady accretion of shipments from Up Front had made it relatively tolerable. Of the fifty or so prisoners who had preceded Barrett to Hawksbill, none remained alive. He had held the highest seniority for almost ten years. Time moved here at one-to-one correlation with time Up Front; the Hammer was locked on this point of time, so that Hahn, arriving here today more than twenty years after Barrett, had departed from a year Up Front more than twenty years after the time of Barrett's expulsion. Barrett had not had the heart to begin pumping Hahn for news of 2029 so soon. He would learn all he needed to know, and small cheer it would be, anyway.

Barret reached for a book. But the fatigue of hobbling

around the station had taken more out of him than he realized. He looked at the page for a moment. Then he put it away and closed his eyes and dozed.

IV

That evening, as every evening, the men of Hawksbill Station gathered in the main building for dinner and recreation. It was not mandatory, and some men chose to eat alone. But tonight nearly everyone who was in full possession of his faculties was there, because this was one of the infrequent occasions when a newcomer had arrived to be questioned about the world of men.

Hahn looked uneasy about his sudden notoriety. He seemed to be basically shy, unwilling to accept all the attention now being thrust upon him. There he sat in the middle of the group while men twenty and thirty years his senior crowded in on him with their questions, and it was obvious that he wasn't enjoying the session.

Sitting to one side, Barrett took little part in the discussion. His curiosity about Up Front's ideological shifts had ebbed a long time ago. It was hard for him to realize that he had once been so passionately concerned about concepts like syndicalism and the dictatorship of the proletariat and the guaranteed annual wage that he had been willing to risk imprisonment over them. His concern for humanity had not waned, merely the degree of his involvement in the twenty-first century's political problems. After twenty years at Hawksbill Station, Up Front had become unreal to Jim Barrett, and his energies centered around the crises and challenges of what he had come to think of as "his own" time—the late Cambrian.

So he listened, but more with an ear for what the talk

revealed about Lew Hahn than for what it revealed about current events Up Front. And what it revealed about Lew Hahn was mainly a matter of what was not revealed.

Hahn didn't say much. He seemed to be feinting and evading.

Charley Norton wanted to know, "Is there any sign of a weakening of the phony conservatism yet? I mean, they've been promising the end of big government for thirty years, and it gets bigger all the time."

Hahn moved restlessly in his chair. "They still promise. As soon as conditions become stabilized—"

"Which is when?"

"I don't know. I suppose they're making words."

"What about the Martian Commune?" demanded Sid Hutchett. "Have they been infiltrating agents onto Earth?"

"I couldn't really say."

"How about the Gross Global Product?" Mel Rudiger wanted to know. "What's its curve? Still holding level, or has it started to drop?"

Hahn tugged at his ear. "I think it's slowly edging down."

"Where does the index stand?" Rudiger asked. "The last figures we had, for '25, it was at 909. But in four years—"

"It might be something like 875 now," said Hahn.

It struck Barrett as a little odd that an economist would be so hazy about the basic economic statistic. Of course, he didn't know how long Hahn had been imprisoned before getting the Hammer. Maybe he simply wasn't up on the recent figures. Barrett held his peace.

Charley Norton wanted to find out some things about the legal rights of citizens. Hahn couldn't tell him. Rudiger asked about the impact of weather control—whether the supposedly conservative government of liberators was still ramming programmed weather down the mouths of the citizens—and Hahn wasn't sure. Hahn couldn't rightly say much about the functions of the judiciary, whether it had recovered any of the power stripped from it by the Enabling Act of '18. He didn't have any comments to offer on the tricky subject of population control. In fact, his performance was striking for its lack of hard information.

"He isn't saying much at all," Charley Norton grumbled to the silent Barrett. "He's putting up a smokescreen. But either he's not telling what he knows, or he doesn't know."

"Maybe he's not very bright," Barrett suggested.

"What did he do to get here? He must have had some kind of deep commitment. But it doesn't show, Jim! He's an intelligent kid, but he doesn't seem plugged in to anything that ever mattered to any of us."

Doc Quesada offered a thought. "Suppose he isn't a political at all. Suppose they're sending a different kind of prisoner back now. Axe murderers, or something. A quiet kid who quietly chopped up sixteen people one Sunday morning. Naturally he isn't interested in politics."

Barrett shook his head. "I doubt that. I think he's just clamming up because he's shy or ill at ease. It's his first night here, remember. He's just been kicked out of his own world and there's no going back. He may have left a wife and baby behind, you know. He may simply not give a damn tonight about sitting up there and spouting the latest word on abstract philosophical theory, when all he wants to do is go off and cry his eyes out. I say we ought to leave him alone."

Quesada and Norton looked convinced. They shook their heads in agreement; but Barrett didn't voice his opinion to the room in general. He let the quizzing of Hahn continue until it petered out of its own accord. The men began to drift away. A couple of them went in back to convert Hahn's vague generalities into the lead story for the next hand-written edition of the Hawksbill Station *Times*. Rudiger stood on a table and shouted out that he was going night fishing, and four men asked to join him. Charley Norton sought out his usual debating partner, the nihilist Ken Belardi, and reopened, like a festering wound, their discussion of planning versus chaos, which bored them both to the point of screaming. The nightly games of stochastic chess began. The loners who had made rare visits to the main building simply to see the new man went back to their huts to do whatever they did in them alone each night.

Hahn stood apart, fidgeting and uncertain.

Barrett went up to him. "I guess you didn't really want to be quizzed tonight," he said.

"I'm sorry I couldn't have been more informative. I've been out of circulation a while, you see."

"But you were politically active, weren't you?"

"Oh, yes," Hahn said. "Of course," He flicked his tongue over his lips. "What's supposed to happen now?"

"Nothing in particular. We don't have organized activities here. Doc and I are going out on sick call. Care to join us?"

"What does it involve?" Hahn asked.

"Visiting some of the worst cases. It can be grim, but you'll get a panoramic view of Hawksbill Station in a hurry."

"I'd like to go."

Barrett gestured to Quesada, and the three of them left the building. This was a nightly ritual for Barrett, difficult as it was since he had hurt his foot. Before turning in, he visited the goofy ones and the psycho ones and the catatonic ones, tucked them in, wished them a good night and a healed mind in the morning. Someone had to show them that he cared. Barrett did.

Outside, Hahn peered up at the moon. It was nearly full tonight, shining like a burnished coin, its face a pale salmon color and hardly pockmarked at all.

"It looks so different here," Hahn said. "The craters— where are the craters?"

"Most of them haven't been formed yet," said Barrett. "Two billion years is a long time even for the moon. Most of its upheavals are still ahead. We think it may still have an atmosphere, too. That's why it looks pink to us. Of course, Up Front hasn't bothered to send us much in the way of astronomical equipment. We can only guess."

Hahn started to say something. He cut himself off after one blurted syllable.

Quesada said, "Don't hold it back. What were you about to suggest?"

Hahn laughed in self-mockery. "That you ought to fly up there and take a look. It struck me as odd that you'd spend all these years here theorizing about whether the moon's got an atmosphere and wouldn't ever once go up to look. But I forgot."

"It would be useful to have a commut ship from Up Front," Barrett said. "But it hasn't occurred to them. All we can do is look. The moon's a popular place in '29, is it?"

"The biggest resort in the system," Hahn said. "I was there on my honeymoon. Leah and I—"

He stopped again.

Barrett said hurriedly, "This is Bruce Valdosto's hut. He cracked up a few weeks ago. When we go in, stand behind us so he doesn't see you. He might be violent with a stranger. He's unpredictable."

Valdosto was a husky man in his late forties, with swarthy skin, coarse curling black hair, and the broadest shoulders any man had ever had. Sitting down, he looked even burlier than Jim Barrett, which was saying a great deal. But Valdosto had short, stumpy legs, the legs of a man of ordinary stature tacked to the trunk of a giant, which spoiled the effect completely. In his years Up Front he had totally refused any prosthesis. He believed in living with deformities.

Right now he was strapped into a webfoam cradle. His domed forehead was flecked with beads of sweat, his eyes were glittering beadily in the darkness. He was a very sick man. Once he had been clear-minded enough to throw a sleet bomb into a meeting of the Council of Syndics, giving a dozen of them a bad case of gamma poisoning, but now he scarcely knew up from down, right from left.

Barrett leaned over him and said, "How are you, Bruce?"

"Who's that?"

"Jim. It's a beautiful night, Bruce. How'd you like to come outside and get some fresh air? The moon's almost full."

"I've got to rest. The committee meeting tomorrow—"

"It's been postponed."

"But how can it? The Revolution—"

"That's been postponed too. Indefinitely."

"Are they disbanding the cells?" Valdosto asked harshly.

"We don't know yet. We're waiting for orders. Come outside, Bruce. The air will do you good."

Muttering, Valdosto let himself be unlaced. Quesada and Barrett pulled him to his feet and propelled him through the door of the hut. Barrett caught sight of Hahn in the shadows, his face somber with shock.

They stood together outside the hut. Barrett pointed to the moon. "It's got such a lovely color here. Not like the dead thing Up Front. And look, look down there, Bruce. The sea breaking on the rocky shore. Rudiger's out fishing. I can see his boat by moonlight."

"Striped bass," said Valdosto. "Sunnies. Maybe he'll catch some sunnies."

"There aren't any sunnies here. They haven't evolved yet." Barrett fished in his pocket and drew out something ridged and glossy, about two inches long. It was the exos-kelton of a small trilobite. He offered it to Valdosto, who shook his head.

"Don't give me that cockeyed crab."

"It's a trilobite, Bruce. It's extinct, but so are we. We're two billion years in our own past."

"You must be crazy," Valdosto said in a calm, low voice that belied his wild-eyed appearance. He took the trilobite from Barrett and hurled it against the rocks. "Cockeyed crab," he muttered.

Quesada shook his head sadly. He and Barrett led the sick man into the hut again. Valdosto did not protest as the medic gave him the sedative. His weary mind, rebelling en-tirely against the monstrous concept that he had been exiled to the inconceivably remote past, welcomed sleep.

When they went out Barrett saw Hahn holding the trilobite on his palm and staring at it in wonder. Hahn offered it to him, but Barrett brushed it away. "Keep it if you like," he said. "There are more."

They went on. They found Ned Altman beside his hut, crouching on his knees and patting his hands over the crude, lopsided form of what, from its exaggerated breasts and hips, appeared to be the image of a woman. He stood up when they appeared. Altman was a neat little man with yellow hair and nearly invisible white eyebrows. Unlike anyone else in the Station, he had actually been a government man once, fifteen years ago, before seeing through the myth of syndicalist capitalism and joining one of the underground factions. Eight years at Hawkskill Station had done things to him.

Altman pointed to his golem and said, "I hoped there'd be lightning in the rain today. That'll do it, you know. But there isn't much lightning this time of year. She'll get up alive, and then I'll need you, Doc, to give her her shots and trim away some of the rough places."

Quesada forced a smile. "I be glad to do it, Ned. But you know the terms."

"Sure. When I'm through with her, you get her. You think I'm a goddam monopolist? I'll share her. There'll be a waiting list. Just so you don't forget who made her, though. She'll remain mine, whenever I need her." He noticed Hahn. "Who are you?"

"He's new," Barrett said. "Lew Hahn. He came this afternoon."

"Ned Altman," said Altman with a courtly bow. "Formerly in government service. You're pretty young, aren't you? How's your sex orientation? Hetero?"

Hahn winced. "I'm afraid so."

"It's okay. I wouldn't touch you. I've got a project going here. But I just want you to know, I'll put you on my list. You're young and you've probably got stronger needs than some of us. I won't forget about you, even though you're new here."

Quesada coughed. "You ought to get some rest now, Ned. Maybe there'll be lightning tomorrow."

Altman did not resist. The doctor took him inside and put him to bed, while Hahn and Barrett surveyed the man's handiwork. Hahn pointed toward the figure's middle.

"He's left out something essential," he said. "If he's planning to make love to this girl after he's finished creating her, he'd better—"

"It was there yesterday," said Barrett. "He must be changing orientation again." Quesada emerged from the hut. They went on, down the rocky path.

Barrett did not make the complete circuit that night. Ordinarily, he would have gone all the way down to Latimer's hut overlooking the sea, for Latimer was on his list of sick ones. But Barrett had visited Latimer once that day, and he didn't think his aching good leg was up to another hike that far. So after he and Quesada and Hahn had been to all of the easily accessible huts and had visited the man who prayed for alien beings to rescue him and the man who was trying to break into a parallel universe where everything was as it ought to be in the world and the man who lay on his cot sobbing for all his wakeful hours, Barrett said goodnight to his companions and allowed Quesada to escort Hahn back to his hut without him.

After observing Hahn for half a day, Barrett realized he did not know much more about him than when he had first dropped onto the Anvil. That was odd. But maybe Hahn would open up a little more, after he'd been here a while. Barrett stared up at the salmon moon and reached into his pocket to finger the little trilobite before he remembered that he had given it to Hahn. He shuffled into his hut. He wondered how long ago Hahn had taken that lunar honeymoon trip.

V

Rudiger's catch was spread out in front of the main building the next morning when Barrett came up for breakfast. He had had a good night's fishing, obviously. He usually did. Rudiger went out three or four nights a week, in a little dinghy that he had cobbled together a few years ago from salvaged materials, and he took with him a team of friends whom he had trained in the deft use of the trawling nets.

It was an irony that Rudiger, the anarchist, the man who believed in individualism and the abolition of all political institutions, should be so good at leading a team of fishermen. Rudiger didn't care for teamwork in the abstract. But it was hard to manipulate the nets alone, he had discovered. Hawksbill Station had many little ironies of that sort. Political theorists tend to swallow their theories when forced back on pragmatic measures of survival.

The prize of the catch was a cephalopod about a dozen feet long—a rigid conical tube out of which some limp squid-like tentacles dangled. Plenty of meat on that one, Barrett thought. Dozens of trilobites were arrayed around it, ranging in size from the inch-long kind to the three-footers with their baroquely involuted exoskeletons. Rudiger fished both for food and for science; evidently these tribolites were discards, species that he already had studied, or he wouldn't have left them here to go into the food hoppers. His hut was stacked ceiling-high with trilobites. It kept him sane to collect and analyze them, and no one begrudged him his hobby.

Near the heap of trilobites were some clusters of hinged brachiopods, looking like scallops that had gone awry, and a pile of snails. The warm, shallow waters just off the coastal shelf teemed with life, in striking contrast to the barren land. Rudiger had also brought in a mound of shiny black seaweed. Barrett hoped someone would gather all this stuff up and get it into their heat-sink cooler before it spoiled. The bacteria of decay worked a lot slower here than they did Up

Front, but a few hours in the mild air would do Rudiger's haul no good.

Today Barrett planned to recruit some men for the annual Inland Sea expedition. Traditionally, he led that trek himself, but his injury made it impossible for him even to consider going any more. Each year, a dozen or so able-bodied men went out on a wide-ranging reconnaissance that took them in a big circle, looping northwestward until they reached the sea, then coming around to the south and back to the Station. One purpose of the trip was to gather any temporal garbage that might have materialized in the vicinity of the Station during the past year. There was no way of knowing how wide a margin of error had been allowed during the early attempts to set up the Station, and the scattershot technique of hurling material into the past had been pretty unreliable. New stuff was turning up all the time that had been aimed for Minus Two Billion, Two Thousand Oh Five A. D., but which didn't get there until a few decades later. Hawksbill Station needed all the spare equipment it could get, and Barrett didn't miss a chance to round up any of the debris.

There was another reason for the Inland Sea expeditions, though. They served as a focus for the year, an annual ritual, something to peg a custom to. It was a rite of spring here.

The dozen strongest men, going on foot to the distant rock-rimmed shores of the tepid sea that drowned the middle of North America, were performing the closest thing Hawksbill Station had to a religious function, although they did nothing more mystical when they reached the Inland Sea than to net a few trilobites and eat them. The trip meant more to Barrett himself than he had ever suspected, also. He realized that now, when he was unable to go. He had led every such expedition for twenty years.

But last year he had gone scrabbling over boulders loosened by the tireless action of the waves, venturing into risky territory for no rational reason that he could name, and his aging muscles had betrayed him. Often at night he woke sweating to escape from the dream in which he relived that ugly moment: slipping and sliding, clawing at the rocks, a mass of stone dislodged from somewhere and came crashing down with an agonizing impact on his foot, pinning him, crushing him. He could not forget the sound of grinding bones. Nor was he likely to lose the memory of the homeward march, across hundreds of miles of bare rock, his bulky body slung between the bowed forms of his companions.

He thought he would lose the foot, but Quesada had spared him from the amputation. He simply could not touch the foot to the ground and put weight on it now, or ever again. It might have been simpler to have the dead appendage sliced off. Quesada vetoed that, though. "Who knows," he had said, "some day they might send us a transplant kit. I can't rebuild a leg that's been amputated." So Barrett had kept his crushed foot. But he had never been quite the same since, and now someone else would have to lead the march.

Who would it be, he asked himself?

Quesada was the likeliest. Next to Barrett, he was the strongest man here, in all the ways that it was important to be strong. But Quesada couldn't be spared at the Station. It might be handy to have a medic along on the trip, but it was vital to have one here. After some reflection Barrett put down Charley Norton as the leader. He added Ken Belardi—someone for Norton to talk to. Rudiger? A tower of strength last year after Barrett had been injured; Barrett didn't particularly want to let Rudiger leave the Station so long though. He needed able men for the expedition, true, but he didn't want to strip the home base down to invalids, crackpots, and psychotics. Rudiger stayed. Two of his fellow fishermen went on the list. So did Sid Hutchett and Arny Jean-Claude.

Barrett thought about putting Don Latimer in the group. Latimer was coming to be something of a borderline mental case, but he was rational enough except when he lapsed into his psionic meditations, and he'd pull his own weight on the expedition. On the other hand, Latimer was Lew Hahn's roommate, and Barrett wanted Latimer around to observe Hahn at close range. He toyed with the idea of sending both of them out, but nixed it. Hahn was still an unknown quantity. It was too risky to let him go with the Inland Sea party this year. Probably he'd be in next spring's group, though.

Finally Barrett had his dozen men chosen. He chalked their names on the slate in front of the mess hall and found Charley Norton at breakfast to tell him he was in charge.

It felt strange to know that he'd have to stay home while the others went. It was an admission that he was beginning to abdicate after running this place so long. A crippled old man was what he was, whether he liked to admit it to himself or not, and that was something he'd have to come to terms with soon.

In the afternoon, the men of the Inland Sea expedition gathered to select their gear and plan their route. Barrett kept away from the meeting. This was Charley Norton's show, now. He'd made eight or ten trips, and he knew what to do. Barrett didn't want to interfere.

But some masochistic compulsion in him drove him to take a trek of his own. If he couldn't see the western waters this year, the least he could do was pay a visit to the Atlantic, in his own backyard. Barrett stopped off in the infirmary and, finding Quesada elsewhere, helped himself to a tube of neural depressant. He scrambled along the eastern trail until he was a few hundred yards from the main building, dropped his trousers and quickly gave each thigh a jolt of the drug, first the good leg, then the gimpy one. That would numb the muscles just enough so that he'd be able to take an extended hike without feeling the fire of the fatigue in his protesting joints. He'd pay for it, he knew, eight hours from now, when the depressant wore off and the full impact of his exertion hit him like a million daggers. But he was willing to accept that price.

The road to the sea was a long, lonely one. Hawksbill Station was perched on the eastern rim of the geosyncline, more than eight hundred feet above sea level. During the first half dozen years, the men of the Station had reached the ocean by a suicidal route across sheer rock faces, but Barrett had incited a ten-year project to carve a path. Now wide steps descended to the sea. Chopping them out of the rock had kept a lot of men busy for a long time, too busy to worry or to slip into insanity. Barrett regretted that he couldn't conceive some comparable works project to occupy them nowadays.

The steps formed a succession of shallow platforms that switch-backed to the edge of the water. Even for a healthy man it was still a strenuous walk. For Barrett in his present condition it was an ordeal. It took him two hours to descend a distance that normally could be traversed in a quarter of that time. When he reached the bottom, he sank down exhaustedly on a flat rock, licked by the waves, and dropped his crutch. The fingers of his left hand were cramped and gnarled from gripping the crutch, and his entire body was bathed in sweat.

The water looked gray and somehow oily. Barrett could not explain the prevailing colorlessness of the late Cambrian world, with its somber sky and somber land and somber sea, but his heart quietly ached for a glimpse of green vegetation again. He missed chlorophyll. The dark wavelets lapped against his rock, pushing a mass of floating black seaweed back and forth. The sea stretched to infinity. He didn't have the faintest idea how much of Europe, if any, was above water in this epoch.

At the best of times most of the planet was submerged; here, only a few hundred million years after the white-hot rocks of the land had pushed into view, it was likely that all that was above water on Earth was a strip of territory here and there. Had the Himalayas been born yet? The Rockies? The Andes? He knew the approximate outlines of late Cambrian North America, but the rest was a mystery. Blanks in knowledge were not easy to fill when the only link with Up Front was by one-way transport; Hawksbill Station had to rely on the random assortment of reading matter that came back in time, and it was furiously frustrating to lack information that any college geology text could supply.

As he watched, a big trilobite unexpectedly came scuttering up out of the water. It was the spike-tailed kind, about a yard long, with an eggplant-purple shell and a bristling arrangement of slender spines along the margins. There seemed to be a lot of legs underneath. The trilobite crawled up on the shore—no sand, no beach, just a shelf of rock— and advanced until it was eight or ten feet from the waves.

Good for you, Barrett thought. Maybe you're the first one who ever came out on land to see what it was like. The pioneer. The trailblazer.

It occurred to him that this adventurous trilobite might well be the ancestor of all the land-dwelling creatures of the eons to come. It was biological nonsense, but Barrett's weary mind conjured a picture of an evolutionary procession, with fish and amphibians and reptiles and mamals and man all stemming in unbroken sequence from this grotesque armored thing that moved in uncertain circles near his feet.

And if I were to step on you, he thought?

A quick motion—the sound of crunching chitin—the wild scrabbling of a host of little legs—

And the whole chain of life snapped in its first link. Evolution undone. No land creatures ever developed. With the descent of that heavy foot all the future would change, and there would never have been any Hawksbill Station, no human race, no James Edward Barrett. In an instant he would have both revenge on those who had condemned him to live out his days in this place and release from his sentence.

He did nothing. The trilobite completed its slow perambulation of the shoreline rocks and scuttered back into the sea unharmed.

The soft voice of Don Latimer said, "I saw you sitting down here, Jim. Do you mind if I join you?"

Barrett swung around, momentarily surprised. Latimer had come down from his hilltop hut so quietly that Barrett hadn't heard a thing. He recovered and grinned and beckoned Latimer to an adjoining rock.

"You fishing?" Latimer asked.

"Just sitting. An old man sunning himself."

"You took a hike like that just to sun yourself?" Latimer laughed. "Come off it. You're trying to get away from it all, and you probably wish I hadn't disturbed you."

"That's not so. Stay here. How's your new roommate getting along?"

"It's been strange," said Latimer. "That's one reason I came down here to talk to you." He leaned forward and peered searchingly into Barrett's eyes. "Jim, tell me: do you think I'm a madman?"

"Why should I?"

"The esping business. My attempt to break through to another realm of consciousness. I know you're tough-minded and skeptical. You probably think it's all a lot of nonsense."

Barrett shrugged and said, "If you want the blunt truth, I do. I don't have the remotest belief that you're going to get us anywhere, Don. I think it's a complete waste of time and energy for you to sit there for hours harnessing your psionic powers, or whatever it is you do. But no, I don't think you're crazy. I think you're entitled to your obsession and that you're going about a basically futile thing in a reasonably level-headed way. Fair enough?"

"More than fair. I don't ask you to put any credence in my research, but I don't want you to think I'm a total lunatic for trying it. It's important that you regard me as sane, or else what I want to tell you about Hahn won't be valid to you."

"I don't see the connection."

"It's this," said Latimer. "On the basis of one evening's acquaintance, I've formed an opinion about Hahn. It's the kind of an opinion that might be formed by a garden variety paranoid, and if you think I'm nuts you're likely to discount my idea."

"I don't think you're nuts. What's your idea?"

"That he's been spying on us."

Barrett had to work hard to keep from emitting the guffaw that would shatter Latimer's fragile self-esteem. "Spying?" he said casually. "You can't mean that. How can anyone spy here? I mean, how can he report his findings?"

"I don't know," Latimer said. "But he asked me a million questions last night. About you, about Quesada, about some of the sick men. He wanted to know everything."

"The normal curiosity of a new man."

"Jim, he was taking notes. I saw him after he thought I was asleep. He sat up for two hours writing it all down in a little book."

Barrett frowned. "Maybe he's going to write a novel about us."

"I'm serious," Latimer said. "Questions—notes. And he's shifty. Try to get him to talk about himself!"

"I did. I didn't learn much."

"Do you know why he's been sent here?"

"No."

"Neither do I," said Latimer. "Political crimes, he said, but he was vague as hell. He hardly seemed to know what the present government was up to, let alone what his own opinions were toward it. I don't detect any passionate philosophical convictions in Mr. Hahn. And you know as well as I do that Hawksbill Station is the refuse heap for revolutionaries and agitators and subversives and all sorts of similar trash, but that we've never had any other kind of prisoner here."

Barrett said coolly, "I agree that Hahn's a puzzle. But who could he be spying for? He's got no way to file a report, if he's a government agent. He's stranded here for keeps, like us."

"Maybe he was sent to keep an eye on us—to make sure we aren't cooking up some way to escape. Maybe he's a volunteer who willingly gave up his twenty-first-century life so he could come among us and thwart anything we might be hatching. Perhaps they're afraid we've invented forward time-travel. Or that we've become a threat to the sequence of the time-lines. Anything. So Hahn comes among us to snoop around and block any dangers before they arrive."

Barrett felt a twinge of alarm. He saw how close to paranoia Latimer was hewing, now. In half a dozen sentences he had journeyed from the rational expression of some justifiable suspicions to the fretful fear that the men from Up Front were going to take steps to choke off the escape route that he was so close to perfecting.

He kept his voice level as he told Latimer, "I don't think you need to worry, Don. Hahn's an odd one, but he's not here to make trouble for us. The fellows Up Front have already made all the trouble for us they ever will."

"Would you keep an eye on him anyway?"

"You know I will. And don't hesitate to let me know if Hahn does anything else out of the ordinary. You're in a better spot to notice than anyone else."

"I'll be watching," Latimer said. "We can't tolerate any spies from Up Front among us." He got to his feet and gave Barrett a pleasant smile. "I'll let you get back to your sunning now, Jim."

Latimer went up the path. Barrett eyed him until he was close to the top, only a faint dot against the stony backdrop. After a long while Barrett seized his crutch and levered himself to his feet. He stood staring down at the surf, dipping the tip of his crutch into the water to send a couple of little crawling things scurrying away. At length he turned and began the long, slow climb back to the Station.

VI

A couple of days passed before Barrett had the chance to draw Lew Hahn aside for a spot of political discussion. The Inland Sea party had set out, and in a way that was too bad, for Barrett could have used Charley Norton's services in penetrating Hahn's armor. Norton was the most gifted theorist around, a man could weave a tissue of dialectic from the least promising material. If anyone could find out the depth of Hahn's Marxist commitment, if any, it was Norton.

But Norton was leading the expedition, so Barrett had to do the interrogating himself. His Marxism was a trifle rusty, and he couldn't thread his path through the Leninist, Stalinist, Trotskyite, Khrushchevist, Maoist, Berenkovskyite and Mgumbweist schools with Charley Norton's skills. Yet he knew what questions to ask.

He picked a rainy evening when Hahn seemed to be in a fairly outgoing mood. There had been an hour's entertainment that night, an ingenious computer-composed film that Sid Hutchett had programmed last week. Up Front had been kind enough to ship back a modest computer, and Hutchett had rigged it to do animations by specifying line widths and lengths, shades of gray and progression of raster units. It was a simple but remarkably clever business, and it brightened a dull night.

Afterward, sensing that Hahn was relaxed enough to lower his guard a bit, Barrett said, "Hutchett's a rare one. Did you meet him before he went on the trip?"

"Tall fellow with a sharp nose and no chin?"

"That's the one. A clever boy. He was the top computer man for the Continental Liberation Front until they caught him in '19. He programmed that fake broadcast in which Chancellor Dantell denounced his own regime. Remember?"

"I'm not sure I do." Hahn frowned. "How long ago was this?"

"The broadcast was in 2018. Would that be before your time? Only eleven years ago—"

"I was nineteen then," said Hahn. "I guess I wasn't very politically sophisticated."

"Too busy studying economics, I guess."

Hahn grinned. "That's right. Deep in dismal science."

"And you never heard that broadcast? Or even heard of it?"

"I must have forgotten."

"The biggest hoax of the century," Barrett said, "and you forgot it. You know the Continental Liberation Front, of course."

"Of course." Hahn looked uneasy.

"Which group did you say you were with?"

"The People's Crusade for Liberty."

"I don't know it. One of the newer groups?"

"Less than five years old. It started in California."

"What's its program?"

"Oh, the usual," Hahn said. "Free elections, representative government, an opening of the security files, restoration of civil liberties."

"And the economic orientation? Pure Marxist or one of the offshoots?"

"Not really any, I guess. We believed in a kind of—well, capitalism with some government restraints."

"A little to the right of state socialism, and a little to the left of *laissez-faire?*" Barrett suggested.

"Something like that."

"But that system was tried and failed, wasn't it? It had its day. It led inevitably to total socialism, which produced the compensating backlash of syndicalist capitalism, and then we got a government that pretended to be libertarian while actually stifling all individual liberties in the name of freedom. So if your group simply wanted to turn the clock back to 1955, say, there couldn't be much to its ideas."

Hahn looked bored. "You've got to understand I wasn't in the top ideological councils."

"Just an economist?"

"That's it. I drew up plans for the conversion to our system."

"Basing your work on the modified liberalism of Ricardo?"

"Well, in a sense."

"And avoiding the tendency to fascism that was found in the thinking of Keynes?"

"You could say so," Hahn said. He stood up, flashing a quick, vague smile. "Look, Jim, I'd love to argue this further with you some other time, but I've really got to go now. Ned Altman talked me into coming around and helping him do a lightning-dance to bring that pile of dirt to life. So if you don't mind—"

Hahn beat a hasty retreat, without looking back.

Barrett was more perplexed than ever. Hahn hadn't been "arguing" anything. He had been carrying on a lame and feeble conversation, letting himself be pushed hither and thither by Barrett's questions. And he had spouted a lot of nonsense. He didn't seem to know Keynes from Ricardo, nor to care about it, which was odd for a self-professed economist. He didn't have a shred of an idea what his own political party stood for. He had so little revolutionary background that he was unaware even of Hutchett's astonishing hoax of eleven years back.

He seemed phony from top to bottom.

How was it possible that kid had been deemed worthy of exile to Hawksbill Station, anyhow? Only the top firebrands went there. Sentencing a man to Hawksbill was like sentencing him to death, and it wasn't done lightly. Barrett couldn't imagine why Hahn was here. He seemed genuinely distressed at being exiled, and evidently he had left a beloved wife behind, but nothing else rang true about the man.

Was he—as Latimer suggested—some kind of spy?

Barrett rejected the idea out of hand. He didn't want Latimer's paranoia infecting him. The government wasn't likely to send anyone on a one-way trip to the Late Cambrian just to spy on a bunch of aging revolutionaries who could never make trouble again. But what *was* Hahn doing here, then?

He would bear further watching, Barrett thought.

Barrett took care of some of the watching himself. But he had plenty of assistance. Latimer. Altman. Six or seven others. Latimer had recruited most of the ambulatory psycho cases, the ones who were superficially functional but full of all kinds of fears and credulities.

They were keeping an eye on the new man.

On the fifth day after his arrival, Hahn went out fishing in Rudiger's crew. Barrett stood for a long time on the edge of the geosyncline, watching the little boat bobbing in the surging Atlantic. Rudiger never went far from shore—eight hundred, a thousand yards out—but the water was rough even there. The waves came rolling in with X thousand miles of gathered impact behind them. A continental shelf sloped off at a wide angle, so that even at a substantial distance off shore the water wasn't very deep. Rudiger had taken soundings up to a mile out, and had reported depths no greater than a hundred sixty feet. Nobody had gone past a mile.

It wasn't that they were afraid of falling off the side of the world if they went too far east. It was simply that a mile was a long distance to row in an open boat, using stubby oars made from old packing cases. Up Front hadn't thought to spare an outboard motor for them.

Looking toward the horizon, Barrett had an odd thought. He had been told that the women's equivalent of

Hawksbill Station was safely segregated out of reach, a couple of hundred million years up the time-line. But how did he know that? There could be another Station somewhere else in this very year, and they'd never know about it. A camp of women, say, living on the far side of the ocean, or even across the Inland Sea.

It wasn't very likely, he knew. With the entire past to pick from, the edgy men Up Front wouldn't take any chance that the two groups of exiles might get together and spawn a tribe of little subversives. They'd take every precaution to put an impenetrable barrier of epochs between them. Yet Barrett thought he could make it sound convincing to the other men. With a little effort he could get them to believe in the existence of several simultaneous Hawksbill Stations scattered on this level of time.

Which could be our salvation, he thought.

The instances of degenerative psychosis were beginning to snowball, now. Too many men had been here too long, and one crackup was starting to feed the next, in this blank lifeless world where humans were never meant to live. The men needed projects to keep them going. They were starting to slip off into harebrained projects, like Altman's Frankenstein girlfriend and Latimer's psi pursuit.

Suppose, Barrett thought, I could get them steamed up about reaching the other continents?

A round-the-world expedition. Maybe they could build some kind of big ship. That would keep a lot of men busy for a long time. And they'd need navigational equipment—compasses, sextants, chronometers, whatnot. Somebody would have to design an improvised radio, too. It was the kind of project that might take thirty or forty years. A focus for our energies, Barrett thought. Of course, I won't live to see the ship set sail. But even so, it's a way of staving off collapse. We've built our staircase to the sea. Now we need something bigger to do. Idle hands make for idle minds ... sick minds ...

He liked the idea he had hatched. For several weeks now Barrett had been worrying about the deteriorating state of affairs in the Station, and looking for some way to cope with it. Now he thought he had his way.

Turning, he saw Latimer and Altman standing behind him.

"How long have you been there?" he asked.

"Two minutes," said Latimer. "We brought you something to look at."

Altman nodded vigorously. "You ought to read it. We brought it for you to read."

"What is it?"

Latimer handed over a folded sheaf of papers. "I found this tucked away in Hahn's bunk after he went out with Rudiger. I know I'm not supposed to be invading his privacy, but I had to have a look at what he's been writing. There it is. He's a spy, all right."

Barrett glanced at the papers in his hand. "I'll read it a little later. What is it about?"

"It's a description of the Station, and a profile of most of the men in it," said Latimer. He smiled frostily. "Hahn's private opinion of me is that I've gone mad. His private opinion of you is a little more flattering, but not much."

Altman said, "He's also been hanging around the Hammer."

"What?"

"I saw him going there late last night. He went into the building. I followed him. He was looking at the Hammer."

"Why didn't you tell me that right away?" Barrett snapped.

"I wasn't sure it was important," Altman said. "I had to talk it over with Don first. And I couldn't do that until Hahn had gone out fishing."

Sweat burst out on Barrett's face. "Listen, Ned, if you ever catch Hahn going near the time-travel equipment again, you let me know in a hurry. Without consulting Don or anyone else. Clear?"

"Clear," said Altman. He giggled. "You know what I think? They've decided to exterminate us Up Front. Hahn's been sent here to check us out as a suicide volunteer. Then they're going to send a bomb through the Hammer and blow the Station up. We ought to wreck the Hammer and Anvil before they get a chance."

"But why would they send a suicide volunteer?" Latimer asked. "Unless they've got some way to rescue their spy—"

"In any case we shouldn't take any chance," Altman argued. "Wreck the Hammer. Make it impossible for them to bomb us from Up Front."

"That might be a good idea. But—"

"Shut up, both of you," Barrett growled. "Let me look at these papers."

He walked a few steps away from them and sat down on a shelf of rock. He began to read.

VII

Hahn had a cramped, crabbed handwriting that packed a maximum of information into a minimum of space, as though he regarded it as a mortal sin to waste paper. Fair enough. Paper was a scarce commodity here, and evidently Hahn had brought these sheets with him from Up Front. His script was clear, though. So were his opinions. Painfully so.

He had written an analysis of conditions at Hawksbill

Station, setting forth in about five thousand words everything that Barrett knew was going sour here. He had neatly
ticked off the men as aging revolutionaries in whom the old
fervor had turned rancid. He listed the ones who were cer-
tifiably psycho, and the ones who were on the edge, and the
ones who were hanging on, like Quesada and Norton and
Rudiger. Barrett was interested to see that Hahn rated even
those three as suffering from severe strain and likely to fly
apart at any moment. To him, Quesada and Norton and Rudiger seemed just about as stable as when they had first
dropped onto the Anvil of Hawksbill Station, but that was
possibly the distorting effect of his own blurred perceptions.
To an outsider like Hahn, the view was different and perhaps
more accurate.

Barrett forced himself not to skip ahead to Hahn's eval-
uation of him.

He wasn't pleased when he came to it. "Barrett," Hahn
had written, "is like a mighty beam that's been gnawed from
within by termites. He looks solid, but one good push would
break him apart. A recent injury to his foot has evidently
had a bad effect on him. The other men say he used to be
physically vigorous and derived much of his authority from
his size and strength. Now he can hardly walk. But I feel
the trouble with him is inherent in the life of Hawksbill
Station and doesn't have much to do with his lameness. He's
been cut off from normal human drives for too long. The
exercise of power here has provided the illusion of stability
for him, but it's power in a vacuum, and things have happened within Barrett of which he's totally unaware. He's in
bad need of therapy. He may be beyond help."

Barrett read that several times. *Gnawed from within by
termites . . . one good push . . . things have happened within
him . . . bad need of therapy . . . beyond help . . .*

* * *

He was less angered than he thought he should have been. Hahn was entitled to his views. Barrett finally stopped re-reading his profile and pushed his way to the last page of Hahn's essay. It ended with the words, "Therefore I recommend prompt termination of the Hawksbill Station penal colony and, where possible, the therapeutic rehabilitation of its inmates."

What the hell was this?

It sounded like the report of a parole commisioner! But there was no parole from Hawksbill Station. That final sentence let all the viability of what had gone before bleed away. Hahn was pretending to be composing a report to the government Up Front, obviously. But a wall two billion years thick made filing of that report impossible. So Hahn was suffering from delusions, just like Altman and Valdosto and the others. In his fevered mind he believed he could send messages Up Front, pompus documents delineating the flaws and foibles of his fellow prisoners.

That raised a chilling prospect. Hahn might be crazy, but he hadn't been in the Station long enough to have gone crazy here. He must have brought his insanity with him.

What if they had stopped using Hawksbill Station as a camp for political prisoners, Barrett asked himself, and were starting to use it as an insane asylum?

A cascade of psychos descending on them. Men who had gone honorably buggy under the stress of confinement would have to make room for ordinary Bedlamites. Barrett shivered. He folded up Hahn's papers and handed them to Latimer, who was sitting a few yards away, watching him intently.

"What did you think of that?" Latimer asked.

"I think it's hard to evaluate. But possibly friend Hahn is emotionally disturbed. Put this stuff back exactly where you got it, Don. And don't give Hahn the faintest inkling that you've read or removed it."

"Right."

"And come to me whenever you think there's something I ought to know about him," Barrett said. "He may be a very sick boy. He may need all the help we can give."

The fishing expedition returned in early afternoon. Barrett saw that the dingy was overflowing with the haul, and Hahn, coming into the camp with his arms full of gaffed trilobites looked sunburned and pleased with his outing. Barrett came over to inspect the catch. Rudiger was in an effusive mood and held up a bright red crustacean that might have been the great-great-grandfather of all boiled lobsters, except that it had no front claws and a wicked-looking triple spike where a tail should have been. It was about two feet long, and ugly.

"A new species!" Rudiger crowed. "There's nothing like this in any museum. I wish I could put it where it would be found. Some mountaintop, maybe."

"If it could be found, it *would* have been found," Barrett reminded him. "Some paleontologist of the twentieth century would have dug it out. So forget it, Mel."

Hahn said, "I've been wondering about that point. How is it nobody Up Front ever dug up the fossil remains of Hawksbill Station? Aren't they worried that one of the early fossil-hunters will find it in the Cambrian strata and raise a fuss?"

Barrett shook his head. "For one thing, no paleontologist from the beginning of the science to the founding of the Station in 2005 ever *did* dig up Hawksbill. That's a matter of record, so there was nothing to worry about. If it came to light after 2005, why, everyone would know what it was. No paradox there."

"Besides," said Rudiger sadly, "in another two billion years this whole strip of rock will be on the floor of the Atlantic, with a couple of miles of sediment over it. There's not a chance we'll be found. Or that anyone Up Front will ever see this guy I caught today. Not that I give a damn. I've seen him. I'll dissect him. Their loss."

"But you regret the fact that science will never know of this species," Hahn said.

"Sure I do. But is it my fault? Science does know of this species. Me. I'm science. I'm the leading paleontologist of this epoch. Can I help it if I can't publish my discoveries in the professional journals?" He scowled and walked away, carrying the big red crustacean.

Hahn and Barrett looked at each other. They smiled, in a natural mutual response to Rudiger's grumbled outburst. Then Barrett's smile faded.

termites . . . one good push . . . therapy . . .

"Something wrong?" Hahn asked.

"Why?"

"You looked so bleak all of a sudden."

"My foot gave me a twinge." Barrett said. "It does that, you know. Here. I'll give you a hand carrying those things. We'll have fresh trilobite cocktail tonight."

VIII

A little before midnight, Barrett was awakened by footsteps outside his hut. As he sat up, groping for the luminescence switch, Ned Altman came blundering through the door. Barrett blinked at him.

"What's the matter?"

"Hahn!" Altman rasped. "He's fooling around with the

Hammer again. We just saw him go into the building."

Barrett shed his sleepiness like a seal bursting out of water. Ignoring the insistent throb in his leg, he pulled himself from his bed and grabbed some clothing. He was more apprehensive than he wanted Altman to see. If Hahn, fooling around with the temporal mechanisms, accidentally smashed the Hammer, they might never get replacement equipment from Up Front. Which would mean that all future shipments of supplies—if there were any—would come as random shoots that might land in any old year. What business did Hahn have with the machine, anyway?

Altman said, "Latimer's up there keeping an eye on him. He got suspicious when Hahn didn't come back to the hut, and he got me, and we went looking for him. And there he was, sniffing around the Hammer."

"Doing what?"

"I don't know. As soon as we saw him go in, I came down here to get you. Don's watching."

Barrett stumped his way out of the hut and did his best to run toward the main building. Pain shot like trails of hot acid up the lower half of his body. The crutch dug mercilessly into his left armpit as he leaned all his weight into it. His crippled foot, swinging freely, burned with a cold glow. His right leg, which was carrying most of the burden, creaked and popped. Altman ran breathlessly alongside him. The Station was silent at this hour.

As they passed Quesada's hut, Barrett considered waking the medic and taking him along. He decided against it. Whatever trouble Hahn might be up to, Barrett felt he could handle it himself. There was some strength left in the old gnawed beam.

*　　*　　*

Latimer stood at the entrance to the main dome. He was right on the edge of panic, or perhaps over the edge. He seemed to be gibbering with fear and shock. Barrett had never seen a man gibber before.

He clamped a big paw on Latimer's thin shoulder and said harshly, "Where is he? Where's Hahn?"

"He—disappeared."

"What do you mean? Where did he go?"

Latimer moaned. His face was fishbelly white. "He got onto the Anvil," Latimer blurted. "The light came on—the glow. And then Hahn disappeared!"

"No," Barrett said. "It isn't possible. You must be mistaken."

"I saw him go!"

"He's hiding somewhere in the building," Barrett insisted. "Close that door! Search for him!"

Altman said, "He probably did disappear, Jim. If Don says he disappeared—"

"He climbed right on the Anvil. Then everything turned red, and he was gone."

Barrett clenched his fists. There was a white-hot blaze just behind his forehead that almost made him forget about his foot. He saw his mistake now. He had depended for his espionage on two men who were patently and unmistakably insane, and that had been itself a not very sane thing to do. A man is known by his choice of lieutenants. Well, he had relied on Altman and Latimer, and now they were giving him the sort of information that such spies could be counted on to supply.

"You're hallucinating," he told Latimer curtly. "Ned, go wake Quesada and get him here right away. You, Don, you stand here by the entrance, and if Hahn shows up I want you to scream at the top of your lungs. I'm going to search the building for him."

"Wait," Latimer said. He seemed to be in control of himself again. "Jim, do you remember when I asked you if you thought I was crazy? You said you didn't." You trusted me. Well, don't stop trusting me now. I tell you I'm not hallucinating. I saw Hahn disappear. I can't explain it, but I'm rational enough to know what I saw."

In a milder tone Barrett said, "All right. Maybe so. Stay by the door, anyway. I'll run a quick check."

He started to make the circuit of the dome, beginning with the room where the Hammer was located. Everything seemed to be in order there. No Hawksbill Field glow was in evidence, and nothing had been disturbed. The room had no closets or cupboards in which Hahn could be hiding. When he had inspected it thoroughly, Barrett moved on, looking into the infirmary, the mess hall, the kitchen, the recreation room. He looked high and low. No Hahn. Of course, there were plenty of places in those rooms where Hahn might have secreted himself, but Barrett doubted that he was there. So it had all been some feverish fantasy of Latimer's, then. He completed the route and found himself back at the main entrance. Latimer still stood guard there. He had been joined by a sleepy Quesada. Altman, pale and shaky-looking, was just outside the door.

"What's happening?" Quesada asked.

"I'm not sure," said Barrett. "Don and Ned had the idea they saw Lew Hahn fooling around with the time equipment. I've checked the building, and he's not here, so maybe they made a little mistake. I suggest you take them both into the infirmary and give them a shot of something to settle their nerves, and we'll all try to get back to sleep."

Latimer said, "I tell you, I saw—"

"Shut up!" Altman broke in. "Listen! What's that noise?"

Barrett listened. The sound was clear and loud: the hissing whine of ionization. It was the sound produced by a functioning Hawksbill Field. Suddenly there were goosepimples on his flesh. In a low voice he said, "The field's on. We're probably getting some supplies."

"At this hour?" said Latimer.

"We don't know what time it is Up Front. All of you stay here. I'll check the Hammer."

"Perhaps I ought to go with you," Quesada said mildly.

"*Stay here!*" Barrett dered. He paused, embarrassed at his own explosive show of wrath. "It only takes one of us. I'll be right back."

Without waiting for further dissent, he pivoted and limped down the hall to the Hammer room. He shouldered the door open and looked in. There was no need for him to switch on the light. The red glow of the Hawksbill Field illuminated everything.

Barrett stationed himself just within the door. Hardly daring to breathe, he stared fixedly at the Hammer, watching as the glow deepened through various shades of pink toward crimson, and then spread until it enfolded the waiting Anvil beneath it.

Then came the implosive thunderclap, and Lew Hahn dropped out of nowhere and lay for a moment in temporal shock on the broad plate of the Anvil.

IX

In the darkness, Hahn did not notice Barrett at first. He sat up slowly, shaking off the stunning effects of a trip through time. After a few seconds he pushed himself toward the lip of the Anvil and let his legs dangle over it. He swung them to get the circulation going. He took a series of deep breaths. Finally he slipped to the floor. The glow of the field had gone out in the moment of his arrival, and so he moved warily, as though not wanting to bump into anything.

Abruptly Barrett switched on the light and said, "What have you been up to, Hahn?"

The younger man recoiled as though he had been jabbed in the gut. He gasped, hopped backward a few steps, and flung up both hands in a defensive gesture.

"Answer me," Barrett said.

Hahn regained his equilibrium. He shot a quick glance past Barrett's bulky form toward the hallway and said, "Let me go, will you? I can't explain now."

"You'd better explain now."

"It's easier for everyone if I don't," said Hahn. "Let me pass."

Barrett continued to block the door. "I want to know where you've been. What have you been doing with the Hammer?"

"Nothing. Just studying it."

"You weren't in this room a minute ago. Then you appeared. Where'd you come from, Hahn?"

"You're mistaken. I was standing right behind the Hammer. I didn't—"

"I saw you drop down on the Anvil. You took a time trip, didn't you?"

"No."

"Don't lie to me! You've got some way of going forward in time, isn't that so? You've been spying on us, and you just went somewhere to file your report—somewhen—and now you're back."

Hahn's forehead was glistening. He said, "I warn you,

don't ask too many questions. You'll know everything in due time. This isn't the time. Please, now. Let me pass."

"I want answers first," Barrett said. He realized that he was trembling. He already knew the answers, and they were answers that shook him to the core of his soul. He knew where Hahn had been.

Hahn said nothing. He took a few hesitant steps toward Barrett, who did not move. He seemed to be gathering momentum for a rush at the doorway.

Barrett said, "You aren't getting out of here until you tell me what I want to know."

Hahn charged.

Barrett planted himself squarely, crutch braced against the doorframe, his good leg flat on the floor, and waited for the younger man to reach him. He figured he outweighed Hahn by eighty pounds. That might be enough to balance the fact that he was spotting Hahn thirty years and one leg. They came together, and Barrett drove his hands down onto Hahn's shoulder's, trying to hold him, to force him back into the room.

Hahn gave an inch or two. He looked up at Barrett without speaking and pushed forward again.

"Don't—don't—" Barrett grunted. "I won't let you—"

"I don't want to do this," Hahn said.

He pushed again. Barrett felt himself buckling under the impact. He dug his hands as hard as he could into Hahn's shoulders and tried to shove the other man backward into the room, but Hahn held firm, and all of Barrett's energy was converted into a thrust rebounding on himself. He lost control of his crutch, and it slithered out from under his arm. For one agonizing moment Barrett's full weight rested on the crushed uselessness of his left foot, and then, as though his limbs were melting away beneath him, he began to sink toward the floor. He landed with a reverberating crash.

Quesada, Altman and Latimer came rushing in. Barrett writhed in pain on the floor. Hahn stood over him, looking unhappy, his hands locked together.

"I'm sorry," he said. "You shouldn't have tried to muscle me like that."

Barrett glowered at him. "You were traveling in time, weren't you? You can answer me now!"

"Yes," Hahn said at last. "I went Up Front."

An hour later, after Quesada had pumped him with enough neural depressants to keep him from jumping out of his skin, Barrett got the full story. Hahn hadn't wanted to reveal it so soon, but he had changed his mind after his little scuffle.

It was all very simple. Time travel now worked in both directions. The glib impressive noises about the flow of entrophy had turned out to just noises.

"How long has this been known?" Barrett asked.

"At least five years. We aren't sure yet exactly when the breakthrough came. After we're finished going through all the suppressed records of the former government—"

"The former government?"

Hahn nodded. "The revolution came in January. Not really a violent one, either. The syndicalists just mildewed from within, and when they got the first push they fell over."

"Was it mildew?" Barrett asked, coloring. "Or termites? Keep your metaphors straight."

Hahn glanced away. "Anyway, the government fell. We've got a provisional liberal regime in office now. Don't ask me much about it. I'm not a political theorist. I'm not even an economist. You guessed as much."

"What are you, then?"

"A policeman," Hahn said. "Part of the commission that's investigating the prison system of the former government. Including this prison."

Barrett looked at Quesada, then at Hahn. Thoughts were streaming turbulently through him, and he could not remember when he had last been so overwhelmed by events. He had to work hard to keep from breaking into the shakes again. His voice quavered a little as he said, "You came back to observe Hawksbill Station, right? And you went Up Front tonight to tell them what you saw here. You think we're a pretty sad bunch, eh?"

"You've all been under heavy stress here," Hahn said. "Considering the circumstances of your imprisonment—"

Quesada broke in. "If there's a liberal government in power now and it's possible to travel both ways in time, then am I right in assuming that the Hawksbill prisoners are going to be sent Up Front?"

"Of course," said Hahn. "It'll be done as soon as possible. That's been the whole purpose of my reconnaissance mission. To find out if you people were still alive, first, and then to see what shape you're in, how badly in need of treatment you are. You'll be given every available benefit of modern therapy, naturally. No expense spared—"

Barrett scarcely paid attention to Hahn's words. He had been fearing something like this all night, ever since Altman had told him Hahn was monkeying with the Hammer, but he had never fully allowed himself to believe that it could really be possible.

He saw his kingdom crumbling.

He saw himself returned to a world he could not begin to comprehend—a lame Rip Van Winkle, coming back after twenty years.

He saw himself leaving a place that had become his home.

Barrett said tiredly, "You know, some of the men aren't going to be able to adapt to the shock of freedom. It might just kill them to be dumped into the real world again. I mean the advanced psychos—Valdosto, and such."

"Yes," Hahn said. "I've mentioned them in my report."

"It'll be necessary to get them ready for a return in grad-ual stages. It might take several years to condition them to the idea. It might even take longer than that."

"I'm no therapist," said Hahn. "Whatever the doctors think is right for them is what'll be done. Maybe it will be necessary to keep them here. I can see where it would be pretty potent to send them back, after they've spent all these years believing there's no return."

"More than that," said Barrett. "There's a lot of work that can be done here. Scientific work. Exploration. I don't think Hawksbill Station ought to be closed down."

"No one said it would be. We have every intention of keeping it going, but not as a prison."

"Good," Barrett said. He fumbled for his crutch, found it and got heavily to his feet. Quesada moved toward him as though to steady him, but Barrett shook him off. "Let's go outside," he said.

They left the building. A gray mist had come in over the Station, and a fine drizzle had begun to fall. Barrett looked around at the scattering of huts. At the ocean, dimly visible to the east in the faint moonlight. He thought of Charley Norton and the party that had gone on the annual expedition to the Inland Sea. That bunch was going to be in for a real surprise, when they got back here in a few weeks and discovered that everybody was free to go home.

Very strangely, Barrett felt a sudden pressure forming around his eyelids, as of tears trying to force their way out into the open.

He surveyed his kingdom from the top of the hill, taking a long, slow look.

Then he turned to Hahn and Quesada. In a low voice he said, "Have you followed what I've been trying to tell you? Someone's got to stay here and ease the transition for the sick men who won't be able to stand the shock of return. Someone's got to keep the base running. Someone's got to explain to the new men who'll be coming back here, the scientists."

"Naturally," Hahn said.

"The one who does that—the one who stays behind—I think it ought to be someone who knows the Station well, someone who's fit to return Up Front, but who's willing to make the sacrifice and stay. Do you follow me? A volunteer." They were smiling at him now. Barrett wondered if there might not be something patronizing about those smiles. He wondered if he might not be a little too transparent. To hell with both them, he thought. He sucked the Cambrian air into his lungs until his chest swelled grandly.

"I'm offering to stay," Barrett said in a loud tone. He glared at them to keep them from objecting. But they wouldn't dare object, he knew. In Hawksbill Station, he was the king. And he meant to keep it that way. "I'll be the volunteer," he said. "I'll be the one who stays."

He looked out over his kingdom from the top of the hill.

TIME TRAVELERS NEVER DIE

JACK MCDEVITT

And once more, as in Paul Levinson's story, as in Gregory Landis's terrifying constructed paradox, here is that inalterability of time, that fierce resistance of paradox becoming the construct for tragedy. Tie these three stories and they are a single gorgeous, ragged short novel, written in three sections eight years apart and all of them on a final awards ballot. Of the three, this, with its equally perverse and inalterable concept of human loss at its center, may be on consideration the darkest section of that hypothetical, aggregate novel. De gustibus and so on.

Jack McDevitt, a retired Naval officer, published his first novel, *The Hercules Text*, more than a decade and a half ago; there are other impressive novels. Of his remarkable body of work, it is a casual short story equally fierce, "To Hell the Stars," and this novella which are my own favorites.

Thursday, November 24.
Shortly before noon.

We buried him on a cold, gray morning, threatening snow. The mourners were few, easily constraining their grief for a man who had traditionally kept his acquaintances at a distance. I watched the preacher, white-haired, feeble, himself near the end, and I wondered what he was thinking as the wind rattled the pages of his prayer book.

Ashes to ashes—

I stood with hands thrust into coat pockets, near tears. Look: I'm not ashamed to admit it. Shel was odd, vindictive, unpredictable, selfish. He didn't have a lot of friends. Didn't deserve a lot of friends. But I *loved* him. I've never known anyone like him.

—In sure and certain hope—

I wasn't all that confident about the resurrection, but I knew that Adrian Shelborne would indeed walk the earth

365

again. I knew, for example, that he and I would stand on an Arizona hilltop on a fresh spring morning late in the twenty-first century, and watch silver vehicles rise into the sky on the first leg of the voyage to Centaurus. And we would be present at the assassination of Elaine Culpepper, a name unknown now, but which would in time be inextricably linked with the collapse of the North American Republic. Time travelers never really die, he was fond of saying. We've been far downstream. You and I will live a very long time.

The preacher finished, closed his book, and raised his hand to bless the orchid-colored coffin. The wind blew, and the air was heavy with the approaching storm. The mourners, anxious to be about the day's business, bent their heads and walked past, flinging lillies in Shel's general direction. Helen Suchenko stood off to one side, looking lost. Lover with no formal standing. Known to the family but not particularly liked, mostly because they disapproved of Shel himself. She dabbed jerkily at her eyes and riveted her gaze on the gray stone that carried his name and dates.

She was fair-haired, with eyes like sea water, and a quiet, introspective manner that might easily have misled those who did not know her well.

"I can't believe it," she said.

I had introduced him to Helen, fool that I am. She and I had been members of the Devil's Disciples, a group of George Bernard Shaw devotees. She was an MD, just out of medical school when she first showed up for a field trip to see *Arms and the Man*. It was love at first sight, but I was slow to show my feelings. And while I was debating how best to make my approach, Shel walked off with her. He even asked whether I was interested, and I, sensing I had already lost, salvaged my pride and told him of course not.

He never understood how I felt. He used to talk about her a lot when we were upstream. How she would enjoy Victorian London. Or St. Petersburg before the first war. But he never shared the great secret with her. That was always something he was going to do later.

She was trembling. He really *was* gone. And I had a clear field. That indecent thought kept pushing through. I had wanted her a long time. She was drawn to me, too, just as she was to Shel, and I suspected that I might have carried the day with her had I pressed my case. But I had never betrayed him.

Her cheeks were wet.

"I'll miss him, too," I said.

"I loved him, Dave."

"I know."

He had died when his townhouse burned down almost two weeks before. He'd been asleep upstairs and had never got out of bed. The explanation seemed to be that the fire had sucked the oxygen out of the house and suffocated him before he realized what was happening. Happens all the time, the fire department said.

I told her everything would be all right.

She tried to laugh, but the sound had an edge. "Our last conversation was so pointless. I wish I'd known—." Tears leaked out of her eyes. She tried to catch her breath. "I would have liked to tell him how much he meant to me. How glad I was to have known him."

"I know." I began to guide her toward my Porsche. "Why don't you let me take you home?"

"It's all right," she said. "I'll be okay." Her car was parked near a stone angel.

Edmond Halverson, head of the art department at the University, drew abreast, tipped his hat, and whispered his regrets. We mumbled something back and he walked on.

She swallowed. "When you get a chance, Dave, give me a call."

I watched her get into her car and drive away. She had known so much about Adrian Shelborne. And so little.

He had traveled in time, and of all persons now alive, only I knew. He had brought me in, he'd said, because he needed my language skills. But it was more than that. He wanted someone to share the victory with, someone to help celebrate. Over the years, he'd mastered classical Greek, and Castilian, and Renaissance Italian. And he'd gone on, acquiring enough Latin, Russian, French, and German to get by on his own. But we continued to travel together. And it became the hardest thing in my life to refrain from telling people I had once talked aerodynamics with Leonardo.

I watched his brother Jerry duck his head to get into his limo. Interested only in sports and women, Shel had said of him. And making money. *If I'd told him about the Watch,* he'd said, *and offered to take him along, he'd have asked to see a Super Bowl.*

Shel had discovered the principles of time travel while looking into quantum gravity. He'd explained any number of times how the Watches worked, but I never understood any of it. Not then, and not now. "Why all the secrecy?" I'd asked him. "Why not take credit? It's the discovery of the ages." We'd laughed at the new shade of meaning to the old phrase.

"Because it's dangerous." He'd peered over the top of his glasses, not at me, but at something in the distance. "Time travel should not be possible in a rational universe." He'd shaken his head, and his unruly black hair had fallen into his eyes. He was only thirty-eight at the time of his death, a polished young genius who loved and charmed women. "I saw from the first *why* it was theoretically possible," he'd said. "But I thought I was missing something, some detail that would intervene to prevent the actual construction of a device. And yet there it is." And he'd looked down at the Watch strapped to his left wrist. He worried about Causality, the simple flow of cause and effect. "A time machine breaks it all down," he said. "It makes me wonder what kind of universe we live in."

I thought we should forget the philosophy and tell the world. Let other people worry about the details. When I pressed him, he'd talked about teams from the Mossad going back to drag Hitler out of 1935, or Middle Eastern terrorists hunting down Thomas Jefferson. It leads to utter chaos, he'd said. Either time travel should be prohibited, like exceeding the speed of light. Or the intelligence to achieve it should be prohibited."

We used to retreat sometimes to a tower on a rocky reef far downstream. No one lives there, and there is only ocean in all directions. I don't know how he found it, or who built it, or what that world is like. Nor do I believe *he* did. We enjoyed the mystery of the place. The moon is bigger, and the tides are loud. We'd hauled a generator out there, and a refrigerator, and a lot of furniture. We used to sit in front of a wall-length transparent panel, sipping beer, watching the ocean, and talking about God, history, and women.

They were good days.

Eventually, he'd said he would take Helen there.

The wind blew, the mourners dwindled and were gone, and the coffin waited on broad straps for the gravediggers.

Damn. I would miss him.

Gone now. He and his Watches. And temporal logic apparently none the worse.

Oh, I still had a working unit in my desk, but I knew I wouldn't use it again. I did not have his passion for time travel. Leave well enough alone. That's my motto.

On the way home, I turned on the radio. It was an ordinary day. Peace talks were breaking down in Africa. Another congressman was accused of diverting campaign funds. Assaults against spouses had risen again. In Los Angeles, there was a curious conclusion to an expressway pileup: two people, a man and a woman, had broken into one of the wrecked vehicles and kidnapped the driver, who was believed to be either dead or seriously injured. They had apparently run off with him.

Only in California.

Shel was compulsively secretive. Not only about time travel, but about everything. You never really knew what he was feeling because the mask was always up. He used to drive Helen crazy when we went to dinner because she had to wait until the server arrived to find out what he was going to order. When he was at the University, his department could never get a detailed syllabus out of him. And I was present when his own accountant complained that he was holding back information.

He used to be fond of saying knowledge is power, and I think that was what made him feel successful, that he knew things other people didn't. Something must have happened to him when he was a kid. It was probably the same characteristic that turned him into the all-time great camp follower. I don't know what the proper use for a time machine should be. We used it to make money. But mostly we used it to argue theology with Thomas Acquinas, to talk gravity with Isaac Newton, to watch Thomas Huxley take on Bishop Wilberforce. For us, it had been an entertainment medium. It seemed to me that we should have done *more* with it.

Don't ask me what.

I had all kinds of souvenirs: coins that a young Julius

Caesar had lost to Shel over draughts, a program from the opening night of *The Barber of Seville*, a quill once used by Benjamin Franklin. And photos. We had whole albums full of Alexander and Marcus Aurelius and the sails of the *Santa Maria* coming over the horizon. But they all looked like scenes from old movies. Except that the actors didn't look as good as you'd expect. When I pressed Shel for a point to all the activity, he said, what more could there be than an evening before the fire with Al Einstein? (We had got to a fairly intimate relationship with him, during the days when he was still working for the Swiss patent office.)

There were times when I knew he wanted to tell Helen what we were doing, and bring her along. But some tripwire always brought him up short, and he'd turn to me with that maddeningly innocuous smile as if to say, you and I have a secret and we had best keep it that way. Helen caught it, knew there was something going on. But she was too smart to try to break it open.

We went out fairly regularly, the three of us, and my true love of the month, whoever that might be. My date was seldom the same twice because she always figured out that Helen had me locked up. Helen knew that too, of course. But Shel didn't. I don't think it ever occurred to him that his old friend would have considered for a moment moving in on the woman he professed (although not too loudly) to love. There were times when we would be left alone, Helen and I, usually while Shel was dancing with my date, and the air would be thick with tension. Neither of us ever said anything directly, but sometimes our gaze would touch, and her eyes would grow very big and she would get a kind of forlorn look.

When we talked, the four of us, the subject of whether it was possible to love two people simultaneously used to come up a lot, although I can't remember who'd start it. We'd all express opinions, but the positions changed from time to time.

Helen was a frustrated actress who still enjoyed the theater. After about a year, she abandoned the Devil's Disciples, explaining that she simply did not have time for it anymore. But Shel understood her passion and indulged it. Whenever there was a revival, we all went. Inevitably, while we watched Shaw's frequently unconscious characters career toward their destinies, Shel would find an opportunity to tell me he was going to take her back to meet the great playwright.

I used to promise myself to stop socializing with her, to find an excuse, because it hurt so much to sit in the awful glare of her passion for him. But if I had done that, I wouldn't have seen her at all. At night, when the evening was over, she always kissed me, sometimes lightly on the cheek, sometimes a quick hit-and-run full on the lips. And once or twice, when she'd drunk a little too much and her control had slipped, she'd put some serious effort into it.

2.

Thursday, November 24. Noon.

The storm picked up while I drove home, reminiscing, feeling sorry for myself. I already missed his voice, his sardonic view of the world, his amused cynicism. We had seen power misused and abused all through the centuries, up close, sometimes with calculation, more often out of ignorance.

He'd done all the research in his basement laboratory, had built the first working models down there. These had been big, room-sized chambers which had dwindled in bulk as their capabilities increased. I was involved almost from the beginning. Eventually, the device had shrunk to the size of a watch. It was powered by a cell clipped to the belt or carried in a pocket. I still had one of the power packs at home.

I would have to decide what to do with our wardrobe. We'd used my second floor bedroom as an anteroom to the ages. It overflowed with rows of costumes and books on culture and language for every period we'd visited, or intended to visit.

But if my time-traveling days were over, I had made enough money from the enterprise that I would never have to work again, if I chose not to. The money had come from having access to next week's newspapers. We'd debated the morality of taking personal advantage of our capabilities, but I don't think the issue was ever in doubt. We won a small fortune at various race tracks. We'd continued to prosper until two gentlemen dropped by Shel's place one afternoon and told him they were not sure what was behind his winning streak, but that if it continued, they would break his knees. They must have known enough about us to understand it wouldn't be necessary to repeat the message to me.

We considered switching to commodities. But neither of us understood much about them, so we took our next plunge in the stock market. "It's got to be illegal," said Shel. And I'd laughed. "How could it be?" I asked him. "There are no laws against time travel." "Insider trading," he suggested.

Whatever. We justified our actions because gold was the commodity of choice upstream. It was research money, and we told each other it was for the good of mankind, although neither of us could quite explain how that was so. Gold was the one item that opened all doors, no matter what age you were in, no matter what road you traveled. If I learned anything during my years as Shel's interpreter and faithful Indian companion, it was that people will do anything for gold.

While I took a vaguely smug view of human greed, I put enough aside to buy a small estate in Exeter, and retired from the classroom to a life of books and contemplation. And travel in several dimensions.

Now that it was over, I expected to find it increasingly difficult to keep the secret. I had learned too much. I wanted to tell people what I'd done. Who I'd talked to. *So we were sitting over pastry and coffee on St. Helena, and I said to Napoleon—*

There was a thin layer of snow on the ground when I got home. Ray White, a retired tennis player who lives alone on the other side of Carmichael Drive, was out walking. He waved me down to tell me how sorry he was to hear about Shel's death. I thanked him and pulled into the driveway. A black car that I didn't recognize was parked off to one side. Two people, a man and a woman, were sitting inside. They opened their doors and got out as I drifted to a stop in front of the garage.

The woman was taller and more substantial than the man. She held out credentials. "Dr. Dryden? I'm Sgt. Lake, Carroll County Police." Her smile did not reach her eyes. "This is Sgt. Howard. Could we have a few minutes of your time?"

Her voice was low key. She would have been attractive had she been a trifle less official. She was in her late thirties, with cold dark eyes and a cynical expression that looked considerably older than she was.

"Sure," I said, wondering what it was about.

Sgt. Howard was a wiry little man with features screwed up into a permanent frown. He was bald, with thick eyebrows, and large floppy ears. He looked bored.

We stepped up onto the deck and went in through the sliding glass panels. Lake sat down on the sofa, while Howard undid a lumpy gray scarf and took to wandering around the room, inspecting books, prints, stereo, whatever. I offered coffee.

"No, thanks," said Lake. Howard just looked as if I hadn't meant him. She crossed her legs. "I wanted first to offer my condolences. I understand Dr. Shelborne was a close friend?"

"That's correct," I said. "We've known each other a long time."

She nodded, produced a leather-bound notebook, opened it, and wrote something down. "Did you have a professional relationship?" she asked.

"No," I said slowly. "We were just friends."

She seemed to expect me to elaborate. "May I ask what this is about?" I continued. "Has something happened?"

Her expression changed, became more intense. "Dr. Dryden," she said, "Dr. Shelborne was murdered."

My first reaction was simply to disbelieve the statement. "You're not serious."

"I never joke, Doctor. We believe someone attacked the victim in bed, struck him hard enough to fracture his skull, and set fire to the house."

Behind me, the floor creaked. Howard was moving around. "I don't believe it," I said.

Her eyes never left me. "The fire happened between 2:15 and 2:30 a.m., on the twelfth. Friday night, Saturday morning. I wonder if you'd mind telling me where you were at that time?"

"At home in bed," I said. There had been rumors that the fire was deliberately set, but I hadn't taken any of it seriously. "Asleep," I added unnecessarily. "I thought lightning hit the place?"

"No. There's really no question that it was arson."

"Hard to believe," I said.

"Why?"

"Nobody would want to kill Shel. He had no enemies. At least, none that I know of."

I was beginning to feel defensive. Authority figures always make me feel defensive. "You can't think of *anyone* who'd want him dead?"

"No," I said. But he had a lot of money. And relatives.

She looked down at her notebook. "Do you know if he kept any jewelry in the house?"

"No. He didn't wear jewelry. As far as I know, there was nothing like that around."

"How about cash?"

"I don't know." I started thinking about the gold coins that we always took upstream. A stack of them had been locked in a desk drawer. (I had more of them upstairs in the wardrobe.) Could anyone have known about them? I considered mentioning them, but decided it would be prudent to keep quiet, since I couldn't explain how they were used. And it would make no sense that I knew about a lot of gold coins in his desk and had never asked about them. "Do you think it was burglars?" I said.

Her eyes wandered to one of the bookcases. It was filled with biographies and histories of the Renaissance. The eyes were dark and cool, black pools waiting for something to happen. "That's possible, I suppose." She canted her head to read a title. It was Ledesma's biography of Cervantes, in the original Spanish. "Although burglars don't usually burn the house down." Howard had got tired poking around, so he circled back and lowered himself into a chair. "Dr. Dryden," she continued, "is there anyone who can substantiate the fact that you were here asleep on the morning of the twelfth?"

"No," I said. "I was alone." The question surprised me. "You don't think *I* did it, do you?"

"We don't really think *anybody* did it, yet."

Howard caught her attention and directed it toward the wall. There was a photograph of the three of us, Shel and Helen and me, at a table at the Beach Club. A mustard-colored umbrella shielded the table, and we were laughing and holding tall, cool drinks. She studied it, and turned back to me. "What exactly," she said, "is your relationship with Dr. Suchenko?"

I swallowed and felt the color drain out of my face. *I love her. I've loved her from the moment I met her.* "We're friends," I said.

"Is that all?" I caught a hint of a smile. But nobody knew. I'd kept my distance all this time. Even Helen didn't know. Well, she knew, but neither of us had ever admitted to it.

"Yes," I said. "That's all."

She glanced around the room. "Nice house."

It was. I had treated myself pretty well, installing leather furniture and thick pile carpets and a stow-away bar and some original art. "Not bad for a teacher," she added.

"I don't teach anymore."

She closed her book. "So I understand."

I knew what was in her mind. "I did pretty well on the stock market," I said.

"As did Dr. Shelborne."

"Yes. That's so."

"Same investments?"

"By and large, yes. We did our research together. An investment club, you might say."

Her eyes lingered on me a moment too long. She began to button her jacket. "Thank you, Dr. Dryden."

I was still numb with the idea that someone might have

murdered Shelborne. He had never flaunted his money, had
never even moved out of that jerkwater townhouse over in
River Park. But someone had found out. And they'd robbed
him. Possibly he'd come home and they were already in the
house. He might even have been upstream. Damn, what a
jolt that would have been: return from an evening in Bab-
ylon and get attacked by burglars.

So they'd killed him. And burned the house to hide the
murder. No reason it couldn't have happened that way.

I opened the sliding door for them. "You will be in the
area if we need you?" Lake asked. I assured her I would be,
and that I would do whatever I could to help find Shel's
killer. I watched them drive away and went back inside and
locked the door. It had been painful enough believing that
Shel had died through some arbitrary act of nature. But it
enraged me to think that a thug who had nothing whatever
to contribute would dare take his life.

I poured a brandy and stared out the window. The snow
was coming harder now. In back somewhere, something
moved. It might have been a tree branch, but it sounded
inside.

Snow fell steadily against the windows.

It came again. A floor board, maybe. Not much more
than a whisper.

I took down a golf club, went into the hallway, looked
up the staircase and along the upper level. Glanced toward
the kitchen.

Wood creaked. *Upstairs.*

I started up as quietly as I could, and got about halfway
when I saw movement at the door to the middle bedroom.
The wardrobe.

One of the curious phenomena associated with sudden
and unexpected death is our inability to accept it when it
strikes close to us. We always imagine that the person we've

lost is in the kitchen, or in the next room, and that it requires only that we call his name in the customary way to have him reappear in the customary place. I felt that way about Shel. We'd spent a lot of time together, had shared dangers and celebrations. And when it was over, we normally came back through the wardrobe.

He came out now.

He stood up there, watching me.

I froze.

"Hello, Dave," he said.

I hung on the bannister, and the stairs reeled. "Shel, is that *you*?"

He smiled. The old, crooked grin that I had thought not to see again. Some part of me that was too slow-witted to get flustered started flicking through explanations. Someone else had died in the fire. It was a dream. Shel had a twin.

"Yes," he said. "It's me. Are you okay?"

"Yeah."

"I'm sorry. I know this must be a shock." He moved toward me, along the top of the landing. I'm not sure what I was feeling. There was a rush of emotions, joy, anger, even fear. He came down a few stairs, took my shoulders, and steadied me. His hands were solid, his smile very real, and my heart sank. Helen's image surfaced.

"I don't understand," I said.

Adrian Shelborne was tall and graceful. His eyes were bright and sad. We slid down into sitting positions. "It's been a strange morning," he said.

"You're supposed to be dead."

He took a deep breath. "I know. I do believe I *am*, David."

Suddenly it was clear. "You're *downstream*."

"Yes," he said. "I'm downstream." He threw his head back. "You sure you're okay?"

"I've spent two weeks trying to get used to this. That you were gone—."

"It seems to be true." He spaced the words out, not able to accept it himself.

"When you go back—."

"—The house will burn, and I will be in it."

For a long time neither of us spoke. "Don't go back," I said at last.

"I have to."

I was thinking how candle-light filled Helen's eyes, how they had walked to the car together at the end of an evening, the press of her lips still vibrant against my cheek.

"Why?" I asked. Hoping he would have a good answer.

"Because they just buried me, Dave. They found me in my bed. Did you know I didn't even get out of my bed?"

"Yes," I said. "I heard that."

"I don't believe it." He was pale, and his eyes were red.

My first ride with him had been to Gettysburg to listen to Lincoln. It had been breathtaking, and Shel talked later about having dinner with Caesar and Voltaire and Catherine the Great. But the second trip had been a surprise. We were riding a large misshapen brown chamber then, a thing that looked like a hot water tank. He'd refused to tell me where we were going. It turned out to be 1975 New Haven. He wanted to see a young woman, barely more than a girl. I don't think Shel realized how young she was until we got there. Her name was Martha, and six hours after we showed up she would fall asleep at the wheel of her Ford while driving to pick up her mother. And Shel's life would be altered forever. "She and I had dinner last night at The Mug," he told me while we waited for her to come out of the telephone company building where she worked. "I never saw her again."

It was 5:00 p.m., and the first rush out the door was beginning.

"What are you going to do?" I'd asked.

He was a wreck. "Talk to her."

"She'll call the police. She's not going to know who you are."

"I'll be careful." And he warned me about paradoxes. Don't want to create a paradox. "I just want to see her again."

A light rain had begun. People poured out through the revolving doors. They looked up at the clouds, grimaced, and scattered to cars and buses, holding newspapers over their heads.

And then Martha came out.

I knew her immediately, because Shel stiffened and caught his breath. She paused to exchange a few words with another young woman. The rain came harder.

She was twenty years old and full of vitality and good humor. There was much of the tomboy about her, just giving way to a lush golden beauty. Her hair was shoulder-length and accentuated her shoulders. (I saw much of Helen in her, in her eyes, in the set of her mouth, in her animation.) She was standing back under the building overhang, protected from the rain. She waved goodby to the friend, and prepared to dash through the storm. But her gaze fell on us, on Shel. Her brow furrowed and she looked at us uncertainly.

Shel stepped forward.

I was holding his arm. Holding him back. A gust of wind blew loose dust and paper through the air. "Don't," I said.

"I know." *Avoid the irreparable act that could not have happened.*

She turned away and broke into a half-run. We watched her disappear around the corner out onto the parking lot.

We had talked about that incident many times, what might have happened had he intervened. We used to sit in the tower at the end of time, and he'd feel guilty and virtuous at the same time.

"They think you were murdered," I said.

"I know. I heard the conversation." Downstairs, he fell into an armchair. His face was gray.

My stomach churned and I knew I wasn't thinking clearly. "What happened? How did you find out about the funeral?"

He didn't answer right away. "I was doing some research downstream," he said finally, "in the Trenton Library. In the reference section. I was looking at biographies so I could plan future flights. You know how I work."

"Yes," I said.

"And I did something I knew was a mistake. Knew it while I was doing it. But I went ahead anyhow."

"You looked up your own biography."

He grinned. "Yeah. Couldn't help myself. It's a terrible thing to have the story of your life at your elbow. Dave, I walked away from it twice and came back both times." He sighed. "I'll be remembered for my work in quantum transversals."

"This is what comes of traveling alone." I was irritated. "I told you we should never do that."

"It's done," he said. "Listen, if I hadn't looked, I'd be dead now."

I broke out a bottle of burgundy, filled two glasses and we drank it off. I filled them again. "What are you going to do?"

He shook his head, dismayed. "*It's waiting for me back there*. I don't know *what* to do." His breathing was loud. Snow was piling up on the windows.

"The papers are predicting four inches," I said.

He nodded, as if it mattered. "The biography also says I was murdered. It didn't say by whom."

"It must have been burglars."

"At least," he said, "I'm warned. Maybe I should take a gun back with me."

"Maybe."

Avoid the irreparable act.

"Anyway," he said, "I thought you'd want to know I'm okay." He snickered at that. His own joke.

I kept thinking about Helen. "Don't go back at all," I said. "With or without a gun."

"I don't think that's an option."

"It sure as hell is."

"At some point," he said, "for one reason or another, I went home." He was staring at the burgundy. He hadn't touched the second glass. "My God, Dave, I'm scared. I've never thought of myself as a coward, but I'm afraid to face this."

It wasn't a good time to say anything, so I just sat.

"It's knowing the way of it," he said. "That's what tears me up."

"Stay here," I said.

He shook his head. "I just don't think the decision's in my hands. But meantime, there's no hurry. Right?"

"Makes sense to me."

"I've got a few places to go. People to talk to. Then, when I've done what I need to do, I'll think about all this."

"Good."

He picked up the glass, drained it, wiped his lips, and drifted back to the sofa. "It was scary out there today, Dave. I watched them throw flowers on my coffin. You should try that sometime." His eyes slid shut. "Are they sure it's me?"

"I understand the body was burned beyond recognition."

"That's something to think about. It could be anyone. And even if it *is* me, it might be a Schrodinger situation. As long as no one knows for certain, it might not matter."

"The police know. I assume they checked your dental records."

He nodded. "I suppose they do that sort of thing automatically. Do me a favor though and make sure they have a proper identification." He got up, wandered around the room, touching things, the books, the bust of Churchill, the P.C. He paused in front of the picture from the Beach Club. "I keep thinking how much it means to be alive. You know, Dave, I saw people out there today I haven't seen in years."

The room became still. He played with his glass. It was an expensive piece, chiseled, and he peered at its facets. "When is the reading of the will?"

"I don't know. They may have done it already."

"I'm tempted to go."

"To the reading?"

He managed a tight, pained smile. "I could wear a black beard and reveal myself at the appropriate moment."

"You can't do that," I said, horrified.

He laughed. "I know. But my God I would love to." He shook himself, as if he were just waking up. "Truth is that I know how I'm going to die. But it doesn't have to happen until I'm ready for it. Meantime, we've got places to go. Right?"

"Right," I said.

He looked past me, out the window.

"I think you need to tell her," I said gently.

His expression clouded. "I know." He drew the words out. "I'll talk to her. At the proper time."

"Be careful," I said. "She isn't going to expect to see you."

3.

Friday, November 25. Mid-morning.

The critical question was whether we had in fact buried Adrian Shelborne, or whether there was a possibility of mistaken identity. We talked through the night. But neither of us knew anything about police procedure in such matters, so I said I would look into it.

I started with Jerry Shelborne, who could hardly have been less like his brother. There was a mild physical resemblance, although Jerry had allowed the roast beef to pile up a little too much. He was a corporate lawyer. In his eyes, Shel had shuffled aimlessly through life, puttering away with notions that had no reality in the everyday world in which normal people live. Even his brother's sudden wealth had not changed his opinion.

"I shouldn't speak ill of the dead," he told me that morning. "He was a decent man, had a lot of talent, but he never really made his life count." Jerry sat behind a polished teak desk, an India rubber plant in a large pot at his side leaning toward a sun-filled window. The furniture was dark-stained, leather-padded. Plaques covered the walls, appreciations from civic groups, corporate awards, various licenses and testaments. Photos of his two children were prominently displayed, a boy in a Little League uniform, a girl nuzzling a horse. His wife, who had left him years earlier, was missing.

"Actually," I said, "I thought he did pretty well."

"I don't mean money." (I hadn't been thinking of money.) "But it seems to me a man has an obligation to live in his community. To make a contribution to it." He leaned back expansively and thrust satisfied fingers into a vest pocket. " 'To whom much is given'," he said, " 'much shall be expected.' "

"I suppose. Anyway, I wanted to extend my sympathy."

"Thank you." Jerry rose, signaling that the interview was over.

We walked toward the paneled door. "You know," I said, "this experience has a little bit of *deja vu* about it."

He squinted at me. He didn't like me, and wasn't going to be bothered concealing it. "How do you mean?"

"There was a language teacher at Princeton, where I got my doctorate. Same thing happened to him. He lived alone and one night a gas main let go and blew up the whole house. They buried him and then found out it wasn't him at all. He'd gone on an unannounced holiday to Vermont, and turned his place over to a friend. They didn't find out until several days after the funeral."

Jerry shrugged, amused at the colossal stupidity loose in the world. "Unfortunately," he said, "there's not much chance of that here. They tell me the dental records were dead on."

I probably shouldn't have tried to see how Helen was doing. But I called her from a drug store and she said yes, she'd like to see me, and suggested lunch. We met at an Applebee's in the Garden Square Mall.

She looked worn out. Her eyes were bloodshot, and she tended to lose the thread of conversation. She and Shel had made no formal commitment. But she had certainly believed they had a future together. Come what may. But Shel had been evasive. And there had been times when, discouraged that she got so little of his time, she'd opened up to me. I don't know if anything in my life had been quite as painful as sitting with her, listening to her describe her frustration, watching the occasional tears roll down her cheek. She trusted me, absolutely.

"Are you all right?" she asked me.

"Yes. How about you?"

The talk was full of regrets, things not said, acts undone. The subject of the police suspicions came up, and we found it hard to subscribe to the burglar theory. "What kind of intruder," I asked, "kills a sleeping man, and then sets the house on fire?"

She was as soft and vulnerable that day as I'd ever seen her. By all the laws of nature, Shel was dead. Was I still bound to keep my distance? And the truth was that Shel did not even care enough to ease her suffering. I wondered how she would react if she knew Shel was probably in my kitchen at that moment, making a submarine sandwich.

I wanted to tell her. There was a possibility that, when she *did* find out, she would hold it against *me*. I also wanted to keep Shel dead. That was hard to admit to myself, but it was true. I wanted nothing more than a clear channel with Helen Suchenko. But when I watched her bite down the pain, when the tears came, when she excused herself with a shaky voice and hurried back to the ladies' room, I could stand it no more. "Helen," I said, "are you free this afternoon?"

She sighed. "People get nervous around weepy doctors. Yes, I'm free. But I'm not in the mood to go anywhere."

"Can I persuade you to come out to my place?"

She looked desperately fragile. "I don't think so, Dave. I need some time to myself."

I listened to the hum of conversation around us. "Please," I said. "It's important."

It was snowing again. Helen followed me in her small blue Ford. I watched her in the mirror, playing back all possible scenarios on how to handle this. Leave out the time travel stuff, I decided, at least for now. Use the story I'd told Jerry as an example of how misunderstandings can occur. *He's not dead, Helen.* And then bring him into the room. Best not to warn *him*. God knows how he would react. But get them together, present Shel with a *fait accompli*, and you will have done your self-sacrificial duty, Dave. You dumb bastard.

I pulled through blowing snow into my garage. Helen rolled in beside me, and the doors closed. "Glad to be out of that," she said, with a brave smile that implied she had decided we needed something new to talk about.

The garage opened into the kitchen. I stopped before going through the door and listened. There were no sounds on the other side. "Helen," I said, "I've got something to tell you."

She pulled her coat around her. Her breath formed a mist. "We aren't going into it out here, I hope, are we?"

I smiled and opened the door. The kitchen was empty. No sounds anywhere in the house. "It's about Shel," I said.

She stepped past me and switched on the kitchen light. "I know," she said. "What else could it be?"

A white envelope lay on the table, with my name on it, printed in his precise hand. I snatched it up, but not before she'd seen it.

"Just a list of things to do." I pushed it into my pocket. "How about some coffee?"

"Sure. Sounds good."

"It'll have to be instant," I said, putting water on the stove.

"Do you always do that?" she asked.

"Do what?"

"Write yourself notes?"

"It's my to-do list. It's the first thing I do every morning."

She got two cups down and I excused myself, slipped out, and opened the envelope.

> *Dear Dave,*
>
> *I don't know how to write this. But I have to think about what's happened and figure out what to do. I don't want to jump the gun if it's not necessary. You understand.*
>
> *I know this hasn't been easy for you. But I'm glad you were there. Thanks.*
>
> *Shel*
>
> *P.S. I've left most of my estate to the Leukemia Foundation. That will generate a half-dozen lawsuits from my relatives. But if any of those vultures show signs of winning, I'll come back personally and deal with them.*

I read it a half-dozen times. Then I crumpled it, tossed it, and went back to the kitchen.

She was looking out the window at the falling snow. Usually, my grounds were alive with bluejays and squirrels. But the critters were all tucked away now. "It's lovely," she said. "So what's the surprise?"

"Son of a gun. I went out to get it and forgot." We strolled into the living room and I hurried upstairs in search of an idea.

I think I mentioned that the wardrobe was also a small museum. There were items of inestimable value, but only if you knew their origin. We had scrolls from the library at Alexandria, a sextant designed and built by Leonardo, a silver bracelet that had once belonged to Calpurnia, a signed folio of *Hamlet*, a pocket watch that Leo Tolstoy had carried while writing *War and Peace*. There were photos of Martin Luther and Albert Schweitzer and Attila the Hun and Charles XII of Sweden. All more or less worthless.

I couldn't bear to give away Calpurnia's bracelet to someone who would not understand what it was. I settled instead for a gold medallion I'd bought from a merchant in Thebes during the fifth century, B.C. It carried a serpent's likeness. An Apollonian priest had insisted I'd acquired a steal. At one time, he said, it had belonged to Aesculapius, the divine doctor, who'd been so good he cured the dead. He backed up his view by trying to buy it from me, offering six times what I'd paid for it.

I carried it downstairs and gave it to Helen, telling her that Shel had wanted me to be sure she got it in case anything happened to him. She glowed, and turned it over and over, unable to get enough of it. "It's exquisite," she said. And the tears came again.

If that thing had possessed any curative powers, I could have used them at that moment.

Snow filled the world. The stand of oaks bordering the approach to the house faded. As did the stone wall along Carmichael Drive, and the hedges on the west side of the grounds. Gradually a heavy white curtain was drawn across the middle of the lawn. "I think we're going to get a foot before this is over," I commented.

She stood by the curtains, enjoying a glass of chablis. I'd started the fire, and it crackled and pocked comfortably. We added Mozart, and I hoped the storm would continue.

"I think so too," she said. A pair of headlights crept past, out beyond the stone wall.

We talked inconsequentials. She had recovered herself,

and I wondered whether it was her proximity to me, with all the baggage I brought to any meeting, that had triggered the emotional display. I was not happy that Shel was still in the field. But during that afternoon, I came to understood it might make no difference. Even if Shel were safely in his grave, I was still the embodiment of too many memories. The decent thing to do would be to fade out of her life, just as Carmichael Drive and the trees were fading now. But I could not bring myself to do that.

She talked about a break in the weather so she could go home. But my luck held. The snow piled up, and we stayed near the fire. I was alone at last with Helen Suchenko, and it was perhaps the most painful few hours of my life. Yet I would not have missed them, and I've replayed them countless times since.

We watched the reports on the Weather Channel. It was a heavy system, moving down from Canada, low pressure and high pressure fronts colliding, eight inches predicted. On top of yesterday's storm, it was expected to shut down the entire east coast from Boston to Baltimore.

She talked a lot about Shel. She'd shake her head as if remembering something, and then dismiss it. She'd veer off onto some other subject, a movie, the latest political scandal, a medical advance that held hope for a breakthrough in this or that. There were a couple of patients she was worried about, and a few hypochondriacs whose lives were centered on imagined illnesses. I told her how much I missed teaching, which wasn't entirely true, but it's the sort of thing people expect you to say. What I really missed was a sense of purpose, a reason to exist. I had that upstairs, in notes detailing conversations with Rachmaninoff and Robert E. Lee and Oliver Cromwell and Aristotle and H. G. Wells. Those conversations would make the damndest book the world had ever seen, reports by the principal actors on their ingenuity, their dreams, their follies. But it would never get written.

We lost the cable at four o'clock, and with it the Weather Channel.

Gradually, the light dwindled out of the sky. I put on steaks and Helen made up a salad. Our timing was perfect because the power failed just as we put everything on the table. I lit candles, and she sat in the flickering light and looked happy. If the clouds had not dissipated, at least for these few hours they had receded.

The music had been silenced by the power outage, so we sat listening to the fire and the whisper of snow against the house. Occasionally, I glanced up at the upstairs bedroom, half-expecting the door to open. I tried to plan what I would do if Shel suddenly appeared on the landing.

It did not happen. We talked into the early hours, until finally she gave out and fell asleep. I moved her to the sofa and went upstairs for blankets. The heating system, of course, was not working, nor was anything else in the all-electric house. The second floor was already cooling off, but I had plenty of firewood.

I settled into a large armchair and slept. Somewhere around two, I woke, listening to the silence. The fire was low. I poked at it, and added a log. Helen stirred but did not wake. Usually, even during the early morning hours, there are sounds: a passing car, the wind in the trees, a dog barking somewhere. But the world was absolutely still.

It was also absolutely dark. No stars. No lights of any kind.

I pointed a flashlight out the window. The night had closed in, wrapped itself around the house so tightly that the beam penetrated only a few feet. It looked like an effect out of a Dracula film. I tried to call the 24-hour weather line. But the phone was dead.

"What is it, Dave?" Helen's voice, soft in the dark.

"Come take a look out the window."

She padded over. And caught her breath. "It's pitch black out there."

We went outside. It was the thickest, darkest night I'd ever seen. We didn't sleep well after that. At about six, Helen made toast over the fire, and I broke out some fruit juice. The lights were still off. And there was no sign of dawn.

I wondered about Ray White, my neighbor. Ray was a good guy, but he lived alone in a big house, and I thought of him over there wrapped in this goddam black void with no power and maybe no food. He wasn't young, and I thought it would be a good idea to check on him.

"I'll go with you," Helen said.

My first reaction was to tell her not to be silly, but you didn't say things like that to her. So I got another flashlight, and we let ourselves out through the sliding door. We had to poke around to find the path to the front gate. The flashlights didn't help much. There's a hundred-year-old oak midway between the house and the stone wall that surrounds the property. It's only a few feet off the walk, but we couldn't see it.

We reached the front gate and eased out onto the sidewalk. "Stay close," I said.

We stepped off the curb. Her hand tightened in mine.

Carmichael is two lanes wide. We started across, but the snow cover stopped right in the middle of the street. It was the damndest thing. There was no snow at all on the other side. There wasn't even *blacktop*. The surface had turned to rock. Where the hell was there rock on the other side of Carmichael Drive? A patch of grass, yes, and some concrete. But not rock.

"You sure you know where we are?" she asked.

"Yes," I said. "Of course."

The rock was black. It almost looked like marble.

We found no curb. No sidewalk. None of the trees that lined the far side of the street. No sign of the low wall that encloses Ray White's sprawling grounds and executive mansion.

We found nothing.

I tried calling Ray's name. But no one answered.

"Are you sure we came out the right way?" Helen asked.

4.

During the summer of 1496, Michelangelo was twenty-one years old, newly-arrived in Rome, and looking for work. He was already a towering genius, but no one knew that yet. Shel had made no secret of his intention to go back and give the young man a commission. "Do him a favor," he'd said, magnanimously. "It will upset nothing, and we'll collect a nice souvenir."

He had never got around to it. And that meant I had a likely place to look for him.

This was the Rome of Alexander VI, a pope who brooked neither heresy nor opposition. It was a bad time for the True Faith, a few decades after the fall of Constantinople, when Europe had given sanctuary to armies of scholars from that benighted land. The scholars had repaid the good turn by unleashing the Renaissance. It was a dusty, unimposing Rome, still medieval, still passive by either modern or imperial standards. Dreary, bootstrap houses lined the narrow, winding streets, sinking into the rubble of classical times. Churches and palaces were everywhere. More were under construction. The Fortress of Sant' Angelo, containing Hadrian's tomb, dominated the banks of the Tiber. The western approaches to the city were guarded by the old Basilica of St. Peter, the predecessor of the modern structure.

I found Michelangelo with the assistance of Pietro Cardinal Riario, who is known to history for his early support of Michelangelo, and for his occasional homicidal tendencies.

He was living in modest quarters not far from the Tiber. The landlord directed me to a dump site, where I found him seated on a low hill at the edge of the facility, contemplating heaps of trash. Michelangelo was an ordinary-looking young man, with clear, congenial features and handsome dark eyes. He did not hear me approach. "Hello," I said, casually, following his gaze. "That's a fairly dismal prospect."

He looked up, surprised. "Hello, Father." (I was dressed in clerical garb.) He sounded preoccupied, and probably hoped I would move on. "Yes," he added, "it is."

We looked out across the smoking mounds. Carrion eaters wheeled overhead. "See that?" He pointed at a broken column. "It used to be part of the Forum."

Two men wheeled a cart loaded with trash past us, proceeded another twenty yards along the crest of the hill, stopped, and tilted the vehicle's contents into the dump. "Tell me," I said, "Are you Michelangelo Buonarroti? The sculptor?"

He brightened. "I am he, Father. Why do you smile?"

"I've heard you are talented," I said. "I'm looking for a friend. He said he was coming here to give you a commission."

Michelangelo got to his feet. "I have not yet established myself," he said. "But I'm happy to hear my reputation is growing. Your friend, is he a priest also?"

I was not sure how Shel might have presented himself.

"He is. But he works among the poor and often dresses accordingly."

His brow wrinkled and he looked as if he had just made a connection. "Is your name David?"

That startled me. "Why do you ask?"

"I was given a message for David. Are you he?"

"Yes."

He studied me carefully. "And what is your friend's name?"

"Adrian," I said.

"*Father* Adrian."

"Yes, that is correct. *Father* Adrian. And the message?"

"Back at the house. It came by courier two days ago. Would you care to walk with me?"

It was a warm, still afternoon. The sun was high and very bright, and the sky was filled with clumps of white cloud. "How long have you been in Rome?" I asked.

It was his turn to be surprised. "Only a few weeks," he said. "How did you know I had just come?"

"You're better known than you realize, young man. What are you working on now?"

"Not very much, I'm afraid. Only Cardinal Riario sends me assignments. I am very much indebted to him."

As are we all. "But you *do* have a commission from Father Adrian?"

"Yes. But I have not yet begun on it. He wants me to render Hermes for him in his role as healer. But I haven't been able to decide what form the work should take."

I used a small Minolta to get a couple of pictures, doing it as unobtrusively as I could. But he saw the camera and asked what it was. "A relic," I replied.

His house was one of a group of nondescript structures crowded around a muddy courtyard. It was halfway up a hill, just high enough to glimpse the Tiber, which looked muddy. Children played noisily in the courtyard. Michelangelo had built a workshop in the rear of the house. While he retrieved the message, I stuck my head inside. It was damp and smelled of wet stone. Tables, benches and shelves were made of planks. A small piece of carrara marble with a child's head just emerging was set atop a pair of boards on the floor. It looked like the long-lost *Sleeping Cupid*.

I took more pictures. Children ran loose, screaming and fighting, and I wondered how it was possible for genius to function amid the bedlam.

"Here it is, Father." He appeared and handed me a yellow envelope with DAVID DRYDEN printed on it. "It does not indicate you are a priest," he added. "It is why I was confused."

"Thank you, Michelangelo. I've enjoyed talking with you." I held out my hand. He shook it, and it was one of those electric moments you get to enjoy if you're a time traveler. Then I gave him a gold coin and watched his eyes go wide. "See you finish his commission properly," I said.

"Oh, I will, Father. You may be sure."

I turned away, and waited until I was out of the neighborhood to open the envelope. It read:

DAVID, COME AT ONCE. I AM IN THE BORGIA TOWER. ACCUSED OF HERESY OR SOME DAMNED THING. GUARDS CAN BE BRIBED.

The Vatican, even at that remote period, was an architectural marvel. Pilgrims filled its courts and streets. The sacred buildings clustered together behind crenelated walls and the Tiber, a sacred camp besieged by the worldly powers. I looked up at Old St. Peter's, in which Pope Leo III had crowned Charlemagne; passed San Damaso Courtyard, which still hosted jousting tournaments; and paused near the Library to get my bearings. The Borgia Tower was an ominous fortress guarding the western flank of the papal palace, parallel with its military-appearing twin, the Sistine Chapel. Guards patroled the entrance. I went up to the front door, as if I had all the right in the world to be there. A sentry challenged me. He wore a blue uniform, and he carried a dagger and a small axe.

"I am the confessor," I said, "of Adrian Shelborne, who I believe to be a visitor here."

The guard was barely nineteen. "Have you been sent for, Father?"

His manner implied that if I didn't have an invitation, I would be barred. And my instincts told me that a bribe would not work. Not with this boy. He was too new. "Yes," I said. "The Administrator asked me to come." I was trying to remember influential names in this Vatican, and my mind had gone blank.

"Ah." He nodded. "Good. Please come with me."

We entered the Tower. "Wait here," he said, and disappeared through a side door. The anteroom in which I stood was decorated with a Domenico Ghirlandaio painting. It was a scene from the Last Judgment. A God who looked much like Jupiter approached his throne in a sunbright chariot, while angels sang and humans cringed or celebrated, according to their consciences. I was tempted to make off with it and come back later for Shel.

The sentry reappeared, trailing a sergeant. "You wish to see Cardinal Borgia?" he asked.

"No," I said quickly. That depraved monster was the last person I wanted to see. "No, I wish to visit Father Adrian Shelborne. To hear his confession."

"Ah." The sergeant nodded. It was a noncommittal nod, putting me in a holding pattern. He looked at me through flat cold eyes. His teeth were snagged and broken. He had a broad nose, and a long scar running from his right ear

across the jaw to his lip, where it caused a kind of permanent sneer. Not his fault, but the man could not have managed a smile without scaring the kids. "Father, surely you
realize where you are. He would not be denied the sacra-
ments *here*."

I pressed a gold coin into his hand. "If you could see
your way clear, *signore*."

He slipped it deftly into a pocket without changing expression. "He must have very heavy sins, Father."

"I would like only a few minutes," I said.

"Very well." He straightened his uniform. "This way."

We went deep into the building. Walls were lined with
frescoes and paintings, likenesses of figures from both classical and Christian mythology, renderings of church fathers
and of philosophers. I saw none that I recognized.

We mounted four flights of stairs and passed into chambers even more ornately decorated than those on the lower
floors. My escort deposited me in a room with an exquisite
statue of St. Michael, wings spread and sword drawn. Not a
good omen. But I was wearing the Watch, and a cable ran
up my arm and down my side connecting it with the powerpack. I had to assume Shel had lost his unit or he wouldn't
be stuck here. But it didn't matter. Mine would be enough
to get us both out.

Moments later, he was back. "This way, please, Father,"
he said, opening a paneled door for me.

I went through into a well-appointed study, and found
myself looking at a young man seated behind a large carved
desk. He was about Michelangelo's age. But *this* youth wore
a Cardinal's red garments. And that told me who he was.

"Thank you, John," he said to my escort. The door
closed softly behind me. I now saw two muscular priests
advancing to either side of the Cardinal's desk. The wall
behind him was dominated by a variant of the papal seal.

Several books, an expensive luxury then, were stacked on a table to his left. One, a treatise on St. Jerome, lay open. Gray light came through three windows whose heavy curtains were drawn back.

This was Cesare Borgia. *Don't drink the wine.* Appointed to the College of Cardinals by his father, Pope Alexander VI. My God, what had Shel got himself into?

He smiled pleasantly, crooked his index finger and signaled me forward. "Good afternoon, Father—?"

"David Dryden, Eminence," I said.

His lips were full and sensuous. The eyes were dark and detached, the nose straight, the jaws lean. He wore a thin smile, rather like a cassock, something to be taken off and put on. "Dryden." He tasted the word. Let his tongue roll around on it as if he were swallowing both it and me. "Your accent is strange. Where are you from?"

"Cornwall." Good a spot as any. "I am a poor country priest," I added.

"I see." He placed his fingertips together. The hands were long and thin and had not seen the sun recently. "You wished to see Father Shelborne?"

"If possible, Eminence. I am his confessor."

His teeth were straight and white. "And where did you take orders, Father?"

"St. Michael's." I inserted pride in my response. Good old alma mater.

"In Cornwall?"

"Yes." I tried not to hesitate. What sort of priest has no idea where his seminary is?

"We've had other visitors from St. Michael's recently," he said. "It has a magnificent view of the Umber, I understand?"

Where in God's name was the Umber? "Actually," I said,

"it is the rolling hills of Cornwall that attract the eye."

He considered my response. "And how do you stand on the matter of the Waldensians?"

The Waldensians were men who gave away their money and traveled the roads of southern Europe helping the poor. By their example, they had embarrassed the more powerful members of the Church, and had therefore been branded heretics. "They should commit to Mother Church," I said.

"That is quite good," Cesare smiled, "for a country priest. Tell me, Father, where does a country priest get gold with which to bribe my guards?"

"I had not intended to bribe anyone, Eminence. I thought rather, in the tradition of the Faith, to share my own largess. I have come recently into good fortune."

"What kind of good fortune?"

"An inheritance. My father died and left his money—"

Cesare waved my story away with a gesture that was almost feminine. "I see." The two muscular priests came to attention. "Who is paying you, Dryden? The French?"

"I'm in no one's pay, Eminence. I mean no one any harm."

He glanced at the priests. A signal. They came forward and took hold of my arms and did the equivalent of a patdown. It was not gentle. One came only to about my eyes, but he was wide as a girder. The other was big and athletic, just beginning to thicken around the waist. He was the type who, in our age, would have been at the Y every day playing squash. The Girder found my Watch within moments and held up my left arm triumphantly, shaking the sleeve back so Cesare could see. He started to remove it, but the cable connecting it to the powerpack wouldn't let go. There was a brief struggle during which I came close to getting strangled. Eventually I managed to get it off without disconnecting the units. The priest held it out for Cesare, who placed it on the desk. They took my gold, and gave that to him too. Then they stepped back.

Cesare looked at the Watch and the powerpack. He took them to the window, without disconnecting the cable, and examined them. "Father," he said, "what *is* this thing?"

I had a feeling the relic story wasn't going to sell here. "It's a timepiece."

"And how does it work?" He squinted at the Watch, whose face was blank, and would remain so until it received the proper command.

"It's broken," I said. "It belonged to my father. I keep it in his honor."

Again the smile. The bastard didn't believe a word. And I realized I'd overlooked an obvious point. He reached down and opened a desk drawer, from which he withdrew Shel's unit. He placed them side by side. "They seem to be twins," he said.

"He is my cousin, Eminence."

"And you both carry these *things*, in honor of your esteemed fathers. I am touched." His smile widened, and snapped off. "David Whatever-your-name-is, let us be clear on one point. Unless you are honest with me, I will have to assume you and your friend are agents of a foreign power, and beyond reclamation. I will then have no choice but to deal with you accordingly." He came around the side of the desk.

"Where is Adrian?" I asked.

Cesare stared at me momentarily, and looked toward the door. It opened, and I saw Shel. He was dirty, bruised, covered with blood. He sagged in the arms of two guards. One was John, the man who had escorted me.

I started toward him, but the priests got between us.

Shel's eyes opened. "You don't look so good," I said, still speaking Italian.

He tried to wipe his mouth, but the guards held both arms tight. "Hello, Dave," he said. "What took you so long?"

I turned back to Cesare. "Why have you detained him, Eminence?"

The Cardinal's eyes were fixed on me. "You have courage, Father, to come here and interrogate *me*. But I don't mind. We know your friend is a heretic. He is probably also a spy and an assassin. A would-be assassin."

"I tried to get an audience with His Holiness," Shel muttered.

"That was stupid," I said in English. "Why?" Alexander VI was the Borgia pope, a womanizer, con man, murderer, father of Lucrezia and Cesare. "Why would you want to see him?"

"Seemed like a good idea at the time."

The girder priest drove his fist into my stomach and I went to my knees. "Please confine your remarks to *me*," said Cesare. "Now perhaps you will tell us why you are here. The truth, this time."

"Eminence," I said, "we are only pilgrims."

He sighed. "Very well." He looked toward the windows.

The center window looked down four stories. They opened it, dragged Shel across the floor, and hoisted him onto the sill. "Wait," I cried. But the bastards held me tight.

Cesare watched my reaction. "Have you anything to say, Father Dryden?"

"Yes. You're right, Eminence. We are French spies."

"Good. Now perhaps you will tell me who sent you?"

"Monte Cristo," I said.

"I'm not surprised." Cesare's thin lips smiled. "What was your purpose? To attempt the life of His Holiness?"

"No. Most certainly not. We hoped to sow political discord."

They leaned Shel out over the street. "I don't think I heard you correctly. Did you say you were here to kill the Pope?"

"Yes," I agreed, seeing that was the only response that would satisfy him. "That is why we were sent."

Cesare gestured and they brought Shel back inside. "I assume everyone here heard his admission?" he asked.

Shel glared at me. "Damn you," he said in English. "They'll kill us now."

Cesare sighed. "Take them away," he told John casually.

"Wait," Shel said. "Perhaps Your Eminence would care to allow us to make a contribution to the Church."

"In exchange for my intercession at your trial?" He looked interested. "What have you to bargain with?"

"I have access to a substantial sum of gold." I watched, certain that no deal would work. They would simply take everything, and we would still end up in the dungeons.

"And where is this gold?"

"Nowhere, just now—." It was as far as he got. Cesare nodded, a barely perceptible movement of head and eye, and John knocked him to his knees.

"Please do not waste my time," he said.

Shel spoke between gasps. "I have no wish to do so, Eminence. You asked about the device we wear on our wrists. It is a *Transmuter*." I could hear the capital T.

Cesare glanced back at the desk. "And what is a transmuter?"

"It converts lead to gold."

The Cardinal looked at me to see how I was receiving this news. I tried to look displeased, as if Shel had just given away a secret. He picked up one of the Watches. "Such a device would do much to spur the mission of the Church."

"Would you like to see how it works, Eminence?" He tried to get up, but the guards held him down.

"Yes," said Cesare. "But I would prefer that your friend show me." He looked at me and I picked up the Watch.

Cesare handed me a lead paperweight. "Proceed." His tone suggested that his expectations had been aroused, and that any disappointment would be ill-received.

The lead weight was a disk-shaped stone, with an image of St. Gabriel appearing to the Virgin.

I set the Watch to take me downstream one minute. Then I smiled at Cesare to be sure I had his attention, and squeezed the trigger. The room and its occupants froze. They became transparent and faded out. Then they reappeared, in somewhat different positions. Cesare's face was twisted with shock; the guards had released Shel and were staggering back toward the door, one in the act of blessing himself; both priests, eyes wide, had retreated well away from where I'd been standing. Shel had got to his feet.

When I reappeared, they panicked. One of the priests thrust a crucifix in my face. I laughed, pushed him away, and turned to Cesare. "You abuse your power, Eminence," I told him. I scooped up our coins and the remaining unit and looked at Shel. Cesare's men hurriedly cleared out of my way. "You all right?" I asked him.

"Yes." He grinned. "It's almost worth it."

I smiled pleasantly at Cesare, whose pale expression contrasted sharply with his red robes. "I'll see you in hell, Borgia."

Shel put the Watch on and set up. "I just realized," he said. "I have to pick up a statue."

"Forget the statue. We need you back home."

One of the guards drew an axe. Shel pulled the trigger. I followed a moment later. But when I materialized in the wardrobe, I was alone.

5.

Saturday, November 26. Late morning.

The Watch, unless instructed otherwise, returns the traveler to the exact time and place of departure. Had Helen been in the room with me, she would not have noticed I'd been gone. But she must have wondered about my energy levels. I'd returned worn out from walking around Rome, and from all the adrenalin I'd pumped. So I went back to sleep.

I woke up in a room lit by a low fire. It was almost noon. "You okay?" she asked. She sounded scared. "I've never seen weather like this."

I got up, collected more snow, and melted it to make water. (You have to melt a lot of snow to get a little water.) There was still *nothing* outside my property lines. I brushed my teeth and tried to draw the bathroom around me, as a kind of shield against what was happening. It was familiar, my anchor to reality.

When I returned downstairs, Helen was putting the phone back in the cradle. She shook her head no. It was still out. We opened a can of meat, added some carrots, and cooked them over the fire.

I needed to make another effort to talk to Shel. I was certain everything was tied into his funeral. There was a possibility that we were approaching, or had already crossed, some sort of logical Rubicon. A dead man was walking around, and we had to set things right. But how could we do that?

I met him again at Thermopolae. He looked good. Tanned. Fit. Almost like a man on vacation.

"Shel," I said. "We need you."

"I know." Below us, the Thespians were examining the ground on which they would fight. Out on the plain, north of the pass, we could see the Persian army. They stretched to the horizon. "I *will* go back."

"When?"

"When I'm ready. When I'm *able*. There's no hurry, Dave. We both know that."

"I'm not so sure. Something's wrong. We can't even *find* the rest of New Jersey."

"I'm trying to live my life, Dave. Do you know how long it's been for me since I watched the funeral? Four years. Four years I've lived with this. Be patient with me. I'll go back and do the right thing. Relax."

"Okay, Shel. Help me relax. Tell me what's causing the weather conditions back home? Why is the power out? Why can't I find my way across the street?"

"I know about all that," he said.

"And—?"

"Look. Maybe it has nothing to do with me."

The Hellenic squadrons were still filing into the pass, their bright mail dusty from the journey north.

"I doubt it," I said.

He nodded. "As do I. But I've promised to go back. What more do you want?"

"Maybe you should do it now."

"What is *now* to you and me, Dave? What does the word mean?" He glanced up at a promontory about a hundred feet over our heads. "Would you be willing to walk off *that*?"

"We're not talking about *me*."

"Not even if I pleaded with you to do so? Even if the world depended on it?"

I looked at him.

"What if it didn't matter whether you did it today or

tomorrow? Or next month? Or forty years from now?"

"We don't *have* forty years."

"I'm not asking for forty of *your* years. I'm asking for forty of *mine*. I'll do it, Dave. God help me, I'll do it. But on my own schedule. Not yours."

I turned away, and he must have thought I was going to travel out. "Don't," he said. "Dave, try to understand. I'm scared of this."

"I know."

"Good. I need you to know."

We passed ourselves off as traveling law-givers. We moved among the Hellenic troops, wishing them well, assuring them that Hellas would never forget them.

"By the way," I asked him, "how did you land in the dungeon?"

He frowned, not seeming to understand. And then I saw that he was younger here than he had been in Rome. For him, the Vatican incident had not yet happened. "Never mind," I said. "You'll find out soon enough."

"Well," he smiled, "I'm pleased to know that when it happens, you'll be there to rescue me." His expression changed as a thought struck him. "You *did* rescue me, right?"

People accustomed to modern security precautions would be amazed at how easy it was to approach Leonidas. He accepted our good wishes and observed that, considering our physical size, we would both have made excellent soldiers had we chosen that line of work. In fact, both Shel and I towered over him.

He had dark eyes and was in his thirties. He and his men brimmed with confidence. There was no sense here of a doomed force.

He knew about the road that circled behind the pass, and he had already dispatched troops to cover it. The Phocians, as I recalled. Who would run at the first onset.

He invited us to share a meal. This was the third day of the siege, before any blood had been spilt. We talked about the Spartan system of balancing the executive by crowning two kings. And whether democracy could really work in the long run. He thought not. "Athens cannot stay the course," he said. "They have no discipline, and their philosophers encourage them to put themselves before their country. God help us if the poison ever spreads to us." Later, over wine, he asked where we were from, explaining that he could not place the accent.

"America," I said.

He shook his head. "It must be far to the north. Or very small."

We posed with Leonidas, and took pictures, explaining that it was a ritual that would allow us to share his courage. Sparks crackled up from the campfires, and the soldiers talked about home and the future. Later, I traded a gold coin to one of the Thespian archers for an arrow. "I'm not sure that's a good idea," Shel said. "He may need the arrow before he's done."

I knew better. "One arrow more or less will make no difference. When the crunch comes, the Thespians will refuse to leave their Spartan allies. They'll die too. All fifteen hundred of them."

And history will remember only the Spartans.

We watched them, exercising and playing games in full view of their Persian enemies. Shel turned to me, and his face was cold and hard. "You know, David," he said, "you are a monster."

6.

Saturday, November 26. Early afternoon.

"What is *happening*?" she asked. "It's *midnight* out there."

"I think I might know what's wrong, but it's hard to explain."

She was lovely in the candle light. "Could a volcano have erupted somewhere? I know that sounds crazy in South Jersey, but it's all I can think of." She was close to me. Warm and vulnerable and open in a way I had never known before. I touched her hair. Stroked it. She did not withdraw. "I'm glad I was here when it happened, Dave. Whatever it is that's happened."

"So am I," I said.

"So what's your theory?"

I took a deep breath. "It's going to sound crazy."

"The *weather's* crazy."

"Shel and I have been traveling in time."

Her eyes rolled. "Seriously," she said.

"I'm serious. He designed a time machine. Years ago." I showed her my Watch. "Just tell it where you want to go."

She looked at it curiously. "What is it really, Dave? A notebook TV?"

"Hell with this," I said. I have to walk to keep my weight down. Three miles a day, every day. Other people walk around the block, or go down to a park. I like Ambrose, Ohio, near the beginning of the century. It's a pleasant little town with tree-lined streets and white picket fences, where straw hats are in favor for men, and bright ribbons for the ladies. Down at the barber shop, the talk is mostly about the canal they're going to dig through Panama.

I pulled Helen close, punched in Ambrose's coordinates, and told her to brace herself. "The sensation's a little odd at first. But it only lasts a few seconds. And I'll be with you."

The living room froze. She stiffened. The walls and furniture faded to a green landscape with broad lawns and shingled houses and gas street lamps. When the street scene locked in, she backed up, looking wildly around.

"It's okay," I said. "We've gone upstream. Into the past. It's 1905." She was making odd murmuring sounds. "Teddy Roosevelt is President."

Birds sang, and in the distance we could hear the clean bang of church bells. We were standing outside a general store. About a block away there was a railroad siding.

She leaned against me and tried to shut it out.

"It takes a little getting used to," I said.

It was late September. People were burning leaves, talking over back fences. "Maybe we should stay here," she said. "Until the other problem goes away."

"I think we're responsible for the other problem."

"*We* are?"

"Well, Shel and me." Cabbage was cooking somewhere. Finally, I told her about Shel, how he had died but was still alive. Her colors changed and her breathing got uneven. When I'd finished, she sat and stared straight ahead.

"He's still alive," she said.

In a way, he'll always be alive. "Yes. He's still out there." I explained about the funeral, and how he had reacted.

I could see her struggling to grasp the idea, and to control her anger. "Why didn't you tell me?"

"I didn't know how."

"You can take us back, right?"

"Home? Yes."

"Where else?"

"Anywhere. Well, there are range limits, but nothing you'd care about."

A couple of kids with baseball gloves hurried past. "What you're saying," she said, "is that Shel should go back and walk into that fire. And if he doesn't, night-at-noon won't go away. Right? Is that what you're saying?"

"It's what I *think*. Yes, Helen, that's what he should do."

"But he's said he *would* do that? Right? And by the crazy logic of this business, it shouldn't matter when."

"But something's *wrong*. I think he never did go back. Never *will* go back. And I think that's the problem."

"I don't understand any of this," she said.

"I know." I watched a man with a handcart moving along the street, selling pickles and relishes. "I don't either. But there's a continuity. A track. Time flows along the track." I squeezed her hand. "We've torn up a piece of it."

"And—?"

"I think the locomotive went into the river."

She tried to digest that. "Okay. Grant the time machine. Dave, what you're asking him to do is unreasonable. I wouldn't go back either to get hit in the head and thrown into a fire. Would you?"

I got up. "Helen, what you or I would do doesn't much matter. I know this sounds cold, but I think we have to find a way to get Shel where he belongs."

She stood up, and looked west, out of town. The fields were brown, dried out from the summer heat. "You know where to find him?"

"Yes."

"Will you take me to him?"

"Yes." And, after a pause: "Will you help me?"

She stared at the quiet little buildings. White clapboard houses. A horse-drawn carriage just coming around a corner. "Nineteen-five. Shaw's just getting started."

I didn't push. I probably didn't need her to plead with him. Maybe just seeing her would jar something loose. And I knew where I wanted to confront him. At the one event in all of human history which might flay his conscience.

"Why don't we just shoot him?" she said. "And drag him back?"

"The question you are really asking, Simmias, is whether death annihilates the soul?" Socrates looked from one to another of his friends.

Simmias was young and clear-eyed, like most of the others, but subdued in the shadow of the prison house. "It is an important matter," he said. "There is none of more importance. But we were reluctant—." He hesitated, his voice caught, and he could go no farther.

"I understand," said Socrates. "You fear this is an indelicate moment to raise such an issue. But if you would discuss it with me, we cannot very well postpone it, can we?"

"No, Socrates," said a thin young man with red hair. "Unfortunately, we cannot." This, I knew, was Crito.

Despite Plato's account, the final conversation between Socrates and his disciples did not take place in his cell. It might well have begun there, but they were in a wide, utilitarian meeting room when Helen and I arrived. Several women were present. Socrates, then seventy years old, sat at ease on a wooden chair, while the rest of us gathered around him in a half-circle. To my surprise and disappointment, I did not see Shel.

Socrates was, on first glance, a man of mundane appearance. He was of average height for the time, cleanshaven, wearing a dull red robe. Only his luminous eyes were extraordinary. When they fell curiously on me, as they did from time to time, I imagined that he knew where I had come from, and why I was there.

Helen writhed under the impact of conflicting emotions. She had been ecstatic at the chance to see Shel again, although I knew she was not yet convinced. When he did not arrive, she looked at me as if to say she had told me so, and settled back to watch history unfold.

She was, I thought, initially disappointed, in that the event seemed to be nothing more than a few people sitting around talking in an uncomfortable room in a prison. As if the scene should somehow be scored and choreographed and played to muffled drums. She had read Plato's account before we left. I tried to translate for her, but we gave it up. I was just getting in the way of the body language and the voices, which, she said, had a meaning and drama all their own.

"When?" she whispered, after we'd been there almost an hour. "When does it happen?"

"Sunset, I think."

She made a noise deep in her throat.

"Why do men fear death?" Socrates asked.

"Because," said Crito, "they believe it is the end of existence."

There were almost twenty people present. Most were young, but there was a sprinkling of middle-aged and elderly persons. The most venerable of these looked like Moses, a tall man with a white beard, expressive white eyebrows, and a fierce countenance. He gazed intently at Socrates throughout and periodically nodded when the philosopher hammered home a particularly salient point.

"And do all men fear death?" asked Socrates.

"Most assuredly, Socrates," said a boy, who could have been no more than eighteen.

Socrates addressed the boy. "Do even the brave fear death, Cebes?"

Cebes thought it over. "I have to think so, Socrates."

"Why then," asked Socrates, "do the valiant dare death? Is it perhaps because they fear something else even more?"

"The loss of honor," said Crito.

"Thus we are faced with the paradox that even the brave are driven by fear. Can we find no one who can face death with equanimity who is *not* driven by fear?"

Moses stared at Helen. I moved protectively closer to her.

"Of all men," said Crito, "only you seem to show no concern at its approach."

Socrates smiled. "Of all men," he said, "only a philosopher can truly face down death. Because he knows quite certainly that the soul will proceed to a better existence. Provided he has maintained a lifelong pursuit of knowledge and virtue, and has not allowed his soul, which is his divine essence, to become entangled in concerns of the body. For when this happens, the soul takes on corporeal characteristics. And when death comes, it cannot escape. This is why cemeteries are restless at night."

"How can we be sure," asked a man in a blue toga, "that the soul, even if it succeeds in surviving the trauma of death, is not blown away by the first strong wind?"

It was not intended as a serious question, but Socrates saw that it affected the others. So he answered lightly, observing that it would be prudent to die on a calm day, and then undertook a serious response. He asked questions which elicited admissions that the soul was not physical and therefore could not be a composite object. "I think we need not fear that it will come apart," he said, with a touch of amusement.

One of the jailers lingered in the doorway throughout

the long discussion. He seemed worried, and at one point cautioned Socrates against speaking too much, or getting excited. "If you get the heat up," he said, "the poison will not work well."

"We would not wish that," said Socrates sardonically. But he saw the pained expression on the jailer's face, and I thought he immediately regretted the remark.

Women arrived with dinner, and several stayed, so that the room became more and more crowded. In fact, no doors were locked, and no guards, other than the reluctant jailer, were in evidence. Phaedo, who is the narrator of Plato's account, was beside me. He told me that the authorities had hoped profoundly that Socrates would run off. "They did everything they could to avoid this," he said. "There is even a rumor that last night they offered him money and transportation."

Socrates saw us conversing, and he said, "Is there something in my reasoning that disturbs you?"

I'd lost the train of the discussion, but Phaedo said, "Yes, Socrates. However, I am reluctant to put my objection to you."

Socrates turned a skeptical gaze on him. "Truth is what it is. Tell me what disturbs you, Phaedo."

He hesitated, and I realized he was making sure of his voice. "Then let me ask," he said in a carefully neutral tone, "whether you are being truly objective on this matter? The sun is not far from the horizon and, although it grieves me to say it, were I in your position, I also would argue in favor of immortality."

"Were you in his position," said Crito with a smile, "you would have taken the first ship to Syracuse." The company laughed together, Socrates as heartily as any, and the strain seemed broken for the moment.

"You are of course correct in asking, Phaedo. Am I seeking truth? Or trying to convince myself? I can only respond that, if my arguments are valid, then that is good. If they are false, and death does indeed mean annihilation, they nevertheless arm me to withstand its approach. And that too is good." He looked utterly composed. "If I'm wrong, it's an error that won't survive the sunset."

Simmias was seated immediately to the right of Moses. "I for one am convinced," he said. "Your arguments do not admit of refutation. And it is a comfort to me to believe that we have it in our power to draw this company together again in some place of God's choosing."

"Yes," said Crito. "I agree. And, Socrates, we are fortunate to have you here to explain it to us."

"Anyone who has thought about these issues," said Socrates, "should be able to reach, if not truth, at least a high degree of probability."

Moses seemed weighed down with the infirmities of age, and with the distress of the present calamity. Still, he continued to glance periodically at Helen. Now, for the first time, he spoke: "I very much fear, Socrates, that within a few hours there will be no one left anywhere in Hellas, or anywhere else for that matter, who will be able to make these matters plain."

"That's *Shel*'s voice," Helen gasped, straining to see better. The light was not good, and he was facing away from us now, his features hidden in the folds of his hood. Then he turned and looked openly at us, and smiled sadly at her. His lips formed the English words *hello, Helen.*

She was getting to her feet.

At that moment, the jailer appeared with the poisoned cup, and the sight of him, and the silver vessel, froze everyone in the chamber. "I hope you understand, Socrates," he said, "this is not my doing."

"I know that, Thereus," said Socrates. "I am not angry with you."

"They always want to blame *me*," Thereus said.

Silence flowed through the chamber.

The jailer laid the cup on the table. "It is time," he said.

The rest of the company, following Helen's example, got to their feet.

Socrates gave a coin to the jailer, squeezed his hand, thanked him, and turned to look at his friends. "The world is very bright," he said. "But much of it is illusion. If we stare at it too long, in the way we look at the sun during an eclipse, it blinds us. Look at it only with the mind." He picked up the hemlock. Several in the assemblage started forward, but were restrained by their companions. Someone in back sobbed.

"Stay," a voice said sternly. "You have respected him all your life. Do so now."

He lifted the cup to his lips, and his hand trembled. It was the only time the mask slipped. Then he drank it down and laid the cup on the table. "I am sure Simmias is right," he said. "We shall gather again one day, as old friends should, in a far different chamber."

Shel stared at Helen. "It's good to see you again," he said.

She shivered. "You're *not* Shel."

A smile flickered across his lips. "I've been traveling a long time." He stood silhouetted against the moon and the harbor. Behind us, the waterfront buildings of the Piraeus were illuminated by occasional oil lamps. He turned toward me. "David, you seem to have become my dark angel."

I was emotionally drained. "I'm sorry you feel that way," I said.

A gull wheeled overhead. "Socrates dies for a philosophical nicety. And Shelborne continues to run when all the world is at stake. Right?"

"That's right," I said.

Helen was still trembling. "What happened to you?" she whispered.

His lips twitched, and he ran his hand over the long white whiskers. He looked haunted. "Forty years, more or less," he said. He reached for her, but she backed away.

I put a hand on her shoulder. Steadied her. "He's been out here a long time."

Her eyes blazed. "What happened to *my* Shel? What did you do with him?"

"He's been living his allotted years," he said. "Making them count for as much as he can as long as he can. Before my conscience here—" lifting his eyes and targeting me, "before my conscience succeeds in driving me into my grave."

She couldn't hold back any longer. The tears came and she looked for help. But when I started toward her, she threw herself into *his* arms.

He held her a long time, and the water lapped against the piers.

"I've tried to go back," he said. "God help me, I've tried. But I could not bring myself to go there and lie in that bed." Anger surfaced. I could not tell where it was directed. "Did you know that my skull was crushed?"

We knew.

He looked very old. And broken. He didn't seem to know what to do with his hands. The robes had no pockets. But he needed some kind of defensive gesture, so he folded his arms and turned to face the harbor. "I am not Socrates, Dave," he said. "I will not drink from his cup." His eyes locked on mine, and I could see him come to a decision. He drew us together, within the field of his Watch, and punched in a set of coordinates. "But I will settle the issue for you."

Helen shook her head no. No more surprises. And everything began to slow down. The harbor winked out, a ship's deck materialized underfoot, and the sky filled with fire.

We were on a Roman galley. The air was thick with powder and cinders, and the sails were down. We were pitching and rolling. The ocean broke across the deck, and men scrambled and swore at their stations. Below us, long oars dipped rhythmically into the waves. It was daylight, but we could not see more than twenty feet.

"How did you manage that?" I screamed at Shel over the hurricane of noise. The Watches had never possessed the precision to land people on a ship at sea.

"It's been a lot of years," he said. "Technology's better than it used to be."

"Where are we?" demanded Helen, barely able to make herself heard.

Shel was hanging onto a ladder. His clothes were drenched. "A. D. 79," he said. "Just west of Pompeii." His eyes were afire. His silver hair was already streaked with black ash, and I suspected that Shel had lost whatever anchor he might have had in reality. Time had become perhaps too slippery for him at last.

The ship rolled to starboard, and would have dumped Helen into the sea had he not grabbed her, and hung on, pushing me aside. "We do not need *you*," he said.

"Why are we here?" Helen demanded.

The sea and the wind roared, and the dust was blinding. "*I* will pick the time of my death," Shel cried. "And its manner."

I was trying to scramble toward him, but I could do no more than hang on.

"I am uniquely qualified—."

We went down into a trough, and I thought the sea was going to bury us.

"—To make that choice. My death will be an appropriate finale to the symphony of my life."

A fireball roared overhead, and plowed into the water.

"Don't do it," I cried.

"Have no fear, David. I'm not ready yet. But when I am, this will be the way of it." He smiled at me and touched the Watch. "What better exit for a time traveler than sailing with Pliny the Elder?" And he was gone.

"What was that all about?" called Helen. We dipped again and salt water poured across the deck. "Maybe we ought to get out of here too."

I agreed, and wrapped one arm around a stanchion, something to hang onto while I pulled thr trigger.

"Wait," she said. "Do you know who Pliny the Elder is?"

"A Roman philosopher."

"I did a paper on him once. He was an essayist and moralist. Fought a lot for the old values."

"Helen, can we talk about it later?"

"He was also a naval officer. He's trying to rescue survivors. Dave, *he will die out here*."

"We can't do anything about that. But we don't want to be with him when it happens."

"You don't understand. He said he was going to die here, too, right?"

"Who did?"

"*Shel*. If so, why isn't he here?"

Good question. I looked around. We were on the starboard side, near the beam. The sails were down, and a few shadowy figures were moving through the volcanic haze. (I would have expected to hear the roar of the volcano, of

Vesuvius, but the only noise came from the sea and the warm dry wind that blew across the deck.) "Let's try the other side," I said.

He was there, on the port quarter, clinging to a line, while the wind howled around him. Even more ancient this time, frail, weary, frightened. Dressed differently than he had been, in slacks and a green pullover that might have come out of the 1930's.

Cinders stung my eyes.

He saw us and waved. "I've been waiting for you." His gaze lingered on Helen, and he looked at the sea.

"Don't," I cried.

She let go her handhold and tried to scramble across the pitching deck.

He was hanging onto a hawser, balanced near the rail.

The ship pitched, went up the front of a wave, and down the back. He raised his hand in a farewell gesture. "Don't worry, David," he said. "It doesn't matter." The sea broke across the deck, and I was thrown hard against a gunwale. My mouth filled with water and I twisted my shoulder. But I hung on.

We were under a long time. When it ended, he was gone. The rail was clear, and the line to which he'd clung whipped back and forth.

Helen grabbed my arm. I followed her gaze and saw him briefly, on the side of a swell, clutching a board and struggling to stay afloat, his white hair trailing in the water. But another wave broke over him and moments later the board popped to the surface and drifted into the haze.

Something in the ship gave way with a loud sharp crack, and the crewmen cried out. I pulled Helen close.

"Dead again," she said.

"Yeah. Maybe this time for good." I pulled the trigger.

7.

Saturday, November 26. Mid-afternoon.

We returned to the wardrobe in separate, but equally desperate, moods.

Helen could not connect the wild man on the galley with Shel, or even the moody septuagenarian on the dock at the Piraeus. Furthermore, she had not yet accepted either the reality or the implications of time travel. Yet, on a primal level, she had recognized him. And for the second time during two weeks, she mourned for him.

And I? I'd lost all feeling. How could I reconcile two graves? I collapsed into a chair and stared at the costumes, arranged in closets on both sides of the room, marked off by period. Damn them. I remembered the planning and research that had gone into their creation. We had felt so well organized in those days. Prepared for anything.

I let it go.

And then I noticed that I was *seeing* the costumes. There was *light* in the room. It was gray, not bright, but it meant that the black mist was gone. I threw the curtains back, and looked out at a rain-swept landscape.

The trees, the grounds, the walkway, the garage, were visible, huddled together in the storm. The wall still circled the property. And beyond the wall, I could see most of Carmichael Drive. *Most of it.* But Ray White's house had vanished. As had the world on the other side of the street. Carmichael Drive now skirted the edge of a precipice, its far side missing, broken off into a void. Beyond, I could see only gray sky.

Terrified, we went from room to room. Everywhere, in

all directions, it was the same. On the east, where the property was most extensive, even the wall was gone. A seldom-used patio had been cut in half, and the stand of elms that used to provide shade for it now marked the limit of the world.

We opened a bottle of brandy and drew all the blinds.

"Can't we replay that last scene?" she asked. "Go back and rescue him? I mean, that's the whole point of a time machine, isn't it? Nothing's ever irrevocable. You make a mistake, you go back and fix it."

I was tired and my head hurt and at that moment I could have killed Shelborne. "No," I said. "It would just make everything worse. We know what happened. We can't change *that.*"

"Dave," she said, "how could we possibly make things *worse?*"

That was a pretty good question.

She eased onto a sofa and closed her eyes. "Time travel," she said, "isn't all it's cracked up to be, is it?"

"It'll be okay," I said. Rain rattled against the windows. "We need to find a way to eliminate the paradox."

"Okay," she said. "What exactly is the paradox?"

I thought it over. "Adrian Shelborne has two graves. One out on Monument Hill. And the other in the Tyrrhenian Sea. We have to arrange things so that there is only one."

"Can we go back and stop the Friday night fire?"

"Same problem as trying a rescue on the galley. The Friday night fire has already happened, and if you prevent it, then what was the funeral all about?"

"It's like a big knot," she said. "No matter where you try to pull, everything just gets tighter."

We were still wearing our Hellenic robes, which were torn and soiled. And we both needed a shower, but there was no running water. On the other hand, we *did* have rain. And as much privacy as we could ever want.

I got soap, towels, and wash cloths. She took the back yard, which was more sheltered (as if that mattered), and I stood out front. It was late November, but the weather had turned unseasonably warm. Hot water would have been nice, but I felt good anyway after I'd dried off and changed into clean clothes.

Then we sat, each in a kind of private cocoon, thinking about options. Or things lost. The rain continued through the afternoon. I watched rivulets form and wondered how much soil was being washed over the edge. Into what? When the weather cleared, I promised myself that I would walk out and look down.

"Who's buried in the grave on Monument Hill?" she asked.

"Shel."

"How do we know? The body was burned beyond recognition."

"They checked his dental records. We can't *change* that."

She was sitting on the sofa with her legs drawn up under her. "We also can't recover the body from the Tyrrhenian Sea. We have to work on Monument Hill. What can we do about the dental records?"

I looked at her. "I don't think I understand."

"We have a time machine. Use your imagination."

Chain-reaction collisions have become an increasingly dangerous occurrence on limited-access highways around the world. Hundreds die every year, several thousand are injured, and property damage runs well into the millions. On the day that we buried Shel, there had been a pileup in California. It had happened a little after 8:00 a.m. on a day with perfect visibility, when a pickup rearended a station wagon full of kids headed for breakfast and a day at Universal Studios.

We materialized by the side of the road moments after the chain reaction had ended. The highway and the shoulder were littered with wrecked vehicles. Some people were out of their cars trying to help; others were wandering dazed through the carnage. The morning air was filled with screams and the smell of burning oil.

"I'm not sure I can do this," Helen said, spotting a woman bleeding in an overturned Buick. She went over, got the door open, and motioned me to assist. The woman was alone in the car. She was unconscious, and her arm looked bent.

"Helen," I said. "We have a bigger rescue to make."

She shook her head. No. This first. She stopped the bleeding and I got someone to stay with the victim. We helped a few other people, pulled an elderly couple out of a burning van, got one man with two broken legs off the road. "We don't have time for this," I pleaded.

"I don't have time for anything else," she said.

Sirens were approaching. I let her go, concentrating on finding what we'd come for.

He was in a blue Toyota that had rolled over onto its roof. The front of the car was crumpled, a door was off, and the driver looked dead. He was bleeding heavily from a head wound. One tire was spinning slowly. I could find no pulse.

He was about the right size, tangled in a seat belt. When Helen got there, she confirmed that he would do. I used a jack knife to cut him free. The EMT's were spreading out among the wrecked cars. Stretchers were appearing.

Helen could not keep her mind on what we were doing. "Your oath doesn't count," I said. "Not here. Let it go."

We got him out of the car, wrapped him in plastic and

laid him in the road. "He does look a little like Shel," she said in a small voice.

"Enough to get by."

I heard footsteps behind us. Someone wanted to know what we were doing.

It was an EMT.

"It's okay," I said, "we're doctors." I pulled the trigger and we were out of there.

His name was Victor Randall. We found pictures of an attractive woman with cropped brown hair seated with him in a porch swing. And two kids. The kids were smiling at the camera, one boy, one girl, both around seven or eight. "Maybe," Helen said, "when this is over, we can send them a note to explain."

"We can't do that," I said.

"They'll never know what happened to him."

"That's right. And there's no way around it."

There was also about two hundred cash. Later, I would mail that back to the family.

We carried him down to the garage and put him in the Porsche. I adjusted the temporal sweep to maximum, so that when we went the car would go with us.

8.

Thursday, November 10. Near midnight.

Mark S. Hightower had been Shel's dentist for seven years. He operated out of a medical building across the street from Friendship Hospital, where Helen had interned.

I'd met Hightower once. He was short, barrel-chested, flatskulled, a man who looked more like a professional wrestler than a dentist. But he was soft-spoken and, according to Shel, particularly good with nervous patients.

We materialized on a lot off Penrod Avenue in the commercial district. The area was always deserted at night. Ten minutes later, we pulled into the parking lot at the medical center. Hightower was located in back, well away from the street.

Victor was in the front seat, wrapped in plastic. He'd stopped bleeding, and we had cleaned him up as much as we could. "Are you sure you know how to do this?" I asked.

"Of course not, Dave. I'm not a dentist. But the equipment shouldn't be hard to figure out. How do we get inside?"

I showed her a tire iron. "We'll have to break in."

She looked dismayed. "I thought you could manage something a little more sophisticated. Why not just use that thing on your wrist and put us inside the building?"

"Because it doesn't home in, and I don't have the coordinates." I was thinking of Shel's ability to move us from the Piraeus to the quarterdeck on Pliny's galley. If I'd tried that with my Watch, we'd have gone into the ocean.

We put on gloves and walked around the building, looking for an open window. There was none, but we found a rear exit that didn't seem very secure. I wedged the tire iron between the door and the jamb and worked it back and forth until the lock gave. I held my breath, waiting for the screech of a burglar alarm. It didn't come, and we were past the first hurdle.

We went back to the Porsche, got Victor out and half-carried, half-dragged him to the door. Inside, we set him in a chair. Then we turned on penlights and looked around. There were half a dozen rooms designated for patients, opening off a corridor that looped around to the reception area. I wandered from office to office, not really knowing what I was looking for. But Helen did one quick turn through the passageway and pointed at a machine tucked away in a corner. "This is it," she said. The manufacturer's label said it was an orthopantomograph. "It's designed to provide a panoramic X-ray."

"Panoramic? What's that?"

"Full mouth. It should be all we'll need."

The person being X-rayed placed his forehead against a plastic rest and his chin in a cup-shaped support. The camera was located inside a cone which was mounted on a rotating arm. The arm and cone traversed the head and produced a panoramic image of the teeth. The only problem was that the patient normally stood during the procedure.

"It'll take six to eight minutes," said Helen. "During that time we have to keep him absolutely still. Think you can do it?"

"I can do it," I said.

"Okay." She checked to make sure there was a film cassette in the machine. "Let's get him."

We carried Victor to the orthopantomograph. At Helen's suggestion, we'd brought along some cloth strips which we now used to secure him to the device. It was a clumsy business, and he kept sliding away from us. Working in the dark complicated the procedure, but after about a half hour we had him in place.

"Something just occurred to me," I said. "Victor Randall already has the head wound."

Her eyes closed momentarily. "You're suggesting the arsonist didn't hit Shel in the head after all?"

"That's what I think."

"This keeps getting weirder," she said.

A mirror was mounted on the machine directly in front of the face. Helen pressed a button and a light went on in the center of the mirror. "They would tell the patient to watch the light," she said. "That's how they're sure they've got it lined up."

"How are *we* sure?"

"What's the term? 'Dead reckoning'?" She punched another button. A motor started, and the cone began to move.

Ten minutes later we took the cassette out, leaving Victor in place until we were sure we had good pictures. The developer was located in a windowless storage room. Helen removed the film from the cassette and ran it through the machine. When the finished picture came out, she handed it to me without looking at it. "What do you think?"

The entire mouth, uppers and lowers, was clear. "Looks good," I said.

She held it against the light. "Plenty of fillings on both sides. Let's see how it compares."

The records were maintained in manila folders behind the reception desk. Helen found Shel's, and sat down with it at the desk, where the counter hid her from anyone passing outside.

"He goes to the dentist every three months," she said. (I couldn't help noticing she still talked about him in the present tense.) The results of his most recent checkup were clipped on the right side of the folder. In the middle of the sheet was a panoramic picture, like the one we had just taken, and several smaller photos of individual sections. "I think they call these 'wings' " she said. "But when they bring a dentist in to identify a body, they do it with *these*." She held up the panoramic and compared the two. "They don't look much alike in detail. And if they ever get around to comparing it with the wings, they'll notice something's wrong. But it's good enough to get by."

She removed Shel's panoramic and substituted the one we'd just taken. Then she replaced the folder. We wiped off the headrest and checked the floor to be sure we'd spilled no blood. "One more thing," said Helen. She inserted a fresh cassette into the orthopantomograph. "Okay. Let's clear out."

"Wait a minute," I said. "They'll know we broke in. We need to do something to make this look like a burglary." As far as I could see, there wasn't much worth stealing. Magazines. Cheap landscape prints on the walls. "How about a drill?" I said. "It looks expensive."

She squeezed my arm. "What kind of burglar would steal a *drill*?" She went on another tour of the office. Moments later, I heard glass breaking, and she came back with a couple of plastic bottles filled with pills. "Valium," she said.

9.

Saturday, November 12. 1:15 a.m.

I had the coodinates for the workshop, so we were able to go right in. It was located in the basement of the townhouse, a small, cramped, cluttered place with a Cray computer front and center, banks of displays, and an array of experimental equipment I had never begun to understand. Moments after we'd arrived, the oil heater came on with a thump.

We had to carry the body up to the second floor. But I'd done the best I could. The math had always been Shel's job, and the only place in the house I could get to was the workshop. We dressed the corpse in Shel's pajamas, turned back the sheets, and laid him in bed. We put his clothes into a plastic bag.

We also had a brick in the bag. Shel kept his car keys in the middle drawer of a desk on the first floor. We'd debated just letting the clothes burn, but I wanted to leave nothing to chance. Despite what you might think about time travel, what we were doing was forever. We could not come back and undo it, because we were *here*, and we knew what the sequence of events was, and you couldn't change that without paying down the road. If we knew anything for sure now, we knew *that*.

I had left the Porsche at home this time. So we borrowed Shel's green Pontiac. It had a vanity plate reading SHEL, and a lot of mileage. But he took good care of it. We drove down to the river. At the two-lane bridge that crosses the Narrows, we pulled off and waited until there was no traffic. Then we went out to the middle of the bridge, where we assumed the water was deepest, and threw the bag over the side. We still had Victor's wallet and ID, which I planned on burning.

We returned Shel's car. By now it was a quarter to two, thirty-eight minutes before a Mrs. Wilma Anderson would call to report a fire at the townhouse. I worried that we'd cut our time too close, that the intruder might already be inside. But it was still quiet when I returned the car keys to the desk.

We locked the house front and back, which was how we had found it, and retired across the street behind a hedge. It was a good night's work, and we waited now to see who the criminal was. The neighborhood was tree-lined, well-lighted, quiet. The houses were middle-class, fronted by small fenced yards. Cars were parked on both sides of the street. Somewhere in the next block a cat yowled.

Two o'clock.

"Getting late," Helen said.

Nothing moved. "He's going to have to hurry up," I said.

She frowned. "What happens if he doesn't come?"

"He *has* to come."

"Why?"

"Because that's the way it happened. We know that for an absolute fact."

She looked at her watch. Two-oh-one.

"I just had a thought," I said.

"We could use one."

"Maybe you're right. Maybe there is no firebug. Or rather, maybe *we* are the firebugs. After all, we already know where the fractured skull came from."

She nodded reluctantly. "Yeah," she said. "Maybe."

I left the shelter of the hedge and walked quickly across the street, entered Shel's driveway, and went back into the garage. There were several gas cans. All empty.

I needed the car keys. But I was locked out now. I used a rock to break a window, and retrieved the keys. I threw the empty cans into the trunk of his Pontiac. "Wait here," I told Helen. "In case someone *does* show up."

"Where are you going?"

"To get some gas."

There was an all-night station on River Road, only a few blocks away. It was one of those places where they concentrate on keeping the cashier alive after about eleven o'clock. He was a middle-aged, worn-out guy sitting in a cage full of cigarette smoke. A toothpick rolled relentlessly from one side of his mouth to the other. I filled three cans, paid, and drove back.

It was 2:17 when we began sloshing gas around the basement. We emptied a can on the stairway and another upstairs, taking care to drench the bedroom where Victor Randall lay. We poured the rest of it on the first floor, and so thoroughly soaked the entry that I was afraid to go near it with a lighted match. But at 2:25 we touched it off.

Helen and I watched for a time. The flames cast a pale glow in the sky, and sparks floated upward. We didn't know much about Victor Randall, but what we did know maybe was enough. He'd been a husband and father. In their photos, his wife and kids had looked happy. And he got a Viking's funeral.

"What do you think?" asked Helen. "Will it be all right now?"

"Yeah," I said. "I hope so."

10.

Sunday, November 27. Mid-morning.

In the end, the Great November Delusion was written off as precisely that, a kind of mass hysteria that settled across a substantial chunk of New Jersey, Pennsylvania, Maryland, and Delaware. Elsewhere, life had gone on as usual, except that the affected area seemed to have vanished behind a black shroud which turned back all attempts at entry, and admitted no signals.

Fortunately, it had lasted only a few hours. When it ended, persons who had been inside emerged with a wide range of stories. Some had found themselves stranded on a rocky shore; others, in a windowless, doorless house with infinite stairways and corridors. Psychologists pointed out that the one element appearing in all accounts was a depiction of isolation. Sometimes it had been whole communities that were isolated; sometimes families. Occasionally it had been individuals. The general consensus was that, whatever the cause, therapists would be assured of a handsome income for years to come.

My first act on returning home was to destroy Victor Randall's wallet and ID. I would have been ecstatic with the way things had turned out, except that Helen still mourned Shel.

The TV was back with full coverage. The National Guard was out, and experts were already on the talk shows.

I luxuriated in a hot shower and changed. Helen was reduced to putting on a rolled-up pair of my slacks and a tee-shirt. By the time she came downstairs, I had made some bacon and eggs. She ate, and cried a little, and congratulated me. "Saved the world, we did," she said. "Or at least, South Jersey."

After breakfast she seemed reluctant to leave, but she announced finally that she needed to get back to her apartment and see how things were. She had just started for the door when we heard a car pull up. "It's a woman," she said archly, looking out the window. "Friend of yours?"

It was Sgt. Lake. She was alone this time.

The door bell rang.

"This won't look so good," Helen said.

"I know. You want to duck upstairs?"

She thought about it. "No. What are we hiding?"

The bell rang again. I opened up.

"Good morning, Dr. Dryden," said the detective. "I'm glad to see you came through it all right. Everything *is* okay?"

"Yes," I said. "How about you?"

Her cheeks were pale. "Good," she said. "Whatever it was, I hope it's over." She seemed far more human than during her earlier visit.

"Where's your partner?" I asked.

She smiled. "Everything's bedlam downtown. A lot of people went berserk during that *thing*, whatever it was. We're going to be busy for a while." She took a deep breath. "I wonder if I could talk with you?"

"Of course." I stepped back and she came in.

"It's chaos." She seemed not quite able to focus. "Fires, people in shock, heart attacks everywhere. It hasn't been good." She saw Helen and her eyes widened. "Hello, Doctor. I didn't expect to see you here. There'll be plenty for you to do today."

Helen nodded. "You okay?" she asked.

"Yeah. Thanks. I'm fine." She stared out over my shoulder. Then, with a start, she tried to wave it all away. "What was it like here?"

I described what I'd seen. Menawhile, Helen poured coffee and everybody relaxed a little. She had been caught in her car during the event on a piece of rain-swept foggy highway that just went round and round, with ho exit. "Damndest thing," she said.

Helen offered a sedative, but Lake declined and asked whether she might have a minute alone with me. "Sure," Helen said. "I should be on my way anyhow." She patted my shoulder in a comradely way and let herself out.

"Doctor," said Lake, "you've said you were home in bed at the time Dr. Shelborne's home burned. Is that correct?"

"Yes. That's right."

"Are you sure?"

The question hung in the sunlit air. "Of course. Why do you ask?" I could read nothing in her expression.

"Someone answering your description was seen near the townhouse at the time of the fire."

"It wasn't *me*," I said, suddenly remembering the man at the gas station. And I'd been driving Shel's car. With his vanity plate in front just in case anybody wasn't paying attention.

"Okay. I wonder if you'd mind coming down to the station with me, so we can clear the matter up. Get it settled."

"Sure. Be glad to."

We stood up. "Could I have a moment, please?"

"Certainly," she said, and went outside.

I called Helen on her cellular. "Don't panic," she said. "All you need is a good alibi."

"I don't *have* an alibi."

"For God's sake, Dave. You've got something better. You have a *time machine*."

"Okay. Sure. But if I go back and set up an alibi, why didn't I tell them the truth in the beginning?"

"Because you were protecting a woman's reputation," she said. "What else would you be doing at two o'clock in the morning? Get out your little black book." It might have been my imagination, but I thought the reference to my little black book sounded irritated.

11.

Friday, November 11. Early evening.

The problem was that I didn't have a little black book. I've never been all that successful with women. Not to the extent, certainly, that I could call one up with a reasonable expectation of finishing the night in her bed. What other option did I have? I could try to find someone in a bar, but you didn't really lie to the police in a murder case to protect a pick-up.

I pulled over to the curb beside an all-night restaurant, to think about it. It was a rundown area lined with crumbling warehouses. A police cruiser slowed and pulled in behind me. The cop got out and I lowered the window.

"Anything wrong, Officer?" I asked. He was small, black, well-pressed.

"I was going to ask you the same thing, sir. This is not a safe area."

"I was just trying to decide whether I wanted a hamburger."

"Yes, sir," he said. I could hear the murmur of his radio. "Well, listen, I'd make up my mind, one way or the other. I wouldn't hang around out here if I were you."

I smiled, and gave him a thumbs-up. "Thanks," I said.

He got back in his cruiser and pulled out. I watched his lights turn left at the next intersection. And I knew what I was going to do.

I drove south on route 130 for about three quarters of an hour, and then turned east on a two-lane. Around eleven, I entered a small town and decided it was just what I was looking for. Its police station occupied a drab two-story building beside the post office. The Red Lantern Bar was located about two blocks away, on the other side of the street.

I parked in a lighted spot close to the police station, walked to the bar and went inside. It was smoky and subdued, reeking with dead cigarettes and stale beer. Most of the action was near the dart board. I settled in at the bar and commenced drinking Scotch. I stayed with it until the bartender suggested I'd had enough, which usually wouldn't have taken long. But that night my mind stayed clear. Not my motor coordination, though. I paid up, eased off the stool, and negotiated my way back onto the street.

I turned right and moved methodically toward the police station, putting one foot in front of the other. When I got close, I added a little panache to my stagger, tried a couple of practice giggles, and lurched in through the front door.

A man with corporal's stripes came out of a back room.

"Good evening, Officer," I said, with exaggerated formality and the widest grin I could manage, which was then pretty wide. "Can you give me directions to Atlantic City?"

The corporal shook his head. "Do you have some identification, sir?"

"Yes I do," I said. "But I don't see why my name is any
business of yours. I'm in a hurry."

"Where are you from?" His eyes narrowed.

"Two weeks from Sunday," I said. "I'm a time traveler."

12.

Sunday, November 27. Late evening.

Sgt. Lake was surprised and, I thought, disappointed to learn
that I had been in jail on the night of the fire. She said she
understood why I'd been reluctant to explain, but admon-
ished me on the virtues of honesty with law enforcement
authorities.

I called Helen, looking forward to an evening of cele-
bration. I got her recording machine. "Call me when you get
in," I told it.

The call never came. By midnight, when I'd given up
and was getting ready for bed, I noticed a white envelope
on the kitchen table. My name was printed on it in neat,
spare characters.

> *Dear Dave,*
>
> *Shel is back! My Shel. The real one. He wants
> to take me off somewhere, and I don't know where,
> but I can't resist. Maybe we will live near the Par-
> thenon, or maybe Paris during the 1920's. I don't
> know. But I do know you will be happy for me.*
>
> *I will never forget you, Dave.*

Love,

Helen

P.S. We left something for you. In the wardrobe.

I read it several times, and finally crumpled it. They'd left the *Hermes*. They had positioned it carefully under the light, to achieve maximum effect. It looked good.

I stood a long time admiring the piece. But it wasn't Helen. The house filled with echoes and the sound of the wind. More desolate now than it had been when it was the only thing in the universe.

I remembered how Helen had sounded when she thought she was sending me to sleep with another woman. And I wondered why I was so ready to give up.

I did some quick research, went back to the wardrobe, scarcely noticing the *Hermes*, and put on turn-of-the-century evening clothes. Next stop: the Court Theater in Sloane Square, London, to watch the opening performance of *Man and Superman*.

You're damned right, Shelborne.

Time travelers never die.